John Bennion is at it again. *Spin* meets *Ruth at the End of the World* and *Ezekiel's Third Wife* in his new novel, *The Dead Fathers: Grief and Poker in the West Desert*, where questions of chance, of environmental catastrophe, of gender and authority and fundamentalist delusions, all collide. Protagonist Christopher Twist deals with his dead ancestors and his living family, philosophizing, wandering, conversing in words sacred and profane. What are prime causes, what are effects? What are the roles of minor individuals in major conflicts? As in all Bennion's novels, there's much to mine here—literally, this time. This is deep stuff, mines and mazes real and metaphorical. Once again, John Bennion invites us into and beyond his characters' twistiest explorations.

—Julie J. Nichols
author of *Pigs When They Straddle the Air*

The Dead Fathers: Grief and Poker in the West Desert is a busy novel set in a deceptively quiet landscape: a multitude inhabits Utah's stark and gorgeous West Desert, manifestations of an old man's fractured mind and heart. The abundant cast conjures myth and magic, philosophy and theology, politics, physics, history, sense and nonsense. Ancestors and descendants compete for validation. Conscience disturbs habits of compliance. Senescence clings to tender nostalgia and primal hurt. All of this makes for an engrossing read, but the plot's through-line is the real reward: accumulating gestures of desire, of mature mar-

ital reinvention despite—or maybe because of—a long season of disillusion. Read this novel with slow pleasure, immersed in dry water—a sweeping yet intimate landscape John Bennion understands like no other author I have read.

—Karin Anderson
author of *Before Us Like a Land of Dreams*,
What Falls Away, and *Things I Didn't Do*

This is a novel obsessed with opposites, starting with its very form. It's a novel about a man who would be alone in deserted space. Yet this novel provides him with all sorts of company, from strangers to his wife, from the living to the dead, from the Three Nephites (one of whom is a woman, did you know?) to cryptobiotic soil. He is visited almost nightly by his dead father, grandfather, and great-great-grandfather. He is visited by polygamists and an Army general. He is discovered by a brilliant Dutch philosopher/scientist. Yet *The Dead Fathers*, for all the noise and chaos, never stops being quiet and still.

—Theric Jepson
author of *Just Julie's Fine* and *Byuck*,
co-editor of *Monsters and Mormons*,
and editor of *Irreantum*

THE DEAD FATHERS

BCC PRESS

BY COMMON CONSENT PRESS is a non-profit publisher dedicated to producing affordable, high-quality books that help define and shape the Latter-day Saint experience. BCC Press publishes books that address all aspects of Mormon life. Our mission includes finding manuscripts that will contribute to the lives of thoughtful Latter-day Saints, mentoring authors and nurturing projects to completion, and distributing important books to the Mormon audience at the lowest possible cost.

THE DEAD FATHERS

grief and poker in the west desert

a novel by

John Bennion

For information contact
By Common Consent Press
972 East Burnham Lane
Draper, Utah 84020

Cover design: D Christian Harrison
Cover photograph: C. Riley Nelson
Book design: Andrew Heiss

www.bccpress.org
ISBN-13: 978-1-961471-23-8

10 9 8 7 6 5 4 3 2 1

In the heav'ns are parents single?
No, the thought makes reason stare!
Truth is reason; truth eternal
Tells me I've a mother there.

—Eliza R. Snow, "O My Father"

The earth rolls upon her wings, and the sun giveth his light by day, and the moon giveth her light by night, and the stars also give their light, as they roll upon their wings in their glory, in the midst of the power of God.

—Doctrine and Covenants 88:45

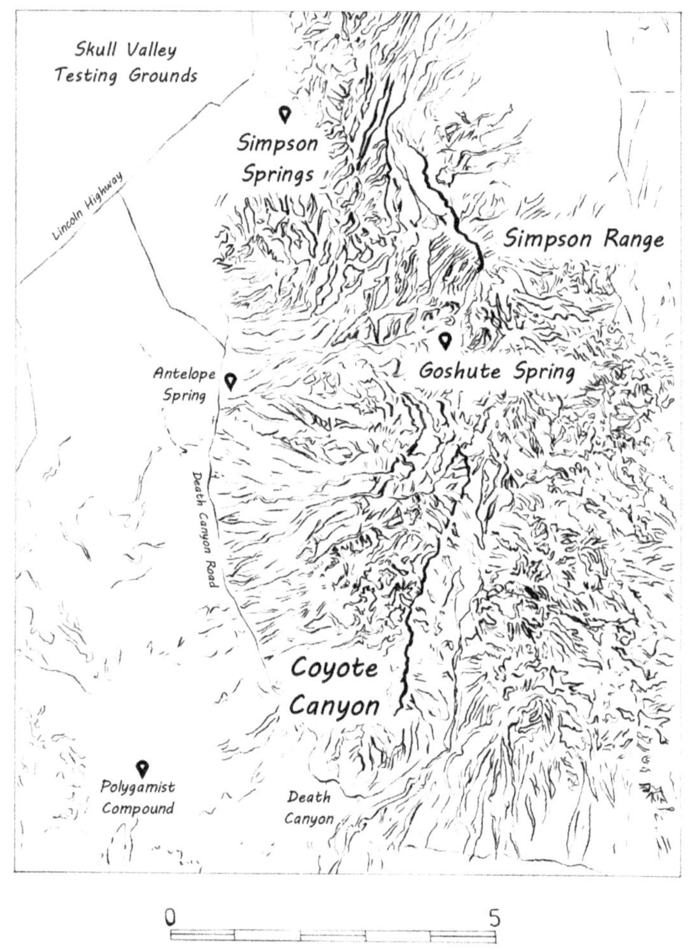

Map, drawn by Hannah Landeen

Christopher Twist Patriarchal Line

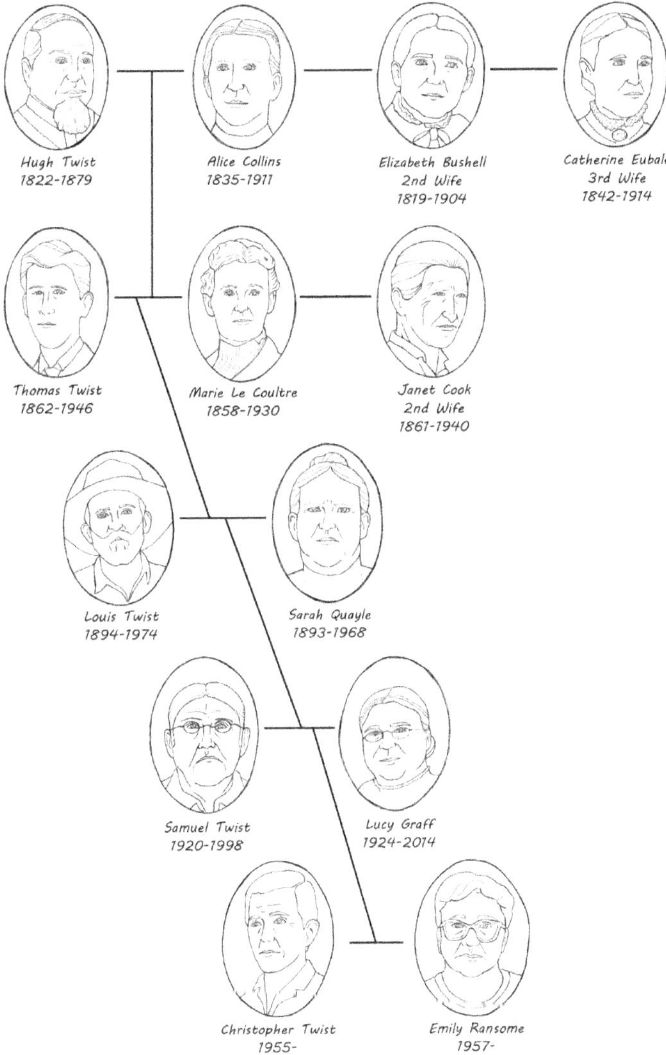

Quist Family Tree, drawn by Hannah Landeen

Playing Solitaire

In the evening they show up in my trailer to play cards, four old men sitting around a table, as if posing for the Cézanne Emily and I saw in London. I never see them coming. What appear to be shadows beyond the edge of the lantern light become hands, arms, and faces. One of us shuffles the cards, someone cuts, and we begin. I don't have a radio and none of us sing well, so our only music is the unearthly yap and wail of coyotes up on the ridge.

The dilapidated travel trailer I'm staying in sits just above the delta of an old creek, where it's been for a couple of decades. From my front step I can see across the flat to the next range, the one after that, and on a clear day, the one after that. Basin and range. The only bright green is the moss in the pond created by Antelope Spring, not far from my trailer. This is no place for Cézanne, who loved the color green. He also loved blue, and I have a thin edge of that in the mountains to the west, eighty miles away on the border of Nevada.

Louis, my grandfather, who died when I was seventeen, rubs his hands together. "Cold as a witch's tits in a brass bra." He had four daughters but never learned to temper his speech. My father Samuel was the caboose, six years younger than the youngest girl, but before he was born the pattern was set: Louis thought he had to define himself against all those women who filled his house.

Hugh frowns at Louis, his grandson, probably judging him for lack of piety, not political correctness. "Let no corrupt communication proceed out of your mouth, but that which is good to the use of edifying, that it may minister grace unto the hearers. Ephesians 4 and 29."

My father Samuel holds his fingers out for two cards. "You haven't touched anybody's tits for more than half a century." Louis's wife left him in his fifties, when he started his seventh homestead in the desert. She'd had enough of poverty and air that dries bread to toast in three minutes.

Louis glares at his son, my father.

I deal myself two cards. "You have never been cruel, Dad. Don't start now."

He looks at the two new cards, throws down his hand. "Sorry. I was really talking about myself." Before my father died my mother Lucy left off sleeping with him because he was drunk every weekend. My older sister, Julie, shared this bit of information with me. When my mother became senile, she thought that Julie, who never married, would be interested in our parents' sex life.

"And I was thinking about myself," I say. "The only living thing in my bed has been an occasional mouse." Once I found a clutch of newborns in my bed. I slid the wriggling bodies onto a plate and put them next to the furnace. They would have frozen outside. Now they live in the cupboards. "And that packrat." While I was outside, one came in from the cold and gathered silverware, pens, and .22 bullets into a nest under my blankets. He was a fellow traveler and a fellow squatter, but I put him out of my bed.

Hugh looks at his cards, smug. From the letters and journals I've read, all three of his wives loved him, but there was friction between the matriarch and the other wives. She couldn't abide having other women in her house. He bets five matchsticks.

"You should get a blow snake," says Dad. "Take care of the rodents." He never smiles when he makes a joke, so I'm not sure whether he's serious.

I lay my cards down carefully, another losing hand.

As generally happens every night, I start thinking about Emily, which makes me melancholy. Not quite a year ago she said, "I don't want to have sex when we don't love each other." It was a warning shot. Half a year later she started an affair with another lawyer. They knew each other from several cases where they were on opposing sides. Somehow their adversarial relationship sparked sexual collusion.

Louis breaks the silence. "Christopher," he says to me, "you're turning whiny and sentimental. Which is one step away from senile." He was a hard-assed desert rancher with perpetual and ill-founded hopes of making a wad of money. Riverbed, his last spread was on land about five miles from here. He points to my blanket covering the entrance. "Unless you get a hold of yourself, your mind will be like that doorway. Not just packrats and mice, but snakes and scorpions will come and go." At the end of his life, he lived in a cabin that was as dilapidated and filthy as my trailer, but at least he had a wooden door. "You'll end up like Sula." Sula was Hugh's daughter who lived a few canyons over. My father told me she was a feral woman and killed a man with an axe.

"And he was driven from men," quotes Hugh, "and did eat grass as oxen, and his body was wet with the dew of heaven, till his hairs were grown like eagles' feathers and his nails like birds' claws." His voice has a hint of his native Welsh.

"Damn right," says Louis. "Nebuchadnezzar lost his shit. Just like you're losing yours." He's talking from experience, because he certainly lost his shit at the end—never cleaning himself, sitting alone in his cabin, telling and retelling a few repetitive, rambling, violent stories. My main memory of my grandfather before his death is of him standing with hip boots in an irrigation ditch while he lays a canvas dam. That and hobbling out to the outhouse on crutches after his knees and hips lost all cartilage. This was before replacements were possible. The pain made him crazy, compounding his dementia. Hopefully not my future.

"You know we won't abandon you," says my father. "Even if you start eating grass."

Cold comfort. "That's what I'm worried about, that you'll never leave me. I thought there were boundaries that protected the living from the dead. Are you supposed to come every damn night?"

The question makes both my father and great-grandfather uncomfortable, but not my rebel grandfather. It makes him angry. "Don't talk to me about boundaries, you whelp, when you defy every one of them yourself. You're the definition of off-the-rails."

When they talk down to me as if I'm still a child, I feel angry and peevish, like a teenager. It's in the Mormon tradition occasionally to be visited by the dead, but "occasionally" is the key word here: they are supposed to have a message to impart. Then they leave, or if needed, they come back two more times. It's like one of God's rules or something: visitors come once or they come three times. But my dead relatives come every damn night, and "you're losing your shit" doesn't seem much like a divine message.

When they first showed up early in December, I was— startled. Even more so when they broke out the cards. After a couple of visits, I shook their hands when they arrived to see if they were resurrected beings. My hypothesis was that Hugh would touch my hand, but the other two, having died as sinners, would refuse. Or worse, they would try and I'd feel nothing. They all had firm grips, tactile. So much for that scriptural test. Worse than useless because it made them livid.

"We're not agents of Lucifer," said Hugh.

"Don't be a damned fool," said Louis.

"Very hurtful," said my father Samuel. "You asked us to come and then you mistrust us."

"I didn't ask you to come." My father glared at me until I remembered that I *had* been thinking about him, and about Grandpa, all the time I'd spent with him in the desert. I may have muttered something about wanting to talk to them again.

Water under the bridge. If I hadn't spoken, I'd be alone. That old hypocrite Louis is right about one thing:

I have let normal human conventions slide. I'm becoming as grotty as he was when he was alive. I look down at my untrimmed fingernails. I also need a haircut. And a shave.

"And a bath," Samuel says. I can't keep them out of my trailer, and I can't keep them out of my head.

The other two nod. "If we can smell you," says Louis, "it's got to be bad." He's winning for a change. I'm out, my father is down to a few matchsticks, and Hugh, who has an uncanny knack for a game he disdained when he was alive, covers his pile with his hand so we won't know how many he has left.

The three of them look at each other, as if they already know the outcome, which makes me wonder again how time works for them.

"I raise you ten," says Louis, glancing at me. "Are you bored, Christopher?"

"Just not into it tonight."

Hugh holds out one finger. I'm not sure whether he's asking for a card or pointing at me. "You think this is just a game?" Everyone is still.

"I guess I do."

"You're as stiff-necked as a neanderthal," says Louis.

Both Samuel and Hugh shove their matchsticks into the middle of the table. "All in," says my father. "You're not letting yourself see the big picture, Son. You're not paying attention."

"War is coming," says Louis. "They want to pull down the whole structure. It's a damned drastic situation."

"War is coming" is new. I wonder if they're finally going to tell me something significant.

"War?"

They all nod, but just keep playing. I was a journalist before I retired, and I want not just what, but who, when, why, and how. None of that is forthcoming.

"How will it start? Will it be an atomic bomb? A rifle shot? A thrown dirt clod? Will I have to flee to the top of Indian Peak? Or are you speaking metaphorically?"

"You really are clueless," says my father.

Which makes me as angry as a teenager. "So inform me!" I shout at him. "You're supposed to enlighten me, but you won't tell me jack shit!"

They look at each other as if they can't believe they spawned such a disappointing creature.

"You pestilent bugger!" says Louis. "Show some damned respect for your elders!"

I smile at him. "I'm just trying to clarify the details of your prophecy. Whole structure of what? The game of poker?"

My father glares at me and throws down his cards.

"Everything!" says Louis. "The whole fucking universe."

Which is clear as ditchwater.

"We're headed for chaos," says my father.

Hugh says, "He that has ears, let him hear."

A knock sounds on the side of the trailer. A woman calls, "Are you decent? It's freezing out here."

"Dammit," says Louis, also throwing down his cards. "I have a full house."

"It's Thomas," says Hugh.

"It's a woman," I say.

"Thomas the traitor," says Hugh. "He's stirring the pot."

They fade into the corners of the trailer.

Thomas? I've never been able to get a clear answer from them as to why my great-grandfather never shows up.

I lift the edge of the blanket door. "Carrie-Anne." My daughter. She visited me just before Christmas, trying to get me to come home.

"If you get out of the way," she says, "I'll come in." I rear back. She steps inside and stands over the stove to spread her hands above the heat. "Dad, are you all right? You look like you just saw a ghost."

When I can speak, I say, "For a second I thought you were your mother."

"She scares you that bad?"

I shrug.

She nods at the table, "Playing solitaire?"

This stops me because it's exactly what Louis said when he and the other two first came to my trailer. "We've come to keep you from playing solitaire." Then he laughed like hell. I hope my daughter is not thinking about me masturbating, but she's not one to balk at a ribald joke, especially not one at my expense.

"I play all the hands," I say, "but I always lose because I can't keep a poker face."

"Dad joke. You should get a door."

"I should."

"Where's your truck?"

"Halfway up the canyon. Something with the transmission. I heard a clank and then there was this horrific grinding noise. The engine runs fine, or did."

She frowns at me. "So if you had an accident or a heart attack or hypothermia, you'd be dead."

I shrug. "People come by more often than you'd think."

She opens the fridge, gags, and shuts it again quick. "You need fresh vegetables. And a bottle of Clorox."

"Spencer will bring my food order next time he comes out."

"At least your books are tidy." I've filled every shelf of the trailer—novels and memoirs and cultural commentary I didn't have time to read when I was a newspaper editor. She opens the door to the toilet, where I built more shelves. "Even in there?"

"The waterline to the trailer froze and burst years ago."

"Where—?"

"There's an outhouse," I say.

She rolls her eyes. "I dreamed about you freezing to death out here alone."

I smile. "A Popsicle."

She rolls her eyes like she did when she was a teenager. "Not funny, Dad. Can you imagine how I felt. It seemed too real for a dream."

I can imagine, but I'm so close to tears that I can't answer her.

"This is different. You are different. What happened, Dad? I mean you used to come out here for a few days or a week, just disappear without warning. But you always came back. This time it's been three and a half months. And this trailer doesn't even have a door now."

"You know what happened."

"Mom's fling with Roger? You would know if you saw her that she still loves you."

"Then why did she do it?"

"Ask her!"

"You say I've changed. True. I feel unable to—I can't navigate—I don't like being with people all the time. And I have my work."

"Keeping vandals away from Spencer Murdock's property?" She shakes her head. "That's not real work."

"That and—"

She leans forward.

I wonder if she'll understand. "I'm looking for a cave."

She turns toward me, every part of her face frowns. "What?"

I know it's a mistake to tell her about my compulsion. "My great-grandfather wrote about a Goshute who escaped soldiers by hiding in it. I want to see it." I want to tell her that finding it seems essential, but I can't explain why. It just is. The idea of crawling where that man hid thrills me.

She bites one side of her lower lip. "I have something to say to you"—her voice hard as glass. "Come home, Dad. This is foolishness." She levels her gray eyes like they are two rifle barrels—eyes just like Hugh's—gray Welsh eyes, his thin face. Her lips and nose from Alice Collins Twist, her great-great-great-grandmother and Hugh's wife. Sometimes I can't keep the generations straight, the repetition of their features. Carrie-Anne also looks like my grandmother, Sarah Quayle. Except the woman glaring at me is tall and thin, and Sarah was short and thin, a tiny Manx woman. Emily once asked me why a lapsed Mormon is so obsessed with his genealogy, but it's something I can't escape. Their genes replicate in my children's faces and their actions mark the landscape I live in. "You need to shave and you stink. You probably have fungus growing in your—"

"I would bathe if the shower worked."

"Fungus, Dad."

I nod. She's probably right because I always have a terrible crotch itch. "There's a fungus amongus."

She doesn't even smile. "This trailer is an abomination. You'll die of hantavirus or botulism or cholera or something worse. Come get in the car."

Now she's fighting dirty. I try to hold my face passive.

"Remember Karin?"

"I haven't been gone that long," I say.

"You haven't seen her since before Thanksgiving," says Carrie-Anne.

"I couldn't bear the thought of sitting with our children and grandchildren over Thanksgiving dinner—pretending everything was normal and well ordered."

"She cried when you were not there."

Karin, Kar-in, Care-in. "That tender soul. When she was born, I couldn't touch her. She frightened me."

Carrie-Anne stares at me. "Frightened you?"

"Tiny, fragile thing. Could have snuffed out just like that. I remember when she was one. That's when she became a person to me." Not a person, a miracle—that clear-faced child. I think about saying "snuffed-out." It's the way Grandpa Louis would have said it. With visitors, even with my own daughter, I lean into the persona of the desert rat, even though I lived most of my life in the city. My occupation was not ranching but reporting on the news and later editing it. Why I pretend to be who I'm not is a question for a psychotherapist.

Carrie-Anne frowns.

"Be objective, Dad. If I left Bruce and the kids and started looking for a hole in the ground, what would you think?"

She's right. The Dead Fathers are right. I have lost my shit. All I have to do is walk out the door with her. Instead I frown.

"Come, Dad. Get in the car." She lays her hand on my arm and pulls at me. "You smell bad, and you have no door on your trailer, and I can't stand to see you like this."

I shake my head. "No. I can't. Some things are too much."

"Too much to forgive?"

"I guess that's what I mean."

"You're not blameless."

"Of course not."

Maybe she sees that I've dug in my heels. Maybe it's like she says, that she can't bear to see me like this. Maybe the smell in my trailer *is* too much for her. Whatever her reasons, she doesn't keep trying to persuade me. She leaves well before I'm ready for her to leave. I think about my life in the city—structured by my job, my neighbors' expectations, and my church. I left them all. Emily and I lived in the house next door to where Carrie-Anne and Bruce live. Emily still lives there. That life feels like it belongs to another person, maybe someone I've read about.

I watch the dust from her car rise in the cold moonlight before returning inside. I think about those other times I escaped my job or my home when those straitjackets became too much for me. Three decades ago there was a cabin here built by my grandfather. Vandals broke the windows and pulled down the walls. Then someone dragged this old trailer here and lived in it for a couple of years. After that I used it a few times, swept the fly bodies and mice turds out, and lay my sleeping bag on the old mattress. Last fall I found that the new owner, an urban redneck, built a barn to stable his horses and ATVs. The door was gone from the trailer, windows broken, skunk and mouse and other scat all over the floor. I swept it out again, boarded up the windows with cardboard, and hung a blanket over the door. It was sufficient for my needs. Still is. Spencer talked with me next time he came out. He was going to ask me to leave, but then he found out that I was Louis Twist's grandson, a maverick desert rancher that Spencer's father, a real estate agent, took him to meet a few times when he was a kid.

I sit at the table. I want to be alone with my sorrow, but they creep back.

"When I first ran sheep out here," says Hugh, "I nearly froze to death. Worse than this drafty place. I had to bed down with the sheep."

"Red sprayed like a pinwheel, a fireworks pinwheel," says Louis, who, like Hugh, is stuck in a primal memory, a GIF that keeps playing through each of their heads. It's one of the stories Louis repeated when he was senile. "That coyote went heads and tails."

"Not here," continues Hugh. "Or not right here—just down where that monstrosity of a barn is."

"Heads and tails," says Louis. "A crimson pinwheel."

Hugh grins. "I had to bed down with one ewe on my left side and another on my right or I would have frozen to death. Living wool blankets."

"The coldest I ever was," I say, "was driving Grandpa's cows between the desert and Rockwood. I'd have to get off my horse and walk to keep warm."

"You were all of five," says Louis. "A little tyke."

"You always liked it out here better than I did," says Samuel, whose career was teaching political science to community college students.

"You can't go home," says Louis. "Don't give in to those women."

I shake my head. "No worry there. I'm too fragile for that."

Dad says, "Not fragile. Strong as a rock."

"Hard as a rock," says Louis.

Hugh purses his lips and looks away from his rude grandson.

"Time to go to Ely," says Louis. "They got women there who can make your old pecker spin like a top."

Hugh's mouth flattens and his brows glower. "You're worse than he is. How will lasciviousness help anything?"

"But we're in total agreement on one thing," says my father, as I watch him cheat at solitaire. "You can't go home. Where would we be then?"

"Where you were before I came here."

"You seem to think we're just here for our entertainment," says my father.

I want to ask them why they blamed Thomas for Carrie-Anne's visit. Hugh said Thomas is a traitor—to what? The Twist family? The Church? But I am too tired and their answers are always less than revealing. I'm also tired from being pulled one way by Carrie-Anne, who didn't know how much I wanted to just get in the car with her, and pulled the other way by the Dead Fathers, who don't know that I won't be a part of their battle, whatever it is.

Sometime after midnight, they finally leave. Their comings and goings are similar to when I saw a coyote in my backyard in the city. It seemed to be a moon shadow, then it was distinguishable as a coyote, then it was gone.

Laid low by Carrie-Anne's visit, or rather by my own refusal to just go home, I stay in bed all the next day. When my father, grandfather, and great-grandfather try to come that night, I put the pillow over my head and refuse to talk to them. They complain loudly about the mistreatment of heavenly visitors. Louis says, "Why are you practicing stupidity? You'll get good at it if you keep going the way you are." Which is kind of lame, even for a dead person.

After they leave, I decide that beyond frustrating them, staying in bed doesn't help anything. It only makes me twitchy and morose.

I rise before dawn and need to pee. It's urgent, so I clap on my felt cowboy hat and slip on my boots. I push through my blanket door to walk to the outhouse twenty yards from the trailer. Finished with my business, I get back inside where it's warmer. I remove my boots, pull on my pants, button a shirt, pull my boots back on, and grab some wood for the stove from the pile I've chopped. I feel better after my morning ritual.

I turn the heat on under the coffeepot and sit on my stoop, which is just railroad ties stacked to make steps. Sitting here is my favorite time of the day, before invaders from the city spew dust trails across the desert. Solitary. Also before my three fathers invade from—where? Certainly not from any paradise, spirit prison, or heaven that I learned about as a child. Still, this early on a Monday morning at the tag end of winter, the people from the city are in their warm beds and my dead fathers are off doing whatever it is they do when they're not bothering me. Hopefully they're taking a seminar in communicating in clear, specific, comprehensible language. Maybe taught by John the Revelator or Isaiah.

Sunlight hits the peak of Turkey Mountain. The sight fills me up and I'm grateful for the subtle pleasures left to me: sunlight, the sound of water running into the pond just down from my trailer, the complex songs of morning birds, the cup in my hand that both warms my hands and clears away my nighttime headache. A new pleasure, the sound of Carrie-Anne's voice, forces itself on me. Unlike the other pleasures, her voice urges me to do something.

Sunlight creeps down the mountain. My second great-grandfather Hugh claimed it looked like a turkey on a platter. Wistful thinking when he was a hungry boy herding sheep. Myself? I generally construe it like my grandfather did—as a woman's breast. This morning I miss Emily intensely. I feel myself at a tipping point, almost ready to return and sort through the tangle of our marriage. Seeing her and my grandchildren and hearing their voices, those simple pleasures, might make it worth the work.

The plain is still in shadow from Simpson Range to the east, behind me. Then the boundary of light rushes toward me as the sun rises. Beautiful—except for the wart on the land, close in, just below me to the left—Spencer's barn, huge as a big-box store. He keeps a few horses there that I feed every morning just after breakfast, a black mare and a chestnut gelding. There's a tack room, full of saddles and bridles, and above that an apartment, where he can stay when he comes out to the desert. Outside he has a horse trailer parked, built like a Cadillac limousine. Would it be vandalism to throw a stick of dynamite inside?

I've read mystical feminist nature writers who say that landscapes are female—part of Mother Earth, but with the possible exception of Turkey Mountain, this part of Utah desert doesn't show feminine curves—just a flat plane and a few rough crags. The hills to the north, inside Skull Valley Testing Grounds, look like plated, ancient beasts, mired in mud.

The desert is deceptive, which my dead fathers might think is a feminine trait, but they are proof that deception isn't gender specific.

I thought this expansive place would be empty of people, like it was when I was a child and teenager. Leaving Emily, I wanted a retreat, solitude so profound that I might see a vision. But my only vision has been of my Dead Fathers, and solitude is rare. The desert has become as crowded as a mall, overrun with people whose desires are worn on the outside, like coats of many colors. Leaving the city, these seekers become unbridled, thinking themselves free to do whatever they damn well please. Rock hounds, ATV drivers, rabbit hunters, pronghorn poachers, polygamists, survivalists and preppers, geocachers, amateur historians following the hoofbeats of Pony Express riders. The trail between way stations turned into the stagecoach and freight route and later the Lincoln Highway. Last week the Army Reserve was on maneuvers, crowding the road with their camo jeeps and personnel trucks and shooting their cannons over the highway into targets out in the Skull Valley Testing Grounds. Occasionally someone interesting stops by. Once, a Saudi climate-change scientist wanted me to tell him how the local plants have changed since I was a boy. He was all right, another child of the desert. I don't mind amateur anthropologists looking for pictographs, birders looking for eagles or meadowlarks, cavers who like to explore abandoned mines, but most people who stop are pests. They rile me up, and it takes more effort than I want to spend to regain my equilibrium after they leave. Every weekend, the campground at Simpson Springs is full of them; every cedar tree along the road between here and the main highway has a huge trailer and muscle-bound pickup parked next to it with lawn chairs arranged around a circle of rocks. The fuckers have the illusion that they're desert people.

Some belong here, like me. Hugh Twist, my great-great-grandfather, ran sheep on the flat below here. His son Thomas herded them. Hugh's infamous daughter Sula married the son of one of Hugh's friends and lived in Death Canyon just around the mountains south of here with her sister wife, Agnes. My grandfather also herded sheep and homesteaded here, raising alfalfa for cattle. Then in the late Forties after this place proved to have too little water or fertile ground for the expansive fields he imagined, he moved his cattle farther west and irrigated his fields from wells. Now polygamists own his former farm and grow corn for the making of ethanol.

I say my people belong here, but the Twists and other Mormon ranchers and sheepmen are relative newcomers.

The Goshutes, their ancestors, and other peoples have been here for thousands of years. In modern times they've been herded onto two reservations, one four hours to the west, the other a half hour to the northeast. Basque, Navajo, and Mexican sheepherders also lived here. Earlier in my life I might have said that none of these people ever left the desert, and meant it figuratively—that their rock foundations, ditches, sheep trails, and roads remain, preserved by the arid climate. Or that they live on only in the retelling of their stories. Recently I've learned from the visits of my dead fathers that literal existence is durable. I knew this as a child, but when I was no longer a child, my belief in my own immortality wasted away from malnourishment.

The word "desert" is also deceptive because it's not true desert, even if it looks barren. It's the eastern edge of the Great Basin. Semi-arid. Teeming with life. The Goshutes ate eighty different kinds of plants, about half as many kinds of insects, reptiles, and small and large mammals. They ate anything that moved or grew. They would have grinned at the irony of a packrat taking sanctuary in their dwelling—grinned and taken out their skinning knives.

After my cup of coffee, I pour a new one and eat breakfast—my last couple of eggs and toast that I have to scrape the mold off of. It is time for a new food order. As soon as those words cross my brain, I laugh, because the phrase sounds like New World Order, which is similar to what the Dead Fathers seem to think is coming, a change that will unseat all the traditions. Paranoid bastards all of them.

I ride my mountain bike down toward the horses. I feel silly riding a bike when there are horses around, but when my truck broke down, Spencer told me I could never touch his mare or his gelding. He's concerned about liability if I get myself hurt. He's especially concerned because he knows Emily is a lawyer. So I asked him to get me a bike. When I get to the barn, the horses nicker and poke their noses over the fence. They don't really like me, but they do like being fed. I dump hay and grain into their bins and check the water.

Then I angle the front brim of my hat low over my eyes to block the sun, and I head for the canyon. First, I ride along the ditch that Louis dug by hand ninety years earlier to carry the water from Goshute Spring up in the canyon to his small patch of alfalfa which was about where Spencer's barn is now. It took all the water from that spring up in the canyon and the trickle from Antelope Spring to be enough for his acre of hay. His ditch sweeps in and out, in graceful curves, staying at the edge of the ridges as it climbs toward the spring. Sine waves mapped on an irregular landscape. A jack rabbit lopes away; a cottontail holds still as a stone. Birds float overhead—ravens now, sometimes turkey vultures, golden eagles, or red-tailed hawks.

About two miles up, I drop down to the road and pass my pickup, which I was able to get out of the way. I think about what my daughter said about being unable to get help if something happened. She's right, but I don't want to do anything about it. I don't have enough money for repairs unless I dip into my retirement, and I want to leave all of that to Carrie-Anne, Todd, Rebecca, their spouses, and my four grandchildren.

Once inside the valley, with its thirteen spills of dirt below the mines, I see seven magpies perched on the old tin building next to the creek. I've never seen so many of the carrion eaters together—a sure sign of something, maybe of the impending war that the Dead Fathers have started talking about. I walk toward the spring and kick up a little buck. After he bounds away, I cup my hand to drink, ignoring the danger of giardia. I'm immune after a lifetime of drinking from streams where cattle and sheep also drink. I leave my bike and walk a mile farther because the road over the pass is too snowbound for the bicycle. I imagine the Goshute and his ancestors walking the same path I walk. Those families had a circle of various camps that they moved between based on food gathering: on the creeks in the spring for greens, higher up for chokecherries and sego lily tubers in the summer, even higher in the fall for pine nuts. I wonder how the Goshute that my ancestor Thomas wrote about saw the plateau. Certainly not the way I see it, but maybe there are some similarities. All desert people have lack of water on the brain. We would have that much in common.

Above the valley of the mines is a high plateau—occasional juniper trees, what Louis called cedars, some sagebrush, Scotch thistles, prickly pear cactus, crested wheat grass introduced for feed for cows and sheep. Somewhere up here is the natural cave that Thomas also wrote about. Escaping from the soldiers stationed at Simpson Springs, the Goshute crawled into a coyote den, one that opened up inside. When I first started my search in December, I just wandered the area. When that didn't work, I marked a map in grids and spent each day searching one grid. That didn't help, so now I'm just wandering again. Maybe the Goshute's long-dead spirit will guide me. Carrie-Anne disregarded my work to discover the cave, but for me it's not a mere hole in the ground but the umbilicus of the earth, or at least of my part of the desert.

I follow cow and deer trails, looking for a sinkhole or a coyote den. I pass an area thick with cryptobiotic soil—something ranchers don't worry much about, although cattle probably do the most damage. I stop and look at the clumps of black, like soot on a casserole, stretching to either side of the thin trail. The desert may seem unchangeable, but it's more delicate than either the tourists or the old cattlemen think. A four-wheeler track will mar the ground for a hundred years.

About a hundred yards to the southeast there's a congregation of sage grouse—a lek, or mating ground. Through my field glasses I watch the grouse mill around, graceful gray hens and larger males, who puff out their white chests. I hear a faint, strange sound, something like the popping noise kids make by sticking a finger in their mouths. It's the mating call the males make by filling air sacs on their chests and throwing their heads back in a jerking dance: "Follup, follup, follup." I watch the males circle each other, some of them bumping chests. The females seem hardly interested.

I feel lucky—few people have seen the mating dance—and hope perches in my soul, a thing with warm feathers, just like in the poem. The display is probably another sign. Trying to figure out what the dance might mean distances me from participating vicariously—which is the way of most organic pleasures. Once you think about the concept of beauty the sensation of it is gone.

On my way back from the valley, I see a truck I don't recognize pulling away with Spencer's horse trailer. I pedal faster but before I can even get to the road, the outfit has driven south toward Six-mile. I'll be up shit creek if I've allowed someone to steal Spencer's trailer. Panicking is useless. I can't chase after them on a bicycle.

So instead of getting worked up, I shrug. My breathing slows, as does my heartbeat. It's my tried-and-true method now of responding to emotion or danger—I shut down. It happened when Emily copulated with Roger and it happened when Carrie-Anne visited. I make myself remember what some Zen master said: life is like boarding a ship that's headed out to sea where it will sink. Facing that sure outcome, nothing else seems significant. Soon I'm calm again. Maybe that's why my editor was glad I chose to leave—the fire I once had in my gut about the powerful screwing over the weak is now just ash.

In the evening as I cook my meal, a truck stops outside and a man calls out my name. It's Spencer, carrying my box of groceries. I take the box and put it on my table. He has never come inside. Even during the winter he made me talk to him in the cold.

I see the same truck from earlier parked on the road. A man and a woman lean against the hood. The woman waves at me. I observe with pleasure her shape, which is defined clearly against the white truck.

"Chris," says Spencer, "where were you today?"

I turn my attention from the woman back to him. "I rode my bike up to the mines. You know I do that every day."

"What if it hadn't been me? What if it had been somebody stealing me blind?"

"The hitch was locked, and I have to get my exercise."

"I pay you to watch my building. If you can't do that, get off my property."

"Tell the fat bastard to stick his measly $10 a day up his asshole," Louis says softly from behind the blanket door.

"Quiet!"

"What?" Spencer takes a step forward. "What did you say?"

I'm caught between two sons-of-bitches, one old and crusty and dead, one younger but just as obnoxious. Both mavericks. Both obstinate. Luckily I'm also a son-of-a-bitch, or aspire to be one. I look him in the eye. "I feed your horses and I watch your property. But I didn't sign on to be on duty twenty-four hours a day. If you need to hire somebody else, go ahead."

Spencer looks up at me, standing on the wooden steps to the trailer, then he looks at the ground. Finally, he grins at me. "You know I can't hire nobody else. Just don't be gone all day."

He turns partway, but then faces me again. "You doing all right? I can get somebody to come out and put a door on this old trailer."

I shrug. "The blanket is just fine." I step back to let him know I'm finished talking. He walks to the truck, climbing in the back seat as the other man starts the engine. As the woman climbs in the front, her jeans pull tight across her butt. I'm grateful that my insensible carcass still responds to some stimuli—the line of sunrise moving across the flat faster than a horse can run, black crusts of cryptobiotic soil, the dance and call of grouse, and the curve of a woman. Yea, these things are too wonderful for me. My own proverbs from the desert.

But I do not look forward to another evening with the three patriarchs. I think of escaping them by heading west to Wendover, spending the night in a hotel room, having a bath, a prime-rib dinner, and an hour with a prostitute. It would be my second time. In January a bitter cold wind blew through my trailer, and I got in my truck to get warm. I drove west, then further west, and then five hours later I was in Wendover. Maybe the second time would be more fun than the first, which was awkward on my part and perfunctory on hers.

But my truck is broken down. There was an old cowboy, also broke-down, living in an old shack on the Grime's ranch over in Footes Canyon, who would give me a ride if I asked him, but he broke his leg in February when his horse fell on him on slippery ground. He's gone back to the city to live with his son. And anyway, tonight I'm thinking of Emily—her blue eyes, clear as sky, her wry smile. Carrie-Anne says that Emily still loves me. How could our daughter know that? I don't want to think that it might be true. Hope is like thinking your boot is empty when a scorpion's down there waiting to sting you.

"One," says Hugh. The old Puritan is winning again, and Louis is stuck in his story again, so it's clear how the evening is going to go.

"Right next to where this trailer is now—" says Louis.

"Was a row of currant bushes," I say.

Louis glares at me.

"Christopher!" says Samuel in his fatherly voice. "Let your grandfather tell his story!"

"Or maybe he wants to tell it for me," says Louis. "Maybe he doesn't know the implications of interrupting the story."

Implications? He's half up out of his seat. Is he going to try to whup my ass? A dead man and a decrepit live one wrestling on a grimy floor. A video of that might get a few hits on YouTube. Or not. I don't know that he'd show up on camera.

"Three cards," says my father, trying to pull Louis back to the game.

Louis sits down again. "The currants are just turning purple and every morning the ripest ones are gone, but I can't tell what animal is eating them. I think it's maybe a skunk or sage hens or kangaroo rats."

I scrape my chair back and walk to the stove and fill my cup. Louis waits until I'm back in my seat.

"So, I go out before first light and see him—a coyote, fat as a tick. He looks up at me from biting at the currants, using his teeth to strip the branches clean. His belly is round, his mouth red. Quick as quick, he turns and runs up the hill behind the garden. I aim the .22 at the base of his tail, at the bung, which looks like a puckered-up mouth. I never miss, and the shot forces the mash of currents out its mouth in a spray of red as the coyote tumbles head over tail, just like a red pinwheel." Louis holds his sides as he laughs.

"Perfect," says Hugh, laying down his cards—another full house.

I say, "I can't figure how you cheat."

Samuel throws down his cards. "He doesn't need to cheat."

"Teaching you a lesson," Hugh says. "Not to believe in the chimera of gambling."

"Chimera hell," I say.

I doubt it's cheating, as in putting cards up his sleeve or dealing good cards to himself, but he always gets great hands. Even seeing the past and future as one eternal round wouldn't help him win like this. Maybe God helps him. Or Lucifer. Or both. Maybe that's the trouble they're anticipating: light and darkness in cahoots like in the time of Job.

With both hands, Hugh pulls the matchsticks toward his side of the table. He levels his gaze at me. "The next few days are momentous."

"Like the spine of the continental divide," says my father, his hand flat, fingers close together. "A drop of water can flow this way or that." He tips the back of his hand one way then the other. "You're teetering on the edge."

"A delicate balance," says Louis.

"Much depends on how you respond," says Hugh.

"So don't fuck up," says Louis.

"Louis!" shouts Hugh. "Language!"

They play silently, glaring at each other. Louis holds up his fingers to show how many cards he wants.

"Fat as a tick," says Louis, his mind still mired in his story.

My father says, "Your mother actually told me 'Lips that touch wine will never touch mine.'"

"They didn't all love each other." Hugh lays down his cards, another winning hand. "But they all loved me. Each of them welcomed me to their beds. Open arms."

My father throws down his cards.

The story I want to hear is one that great-grandfather Thomas wrote in his journal. But he never shows up to answer my questions. The story of the Goshute and the cave. I have a typescript of the journal in my trailer along with all my other books, but every time I look for it, it's in a different place, as if the Dead Fathers don't want me to read it, even though I've already read it many times. After the three are gone, I search, and finally find it buried under the stove wood. Maybe they hoped I'd throw it in the fire by mistake. It is a horrible story, but I don't think they were worried about my sensibility. When I first read it, I was just back from my mission to the Ojibway Reserve in Manitoba, Canada. I wept and my father, even though I was grown, held me in his arms, trying to console me. The impact of the story has hardly faded, so I don't know why I feel compelled to read it again. I train my flashlight on the yellowed pages of Thomas's journal:

My Goshute friend told me about what happened to his father, who was the leader of a family in the late 1850s. One day he returned from checking his rabbit traps to watch a white soldier ride after his daughter-in-law and scoop her across his saddle. He saw two other soldiers with their rifles out, and then he saw the bodies of his son, his wife, his daughters, the patches of red, the pools of black. One of the three soldiers rode toward him, so he dropped the rabbits and ran as bullets whistled past his ears. He knew he could outlast their horses, but over a short distance the horses could sprint faster than him. He twisted his body into a hole in the ground that he had seen coyotes use for a den. Inside it widened into a natural cave. He pulled a boulder after him to partially cover the opening. He crept down the cave in the darkness until he saw light. When he crawled to the surface, he found another den at the base of a shelf of rocks. From the mouth of that den he watched the soldiers searching for him. Of course they never found him. They took the girl back to the Simpson Springs station, where the Goshute didn't dare go, because of the dozens of soldiers there. He mourned his family, wrapped their bodies in their blankets and thrust them down into a branch of the cave that had saved his life. Then he watched the soldiers from the ridge behind the encampment. After a week they dumped the girl's body in a ravine, and he had to wrap her in a blanket and bury her in the cave. The next day the three soldiers left, transferred to a new station farther west. Goshute boys sometimes ran parallel to the stagecoaches, turning cartwheels and handsprings. When the coaches stopped at the next waystation in Riverbed, they begged for bullets or food from the passengers. This Goshute, the father, didn't do gymnastic tricks, but he tracked who came and went on the stage. The night of the transfer, he and other Goshute men circled the station. At dawn, they shot and killed the soldiers as they came out of the cabin, but they spared the stationmaster and the stage driver.

Thomas's story is one of a thousand about how European colonists raped and killed those less powerful than them. I wonder how the Goshute had a son if the soldiers killed his family. Presumably he got together with another woman.

Emily was grossly offended by both the story of the killed coyote and the raped woman. The first story made her think that my grandfather was cruel, a man without pity. She thought my great-grandfather was a much better person. During my life, my grandfather was reserved with me—a child. Now I know his nature better than I ever did before—his sexism, foul mouth, self-centeredness. I wonder if it would be the same with Thomas: knowing him would burst my illusions. Or it could be that Emily's judgement is correct about both of them. And now I'm stuck again thinking about Emily, the paradox of her powerful mind, inflexible will, and kind heart. And of course my own tangle of anger and longing.

TWO

Three Propositions
and a Countersuit

Two mornings later I sit on my stoop drinking my coffee and waiting for the sun. Discontent has brewed since Carrie-Anne's visit. To continue the metaphor: she stirred up grounds that I didn't want stirred up. I'm thinking about the stories Emily and I told each other when we still told stories. The first time we saw each other, I was wearing red-dyed cowboy boots, which she thought were ridiculous. When she had labor pains with our first baby, Emily thought it was just gas. Carrie-Anne was born not breathing. Todd eloped with his wife Rhiannon rather than have a big wedding and reception.

A white pickup stops in the road. It has a logo on the side—BSB, with the head and tail of the S curled around the Bs, as if it's a snake slithering between them. "Keep going!" I call, channeling my grandfather Louis. At the end of his life, he would have gotten his rifle from inside his cabin. Laid it across his lap. They either don't hear or don't believe I'm serious. A man dressed in khaki cargo pants and a daisy yellow overcoat gets out and walks toward me. With him are another man and a woman, the same number as when Spencer stopped to ream me a new one. Same as the Dead Fathers. I'm afflicted by threes. The other man has a coat as big as a sleeping bag, and the woman wears straight black slacks that make her look elegant. Even after she gets desert dust on them, she'll still look elegant. My curiosity doesn't keep me from also being irritated at them for interrupting my solitude.

"I'm Christine Parker," says the woman. She starts to extend her hand to shake mine but puts it in her pocket instead, as if that's where she wanted it in the first place. She's right to not want to touch my dirty paw, but still that bothers me.

"I'm Mike Simmonds," says the man in the yellow overcoat, the taller of the two men. "This is Albert Rich, our geologist. Chrissy is our financing expert. I'm the idea man. Spencer Murdock told us you ride your bike up to the O.K. Silver Mine every day."

Too many names. "Is that an accusation or a revelation?"

He frowns, struggling to slot me into what he expected of an old man living in a doorless trailer, but then his visage softens. "Something else entirely. A request and an invitation. If you've been down in the mines, we'd like to hire you as a guide."

I point to the woman. "She's not dressed for going into the mines."

She lifts a pant leg and shows me both her calf and sturdy leather hiking boots. "We have helmets and lamps in the truck." What did she say her name was? Carlie or Tina or something. Their names have already drifted away, probably because they and their interests are inconsequential to me. "So we'd like you to show us the mines."

"What do you want to see them for?"

They look nothing like the spelunkers who asked me for advice on exploring the mines. Those people were dressed in clothing they could get dirty in. Those came for the pure joy of walking under the earth. Pleasure for these three, I highly suspect, is more specific.

"We're thinking of buying the mineral rights."

"They were played out a hundred years ago," I say.

She smiles as if she knows something I don't.

"A hundred dollars an hour," says the other man from the depths of his coat.

"A waste of your money. I'm no mining expert."

The woman steps forward. She tips her head to one side and smiles at me. "You really won't help us?" She thinks I'll be susceptible to her smile, and I am, but not enough to make me want to spend my day with them.

I look at her svelte slacks, her boots. "No. Those mines are dangerous. You could wander into the shaft where rotten logs hold the ceiling from caving in."

"You could help us avoid the dangerous places, right?" says the man with the yellow coat.

"The best option is to just stay out of them."

The woman says, "It would really help us out if you showed us around, informed us where the dangerous shafts are."

"There are no maps of the old mine," says Yellow Overcoat.

"In an afternoon, you can make $500," says the woman. She leans forward and touches my forearm.

"No," I say, standing and stepping off my stoop. "I'm not interested." I don't like the idea of them opening the mine again, maybe bringing in heavy equipment that miners didn't have a hundred years ago. I wonder if they've gotten mineral rights or if they're still just exploring. Just as I did when I was a journalist, I smell their greed. They will do anything to get what they want. Like the sulfur smell of a spoiled egg. That smell led me hundreds of times in my career to uncover what people didn't want the light to shine on. I feel the edge of adrenaline nudging me toward action. I could contact whoever owns the valley, probably the Bureau of Land Management. I could call the mine exploring club; they would help. That would lead to another call and another, and soon I'd open the whole sordid story to the light.

"Two hundred dollars an hour," says the other man. "You could save us time and money by helping us out."

What I feel is a great boredom at all of that enterprise. "Still no. Now please leave me the fuck alone. I'm in the middle of breakfast."

"We'll do our explorations without your help," says Boots. She steps closer, clearly trying to make me step back. "You refusing won't stop us." When I don't move, she glares at me and turns away.

"Well, we tried," says Yellow Overcoat. "You could have made some good money." I can see only the puff of his breath.

As they walk away, Boots gestures to the other two, chopping her hand, as if she wants my neck or some other skinny part of my body under her axe. I wonder why I went after the woman more ardently than the others. Maybe it was a sexist act. Or maybe it had nothing to do with gender; maybe it was just that she was the one who got in my face. They drive their truck north on the main road but turn at the road that leads to the mines.

As I ride my bike toward the valley where both the mines and Goshute Spring are located, I think about how quickly I became excited at exposing them and how much more quickly I backed down. Bewildering. What used to consume my life just doesn't feel important anymore.

As I walk, I'm still afflicted in sets of three: three ravens caw in the juniper tree I pass, three deerflies land on my coat sleeve, three jacks lope across the opposite hillside. This cosmic unsettlement is deep and pervasive, reaching up into the sky and far into the earth. Three magpies sit on my truck. They are carrion eaters so it seems appropriate.

The human carrion eaters parked their truck next to the tin building. They have disappeared, apparently into one of the mines. Hopefully, the roof will collapse on them. I drop my bike near Antelope Spring and walk up the slope where the snow is too deep for my bike. A rattlesnake slithers into the road ahead, and then feeling the tremor of my footsteps, coils in front of me. The sun is warmish and the snow is melting, but it's too early in the season for a snake to be out of hibernation. It points its head my way, its black tongue flickering in and out. I know it isn't a threat, more like a warning sent by a friend, but I leave the path and walk around it. Its buzz shakes me to my bones. Not a hundred yards later, a coyote slinks up the ravine below me. Finally, when I leave the road to begin my search for the navel hole, there's a badger stalking through the sagebrush. I'm in its path so it rushes at me, and I have to run like hell. Three more creatures warning me.

Because of these signs, I'm jittery all day. If my dormant spidey sense could drive me to get to the root of any mystery, there is one close at hand. I discover I'm frightened of what I might uncover. Not only has lassitude overtaken me, but cowardice. Sitting on a boulder and eating my sandwich at noon, I scan the ground around me for scorpions and snakes. There's a red ant hill nearby and it's swarming, as if I have just kicked it. I finish my sandwich and move farther away, but there are ant hills everywhere.

I've been reading Carlos Castaneda's *The Teachings of Don Juan*, which is sometimes classified as anthropology but generally as fiction. The Yaqui sorcerer in that book teaches that we should all be aware of the earth and what other creatures have to communicate to us. What the pack rat communicated was clear—he wanted to take over my bed. I understand our conflict over territory. But the people, ravens, magpies, deer flies, the snake, coyote, badger, and now the ants seem to be agents of a deeper message. What they impart is ambiguous. Their appearance might be random or the result of following their own inclination. It's too much to be mere coincidence, but as Emily once told me, even the stars seem clustered to human eyes. Random chaos is always an option. But I have the feeling that they are communicating something. Should I read their aggression as a warning or an attack? Their messages, if they are messages, are even more opaque than those of the Dead Fathers. What seems certain is that their behavior is unusual—outside the realm of what's natural to them. It seems that the whole ecosystem is on edge. *They had better be more specific about what they mean by war,* I think. But I don't have confidence in the possibility of clarity. It has not been their strong suit.

This evening when I ride my bike back home in the dark, the Milky Way is so bright that the desert transforms. Generally, it's pastel—beige soil, yellow grass, blue sky; the nearly black green of junipers and pines. Now, the night is as stark as a bad dream, all shades of black, shadows like deep pools. As I move the blanket to enter the trailer, my previous visitor, the pack rat, rushes out, a piece of tinfoil in its mouth. I jump back because he seems as big as a house cat.

I feel as if I've been beaten over the head with signs. I think about what the Dead Fathers said about Nebuchadnezzar, who lost the ability to keep his head screwed on straight. All these omens either portend some shift in the space-time continuum or some shift in my feeble brain toward senility. Trouble with omens is you can't tell the difference between revelation, natural coincidence, and a psychotic break.

"You had visitors today," my father Samuel says. "Three cards." He has arranged his matchsticks in the form of an arrow, pointing across the table at me. Louis hands him a card in a deliberate manner, as if they are actors on a stage, emphasizing the importance of every crisp act.

"Three of them," I say. "Do you know what they're trying to do with the mines?"

None of them meet my eyes.

"Entrepreneurs are everywhere," Hugh says.

"Just like horseshit," says Louis. "But just like horseshit, they fertilize the ground and do no real harm. You don't need to try to thwart their desires. Those old mines aren't useful to anyone. They might make themselves wealthy."

"The mines give me pleasure. I don't want them to ruin it for me and for cavers."

"Selfish," says Hugh.

"Their blasting and drilling work might even seal off the lower entrance," Louis says quietly.

Hugh says, "Shut your loose mouth."

Louis glares at his grandfather, but he does shut his mouth.

"The lower entrance to what?" I ask.

"Never you mind," says Hugh.

Samuel lays down his cards, a flush in hearts, king high. "You were—abrupt with those people."

"You were pretending to act like me," says Louis. "I'm nothing like that. A damned insult."

My father covers his face with his hands. I'm sure he's laughing.

"I don't like the idea of them thundering around with heavy equipment, collapsing mines."

"But it might be a good thing," says Louis. "Shake things up."

I say, "The shaking could collapse Thomas's cave."

The three of them look silently at each other. Finally Samuel turns toward me. "Thomas's cave? He doesn't own a cave."

"Come on," I say. "The cave I've been looking for. The one you warned me not to go down in." I'm perplexed and infuriated by their games with me.

"You weren't just abrupt," says Hugh. "You were downright rude."

"Surprising," says Samuel. "You're generally a reticent person."

"If you can see all of time," I say, "then you already knew what I'd say to them, so it was inevitable."

Hugh shakes his head. "That's quite simplistic."

Louis says, "Like the coyote I shot. It's part of the fabric. Always vomiting red. Always wheeling, always ready to wheel."

Samuel stands and parts the blanket. "When isn't really the issue."

Hugh stands as well. "*When* isn't. And *who* isn't either. What either. None of them really matter." He points outside.

After I turn out the lights and let my eyes adjust, I see on the flat in front of my trailer a pronghorn, which isn't that unusual because a pronghorn buck and sometimes a small group of females come in the evening to drink from Antelope Spring. Spencer has piped water from there to water his horses. What's startling is that there is also a badger and a coyote there. Something slithers under their feet.

"It's that fucker Thomas," says Louis. "He's fucking with things again."

I'm not sure what he means by again. When has Thomas confounded them before? Maybe this animosity between them is the reason he never has come to my trailer to play poker. But what springs into my head is the unity of noun and verb in what Louis said, fuckers fuck, meddlers meddle, like badgers badger, or snakes snake.

"You're onto something," says Hugh to me. "Everything manifests itself."

"You should be the same," says my father. "Fulfilling the measure of your existence. Christopher Twist twists. Manifest yourself!"

What the hell does he mean by either verb—twist or manifest? My father has seldom been so emphatic and unclear in his advice. By the time I was fifteen, he had stopped trying to tell me what to do. Now he's pushy and manipulative, like he was when I was twelve.

"When can I talk to Great-grandpa Thomas?" I ask.

"When?" says Hugh. "You haven't been listening."

My father leans forward across the table. "Time is like this. Once during a dry, dry summer, I was walking with my dad on his farm."

Louis says, "Nothing would grow."

"All the cows were poor, and we'd had to haul off a couple of carcasses. We came to one poor cow, who didn't even have enough water for her body to function."

"Her back was arched," says Louis. "And she was trying to push out this hard little turd. But nothing worked because she was constipated from too little water. She pushed and pushed and that turd just showed its tip. Then she just gave up and it sucked back in."

Now my father Samuel grins as if telling the punchline of a joke. "And Dad said—" He stops and giggles for a minute. "He said, 'Maybe tomorrow.'"

Now Louis is laughing.

"And that's time," says Hugh. "Precisely."

"Nothing happens and yet it always happens."

"Perennially."

After they leave, I lie on my bed but I can't sleep—turning and turning, my mind too frenetic to read, as I consider what they've said. Why is it that when the dead visit me they have no essential message? The words of these three are as impenetrable as those of the Sphinx. Later, when it's too late, the precise meaning may be clear. What is clear is that something or many somethings are coming. I'll face unwelcome visitors again.

As if by prophecy, before I finish my coffee the next morning, Nephi Johnson's SUV pulls up. Nephi is the patriarch of a small polygamist clan that has settled on my grandfather's former farm. I have driven my truck or ridden my bike down a few times to talk to another human being who is not a tourist and to look over the old place. He's shown me his operation, growing corn and distilling it into ethanol. Or more precisely: that's what he pretends to do. Every summer the corn is too patchy to make a good crop. Also, he's never deigned to show me his distilling equipment. I don't know how they make it work economically, but I'm sure it has something to do with government subsidies. The conservatives who complain the loudest about gov'ment handouts are first to grab and misuse them.

We have also had lively conversations about the implications of Joseph Smith's revelation about Celestial marriage, the Adam God theory, the Divine Feminine and Masculine, and the fundamentalists' relationship to the Mother Church. I have enjoyed talking with him. But this morning, I can see from his set face and determined gait that he has a mission. I feel the grump coming on inside me.

He's here with three of his daughters. They all get out, and the women, who are probably in their older teens, maybe early twenties, stand against the car as if in a line-up—pink, gingham, blue dresses, with long skirts and long sleeves.

As if I'm already one of the Dead Fathers, I know what's going to happen before it happens, and I want him to just load them all back in the car and drive away.

"Happy birthday, Brother Twist." He takes off his hat and turns it in his hands.

He's right. It is my birthday. The seventh of March.

"Your sixty-seventh."

I wonder how he knows all this. I've certainly never told him.

"How are you on this chilly morning?"

"I was enjoying my solitude."

"Ah, solitude. Something to be relished." He looks out at my vista. "But even solitude, every night sleeping alone, must feel lonesome sometimes. Cold and lonesome."

"I haven't had the chance to get lonesome." I clear my throat.

"I'll get to the point then." He clasps his hands together, either in prayer or to signal eagerness, maybe both.

"Thank you."

"I want you to join with us. I know you used to be Mormon but you're disaffected."

"And you plan on re-affecting me," I say.

"You are a member of a pioneering family. Four branches of them: Twist, Quayle, Shumway, Young. Royal blood."

"I don't understand," I say, even though I probably do.

"I've decided that your seed would benefit the genetics of my family."

Damn if he doesn't get to the point quicker than I imagined he would.

"I need some children more intelligent than my idiot converts can produce." He nods toward the station wagon, where the three girls have grave misgivings inscribed on their faces. One of them is on the edge of weeping. What kind of father would force his young daughters into a relationship with a man old enough to be their grandfather? I think about Karin, who is not much younger than these girls. Nephi doesn't want romance or even love for his daughters. I have my doubts about the long-term value of romance, but Karin and other young people look forward to it. Right now I can't stand his damnable face. "I will not sow my seed illegitimately," I say, even though it isn't true.

"Oh, you'll have to marry them."

"You want me to add to the sorrow of your children?"

This seems to surprise him. He opens his mouth, shuts it again. "It's what God wants for them. And for you."

Now he's made me angry, just like the woman the day before—spoiling my equanimity. "I will not marry your daughters. Will not, not even if God himself told me in person rather than through a retrograde and fallible human."

"You don't need to get so starchy, Christopher. At least consider my offer." He places his hat back on the crown of his head and turns suddenly to stride back to his vehicle, which could have held twelve women rather than just three. It still isn't big enough for his whole family, his ego, and his dishonesty.

Despite my idealistic words, my mind clings to the image of their shapes against the car, and I'm disgusted with myself. I walk fast up the ridge behind my trailer. I try to wrap my mind around Nephi's motives for asking me—a wayward, aging man—to marry his daughters. There is nothing about me that would lighten their hearts. Apparently he doesn't care about what they want, but it's not clear why he would choose me. I'm in the neighborhood, but I know his family is a branch of a polygamist group centered in American Fork, and that's not that far away. There must be other men there he could choose from. He said it's my blood that comes from the Mormon aristocracy, but that seems silly. His claim that he's just relaying God's message for me is as dishonest as the rhetoric of the Dead Fathers. I'm not rich or righteous. He'd probably be as good at poker as the Dead Fathers, because I can't discern what he's really thinking.

From the top of the ridge, I see the plume of dust as his truck drops into the ancient river bottom. He crosses into his fields that once were my grandfather's. But Nephi grows corn instead of alfalfa. He isn't the first person in the desert to try to deceive the government. To repeat my father's pun from the night before: the Twists have all been good at dishonest twisting. Louis was entitled to only 160 acres from the Desert Land Entry homesteading act, but he filed for homesteads for his wife, each of his children, and each of their spouses. He lived in a trailer that he moved from place to place, built hundreds of miles of fences, and built portable sheds and corrals that he also moved around like a shell game. He dug three wells to tap into the underground river, which, when it was above ground, had connected one branch of Lake Bonneville to another as the ancient lake shrank. These were the two parts of his foundation story—the beauty of free land in America and the necessity of water for that land. He proved up on about three-quarters of the properties but went bankrupt buying machinery to harvest alfalfa. His obsession cost him his wife. She got tired of scraping by in this desolate land and moved back to the city. Also, she was allergic to dust and had sinus trouble all the time when she lived out here. That she even tried to live with him was heroic.

As a journalist one of my talents was getting to the cultural core of human action—how what people did grew out of who they were and who we all are. My fathers' stories weave around a few subjects: land, family, religion, and livestock. The thumb to those four fingers, the one story to rule them all, is the story of water. Hugh's story is the getting of land, livestock, and progeny. At the expense of the delicate plants that grew where he put his cattle. Louis added money to that same formula, as if he could get rich ranching in arid country. Thomas kept his enterprises in proper proportion, hoping to live lightly on the land. My father found the wisdom of just getting the hell out of a place where rain didn't fall.

We all think of the plains of the Great Basin as a desert. "Let's go out to the desert," my father would say as we left for his father's farm in Riverbed. Whether this area of the Great Basin is desert or shrub steppe is an argument that often engages us during poker games. Is the area full of life or destitute of life? It all depends on water. I think of the area more in terms of water than of land: Simpson

Springs, Goshute Spring, Antelope Spring, Grassy Creek, Lost Creek, Footes Creek, Judd Creek, the hot springs toward Delta, Fish Springs. These springs and creeks constitute an archipelago, not islands in a sea, but pockets of water in a sea of dust. Underground it's similar, not one massive aquifer but random pockets of water. Ranchers like my father and grandfather took chances when they dug wells to irrigate their crops. Now, city dwellers in Las Vegas and Salt Lake lust after and try to claim this water.

I remember the sound of the diesel engines that drove the six pumps, the different pitches rising and falling as air moved between each engine and me, wherever I was playing or working. I swam in the ditches along with toads and blow snakes. The water was clear as air as it spilled out of the well. The ditches grew shallower as they branched from the main canal. Where the water went, alfalfa grew between two and three feet tall. Where it didn't, the alfalfa crowns dried up, dead in a month. The water tasted flat then and still does because it contains different minerals than the water from the town where I grew up. I remember not only swimming in the water, but drinking from jugs covered in burlap and kept wet so the water would be cool when the temperature was 100 degrees and the air dry as an oven. I sucked down water after hauling hay, gulped water right from the pipe, the force of it pushing against my face. Once in the city of Orem when I was about six, after picking cherries in the orchards where my cousins lived, I watched one of the adult pickers pour his jug out on the ground. "No!" I shouted, holding my hand out as if I could stop this water from falling. He was surprised and mystified by this furious child.

Lack of water is the story all of us Twist men tell over and over again. Sitting on the ridge, I find myself thinking about my grandmother, who seemed to love my grandfather even after she left him. My own mother had to deal with my father's alcoholism. Thomas's wives had married a homosexual man. Had he told them when he proposed? Probably not. These women, except for my mother, married men who loved farming more than God. What were the stories of the women? Maybe adaptation. It seems universally unfair that their lives were like water flowing around the rock of their obsessed and obstinate husbands. What would their stories have been if they could have followed their own impulses? They might have been like Emily, and suddenly I am washed over with longing for her brash manner. Then I'm think about my smart and lovely but morose mother and my kind grandmother, who fed me ginger snaps or rye crisps with real butter on them. I realize that it's probably inaccurate to say that those strong women didn't choose the career of their lives. What are they like now? "Why can't you be the ones who visit me?" What would they tell me?

They don't appear, so I stand and make my way down the ridge.

This afternoon, on my normal ride to look for the hole in the ground, I am wary. I scan the ground in front of me and to either side. Nothing out of the ordinary appears. But then as I pass the place where my truck was, I find nothing but dual-wheel tracks. Someone has come with a tow truck and taken it away. Was it the BLM impounding it or just an enterprising thief? I didn't want to get it fixed, but it still was my truck. I feel the loss now that it's gone.

After dumping my bike in the mining valley and walking up to the cedared flat, I see someone sitting under a cedar tree. Walking closer, I recognize my great-grandfather, Thomas, whose face is familiar from early photographs. He smiles and lifts his hand in greeting. "I've been waiting for you."

I walk quickly toward him. "I have so many questions."

"And I have so much to ask you," he says.

"I've read your journal, except for the pages that were ripped out."

He leans back and props his head against the trunk. "And you want to know what's in those pages." He turns his head so we're eye to eye. "What do the other men say?"

If he's been observing their visits, why doesn't he know what they say? I had assumed they had no secrets between them. "Nothing about that. And generally nothing that makes sense."

He nods, and his eyes and smile are distant, as if his eyes see other landscapes or as if his mind is on other matters. "Sometimes nothing is all that makes sense." I wonder if he is senile or if that is even possible.

I say, "You've appeared to me in the daylight."

He nods happily. "I color outside the lines. Ask your questions. I probably won't have answers but it might help you feel better."

"Where are all the dead mothers?"

He spreads his arms wide and I see faces all around me, like light glancing off a pond. He smiles when he sees that I've perceived them. I wonder why I don't see them as I see the Dead Fathers.

Then I see them, at least Mom and Grandmother Twist. "It's good to see you," says my mother. "You always were a stubborn boy."

"We wanted to visit you," says my grandmother Sarah, "I'm glad you finally thought to ask." I stand and hug her, and her smell envelops me, lilac and something else. I'm taller than when I last hugged her, which was almost six decades ago, just before she died of colon cancer. Her voice is melodious and kind. When I was young, she let my father build a house on a lot she owned, and lived next door. I would run through the yard and go inside to watch her paint. Her paintings were of the desert, even though she didn't live there anymore. Not as stylized as Georgia O'Keeffe or Maynard Dixon, more realistic but with the same feeling of depth—universal Jungian forms perhaps. Now Carrie-Anne lives in her house.

"I've missed you," I say.

Then I step back and absorb them with my eyes. They both seem—what?—full of joy. Like it's their birthday. Or like it's my birthday and they are pleased to see me. The Dead Fathers seem to be themselves, almost as they were when they were alive. Louis is crasser, but maybe he held back when I was a child. He's also more loquacious now, but that could be because his swearing is like grease in the machine of verbal expression. My mother and grandmother are also themselves but amplified. Both of them seem happier and more relaxed than I remember. Unbounded. As they look at me, I remember once, when I was hunting deer, turning and seeing a cougar padding along behind me. She looked at me, fierce and wild. I brought my gun up, but then she turned and ambled away. I've always felt safe with my mother and grandmother. Even as a teenager, I argued with my father but not my mother. But now I wonder if I didn't argue because it would have been a mistake to cross her.

"Ask the question," my grandmother says.

"You look wonderful," I say.

"You mean wonderful for dead people," Mom says.

"Death released us." Grandma smiles.

"From what? From your husbands?"

"Release from Samuel? Not exactly. I still love your father."

"And I still put up with your grandfather."

"Release from expectation," says my mother. "We've been able to be more like your Emily. Who is as unsuppressed a woman as I've met." She touches my face, and I feel her freedom from being second to my father, or not even him, but always second to every man. It's as if restrictions or reticence sloughed off her when she died. Or before that. At the end of her life she was senile and spoke in word salad. She was angry a lot. Several times she tried to ram me with her walker. Which was kind of funny, but mostly not. Sometimes she didn't speak in word salad. She said stuff like, "They won't let me"—a common phrase for her. Or "Everyone is larger than me. I can hardly breathe." When she was angry at me because I wanted her to eat lunch or take her pills, she said, "Who are you to tell me what to do?"

I glance at Thomas, who is still visible. "They, the Dead Fathers, said you're at war with them. Is that true?"

"Do we look like we're at war?" he says.

"Your father and the others are all worked up," says my mother. "It's just because they're worried."

"They're nearly frantic," I say. "But you're not worried."

"Things will work out," says my grandmother. "You can have confidence in that."

Then they are gone, leaving only mottled patterns of light on the ground. I'm peeved because I didn't take the chance to ask Thomas about the location of the mouth of the cave.

A military vehicle drives up to my trailer at dusk, and I'm filled with dread. A man who seems a little younger than me gets out with a much younger driver. The older man gives me a look fierce as a hawk's, and then he tries, unsuccessfully, to soften his gaze with a crooked smile. I can see how it's going to go all week—a carnival of whackos, a parade of fanatics—capitalists, fundamentalists, and militia-ists. People who reverence the system they swaddle themselves in. I've gone weeks without anyone coming to my home, but the past few days have been constant invasion. I suspect that it has something to do with the Dead Fathers and their talk of an impending battle. It seems no coincidence that they are all people who rely on and love hierarchy. I notice this only because I feel that I'm drifting daily closer to anarchy.

"I suppose it won't do any good to say I don't want whatever you're selling," I say.

The old man laughs. "I'm not selling anything."

Damn liar!

Both men wear army uniforms. The older man looks around for a place to sit, but I don't move to get him anything. Finally he turns over a five-gallon can and sits. The younger soldier won't sit down but stands to the left of his superior officer, as if he's keeping his eye on me. Neither of them introduce themselves, and I don't offer up my own name either. We sit and watch the light fade across the desert. As if he's a cliché, the older man brings a flask out of his pocket and offers me a drink. I take one, smoothest whiskey I've tasted, and hand the flask back.

"Christopher Twist. I'm General David Torrey, posted at Skull Valley Proving Grounds early in my career and again during the past decade. When I was a young officer here, the older soldiers took me to spotlight deer who came to eat in your grandfather's fields. We did him a favor to thin out the herd that was decimating his alfalfa and he did us a favor by giving us sport. We never were caught by Fish and Game officers."

"I remember my grandfather telling me about that when I was a teenager." I watch the pronghorn buck who has come, as always, to drink at the pond.

"I retire in a month," he whispers. Then he nods at the driver who walks to the car and retrieves a rifle and a night scope. "I thought I might have one last shot."

"No," I say. "Absolutely not."

"You don't own them."

Still in his chair, he takes the rifle and takes aim, but I bump the barrel at the last instant and the shot goes over the buck. He disappears like the Dead Fathers.

"You son of a bitch," says the old soldier. "I wanted this."

"But I didn't."

"The older officers said that your grandfather was as good a man as you can find anywhere. It's sad to see his blood descend to a weenie like you."

I haven't been called a weenie since junior high school.

He seems ready to turn the rifle on me, but the young man steps close and takes it out of his hands. He tries longer to persuade me to let him come back, but I'm firm with him.

"This is not the end," he says, a line so dramatic that he could have borrowed it from a movie. Together they walk back to their vehicle, and I watch until the taillights disappear.

Louis and Hugh come out of the trailer. Hugh sits on the bucket, Louis on a boulder. Samuel stands behind them.

Louis asks, "You think I was wrong to shoot deer, antelope, rabbits, all creatures that ate my alfalfa?" He's always called pronghorns antelope, which is an indication of his stubbornness. He does things because he's always done them. Unchangeable.

I shake my head. "I wasn't making a universal statement. I just didn't want him to shoot the pronghorn. I like to watch him every evening."

"I didn't usually shoot coyotes," Louis says. "They might eat a fawn or a rabbit. Just that once I shot one." He grinned. "Head over heels, a red pinwheel."

I am frightened he'll tell me the story again, but Hugh says, "You boys ran cattle. I did as well, but I also ran sheep. Coyotes were a problem for our sheep herds, so I killed them when I could. Cold nights we had to bed down with the sheep or we'd have frozen by morning."

My father Samuel says to me, "You talked to Thomas." They all look at me.

"He seems happy," I say. "He didn't try to make me *do* anything. Unlike some people I know."

"Do!" says Louis. "What has doing got to do with it?"

"Your ignorant assumptions astonish me," says my father.

"It's more a manifestation of will," says Hugh. "What you will, what you won't will."

"He's going to fuck everything up," shouts Louis.

I don't know whether he is talking about me or Thomas. Maybe both of us.

"He walks to and fro upon the earth," says Hugh. "Just like Lucifer."

"He won't stick with you like we do," says my father.

"Mercurial," says Hugh, as if that's a bad thing.

"A damned flash in the pan," says Louis.

"Mom and Grandma were with him," I say.

Louis rolls his eyes. "Of course, they were."

"Did you see them with your eyes?" asks Samuel.

I nod.

Hugh strokes his chin.

"I asked him what he wrote on the missing pages of his journal. Just like I asked you three."

"Did he tell you?" asks Hugh.

I shake my head.

"There's no reason to keep it from him," says my father.

"I tore them out," says Louis. "Full of blasphemy. He married two women and then they parted, and he joined in a carnal relationship with two men."

"Polyandrous relationship," I say.

"Poly something," says Louis. "A damnable abomination."

I think about Thomas's soft speech, good humor, and gentle manner. "He said he colors outside the lines."

"Understatement of the century," says Samuel.

"Understatement of the millennium," says Louis.

Hugh says nothing, but his frown deepens. "You should stay away from him and marry Nephi's daughters."

"I should? Why?"

He doesn't answer.

Louis finally speaks. "The desert is a violent place."

Hugh looks at him. "Sula and Agnes."

They all nod.

"Tell me."

"They lived a couple of canyons over with their husband," says Hugh. "Son of my friend Jacob Roberts. He married both my daughter and her friend, Agnes Cook, on the same day. His first two wives."

"And his last two wives," Louis says. "He moved out here to get away from the Feds who were hunting down polygamists. That first winter, cougars got their five cows and small herd of sheep. By spring they were starving. Jacob died of the cold, but before that he was able to get both of them pregnant. They ran out of food and the nights were as cold as in Antarctica. Desperate, they walked to the next canyon over, where there was a lone man named Arthur Flinders, who had disobeyed Brigham Young and had started a gold and silver mine. He could work the mine even in the winter, because deep in the earth, it was the same temperature all year round. They went over to his cabin and asked for food. They were desperate to keep themselves and their unborn children alive. He told them he only had enough for himself. But then he looked at the two women. Sula was certainly not ugly, and Agnes was one of the most beautiful women ever to grace the desert. He said he could share if they lived with him as man and wives. He was an apostate, so they said, "No!" He shut the door in their faces. Sula took an axe that was next to the door. She bashed the lock, opened the door, and buried the axe in his head before he could get his rifle up."

"So now it's called Death Canyon." I show my teeth in what I hope is a feral grin. "What's the lesson I should get from this?"

"Don't live alone in the desert," says my father.

"Violence is just around the damn corner," says Louis.

"Murdering an apostate is no sin," says Hugh.

They don't seem in any mood to play cards, but they also seem to think it's a ceremony they can't skip. We go into the trailer, and for the first time since we've been playing, I'm winning steadily. I hear a vehicle engine approach and then stop. I'm sure it's another crazy wanting to get something from me, so I don't move, waiting until a knock sounds on the side of my trailer. The Fathers stand from the table and drift away. I lift the blanket to one side and peer out—Emily Ransome, my wife, and she has a grocery bag in her arms. "Can I come in?" she asks. "I decided to try to forgive you for being an asshole."

THREE

Fight or Flight

My first instinct is to flee. I could push the cardboard out of the window casing above my bed and escape. I could find a place to hide outside in the darkness. Maybe I'll walk down to Nephi's homestead, tell him I've changed my mind about joining up. All this flashes through my head in an instant. I came to this place to get away from Emily, and right now I don't have the resolve to face her or the tangle of fault and counter-fault she brings with her. But her visit is the fourth of the day—a disruption of the pattern of three signs clustered.

I move out of the way, and she ducks under the blanket.

"This trailer used to have a door." She steps inside but doesn't sit, holding her bag in her arms as if it will protect her from me. Or maybe she's just afraid it will get filthy if she puts it on the table or counter. She's right to be worried. I see my squalor through her eyes, and I wish I'd cleaned up. Could have if I'd had any warning. Maybe she worried that I'd run if she gave me notice. She knows me well.

Her hair is slightly longer than it was when I left. I should ask if she's growing it out again, but I don't. She's wearing a coat with a western cut, a style I've never seen her wear. The coat is open and under it she's wearing a white blouse and blue jeans with hiking boots. I didn't know she even had a pair of boots. Her face is—what?— unsettled, vulnerable. A face she would never have allowed herself to wear when in any courtroom. Maybe she hasn't come to argue.

I relax slightly, but I still don't know what to say. She's the last person I thought I'd see at my door. My anger from when I first moved out has waned a little, but even that is undercut, sent spinning off, by the shock of seeing her. Shock and—I discover—pleasure. The weight of silence, apathy, and unfaithfulness between us seems suspended, not gone, but held back for a moment. I can't stop looking at her. My nose catches a whiff of my own odor; it's been several weeks since I bathed. I take a step back.

"Don't worry," she says. "I've already eaten." Something catches in my throat when I look at her. She's nearly as tall as me, so at this distance neither of us has to look up at the other. Her eyes are bluest blue, and her response to my close gaze is to mask emotion, shut her face like a closed door. She looks away from me. Apparently, she's unable to read my face either. "Didn't your father always win the ugly beard contest on the Fourth of July?"

"Yes."

"You inherited his genes."

"You've said that before." I smile. "Do you want something to drink?"

She finally puts her bag on the table. "Something from a can if you have it. Water if you don't."

I get out a beer and offer it to her. Then I get a glass from the cupboard. She inspects the glass and hands it back to me. She opens the beer and sips. "Can we talk outside?" She wrinkles her nose. "It's even riper in here than your grandfather's cabin was back in the day."

I grab a chair and set it outside facing my stoop. She sits on the chair and I sit on the stoop. "This is a surprise."

"To me as well," she says. "I'm regretting my decision already."

"You don't have to stay. You can get in your car and go back home." I realize that the jury's still out on whether I want her to stay or leave. But I say, "I'm glad to see you." As the words leave my mouth, they become true, like magic doves flying out of a hat.

"I guess you are. I can't be sure. If you really wanted to see me, you would have come home."

"With you and Roger Finley?" My head is invaded by a Seventeenth-century pun. *Rogers roger*. I try to keep my face straight but don't succeed.

"Stop it. You have the mind of a thirteen-year-old."

Can she read my mind as well? Maybe she thinks I imagined a threesome. "Sorry."

"No you're not." She shrugs. "I haven't seen him for a couple of months." She shows her teeth in a forced smile, making her look like a wolf. "I got bored with him. Or maybe he got bored with me."

"You—"

"I had a dream," she says.

"What do you mean? Of a life with Roger?"

"Of course not." She's giving me her *you numbskull* look. "A night dream where a man told me to come out here."

"What the hell?" She has always rolled her eyes when her pious sister talks about dream visions.

"So I tried to ignore it."

"Tell me."

"So you can interpret? It's my dream." She looks to the west, across the flat toward Turkey Mountain, a peak she's thought unimpressive on the rare occasions she's come out to the desert with me. "It's not really a dream that needs interpretation. I saw a man sitting under a juniper tree talking to a young woman. He wore clothing from a century ago—a vest and trousers, a white shirt buttoned to the top. She wore modern clothing, shorts and a T-shirt. He turned from the woman and spoke to me, but I didn't understand what he said. It didn't feel like a dream—more real. Spooked the hell out of me even though it wasn't really a frightening dream. The granularity of it spooked me. The same dream happened a second night, him talking to a girl and then turning to talk to me, but I still couldn't understand him, except he said my name. That part I understood. Then the third night, I understood. He said, 'Go see Christopher. He misses you, and you both have work to do.'"

"Work to do?"

"What he said. I've probably lost my mind. I didn't want that strange man to appear again tonight, so I came. Bought new boots and a truck."

That makes me think she really has lost her mind— Emily, a truck? I didn't know that she was anything but rational, which, as a lawyer is essential to her—facts and the law, rhetoric and logic. That she bought boots and a truck and came to see me because she had a dream boggles my universe.

"I thought I'd need one if I was going to drive out here."

And this sends me spinning again—spinning in a way even the Dead Fathers haven't achieved. She wouldn't buy a truck for a single trip.

"Do you?"

I'm still reeling. "Do I what?"

"Miss me."

"Yes."

She gives the slightest smile, and I'd give anything to see it again.

"He said his name is Thomas."

Another solid blow. "Thomas?"

"Yes."

"My great-grandfather."

"Really?"

"Our children know his name."

"Not my monkey, not my circus." She looks around. "I brought a sleeping bag and a pad. I'll sleep in my truck."

I have more to ask, but it's clear she's finished— enough talking for one night after a famine of nothing for half a year, barely anything for ten years before that. Too much talking all at once and we might just vomit it all up again.

She goes inside and holds her grocery bag in one arm as if it's a small child. She opens the refrigerator door, looks inside, and shuts it again. "It'll be cold enough outside for this to keep."

"It's full anyway."

"Full of rotten food."

She puts the bag in the cab of her pickup and crawls in the back, shuts the tailgate and the window of her shell behind her.

I'm left in turmoil, but I fear there isn't much time for me to gather my wits before the Dead Fathers return. After sex a year ago, the last time, she said that I had stopped seeing her. She wasn't talking about my habit of closing my eyes during sex, or maybe she was. Later she hooked up with Roger, so I left. Now she thinks I'm the asshole. And Thomas apparently thinks I have a message for her. A half hour earlier I thought my life was complicated, now I can't begin to make sense of what is happening.

"You can't let her get her nose in the tent," says Louis. "She'll take up more emotional space than three camels."

They're back, too soon. And they'll make things even more tangled.

"And she'll invite other devils," says Hugh. "Thomas has twisted himself into her nocturnal mind."

Which makes me smile. I'm the punster, me and my father. Not Hugh.

"It's not funny," says Louis. "Lilith, Judith, Huldah, Emmeline, the whole band of misfits."

"Emily brings a hell you can hardly imagine," says Hugh.

"This is my wife you're talking about. She's not in league with either devils or Thomas. She's taken three giant steps back from religion. She's not involved."

"Who said anything about religion?" asks Louis. "As in being a churchgoer or not a churchgoer? I'm not a damn churchgoer."

"Religion is not relevant," says Hugh.

"And Emily's already involved," says Samuel.

"And Eve," says Hugh. "She betrayed the Father."

"What are you talking about?" I ask. The idea of Eve and Father God at odds with each other won't fit in my head. It feels like the DFs are perpetuating the stereotype that Eve was God's enemy. Eve and the Father worked together to give humankind agency. If he'd been alone, Adam would have mucked it up.

"Don't believe it!" Hugh grabs my forearm. "She disobeyed!"

"But she had to."

"Just like Lucifer had to," says Hugh. "That doesn't mean we should praise either one of them."

"I disagree," I say.

"Disobedience is disobedience," says Hugh.

"And that's why you're going to hell," says Louis. "In a handbasket. You're a disobedient son of a bitch."

"Eve was made from his rib," says Hugh. "Rejecting that symbolism is the root of your problem."

"Where are your wives?" I ask them. "I want to talk to them again. Maybe they'll be clear with me."

Now they won't meet my eyes.

"Are you separated from them?" I ask. "Is it like it's been with Emily and me? A trial separation?"

Louis and my father look at each other. "We've kind of taken different paths," says my father.

"Sarah flew free of me before she died," says Louis. "She's on the same damn trajectory as Lilith and Eve."

"My wives are with me," says Hugh, smug as ever.

"Not all," say Louis.

"There is a renegade," says Hugh. "But Elizabeth and Catherine are not faltering."

"Maybe you're right," says Louis, "or maybe they've lulled you into complacency. They're all daughters of Eve, and you can never tell which way a woman might jump."

When my grandfather was alive, I didn't know that he looked down on women. But then I remember when I was very small, my sisters and I went out to the ranch. He took me out on the tractor but not them. I wanted them to go too, but when I asked him he told me, "You're stronger and smarter than your sisters." Even then I knew that wasn't true.

"Now a second war in heaven is coming," says my father. "You have to choose sides."

"Wait! What did you say?" *A second war in heaven*? That news freezes my brain.

"This will be worse than the last," says Hugh.

My father looks at the other two and they nod. He takes a deep breath. "Mother and Father God may have decided on a trial separation."

I'm too shocked to speak. Father and Mother God separated? Impossible! That's for foolish mortals like me and Emily.

I sit at my table and try to process what is un-processable. This war won't be between God and Lucifer like the first one that happened before the earth was formed but between God the Father and God the Mother. An uncivil war. A divine divorce. This can't be true.

"Breathe!" My father's voice in my ear.

"Go away," I say.

"You don't believe us," says Hugh.

"Of course I don't believe you."

"Give it some time," says my father. "You'll see."

"I need to sleep," I say.

"Damn right," says Louis. "You're going to have to be on your toes, your damn eyes wide open."

My father rests his hand on my shoulder and I feel it there, slight as a feather. "Don't let Emily knock you off your horse. Stay in the saddle."

Whatever the hell that means. It's an odd metaphor for him because he left his father's ranch as soon as he could.

Even after they are finally gone, I still am too wakeful and twitchy to sleep. I feel weight on the bed and open my eyes. Thomas sits next to me.

"Is there really going to be a second war in heaven?"

"Probably. Possibly a war on both sides of the veil. It's so uncertain."

"More uncertain than usual?"

"Definitely. Mother and Father God—are not together right now. Or *apparently* they're not. He's holed himself up on a planet near Kolob. Nobody's seen him for some time. And she's been seen on a planet with a different sun—one she called Penthesilea, after the queen of the Amazons."

I've always thought that, when the scriptures say the dead return to be with God, they mean that they would be always in the presence of the Mother and Father. Now I know that people come and go, meet and part, just as they do in this life. Thomas is gone, but my grandmother is here, along with a woman I don't recognize. Like Joseph Smith and Scrooge, I'm going to have three sets of visitors on this momentous night. Which is actually quite comforting. A familiar pattern. I sit up.

"Thomas told me—"

"Thomas is a little frantic himself." The woman has a French accent. "He needs to calm down." I realize that she's Marie le Coultre, Thomas's wife, a Swiss. I've only seen her face in pictures. She's wearing Levi's and a button-down shirt, not what I'd expect for a woman who lived the same time as Queen Victoria. But in another country.

"Things are not as bad as he thinks," says my grandmother.

"Many believe that everything will fall apart unless they reaffirm authority all across the hierarchy," my grandmother says.

"On both sides of the veil," says Marie, "they all have—what is the current saying?—their panties in a bunch. Which always makes me think of cross-dressing." She touches my arm. "Can you imagine Hugh wearing women's underwear?" She giggles.

It is an image that demands attention.

"Let's get back on track," says my grandmother. "If it was just Samuel, Louis, and Hugh, it might be a tempest in a teapot. But it's many, many others. Not even just people."

"What do you mean?" I shake my head. "Animals?"

"Yes, plants, bacteria, the earth herself." Marie puts her hand on my arm. "No such thing as immaterial matter and all that. Aristotle, Giordano Bruno, Spinoza, Henry More, Herbert Spencer, Joseph Smith, American Transcendentalists, Goshutes, Navajos, New Age Spiritualists. Do you want me to keep going?"

"That's enough for now," I say. "Thank you."

"I don't think you paid attention to the other thing I said. Not just the dead. Also the living. The veil is mostly an imaginary construct."

Who is she talking about? Is Nephi involved? Is that why he wants to bring me into his fold?

"Nephi certainly is involved," says Marie. "And the General, though he's an unwitting participant. He thinks he's following his own selfish desires. Patriarchal authority feeds on itself. This is its nature and disposition. The will to live becomes the will to control. Schopenhauer, Nietzsche, and Joseph Smith."

"Yes, Marie. Thank you." My grandmother smiles. "We don't think that shoring up patriarchal authority is a good move, especially when it's done in a panic."

"Nothing should be done in a panic," says Marie.

This makes sense to me. But I am in a panic.

Marie is not finished. "Take therefore no thought for the morrow: for the morrow shall take thought for the things of itself. Sufficient unto the day is the evil thereof. Jesus. Before him, Epicurus, the Buddha."

"Emily is key," says my grandmother, and they're gone.

I get out of bed and look through the window at Emily's small pickup. The sight calms me a little. She has a light on, maybe so she can read, but it goes dark as I watch. I hope she will sleep peacefully. I want to trust her, just like my grandmother said, but my bullheaded soul resists. I'm glad that she came for me. She crossed a barrier when I didn't have the courage to.

Through the years, when I had to escape suburbia and the life I'd swaddled myself in, Emily almost never came out with me. She came for a few day trips when my grandfather was alive and stayed once when this trailer was in better repair, but this whole desert is still foreign ground to her. This has been my space, even before she became obsessed with her lawyer work. I'm touched because she descended into what must seem like a hell of squalor and chaos when she came to see me, even if it's for just one night. Hopefully for longer than that.

The next morning, early, I sweep all the mud and spilled food out the door and mop the floor. I spray a bleach solution on the table and counters and wipe them down. The fridge will take more time than I have. I start a new pot of coffee and start frying some potatoes. Then I watch the blanket door, thinking it's the dirtiest piece of cloth I've ever seen. This morning I feel much calmer. All I want to do is spend the day with Emily, not worry about the cosmos.

She lifts the blanket and comes in with her grocery bag. "Smells good. Is that coffee?"

I nod. She wears a blue sweater, and I can't help noticing that it matches her eyes. Maybe the Dead Fathers are right: she is a dangerous woman because she has become unpredictable. I'm not a threat to anyone because I have become predictable—every day sitting on my stoop, looking for the cave but not finding it, playing cards.

"I brought oranges." She sets the bag on the table. "Maybe you should clean out the fridge before you put them in it."

"I like your sweater. It matches your eyes."

"I know," she says, but I don't ask which part of my statement she knows. It's probably clear I'm pleased as I look her over. I think maybe I should tear down the blanket and find a door. Maybe then she'd feel like sleeping here instead of in her truck. I look back at my tangled nest of blankets, where the packrat and the mother mouse invaded. She's probably not ready for that.

"You should get a door," she says.

If she can read my mind like the Dead Fathers, I will never, ever be alone again. I fry eggs to go with the potatoes and toast, and she opens a couple of oranges. We sit together on the stoop to eat and drink our coffee.

"It's not instant," she says.

"You know I can't stand it."

"Cowboy coffee." She wipes a few grains off her tongue with a napkin.

She asks me to name the mountains for her: Goshute Peaks, Lion Mountain, Keg. "And Turkey Mountain," she says. I ask about Carrie-Anne and her children. She tells me about their school. She's keeping us on safe ground. She doesn't talk about her work. She thinks I'm jealous of her success as a lawyer, but that's not the whole story. She used her work as an escape. I don't talk about my feelings of betrayal. The troubles were caused by both of us, and there's time to take it slow.

After breakfast, while Emily works on her laptop, I sit next to her and let my mind wander. I see dust—Nephi's again. Knowing he's somehow in league with the DFs makes me even less eager to talk to him.

When I tell Emily whose Suburban is approaching, she says, "Oh, hell, not him." I wonder how she knows anything about my polygamous neighbor, but before I can ask, she gets up and goes inside as the vehicle pulls into my lane. This time Nephi is accompanied by his brother, Frank. In this chaotic universe, they are as anchored as two bulldogs guarding their way of life.

Something about the firmness of their strides as they walk up makes me wary that they are even more determined to assuage my loneliness. They don't know they will fail again. Even if I didn't have a queen up my sleeve, they would fail with me. They are followed by a woman as old as they; her face shows that she has no more illusions—another kind of bulldog steadiness. And one of the girls from the other day. She's maybe eighteen, probably younger. They all stand in front of my trailer just outside the half circle of rocks I use to define my estate.

Nephi speaks first. "You look well, Brother Twist."

Frank says, "Your parents should have named you Oliver."

Which was one of my many nicknames in grade school. He should be smart enough to know his joke is old and tired.

"Is that Spencer Murdock's truck?" Nephi nods toward Emily's vehicle.

"No."

"Yours? Did you get a new one?"

I don't answer. I see the wheels turning in their fevered brains.

"We wish you would at least join us Sunday for our service," says Nephi. "We would certainly enjoy your company."

"It will be familiar to you," says Frank. "We're fellow Mormons."

"We are the father church with all the priesthoods and power," says Nephi. "Your branch of the church is the mother. You have fed on milk, but we sense that you're ready for meat. You belong with us. We can help each other, both communally and personally, both in terms of mammon and spirituality." It's rehearsed—a speech he's delivered to other men before. No wonder he doesn't persuade many converts.

"I'm not much for religion anymore."

"It's not about religion," he says, and the echo of the Dead Fathers wakes me up. "Not about what people say to each other about God. Don't you believe in the afterlife?"

I am obliged to believe in the afterlife. "I didn't say that. I used to value the community of faith, but I'm even tired of that."

"We're just sad that you're here alone," says Nephi. "He looks at the truck. "Or that when you're not alone it's most likely with someone—ah—not worthy of you." He swallows. "Have you considered our offer?" He glances back at the girl, who is certainly beautiful, skin clear as cream on the surface of still milk. But she's just a child and shouldn't have any man forced on her. Especially not someone as old and unwashed as I. If they are unable to find anyone else, Nephi will end up giving her to Frank. I remember that the last time he was here, I called Nephi a fallible human. Now I have to revise my opinion for the worse. In his eyes, his own daughter is chattel; he is the patriarch and gives those under him, like this girl, no volition. Too much like the soldiers who stole the Goshute girl. I want to walk down and punch him in the face, but I've never been physically violent.

I look at the older woman, her strong and clear face. She's probably his first wife. He might be surprised if he tries to do something she doesn't approve of. Why she wants to marry this girl to a stranger is beyond my ability to discern.

I shake my head. "I'm still in the 'no' column."

"It's not good for man to be alone," says Frank.

In fact, that would be very good. On the eighth day, after a much too short period of rest, God smiled at the prospect of emptying heaven, shipping all those wives and clinging children off to have their own adventures. Finally alone, he savored his solitude. Actually, that's an exaggeration. I don't believe God the Father is polygamous. Some of his children are avid polygamists, but he seems like a one-goddess kind of being.

I hear movement and Emily stands next to me on the porch.

"I agree," she says. "When this one's alone he tends toward not taking care of himself. You should see the inside of this trailer—filthy."

What message should I read from their faces? Certainly disappointment, but also some anger—because she represents a new variable in an equation they thought they were close to solving.

I introduce them to her and watch their resolve melt.

"I'm glad to see you're not with someone disreputable," says Frank.

Emily doesn't react, except a small twitching of her mouth, which happens when she's pissed at someone but doesn't want to show it. I wonder how she became angry with them so quickly, and then I remember that she knew about them as soon as I mentioned their names. Neither man seemed to recognize her, which just adds to the mystery.

The young woman is especially glad, but her mother probably knows that the girl is not out of the woods yet. I can see why a mother would want to give her daughter to me instead of to Frank. But the girl should have more choices, an infinity of choices.

"Even though he thinks that's the natural state of man," Emily says. "Solitude. Playing solitaire."

Like daughter, like mother. I try to keep from smiling.

"Maybe so," says Frank, "but deep down, no man wants to be cut off from his family."

Emily looks doubtful, but she says, "It's a comfort to know the old grump has friendly neighbors." She walks toward the girl. "How old are you?"

She turns to her mother, who shakes her head, a slight motion, hardly discernible. In Nephi's household, females must learn to communicate without speech. Nephi has always been even tempered with me, but not so with his children. A month ago when I rode my bike down to his place, he whipped a teenaged boy right in front of me. The child had been slow in doing some chore. I haven't been down to visit him since then.

Mother and daughter turn to walk back to their Suburban.

Emily next faces Nephi. "Christopher tells me you grow corn for biodiesel."

I told her no such thing. I haven't had time to say fifty words to her.

"Yes, we do," he says. "We make enough money to manage out here in the desert."

"I—Christopher has seen your operation, but I haven't. If it would be all right, I'd like to see the good work you're doing."

His face changes, both their faces do, and now he's suspicious. He should be. Emily is up to something. They shouldn't just be suspicious; they should run for their lives. She'll yank their pants down and flay their behinds.

"Maybe sometime," he says. "When we're not so busy." He seems anxious to get away.

After they leave, I turn to Emily. "How do you—"

"This isn't their first time to offer you their daughter," she says.

I nod. "Last time they brought three girls."

"Repulsive men," she says. "I'm surprised you didn't join them."

I'm not sure whether she's teasing me or not. "You know me better than that."

"Do I?" she says. "Know you better than that?" Before I can respond, she goes on: "I've been doing some consulting for the county attorney who is working with the FBI. Apparently, Nephi and Frank grow very little corn and make even less biodiesel. They're selling tax credits for more biodiesel than they could possibly make. We think they have a partner at the refinery who doctors the shipping manifests. They don't actually unload the biodiesel they sell. They just drive the same truckload back and forth. They get money for the tax credits and for selling the biodiesel. Quite a racket."

"You came out here as part of your work?" I thought she came solely for me.

She looks at me. "That's not the only reason."

"It's not your usual schtick." She's all over anything that has to do with environmental protection or social justice, but this is a criminal prosecution.

"No. But when it came up, I was interested. Because of you being out here." She looks at their dust trail. "I don't need to be here to prove what they're doing. But then I thought about looking those bastards in the face when they're arrested." She turns toward the trailer. "That would be something, wouldn't it?"

She has never been one to leave her work at the office. She multitasked me into second priority in her life. One part of me says, *This is the way she is, you should have gotten used to it by now*. But the other part says, *No! I deserve her undivided attention at least some of the time*.

After Emily and I walk down to feed the horses, she works on her computer and I work on the fridge, putting into a trash bag the wizened apples, the solidified can of evaporated milk, the stew with a skin of mold on the top, the wilted and rotten vegetables, petrified mac and cheese. I dump the mess into the fifty-five-gallon barrel I use for burning trash. I wipe it out and put Emily's oranges and the fresh stuff that Spencer brought me into the fridge. There wasn't room before. As I finish, Emily snaps her computer shut.

I sit across the table from her. "What's on the docket for today?" I've chosen my words carefully. *What work do you have today that you're going to do instead of talking to me?*

"Nothing," she says. "Nothing on my docket."

"I don't believe it."

"I'll give you the chance to believe it. Carrie-Anne told me about your search for a hole in the ground." She considers what to say next. "Can I tag along?" Again, she surprises me. "I want to know why you're so interested in this cave."

I tell her about the Goshute who hid there.

"That's not your real reason," she says.

"It's a good reason," I say. "I want to crawl inside the hole where that Goshute man hid to save his life."

She frowns. "An obsession."

"Something like that."

Before leaving, we make sandwiches from the food she's brought. She drives the truck until we're stopped by mud in the road from melted snow. Then we walk up through the junipers on this cold bright morning. The air is full of light and every tree or cluster of trees feels distinct and clear. I sing, "Morning has broken like the first morning." Even the sagebrush is a vibrant gray, which seems like a contradiction but isn't.

Though I'm leading the way part of the time, part of the time we're on an old track and walk side by side. Emily wears a rose-colored coat, a pale blue hat, and her hiking boots—and she seems an essential aspect of this wonder of a day.

She tells me the news of the family. "Karin is even more into women's rights and the environment. She wants to intern with me. Several times she and I have made posters and marched in protests. Peter is starting to think he's too old to sit on my lap while I read to him. Soon he will just refuse. He's already reading chapter books. Erica is driving Carrie-Anne crazy. She couldn't remember that the fireplace screen was hot and kept burning herself until they stopped turning it on."

Our other two children, Todd and Rebecca, live in Denver and Ohio, respectively. I want to ask about them, their children, and their spouses, but I don't. They all flew to Utah for Thanksgiving, the one I fled from, and I wonder if they'll forgive me. But I have learned not to let my mind wander that direction. What happened inside me when she was talking about Karin, Peter, and Erica was terrible and exciting. My soul might fragment if I loosen my grip on its reins but losing control might free me.

It takes an hour to reach the valley of mines, where we walk up along the stream to Goshute Spring. Like the air this morning, the spring bubbles with light.

"This precious world," I whisper.

"What?"

"Nothing." I don't want to open my feeling to her. I'm not used to being vulnerable.

"Christopher," she says, "please tell me."

I shrug. "This is a lovely spot."

"Owned by Cannon-Sharp."

Some of the brightness goes out of the morning. I should have suspected she had more on her mind than seeing me or watching Nephi be arrested. "You've researched it. Of course you have. Why?"

"No reason. Just curious about your neighbors."

She's lying or maybe it isn't lying to leave out the truth of what she's doing—manifesting her multitasking, finger-in-every-pie nature. Just like coyotes or badgers fulfilling the measure of their existence, Emily fingers everyone's business, as if she's blind Justice herself. Just like I used to do as a journalist.

"Who has you on retainer?" I ask. "Cannon-Sharp?"

"No. The Utah Ghost Town Association. Someone wants to reopen the mine. They want to do a sonic test before buying the mineral rights from Cannon-Sharp."

I think about the three people who asked me to guide them. They deceived me or tried to. Emily has also. It's not accurate to say she actively deceived me. She just didn't think it necessary to tell me all her business. I know from my career that that's what men always do. Not just men. People in power. I'm sure I did it when I was obsessed with my stories. Whether I was working on a story about the death of a patient in a survival therapy program or the state legislature passing a bill to stop Park City from banning plastic bags in grocery stores, I didn't explain why I got home late. If I was that way, Emily is now that way in spades. Her motives are never simple or straightforward. This is something we need to talk about, but maybe not now. Despite this tangle, I am glad that someone of Emily's ability and ferocity wants to protect the mine. With Emily as a hired gun, the mines will be safe.

"There's a spelunking club that has gone down in this mine," I say. "They might be able to help."

We sit silently and I see the wheels turning in her head, making lists, and planning strategies.

"The area the cave might be is about a mile farther." I stand and she puts her water bottle back in her backpack. I cut two walking sticks from the willows just down from the spring and hand her one.

She smiles. "Thank you."

I remember that smile from before the coldness set in. I smile back. She looks at me and her smile falters—too much history, too close to the surface.

"Did you miss me?" I ask.

She smiles and touches my hand. "Of course I did. I missed you long before you left."

Right. I try to smile back. I thought that was my line, that she had disappeared into law school and her work a decade ago.

As we climb to the low pass above the valley, I anticipate Thomas showing himself to me again. I have more questions for him. Emily and I come out on top, and on the other side, the land slopes gently down to the next valley, about three miles east of us. I show her the lek and the birds still there, dancing. "They might stay here for a month—at least that's what I've read."

She looks at the dance through the field glasses. "Wow!" She sits on a rock and watches. I'm happy to wait, hoping she'll savor this wonder I've shared with her. For what I think is almost a half an hour, she's entranced. So gratifying. I'm sure she's caught up in the beauty of it. Then she hands me the field glasses.

"We can use that," she says. "To stop the mining."

I'm disappointed that this is her first thought—the utility of the lek. "Because they're an endangered species?"

"Not listed, but Utah is bending over backwards to keep that from happening. They won't let mining happen near a lek."

"It's gratifying that you're so invested in the mines and in my neighbors, Frank and Nephi. So good of you."

She glares at me. "Sarcastic as ever. You should be pleased with my work." She slowly walks to a small rise and takes a camera with a telephoto lens out of her backpack. She shoots pictures of the lek. Then she steps toward me. "But today is not for that business. What are we looking for? The mouth of a cave can't be that hard to find."

A little of the pleasure of looking for the cave with her has dissipated. I *am* still stuck in the romantic idea that she was giving me the gift of her whole attention, this one day. I shrug. "Might be a small hole. Might look like a gopher or badger hole, maybe a coyote den. But it will open up inside—a long cave, one that goes deeper and deeper."

"Journey to the Center of the Earth."

"Not that far."

"I was teasing you." She looks at my face. "But this is too important for teasing, isn't it?"

Her teasing about the cave wasn't the cause of my tightness. I freely admit to myself it's a pissy attitude, to wish for all of her focus today instead of eighty percent of it, but I can't just shake off the feeling.

At first, she accompanies me as I wander. I poke my stick into mouse holes next to boulders, peer at cracks between car-sized boulders of quartzite, bend to look under the occasional shelves of limestone. "Caves are more likely to form in limestone," I tell her. She's trying hard to stay with me, but then she starts marching up and down in a pattern. She walks to the tree and moves over ten yards before walking back—meticulous as always. I point out the dark clumps of cryptobiotic soil, and after that she doesn't walk in straight lines anymore.

I look up the hill and see someone sitting under a juniper, but it isn't Thomas, just a dark rock.

After about a half an hour, Emily gives up and sits in the sun against a rock face. She keeps looking at the lek through the field glasses. I'm surprised she hasn't gone back to her computer in the trailer.

We eat our lunch silently, and I wonder if this trial reconciliation has lower odds for success than a snowball in hell. I continue searching for the cave. After another hour, I return and she's napping on the ground, her head on her small pack. As I watch her, something turns around in my head. I think about her waiting for me as I do what I think of as my work—looking for the cave. Did I give her eighty percent of my focus today? Probably much less than that. But I was so focused on what she wasn't giving to me, that I couldn't see my own shortcomings. I feel emotionally stunted—as fussy and self-centered as an infant. I back up three steps, trying to get a better look at the problem. We have had a decade of not focusing on each other at all. Circling like twin planets. Calculating percentages of attention is missing the point.

"Emily," I say, and she sits up.

"Aren't you cold?"

"This is a good coat." She gathers her legs under her and stands. "Maybe a little cold. But I'll be warm again if we walk."

"Thanks for spending the day with me," I say.

"Thanks for showing me the lek. That will help a lot."

I want to tell her my insight, but when I open my mouth, what comes out is "I wish you'd told me about your lawyer reasons for coming out here." A retrograde comment.

"I didn't think it would be important to you," she says, "but point taken."

We start down the road to the valley of the mines. For a while we walk silently. It feels so nice to be with her that I almost forget our history—her marriage to her job, my waning engagement with mine, distance, her affair, my escape.

She says, "The whole desert is more beautiful than I remembered. It just seemed so dry. It's not dry now."

"You only came a few times, in the heat of summer or in the fall. It is dry then."

"It's why your grandmother left," she says. "The dry, dry air. I couldn't live out here permanently. It's always been your place, not mine."

"I'm happy you're here."

"But." She keeps walking.

I stop in the road. "But what?"

She says, "You're happy I came out here, but." Even before she was a lawyer, she picked at words when we argued. I'm sure I've done the same.

I walk fast to catch up. "Are we going to talk about what happened?"

Her eyebrows arch just a bit, as in "go on." She's in her lawyer mode with me, which I've never liked. She's good at waiting until her opponent speaks and trips himself up. It works better in the courtroom.

I say, "You probably want to know why I left."

"I think I know, but maybe you need to tell me anyway."

"You hurt me, so I left."

I'm not following, so she turns in the road. "Can't we walk and talk?"

I catch up to her.

"Chris, we hurt each other."

"You mean when I left? Or when you took up with Roger? Both?"

She moves her head in an ambiguous motion. I'm not sure what she means, yes or no. An inconvenient memory pushes itself into my head. After I finished, the prostitute stood in front of the bathroom mirror, fixing her lipstick before her next client. I could see her from the bed. But Emily doesn't know about that, and the memory doesn't keep me from blundering on. "The first thing you said to me was that you forgive me for being an asshole. I know I'm a perpetual asshole."

"No. Only occasionally."

I keep going. "Why did you have an affair? What did you want from me? Romance again? Mystery?" I want to make her see what she did. I feel guilt over hiring a prostitute, but my anger at her is heavier. Which just shows how sexist I still am. My act seems almost accidental, hers seems premeditated. I read a poem by the Scottish poet Robert Burns about a woman at home waiting for her husband: "nursing her wrath to keep it warm." It doesn't really help that I know I'm doing the same.

"I don't know what I wanted. It was impulse."

My mouth keeps going. "Did you find it again with Roger?" I discover that I want to hurt her with words. "I need to pee."

"What?" she says to my back. When I don't turn, she says, "Find what?"

"Mystery, romance."

"Of course not."

Then I'm behind a juniper. "I don't want to just fight with her," I whisper. "What can I do?"

A phrase comes into my head. "The tongue leads and the mind follows." I try to remember where I heard that, but I don't have a clue. I zip myself up and come from behind the tree.

Emily pokes her stick into the dirt a few times and connects those points with lines, making an odd shape— something like a cubist map of Florida. "It was exciting for a bit. Something different. I want to talk about what happened before that. I felt claustrophobic. I wanted to smash something. So I did." She says it in a flat tone, as if she doesn't feel remorse or any other emotion.

"You could have smashed a vase, broken a few dishes."

She rolls her eyes. "Be serious."

I nod.

"Neither one of us does hysteria well," she says. "It might be better if one of us did."

As if a camera comes into focus, I recognize my emotion. Not hysteria, or even hurt, but righteous indignation—the duty to be angry with her. As soon as I see what I'm doing, the rest of my anger drains away, leaving me feeling stupid.

A rabbit lopes across the old road. It stops and stares at us, seemingly unworried.

"I went to a prostitute last January," I say.

She doesn't react like I thought she would—with anger, maybe commensurate to the anger I felt. Instead she smiles. "Did you find mystery and romance?"

"Of course not."

She strides down the hill. Now she's angry. Her hands make fists.

"Wait," I say.

"You damned hypocrite!"

"Wait, please!"

Finally, I catch up to her. "I wanted to get back at you. I think that's why I did it."

"That's understandable. Completely understandable. But just now you were trying to shame me for what I did when you also cheated. I can't believe it."

I lean forward on my stick, suddenly tired. "Neither can I."

She glares at me. "What do you want me to say—that we're both sinners?"

"I don't think you're a sinner," I say, but that's not the whole truth. I know it's a damned Victorian Mormon double standard, but I still feel that what she did was worse. "And I don't think that visiting a prostitute is my worst sin."

"What is your worst sin?"

"Running away. Like you said, I'm an asshole."

She nods. "I didn't say that I wasn't also an asshole. We're a pair." She walks on but not as fast as she did before. I know that if I say anything too soon, I'll just muck it up again, so I follow her for about ten minutes. Then I walk faster to catch up.

"Can we sit down?" I point at two boulders on the side of the road.

"Only if you promise not to talk like a dolt."

"I can't promise that."

"At least don't act like you have no self-awareness. You are maybe too self-aware."

"Thank you, I guess. I'll try."

"I'll try also. I don't want to have driven out here for nothing."

I open my mouth, shut it again before more stupidity can escape. "That's what we're trying to find out, isn't it?"

She sits on one boulder and I sit on the other. We sit for a while and look at each other. I'm wary of saying anything. Soon she stands. "It's just too much. There's too much to work through. I'm not sure where to start."

"Let's talk about what we don't need to talk about."

She nods and sits back down. "I hope we don't need to talk about Roger anymore. He was an effect. I don't want to talk about effects, just causes."

"Logical," I say. "But how can we tell what is a cause and what is an effect?" Still I take a stab at it, using her rhetoric. "We don't need to talk about me doing all the cooking and cleaning when you worked a hundred hours a week."

That catches her attention. "We don't? You don't resent that?" The line in her jaw twitches and I'm not sure she believes me.

"I really don't. I resented you never being home, but not because I had to do the housework." I take a breath. "I resented the waning of my career because of the web and social media, and I thought that when you finished law school you'd be more available. Then I thought that once you quit that firm and started working for yourself, you'd be more available. Both times I was wrong."

"You worked long hours early in your career," she says. "This is also hypocritical of you. You were obsessed with your work. Always, always chasing after some corruption that only you could unearth. You were gone every night."

She wants to argue. *The tongue leads.* So do I. I want to ask her if it makes what she did all right just because I did it first. I think about what the Dead Fathers told me about time being non-linear, but cause and effect always seem linked—a temporal chain. I'm not sure how to talk about what happened to us in another way. Maybe we can talk about how we talk. "Your propensity will be to argue everything like a case."

She prepares to stand again, so I speak quickly. "But I do it as well. I really, really wanted to argue just now. To blame you."

"There's enough blame to go around." She relaxes again.

"I wish that instead of smashing things, we could have talked. Like we're doing now. But we couldn't. There was too much—fog."

"Fog?"

"Apathy," I say. "And distance."

She asks, "What's the difference?"

"I don't know."

She folds her arms, glaring at me. "I thought you were distant, so I made myself apathetic."

"What did I do that made you feel that I was distant?" Despite our promise to try, we're still talking past each other. I want her to say that it was her work that was the problem, the reason I became distant.

"You stopped seeing me," she says. "Your eyes just passed over me."

"*I* stopped seeing *you*?"

"OK, we stopped seeing each other."

"There's something we can agree on. We stopped being open to each other. Stopped caring like we used to. We functioned as partners but nothing more than that."

I still want her to say that she stopped caring first. But I can't make her say anything, so this time I keep my mouth shut.

"You're learning," a voice says. Probably my own head talking to itself. But it sounded like a woman. I look around.

"What?" says Emily.

I don't know how to tell her that I hear and see spirits of dead people. But I'm also bothered that someone's watching me, invading my head and urging me to do the right thing. I'll get performance anxiety. And I want to find my own way. I hope the voice doesn't speak again, but then that's what I'm thinking about, so I'm distracted.

Emily's watching me closely. "I had a good time being with you today. We don't have to work through all our problems in one day."

She's right, but I wanted to make more progress. We have really just talked in circles so far. I'm not ready to stop.

She stands and walks down the road, and after a minute, I follow. Within minutes we reach the floor of the mining valley. She is walking ahead, but she stops at Goshute Spring to look at the watercress. I gather some and put it in the plastic sandwich bag.

She smiles. "We can make a salad. I brought some to-matoes." She looks up at me. "As I said, I can see why you love this place. But it's so lonely here."

Little does she know. It's not nearly lonely enough, but if it was just her with me, not all the polygamists, not all the other crazies, especially not the Dead Fathers, it might be about right. I hadn't thought that I would ever not want to be with my grandfather, who had always seemed like a giant to me. A friendly giant. As rough as he was to everyone else, he was kind to me. I feel the loss of that idea of him. Now he's just a sexist, abrasive old man.

As we walk down, I say, "We need to keep talking."

"Yes, we do. But we don't need to push it past our capacity to be civil and logical."

Or maybe we have to shout at each other, get angry. If we're too frightened of anger, we might not dig deep enough. She's watching me, so I nod again, even though I don't agree. Then, after we walk across the stream, past the tin building, and partway down the lower canyon, she takes my hand. Despite my peevishness, I'm grateful; holding her hand is a pleasure I'd forgotten.

As we walk, I think about how soon she might sleep in the trailer, which would be even more pleasurable. It might also drive away the Dead Fathers and free me of their persistent fellowship. As we leave the road to cut across to the trailer, we have to walk single file, and my emotions shut down again. I remember the years-long deadness between us. Or not only that, but a heaviness in the universe. Even if we wanted to, we couldn't affect the inertia of time and space that wears down the love between husbands and wives.

FOUR

Mining for Common Ground

As usual, I sit in the early morning and watch the line of sun move steadily down Turkey Mountain and toward me across the alkali flat. I'll never get bored of this vision. This morning instead of just enjoying the view, I'm afflicted with a ruminative mood, chewing over the many things that have happened during the past week. It's been seven days since Carrie-Anne came, three since the mining people, two since Nephi and the General interrupted my peace and Emily parted my blanket door. One since I learned that War in Heaven II may be coming down the pike. I glance at Emily's truck, which is quiet. She has disrupted my life in ways I can't measure yet. Hopefully a blessed upheaval.

Out on the flat the line between shadow and light marches toward me like the front line of an army. A group of doe pronghorns graze near the pond. They generally eat white sage but clearly the taste of greening grass pleases them. Before long an SUV raises a line of dust coming from the campground at Simpson Springs. The people stop, and instead of watching from their vehicle, they all jump out with their cameras and phones and the pronghorns dash past Spencer's barn and out onto the flat.

Louis might have shot over their heads to scare both the pronghorns and the tourists off his property. I might want to shoot over the heads of the humans, but I wouldn't. This morning I decide it's time to sort out my emotions. I escaped to the desert to be alone and shuffle toward death. These hapless tourists frightened away the sight I wanted to enjoy longer. But at least they don't seem to want anything from me, unlike most other people who come to my trailer. If it isn't to watch their property, help them explore the mines, fill their daughters with seed, let them shoot an animal I admire, help prepare for an apocalypse, it's something else. What they want me to do makes sense from inside their various authoritarian and bureaucratic systems, but their desires are abhorrent to me. Emily used to say I am an anarchist. Maybe when I find the cave, I can crawl in there to be alone, not a part of anyone's ideological edifice. I have long felt comfortable abiding in the natural chaos of the universe, outside the straitjackets we weave for ourselves, but the Dead Fathers want me to accept that there is a strict and essential cosmic structure.

When Emily first showed up, I thought she wanted ed me to come home immediately, settle back into that fabric like Carrie-Anne wants me to. Maybe Emily wants that, but she also bought a truck and seems to plan to stay awhile. She came partly because this location made her plans easier—uncovering the polygamists' practice of defrauding the government and the mining company's scheme to exploit someone else's mineral right and ruin a historical site. It doesn't seem that either of these projects will require much of me. They are a channel for her ardent will, leaving me free to do nothing or something—as I choose. She wants to talk, but she also wants to be with me, as evidenced by her spending most of yesterday just following me through my day. She held my hand—indicating what? That she wants me again or that she never stopped wanting me? The revival of possibility between us has unsettled me. And her dream, where Thomas came to her—profoundly unsettling.

Thomas's appearance also unsettled me but in a different way. He doesn't seem to want anything from me. Why is he so different from the other Dead Fathers? Thomas may be pleased for me if I find the cave, but he's not pressuring me. He seems to think that discovery will come in its own time and season. I think about crawling inside the umbilicus of the earth or at least the umbilicus of this edge of the Great Basin, and just imagining it gives me pleasure. My desire is in no way rational, which is also freeing.

Finally, the sun reaches me. I stand and stretch, satisfied with my mental perambulations, which this time lead to a feeling of peace in patience. At the same instant, the tailgate opens and Emily emerges, dressed in jeans and a red shirt that reflects in her face, making the pink of her skin show more vividly.

"Coffee?"

She nods. I step inside and pour her a cup. We sit together on the stoop and she takes a long draft. She glances at me, then away, opens her mouth, shuts it again. I've seldom seen her so indecisive.

"Come on," I say. "You've never been one to hold back."

"Oh, I don't say half of what I'd like to. I can talk all day in the courtroom, and you could write news stories all day, but neither one of us is good at intimate conversation."

"Right." I go inside and mix up some hotcake batter. Soon the cakes are browned, and I slide two onto a plate, apply butter and syrup, and take them out to her. I make myself a plate and sit next to her. "What were you going to say?"

"Your grandfather ruined you. He and his cabin. He gave you the idea that living in squalor is all right. This is even worse than Carrie-Anne said."

I look at the steaming hotcakes. "I stopped caring."

"That's a problem." So she does want me to do something—take a bath. That seems reasonable, hopeful even. I wonder if Spencer would let me shower in his apartment. Probably not. The only other option is the shallow, muddy pond. I'd come out smelling different but not necessarily better. Maybe a sponge bath is in my future, but that probably wouldn't be the end of my aroma. I need a real dunking in hot water and ample soap—multiple times.

What I would like to do is to stare at her from behind a two-way mirror or some other veil so I could sort out my complex feelings, but when I look at her too long, she becomes uncomfortable. I have to keep glancing away. It isn't as if staring at her would give answers, because gazing is both answer and question; looking at her is something I need to do because I'm curious. Also, her face is pleasant and looking moves me and opens me to feelings I worried were lost.

"What do you want to know?" she asks me.

"You came to gather evidence on the Johnsons."

"Yes. In part. But I already had evidence to get a warrant, so I didn't need to come out here for that. In court it will help if I see their operation and can talk about what I observed."

"You want to see Nephi sweat."

"I do."

"Not very admirable."

"Trying to get his daughter to hook up with an old fart like you is much less admirable. Especially someone who won't bathe."

"Daughters. I told you that he offered me three of them earlier."

She grimaces. "Maybe if he hadn't overdone the offer, you might have joined him."

"Are you jealous?"

She gives a bark of laughter. "No. I'm glad you're not a pedophile."

"The one was probably eighteen."

"Nor a rapist."

I nod. "Thanks, I guess." One thing I know from this conversation, underneath it all we are both lacking in trust. We don't trust each other's motives. "It's odd that someone wants to protect the O.K. Silver Mine from development. A man-made hole in the ground is not something to protect like a ghost town. Well, there's a tin building and a fallen down hotel."

"They care about those but they also care about the mines."

I shake my head.

She smiles. "Yes. It is ironic."

"But you didn't need to be here to do that either."

"No, I don't."

"What else is there?"

"What do you mean?"

"What else have you got going out here? How many irons do you have in the fire?"

She looks away for a moment, then back to me. "In 1968 the military tested a nerve gas they had developed. They hadn't bothered to check the weather and the wind blew it the wrong way. An Anglo rancher who grazed his sheep east of the testing grounds lost most of his herd. He was finally reimbursed, but the Goshutes believe the same incident killed a few elders. And they think it wasn't the only event. They're filing a new lawsuit against the army. They think that with all the public talk now about reparations for Blacks and Native Americans that they might make some progress."

"After all this time. Did you go looking for any of this business?"

"No," she says. "These cases just came up. Very unusual."

"I don't believe in pure coincidence. There's always a will behind things, shaping them."

She nods. "I wondered about that: of course I did."

"I was talking about your will," I say.

"I didn't go hunting for these. They came to me. And then—"

"Go on!"

"And then the dreams came."

I fold my hands on the table.

She sighs. "You've certainly been on my mind. But how could I just show up after all this time?"

"You needed an excuse."

"Petty."

"I don't know about that," I say. "I was also looking for an excuse, but I hadn't found a good one yet. You beat me to it."

She looks at me and neither of us looks away. It feels more like two bull elks circling each other than two lovers soaking up each other's gazes. "I couldn't do it, Chris. Ever since you left, I couldn't see a way out. I had to give in or you did. I didn't want to give in. I needed help to make a move."

I put my hand on hers from across the table. I look at her for a long time and she looks back. For a second, I let myself feel how nice this is, but then I get frightened and move my hand away.

"Let's go look for the navel," she says. It's clear she's once again had enough of wrangling. "Maybe if we contemplate it, we'll become enlightened."

Actually that's what I hope for, and she's being flippant about it. "First, I have to show you the mines." It will be good for her to see what she's protecting.

We walk up along the ditch my grandfather built. Most of the time we walk single file, but when we cross meadows or open hillside, we go side-by-side, she on one bank of the old, filled-in ditch and I on the other.

I sing a song by Donovan that we liked when we were younger. Back then I changed the words: "Lady, kiss me once more, give me some love."

"So silly," she says.

"But it worked," I say. "You did kiss me, did give me love."

"I felt sorry for you because you couldn't and still can't hold a tune." She sings the whole verse perfectly. "I did love how much a country boy you were, corny as hell, but very disarming." Her face is animated, as it was in the old years when we talked and talked about anything and everything—stuff we'd read, stuff we'd thought about, experiences and people and politics and religion and music. Nothing was off limits.

I sing again, "Can't get no satis—"

She sings over the top of my song, much louder and more on tune: "You don't—"

"—faction."

"—own me."

I stop and let her finish her song. "I'm not just one of your toys."

We leave my grandfather's ditch and cross a ravine to join the road that goes to the mines.

"What are you trying to do?" she asks. "Take us back to elementary school?" We were both ten in 1965.

"I am feeling nostalgic. I was thinking this morning about how I thought I would be alone in the desert. My life would be simple and uniform. Nothing would change. This past week I've seen cataclysmic change. I had three sets of visitors. And then you."

"Cataclysmic."

"Those others were," I say, "but your coming was cosmic. Not a cataclysm."

She smiles, and then immediately frowns. "Can you walk behind me? I don't like being downwind from you."

I grin at her.

"You think I'm kidding?" She strides forward and puts some distance between us.

"I don't think you're kidding. I'm thinking how much you love me if you're willing to put up with my smell."

"Don't push your luck," she says without turning.

I want to talk more about the difference between distance and apathy, how to replace them both with something more substantial. They built between us for more than a decade. Nothing will change easily or quickly. If I took a bath, would she be more ready for the work? Something I should try. Maybe moss and leeches would be worth it.

Before long we come to the valley of the mines—thirteen dark mouths scattered across the steep hillsides. We stand next to an old tin building with "AN UNARMED MAN IS A SLAVE" shot into the rusted wall. Emily smiles at the words.

"An armed man is a danger to himself and others," she says. I remember what Louis told me when I was a kid, that I should never call my rifle a gun. In the army a gun meant something else entirely.

"It took a lot of focus for someone to shoot those words."

"Someone with too much time on his hands. Was it you?"

"You know it wasn't me."

"I do. I was teasing you. Your grandfather maybe."

"He wouldn't have thought he needed to write it out."

I point to a white spill of dirt about a hundred yards up the hillside. We clamber up, and I walk into the mouth, an arch about eight feet tall and just as wide. Iron tracks for hauling out ore disappear into the darkness. I switch on my flashlight and hand her another one.

The air inside is wet, the musty smell of dirt and dank water.

"It's hard to walk on the ties," she says.

She's right; the distance from one tie to the next is too short for a step, but two ties are too long. We stride deeper into the mine until there is no sign of light from the opening behind us, even though it's a straight track to the outside.

She clicks her light off. "Turn yours off also."

We stand in the absolute darkness and I hear water dripping and her breathing and my own. Nothing else.

"This is what I used to imagine death is like," I say.

"Morbid."

"Not really. No worries. Perfect peace."

"Should I confiscate your gun?"

"Of course not. I don't think death is like that anymore. It's continual busy-ness. Clamor."

"And how would you know?"

I turn my light on again. We walk deeper into the mine. I glance sideways at her, flashing the edge of my light across her face, and she's grinning. If I'm not mistaken, she's excited about our little field trip. She's never been interested in geology, so it must be something else. Maybe she's just happy to be doing something with me. I hope that's it. "Not much farther."

We come to a T and turn left. Soon the shaft widens into a large cavern with three side tunnels branching out from it. I lead her to the opposite wall, where a fall of dirt and rock rises to an outcropping that shines yellow when we flash our lights on it. Most of the crystals are small and dark, mixed with other rocks and dirt, but a few crystals are larger, an inch in diameter.

"Fool's gold, right?"

I nod.

"Still lovely." She touches the crystals with her fingertip. "Why is this not as valuable as gold?"

"Maybe because fool's gold decays. Specifically it rusts. Iron pyrite."

"Lay not up for yourselves treasures upon earth, where moth and rust corrupt, and where thieves break through and steal."

"You sound like Hugh," I say. "Quoting scripture."

"Hugh?"

"My great-great-grandfather."

She turns toward me but I can't see her expression, not without flashing my light straight into her eyes.

"I memorized it when I was a girl and it's still in my head." She touches the crystals again. "You talk as if you've just spoken to him."

I almost start to tell her about the DFs, but then I lose courage. That news would certainly disrupt the moment.

"You worship your family," she says. "I used to wonder why. Now I know that it's because you think you're descended from nobility."

"Fool's gold nobility."

"But you don't really think that. None of them, not even your father, is merely human to you."

"Oh, I know they're human." I think of their talk during our poker games.

"I'm not convinced. I think that you have wanted all your life to become them. But they were fallible people, just like you."

"This bothers you about me."

She nods. "You're a better person than either your father or your grandfather."

"You just don't know them well." Which is a little deceitful of me. Now that I know them better, they seem bossy and manipulative.

Emily shrugs.

"That's not all I wanted to show you." I walk to the middle shaft and we continue until we come to another large cavern. On one wall a ladder made of new wood goes up about thirty feet to a ledge with the entrance to a shaft beyond it.

"Did you build this?" she asks.

"No."

"Who did?"

"I don't know. I found it just like this."

She places her hand on the ladder as if to climb it. "What's up there?"

"I don't know. I haven't dared go up."

"Why not?" She lifts herself onto the first rung.

"It's not beyond the realm of possibility that someone is up there."

She takes another step higher. "Do you think it's Blythe, Blythe, and Smith?"

"Who?"

"The mining company that's trying to open this mine again."

"This was here before they came," I say.

She takes another step.

"I once started up and then had the clear feeling I didn't want to keep going," I say.

Her flashlight still pointed up the ladder, she looks over her shoulder at me, and then she steps back down. She points her flashlight at the ground—a slab of rock with a faint layer of dust on it. "Have there ever been footprints?" I do the same and can no longer see her face clearly.

"I've never seen any," I say. "Except for my own. I've already stepped there."

"I'm not going up there either."

"Smart," I say.

"Or dumb," she says. "Why would someone build a ladder here now unless it has something to do with the new exploration for ore?"

I shake my head. "I don't know. Maybe it was built by a crazy hermit and he's up there with a shotgun."

I hear her steps as she moves toward me; her shadow reaches the periphery of my flashlight. "Why did you bring me here?"

I shrug. "Miners used to walk here and I like seeing the work that they did to manifest themselves."

"Their work was primarily a benefit to someone else."

"True," I say. "But their work still seems significant. They made miles and miles of tunnel here."

She touches a rock where there is a clear mark made by a pick.

"Not all of it was by hand. They also used dynamite."

She turns to point her light up the ladder again.

I say, "I thought you might be interested. You know—because you're helping to preserve the mines. There are secrets down here."

She turns her light toward me and blinds me. "Soon you'll just be another crazy."

"Am already," I say.

"Let's get out of here and go look for the navel hole that you're obsessed with." Then she laughs and can't stop chuckling at her joke that wasn't even a joke.

As we return through the tunnels, I decide I was smart not to tell her about the visits from my dead ancestors. She'll think my mind as well as my body has descended to squalor.

FIVE

Bleeding Lucifer

The next morning, Emily asks me to go with her to visit the polygamists.

"You want to take up with a couple of their lost boys?"

Her face clouds over. "That's a stupid thing to say."

"A little bit clever."

"It's the kind of thing a man says when he's daydreaming about the daughters." She gives me a wolf smile.

I consider. They were comely, but they reminded me of my own grandchildren and my daughters when they were teenagers. "They shouldn't be afflicted with me."

"Right. You're a filthy old man. In more ways than one."

"They would never have anything to do with me if they weren't forced by their father."

"True." She rolls down the window even though it's still chilly outside. "Tell me another truth. When did you last bathe, really?"

"In February when I went to Wendover. Before that— at Christmas. I drove to the hot springs south of here. After the polygamists, we can go there."

"OK. But it may take a pressure hose to get you clean."

We drive along the Six-mile Road to where it branches down into the river bottom and leads to the polygamists' farm on my grandfather's former land.

Ahead of us is a pickup with someone crouched next to it. Closer I see he's Bennie Bullcreek. He stopped in once to ask me about the petroglyph panel in the next canyon over. He's one of the few people I've met who I enjoyed talking with. He's a Goshute from the Skull Valley band, whose reservation is twenty miles to the north.

Emily stops the truck and gets out. Bennie is dressed in a suit and tie, crouched above a rabbit he's gutting. He has on a pair of rubber-surfaced gloves. He cuts the head mostly off and then pulls downward while holding the rabbit carcass with his other hand, and the skin peels off in one clean motion. I notice that he stuffed his tie between the buttons of his shirt to keep it from hanging down into the blood. He turns and looks at us. He nods at Emily and I wonder how they know each other.

"What's so damn funny?" he asks me.

"It's disjunctive. You in a suit skinning a rabbit."

He smiles. "So Christopher, I should be as filthy as you before I take care of a rabbit I hit with my truck?"

I wonder if the whole universe is colluding to make me bathe.

"I want the skin for a blanket I'm making. I can feed the carcass to my dog."

Emily gets out, passes in front of the truck, and stands with one hand on the hood, watching him work on the rabbit. "You know each other?"

"Christopher is the local expert about this area," says Bennie. "His family has been here for five generations. Mine's only been here for a few hundred generations."

She motions her hand toward me. "Chris is my—ah—husband."

"Your husband," Bennie says. "Now *that* is disjunctive."

She turns to me. "Bennie and I are working together to keep atomic waste off the reservation."

It's another project out here that she somehow forgot to mention.

"Again?" I say. "I thought that was settled decades ago."

"They keep trying new ways of shipping radioactive dirt here." Bennie rolls the skin up and places it and the body in the bed of his truck. "It feels like an eternal fight." He takes a gallon jug in the crook of his arm, tips it, and washes his gloves.

"Emily!" I say. "How many damn projects do you have going out here? I thought you told me about all of them."

"I could do all this from home," she says, understanding me immediately. "Or by taking a few trips out. I didn't need to see you at all. Instead I chose to stay near your trailer for a week or so. Why? Because you're here."

"You haven't been honest with me." I sound pitiful even to my own ears.

She shrugs. "When I came in the trailer door, did you tell me you're looking for the earth's navel?"

"I wish you two would fight in private." Bennie peels off the gloves. "It's embarrassing when you argue in front of me as if I wasn't here."

"Sorry," says Emily.

"You on your way down to nail the polygamists?"

She shakes her head. "Just for research. They even invited us. Like lambs bleating for their butcher."

Actually she invited herself. And I'm not surprised by the violence of her image. I sometimes watched her lawyer in the courtroom. When she finished with one man who had been dumping paint waste into a well near the Jordan River, he shook with fear and anger.

"They're not half as smart as they think they are," Bennie says as he climbs in his truck. "But maybe none of us are."

Emily walks around to the driver's side, and we continue toward my grandfather's former ranch in the dry river bed. Bennie's truck generates dust behind us. She looks at me and sniffs the air, her face sour. She pushes the buttons and rolls down all the windows. I glare at her and crank up the heater all the way.

"How many more secrets do you have?"

"I have as many secrets as you have fleas."

"I don't have any fleas."

She points to red marks on my arms.

"Bedbugs."

She nods as if she's just won the argument. And I guess she has. I'll have to burn all my bedding, maybe fumigate. Maybe poisonous gas that seeps into every part of my trailer will also get rid of the Dead Fathers, but I'm not going to get my hopes up.

Emily stops her truck on the bench where the road branches, the main track going on to Six-mile Canyon and the other passing down into the river valley. She gets out and looks at the spread through a pair of binoculars.

"They claim they've invented a simpler way of producing ethanol," she says. "More elegant." She looks at me. "Speaking scientifically."

She's excited but not about the science of ethanol production. And excited is not the right word. Confident. She's like a wolf I once saw in Denali following a young caribou, a quarter mile behind. Both the caribou and the wolf knew the outcome as if it had already happened. The adolescent caribou was frantic and the wolf's tail wagged. I glance at Emily's face again, her familiar predatory look. Very attractive, just as it was forty years ago. It's one of a constellation of characteristics that both made me love her and made us fall apart.

I have mixed feelings whenever I visit my grandfather's last farm, which he homesteaded after Antelope Spring. I made so many memories here; you could even say that my identity was forged here: not just my tolerance for what Emily calls squalor, but my love of this gray desert, as different from red-rock country as the moon is from Mars, and my appreciation of anyone, Nephi included, who can make a go of it in this arid place. Especially my appreciation for the value of water, which is life. Generations have tried, but the Goshutes were probably the best at it. Like Bennie said, they've been here for generation on generation. Before them, some other people was here living on insects and lizards and whatever they could get their hands on. Both these cultures lived in what Emily and many others might call squalor, but they were and are adaptive, as evidenced by Bennie with his suit and education. Also, they bathed as infrequently as I do. I don't really want to trade my eggs and canned food for insects, but I still feel connected.

Even though it's too early in the spring for the pump engines to run, bringing water up for irrigation, I listen for the sound, three pitches in a tangled harmony. Instead, I hear only Emily breathing and the breeze rattling a clump of tumbleweeds. As a kid, when I visited my grandfather, I went to sleep and woke to the wavering pitch of diesel engines. That sound meant water rushed up and flowed into ditches. During the days, I swam in the ditches or tried to. The main trunks were three feet deep but the branch ditches were less and I clawed the mud to pull myself forward, feeling like a toad or an alligator. I had to watch out for snakes, not the blow or water snakes but the rattlers, because the water made it so they couldn't sound a warning.

"No sprinklers," I say. "They're still flood irrigating."

"Four hundred acres," she says. "They claim to have sold 130,000 gallons of ethanol last summer."

I shrug. "And?"

"They shouldn't be able to get that much ethanol from so little acreage. Do you want to know the figures?"

"No."

"Well. It's more bushels per acre than they grow in the Midwest. Do those look like high-producing fields to you?"

I shake my head. "No." I've only seen them in their winter-dead and harvested states, but the stumps of the stalks seem patchy.

She gives me a look. "Maybe they'll show us the ethanol distilling equipment they claim is so efficient."

"Maybe they won't let me look at it with you here. You'll ask a million questions, and he already knows you're up to no good."

"Right." She climbs back in her truck.

The road winds down the foothill to the floor of the ancient riverbed. At the entrance to the farm, she stops and I get out to swing the gate open, a fancy gate welded from inch pipes. In my grandfather's day it was four strands of barbed wire. We drive closer, and I see fields with only corn stubble. A massive tractor works a twelve-bottom plow to the south of us.

"That's an expensive tractor," I say.

"A hundred and twenty thousand," she says.

Ten years earlier all this would have put me on point like a bird dog. And even now I feel an itch of curiosity. What is Nephi up to?

We drive past where my grandfather's corrals were, the space now filled with three buildings—orange-yellow aluminum siding. Emily stops a half mile farther, where my grandfather's last cabin stood. It was covered with black tar paper, never finished. In its place stands a two-story ranch house and beyond that another one—Frank's and Nephi's homes. Probably ten bedrooms in each one.

Nephi walks out to meet the truck. He's smiling. "You came to join us for our Sunday meetings. I'm so grateful you changed your mind."

"It's Sunday?" I say.

"All day," says Emily. She takes my hand and smiles demurely. "Actually, we're here to look at your operation. If you're not too busy today."

He pauses. "I suppose a short tour doesn't break the Sabbath, but if I do, you must stay for Sacrament Meeting." He turns before either of us can answer.

"You grow corn?" Emily asks.

"For ethanol. Because the government thinks of it as a renewable resource."

I say, "You don't agree? We can grow more corn, but we can't grow more dinosaurs." I'm baiting him because he thinks the earth is seven thousand years old. Oil was placed in the earth by God to bless the lives of His children.

"I am happy to get more from my farm than I would get from growing alfalfa." He points toward his house. "Better than your grandfather's shack, right?" He turns toward his truck. "Follow me." He drives before us back to the yellow buildings, and parks in front of the southernmost one. Outside is a kind of lean-to, appended to the larger building. I walk over and see a large generator run by a gasoline engine.

Emily takes out her phone.

"No pictures," Nephi says. "We have our process copyrighted, but I still don't want to have pictures floating around that someone else can use to duplicate what we're doing here."

"Why is the engine outside?" I ask.

"Fire danger," he says. "Corn dust is flammable."

He turns to Emily, who has managed to stay quiet. She glances at him and then looks at the ground. I realize she's trying to fit his idea of how a woman should behave. It's not going to work. He's not stupid or unobservant.

He studies her for a moment, and I know he sees right through her. Maybe he doesn't know exactly what she's up to, but he's not going to show us anything he doesn't want us to see. Finally, he smiles, opens the door, and steps inside. We follow, me first and Emily behind. I see mounds of corn with some scoop shovels stuck into a mound. Face masks are looped over the handles. Near that is a hopper with an auger underneath. It's odd that all this equipment is still. Is it just for Sunday that it's shut down, or does it lie silent most of the time?

"This is our grinder."

I glance at Emily, who grins back. She's not as good an actor as she thinks she is.

"You still have corn," I say.

"We do small batches throughout the year. Small and steady. That's one of our secrets. Our equipment investment is smaller that way."

I think about the massive tractor.

He leads us back outside and points to a tanker truck. "Every week we send a truck to the refinery. We can make money by keeping our operation small—a family business."

He puts his hand on my shoulder. "You should join us."

"That's what I don't understand," I say. "Why you want me to marry your daughters, why you want me to join you. Doesn't make sense."

"You underestimate both your potential and my charity. You can't pretend that you're happy or that you feel you're living a satisfying life. You can't pretend that you're being challenged. Right now you're wasting yourself. Both of you are."

He looks at Emily to see how she's taking this. He's trying to needle her. Does he think I'll do something that she opposes? Clearly he does.

The line in Emily's jaw tightens. I wonder if it will start twitching. But she just smiles at him.

"Sister Twist, are you out here permanently? Or is this just a visit?"

"Permanently," I say. Her thumbnail digs into my palm. I succeed in not wincing. "Or maybe just a visit."

Somehow Emily keeps her face passive. "That's still to be decided."

"Drive for us," he says to me. "You're stagnating in that trailer."

There's another building, one with a large padlock on it, with a tempered steel chain. He's not about to show us that building.

I look across the fields of corn stubble. The snow has melted and the dirt is dry on the surface. Where the plow has passed the soil is darker, but not as dark as soil in Rockwood. "How much is your yield?"

"Two hundred bushels an acre." He's smug, like a fisherman who's just told a story about a big fish.

I nod as if I care.

He takes a few steps back toward his truck. The tour is over. Over his shoulder I see Emily walk to the building we didn't see. She pulls at the padlock, and then peers in a window.

He turns to face me. "Where's Emily?"

Now she's out of sight. "I think she had to pee," I say.

"She should have said something." He steps closer to me. "Christopher, I wish you'd reconsider. We're not getting great converts. I can't have my daughters marrying their brothers or their cousins. Or their uncle. We're to that point."

He seems genuinely interested in me. But there's a dark underbelly to his offer. He wants me to break the law and marry his girls—against their will. In my mind there's no sin worse than stealing someone's volition. I wonder if that's what he wants—to bring me into his fold so he can control me. But that doesn't make sense either. There's something here I'm not seeing.

He takes my hand and pulls me close. Then he puts a hand on each of my shoulders. I try pulling away but he holds me. "I've had a revelation." His voice wavers as if he can't bear up under the emotion. "I should have told you before. I had a dream. It's your destiny to marry my daughters, join with my family. That's why I came to your trailer. I was commanded by God to give you this message. You are to let your sinful wife go her own way and marry my daughters." He nods back toward his and his brother's houses. "We'll build a third house, just for you." He leans forward and whispers in my ear. "You can help us bleed Lucifer dry."

I consider asking him what that means, but I don't want to know, so I shrug and turn from under his heavy hands. Emily comes from behind the building and steps up into her truck.

He grins. "A young wife keeps an old man young. You know in your heart that what I'm saying is ordained to happen."

"Thanks for showing us your operation," I say.

"Stay for the meeting. That was the agreement."

I shake my head. "It was your idea, not mine."

He glares at me as I walk toward Emily's truck. She doesn't talk until we're off the property.

"He looked like he was giving you the holy kiss."

"Just offering his daughters again. He said he had a vision that I should join his commune."

"I thought I didn't believe in Lucifer," she says. "But that man is evil."

I look at her. I might have gone weeks without hearing that name, except from the Dead Fathers, so I'm surprised to hear it twice within a few minutes.

"Not evil," I say. "Just has problematic assumptions. In my ear he said something about helping them bleed Lucifer dry."

She looks at me. "That's code for defrauding the government. Government is Lucifer, so taking money from the government is helping destroy it."

Her tire runs against the shelf of dirt at the edge of the road.

"Watch your driving," I say. "I was distracted when you explained this before. Something about tax credits. Tax credits aren't money. They would just reduce taxes owed."

"It's more complex than that. Oil refineries in states like Texas, where they don't want to mix ethanol with gasoline, have to pay tax credits to refineries that do. So the refinery where Nephi and Frank send their biofuel makes a massive profit from selling tax credits."

"Too complex for me," I say.

"Liar. They're doctoring the records at both ends, so they can claim more credits than they deserve and the Texans can keep more of their money. We think he's trucking ethanol to the plant, where it's recorded, but then they don't unload it. He sells the same tank over and over."

She turns toward me and nearly runs off the road again.

"Just stop the truck," I say. "We're not in a hurry to get anywhere."

She parks in the middle of the road. "I wish I knew what he had in that second building. It had an engine outside, just like the first. If it's just another ethanol distillery, why didn't he let us see it?"

"You think there's another part to the con?"

"Yes. They're bleeding Lucifer from both arms, his neck, and maybe his femoral arteries." She pauses. "It smelled like alcohol."

"Ethanol is alcohol. Maybe they have another distillery in there, just like the one we saw."

"I looked through the window. It didn't look like an ethanol distillery. I wonder if he's making whiskey in there."

"He's a fundamentalist! He wouldn't distill whiskey. It's against the Word of Wisdom."

"Well, I still think it was whiskey. Maybe he doesn't think it's wrong to sell it to Gentiles."

She starts the truck again and turns off the main road onto the one that cuts up toward Spencer's land. I realize we've both forgotten about the bath. The hot springs are back through Nephi's property and another hour of driving to the south. I don't have a swimsuit and I doubt she has one either, so breaking my bath fast with her seems appealing.

"We forgot about my bath."

"Damn!" she says. "How far is it?"

"Forty miles south."

She focuses on the road. "Not now. Too much to think about. Too much to do."

At least I've had most of her attention for a couple of days. If all this is an exploration of whether we should get back together, I am convinced we should. I hope it's the same for her.

She's silent the rest of the way back to my trailer. Instead of pulling into the lane to my trailer, she drops me off on the road. "I'll be back soon. Maybe tomorrow night, maybe a bit later." She touches my left hand as I open the door. Then her truck pulls away, leaving a plume of dust that sinks to the ground because there is no breeze now.

Wait! I'm not ready for her to go. What if she doesn't come back? What if my rank odor has driven her away? When her dust dies, I turn and walk toward my trailer. Despite her leaving, or maybe because of her leaving and the loss I feel, I can't give up.

I finish my dinner, a cold can of pork and beans flavored with a squishy cube of fat. At least I have a warm beer to chase it. I wipe my plate with a piece of bread, eat the bread, and put the plate in a cupboard. It's too dry for any bacteria to grow. I might as well be living on Mars.

Just as I finish my beer, I notice that they're back.

"I told you to take Nephi up on his offer," says Hugh. "You'd be settled and progressing. Instead you're swimming in the opposite direction."

"It's good for a woman to feel she has competition," says Louis.

"You are really losing it," says my father, pulling out a chair and sitting in it. "You're standing on thin ice."

"Soon it will be spring, and the ice will melt. I'll just take a swim."

"It's not just cold water you'll fall into," says Hugh, "but the gulf of hell."

"That damned harpy Lilith will crawl up to earth on your back," says Louis.

"How will getting into bed with the polygamists help anything?" I mean it as a joke, but none of them crack a smile.

"You're missing the point, you obtuse bastard," says Louis.

"You want me to help them bleed the government? Do you think the government is Lucifer?"

"The government is irrelevant," says Louis. "A circle jerk of narcissists."

"Ineffectual," says Hugh.

"Well then what is relevant?" I ask.

"You are," says my father. "You are the fulcrum. The angle of repose. The particle that makes critical mass."

"I don't have a clue what you're talking about."

"Blind mouth," says Hugh. "O foolish people, and without understanding; which have eyes, and see not; which have ears, and hear not. In this war in heaven you have an essential part to play."

More disturbing news. I almost long for the time when they had no messages for me. "Preposterous! I'm no general."

"No," says Louis. "Not even a good warrior. But we don't get to decide these things."

"When will I be required to act?" I ask.

"Too soon," says my father.

"You imply that you're on the good side and that Emily and your wives are on the other. None of them are evil!"

They bend close over their cards.

"Is Lucifer not involved in this war or is his part a covert operation?"

Clearly, they're done talking.

"I wish you'd just communicate without all this silly obfuscation."

They stare at me as if I've just blasphemed. I admit the word does sound like an obscenity. And then they drift away. I can never mark a point where they disappear, but we're eyeing each other mistrustfully, and then they're gone. Most disturbing is the Dead Fathers' assertion that I have something to do with how this war is going down. By my nature I'm a blunderer. When I was a reporter, that was my method: blundering around where there was the stench of something hidden, knocking vases over, careening into China cabinets, tripping over throw rugs, until I found the stinking thing. This seems more delicate: blundering might make everything worse. I can't count on the Dead Fathers to say anything that might help me make good decisions; Biblical Isaiah is crystal clear compared to these obfuscators. With them, left might be right, up might be down, yes might be no.

The next morning six or seven trucks raise clouds of dust as they caravan up the canyon. The first one is the pickup with the BSB logo. I jump on my bicycle and follow them toward the O.K. Silver Mine. With every turn of the wheels, my anger builds. The tracks sink deep into the margins of the dirt road, so I know they're carrying weight.

I'm about a third of the way up when I hear an explosion and the ground shakes. "Those sons of bitches!" I say. Right after that, I hear another blast, and another, five in total. I pedal harder and soon get to the valley. Plumes of dust still hang in the air. One truck is parked next to the old tin building, another up by the spring, another to the north. The trucks have wires coming from the back that are plugged into rods in the ground.

The man I met before walks down the hill toward me; he's still wearing his yellow overcoat, even though it's not as chilly as before. "We managed without you."

"What are you doing?" I scream.

The woman follows him. "We think there's another vein of silver, running beneath the abandoned mines."

Yellow Overcoat says, "The mine was mostly played out by the 1930s, but we think there may be ore they didn't have the equipment to discover."

The second man says, "We've had luck sonic mapping other played-out mines."

"Sonic mapping?"

Yellow Overcoat speaks up. "We explode five charges at once and the computer records what's under the ground. You could help us be more exact about where to place the explosives."

My first thought: *I don't want explosives anywhere near that valley.* I say, "This isn't your land."

"Right, a corporation in Salt Lake owns it—Cannon-Sharp," says Boots. "We bought the mineral rights from them."

"Won't the explosions make the mines unstable?"

He squints at the sun. "Might collapse a few unstable mines. Make them safer, like shooting a cannon to cause an avalanche."

"For every tunnel you collapse, three more would be made more unstable."

He doesn't seem to hear me.

"We also want to set them off on the plateau above the mining valley."

I glare at him. If they set off explosives up there, they might close off the navel hole that I haven't yet found. They would certainly scare away the lek. "That would be bad."

"Bad?" says Boots.

"There's a cave up there," I say. "And a lek."

"A what?" Boots asks.

"Where sage grouse mate."

"Neither the cave nor the sage grouse grounds is on any map." I can't even see Yellow Overcoat's face.

I realize that raving at them will do no good. The damage is already done. He glances toward the east, toward the place where I've been looking for the earth's navel. "We'll have to clear a better road onto the plateau. We'll need to bring in a bulldozer to remove the boulders from the road in the canyon."

"No," I say.

"You can't legally stop us," says Boots.

"But we can write to all the mine spelunkers. And to the people who love visiting ghost towns. And to the state people who set up state heritage sites."

"We?" says Yellow Overcoat. "You and who else? Spencer said you're all alone out here."

I'm not going to give him any warning about Emily. She'll be into them like a torpedo. But she'll have to hurry.

"I'll bet you don't even have internet," Boots says.

"I might have to make a trip to town."

"By then we'll be finished."

I get on my bike and continue along the road.

"You're trespassing!" Yellow Overcoat shouts.

I stop. "This is a public right of way." I don't even know if that's true.

"It's not safe," he says.

I turn and keep riding—past the truck next to the spring, which is bubbling murky water, a sign of internal bleeding.

"You can't go there! It's dangerous!"

It probably isn't dangerous because they're finished blasting here. I walk my bike up the incline on the far side of the valley and the landscape opens up. Instead of searching, I dump my bike next to the juniper where I saw Thomas before and wait. I look at the lek through my field glasses. The birds are still there, but they're not doing their dance. I am sure that they were upset by the loud blasts that shook the ground. I just hope they go back to their mating dance, and I hope to hell the blasts haven't collapsed the cave.

I begin to wish I had a gun to threaten the mining team with, but I know I wouldn't really do that. I'm not sure why it also bothers me that some mineshafts near the blasts might have collapsed. They were mineshafts after all—dug by humans into the earth. If they could find more minerals under those mazes of tunnels, why shouldn't they go for it? But I had walked there, had drawn some pleasure from the cold, wet darkness, from looking at the iron pyrites and the ore-laced rock walls. And they're not finished. I'm desperate that their charges up on the flat might collapse the cave. Then there's the lek. Explosions so close will drive away the birds. They're not finished. I'm desperate that their charges up on the flat might collapse the cave. Then there's the lek. Explosions so close will drive away the birds.

Instead of hunting for the opening, I climb onto my bike and ride back through the valley of mines. The trucks are still there, and a scattering of tents have sprouted like toadstools, blue, yellow, orange. People sit in a cluster of chairs and hold plates of food on their laps. Some watch me pass. I could pull down their tents, chain myself to one of the trucks, but alone I can't stop them. I want an army of spelunkers and ghost town hunters, but there isn't time. At least they aren't moving to the upper valley this evening, so I have until tomorrow morning. "Damn you to hell, you sons of bitches!" I shout as I pass their tents. Several more turn to look at me. A man packing a pistol comes out of his tent and rests his hand on the butt of it. I speed down the road on my bike.

Back at my trailer, I open the door to see Thomas sitting at my table, which is much more startling than being greeted by the pack rat that had taken over my bed.

"Christopher Twist," he says. "We need to talk. How much sugar do you have in your trailer?"

SIX

Monkey Wrenching

His hands shake and he wears a profound frown. I sit across the table from him.

"What do you want with sugar?"

"Damnit, Christopher. Monkey wrenching!"

My heart is stirred because he cares as much as I do about what's happening.

It takes some time to talk Thomas out of putting sugar in the tanks of the mining company trucks. He thinks this would prevent them from setting off explosives up on the flat near the cave. For one thing, I tell him, there are supervisors, technicians, grunt laborers camped all around the trucks who will stop us. Second, even if we can somehow sneak past them all, it will be no mystery who did it, and I'll end up in jail, which he agrees would be a bad thing. For a third, it's a myth that sugar ruins an engine. Sugar doesn't dissolve in gasoline; it just sinks to the bottom of the tank. He processes this but still doesn't quite get it.

I tell him it's time he shows me where the cave is, but he changes the subject. Instead he tells me General Torrey will come back after dark the next night and try again to shoot the pronghorn. He will probably be drunk.

Which scares the hell out of me.

He stands as if to go. But then he turns back. "And Nephi."

"What about Nephi?"

"Don't worry, drunks and people consumed with anger are generally poor shots."

But before I can get my mouth open to ask what the hell he means, he's gone. Frustrating. Poor shots? That isn't nearly the comfort he seems to think it is. I don't understand how he could know these things and not understand that putting sugar in the tanks won't work, but he insists that prognosticating the workings of a human mind and fathoming the workings of infernal engines are not similar skills.

It turns out we don't need sugar or any other ecoterrorist device. That afternoon I see dust from the north, and a caravan of four official Department of Natural Resources vehicles appears and turns up toward the O.K. Silver Mine. I want to see what is happening, so I ride my bicycle up along the road. Just before I reach the mining valley, the trucks with their equipment drive down. In the last truck are the three who started the trouble. They glare death at me, especially the woman, who does the clichéd thing with two fingers, pointing at her own eyes then at me. She doesn't know I wasn't the instrument of their undoing.

I ride on up, passing all the official vehicles. When I reach the higher flat a half hour later, tire tracks show that trucks have been up there as well, certainly the mining company vehicles, but they must not have had time to set their charges. The lek is quiet. The birds hunker down, as if waiting for a storm to pass. At least they didn't have to suffer blasts right next to their lek.

The next evening I'm crouched above the pond, watching for the General's vehicle. The pronghorn appears at dusk, drinks, and starts grazing. Once it is full dark, just as Thomas said would happen, I see a truck creeping along the road, headlights out. Even though my hands tremble from fear as much as Thomas's did from anger, I throw a rock that splashes into the pond and the buck disappears.

The vehicle runs into the ditch near my trailer, and the door slams. I can't see him, but then I throw another rock into the pond, and I hear him cursing steadily. Then he shouts, "Where are you, you son of a bitch?" His words slur. He shoots a round into the pond, and I throw myself to the ground, lying as flat as I can. He seems to be alone, so there is no assistant to curb his antisocial impulses. He shoots again, this time through the trailer, which will do little damage unless it hits a propane line. Or, heaven forbid, the tank. I don't want to see my trailer and all my books explode. He swears some more and then climbs back into his truck. At first, he's stuck in the ditch, but then he spins a cloud of dust and finally rockets in reverse back onto the road. He turns the truck around and soon the sound of his engine disappears.

I wait until my breathing and heart rate slow before I walk back down the hill. I go near my trailer and sniff. I can't smell propane, but some odor lying on the surface of the air lets me know the Dead Fathers are back. I turn on the light, which also missed being hit by a bullet. Louis holds the pack of cards and has dealt everyone a hand. "We've been waiting for you," says my father. "Let's get started."

"Wait a minute," I say. "That bastard just shot at me. I'm still shaking. And I want to find out where the bullet hit."

Samuel points at my bookshelf.

One book has a hole in the spine and I slide it out—*The Teachings of Don Juan*.

"Apt," he says. "It should have a bullet through it. I've never understood why you like that mystical drivel."

Which stops me. He doesn't seem to think of his own appearance as anything mystical. When I first read the book as a fourteen-year-old, he read it also. At that time he was still trying to keep me from dangerous ideas.

"A bullet through your trailer is the least of your worries," says Louis. "You have no idea of the shitstorm headed your way."

"I know that Mother and Father have separated. Is the world going to end? Will Emily and my children be safe? Would you be clear for once?"

My father just frowns. "We don't know. But we do know that you're not helping yourself."

Louis just glares at me, unable to even swear at me.

"You've always had a disobedient heart," says my father.

"What the hell does that mean?"

"It means you're a contrary son of a bitch," says Louis. I knew it wouldn't be more than a moment before he found his tongue again. "You're always putting a wrench in everyone's operations."

"That might have been true when I was working for the newspaper, but how does killing or not killing a pronghorn affect the universe?"

"You can't pretend not to know about the butterfly ef-fect," says my father. "Everything is connected."

"Interlocked," says Louis.

"Speaking of which, can we please resume our game?" says Hugh. "I feel lucky tonight."

The next morning, I sit on my stoop and drink my coffee. If anything could be an anchor in what Louis rightly de-scribed as my shitstorm-tossed life, this is it. *You could go home*, a voice says in my head. She sounds like my mother, but I'm not sure. Why don't I go home? My excuse has been that I have no vehicle, but now Emily could take me. Also, I don't want anyone, not even my mother, to tell me what to do. I'm as stubborn in my way as my grandfather is. I feel calmer than I did the night before, and the possi-bility of a cataclysm that involves both heaven and earth seems less plausible.

The morning is warmer than it's been and the desert is turning green. Even though it will last only a couple of weeks before the cheatgrass turns yellow again, I want to see the greening. There is unfinished business here—both inside me, where Emily's visit is the very beginning of a greening, and outside me, where things are cosmically unsettled. I'm a pawn in the universe—without any clear vision of the game others are playing, but I'm also curious, my own deadly sin. I want to find out what will happen. I won't have to wait long. The faces of the Dead Fathers as we finished the night before, their smug smiles, let me know that whatever catastrophe is headed my way is im-minent, a hand-sized cloud on the horizon that will short-ly fill the sky.

Before I finish my cup, I see the dust coming from the north. It's Spencer in his huge pickup. He parks in the road and walks up the lane toward me. I can tell from his stride that he bears unpleasant news.

"Chris," he says. "I have to let you go. I'm going to burn this stinking trailer and haul away the remains."

"Who will watch your building? As you said before, people will steal you blind."

"You're not here most of the day anyway." He kicks one of the rocks that forms the boundary of my yard, disrupting the circle. "I hate to do this because I admired your grandfather, his independence and spirit. But you are nothing like him." He created his idea of my grandfather out of stories I told him and his own grandfather told him. His picture has little to do with reality. Then he walks to the trailer where a panel hangs almost loose and rips it off. Technically it's his trailer, but I wish he wouldn't start dismantling my home before I'm moved out. "I've found a replacement. You're not going to believe it, but she's from the Netherlands. Claims it's going to be underwater soon from climate change." He grins and even snorts a little. Our brief conversations about politics taught each of us that the other was intractable. Like me, he's not much of a churchgoer, but unlike me, he believes the earth is in God's hands and humans are vain if they think their actions can affect its eternal destiny.

"She'll live here for food and lodging. Doesn't seem to want anything else—as kooky as you are. She'll stay in the apartment I use when I come out." He smirks, probably assuming he'll get more than guard duty out of her. He is a despicable human.

"How the hell did you find her?"

"I put an ad online and she answered." He looks at me and shrugs. "This trailer should have been junked years ago. It's an eyesore. You're an eyesore. You never bathe and you're crazy as a coot."

I mentally shrug at his comments.

"When?" I say.

"Tomorrow. She's coming on Friday."

I shake my head. "She can take over even if I'm still in the trailer."

"By Saturday then."

It's Wednesday, so that gives me basically three days. I notice the physical signs of anxiety; my breathing and heartbeat speed up. I try to tamp my fear down, but it's not happening. I've just been thrown out of my home, or at least my domicile.

"Go back to your wife," he says as he walks away. He drives down to the horse barn. I resent this even more than when my mother gave me the same advice. He can fire me and burn down the trailer, but he sure as hell can't tell me where to live. Then my anger disappears and I feel calm and even dispassionate again.

"The Netherlands." I return to the trailer and look around at my books, my few belongings. Everything, including my bicycle, could fit in the back of Emily's truck. I should still be upset, but I feel as dead as I did before Emily appeared at my door. Maybe she'll come back before Friday, or maybe I'll have to borrow Spencer's wheelbarrow, the one he has me use to haul horseshit out of the barn. I can set up on BLM land, make a tent out of a tarp. Except I don't have a tarp. I have enough canned food to last about another week. Then there's the oranges and vegetables that Emily and Spencer brought. They'll be fine at night, but in the day I have no way to keep them cold.

I sit inside my trailer reflecting on the fact that my will has sunk to almost nothing. Even if I rise up and fight the troubles that beset me, nothing will change. It strikes me that I face a much more ambiguous situation than Hamlet, who only had to decide whether or not to kill his uncle. But I recognize I'm being melodramatic. I don't have to kill anyone. Like Hamlet, however, I'm indecisive because I don't know how to interpret my recent experiences. Also like Hamlet, I'm too morose to be good company even to myself. I climb on my bike and ride eastward. I'll continue to look for the cave that I haven't found in six months of looking.

Once I reach the plateau, I look through the field glasses, and the birds are still there, but only one small male is flashing his chest at the females, who cower against the ground, too upset to pay attention to him. Finally, he too gives up. We are brothers, that bird and I.

In the evening, after another bootless search, I ride my bike back to the trailer, hoping that Emily has returned. I like the word "niggling." I have a niggling worry that she won't come back. When I get closer, I see that someone is at my trailer. But instead of Emily, it's Nephi waiting for me. He's alone this time. "I hear you've been evicted."

I wonder how the hell he heard that, but I'm not sure I want to know the answer. What commerce could he and Spencer have, a Mormon fundamentalist and an urban redneck?

"It's time for you to make a decision," he says. "I'll build you a house and you can drive truck for me. I need someone I can trust. And you need to place your wayward soul in a yoke. You're a fine man, but you need some parameters."

Fine man? Yoke, parameters? Like most everyone else, he wants to bind me into the straitjacket of his expectation of me. Reduce my volition. Fit me into his own structure. "I want to understand your motive."

"I told you. I received a vision. This is what you are to do."

"You received a vision for me? Why didn't God send me a vision?"

His mouth twists in a kind of grimace. "Do I really need to tell you that? He could knock forever on that thick skull of yours. He could set off a charge of dynamite and you'd hardly notice."

Dynamite jokes are too close just now. "Tell me about this vision."

He hesitates. "You are to marry a handful of my daughters, engender children on them, and drive my ethanol truck."

"Your whiskey truck."

He shrugs. "Not that much difference between the two."

"Except one is against the Word of Wisdom."

"I'm not going to drink it! Speaking of the Word of Wisdom, you'll have to give up coffee if you come to live in our compound."

"I'm still thinking how odd it is for you to distill whiskey. Is it the money?"

He shrugs. "I don't care much about earthly wealth."

It isn't true. As long as I've known him, he's talked about how godliness will lead to prosperity. But I let it go for now. "I could go to prison if I work for you. That's where you're headed if Emily has her way." I see from his face that this isn't news to him.

"Not if you're part of my operation. She'll back down."

I shake my head. "You don't know her. You think I'm thick-skulled, but she's worse. She never deviates a fraction of an iota from her course."

"You told me when you came out here to live that she had an affair. That's a deviation. Or maybe it's not, which would be even worse for you. But I could see the other day that she still has feelings for you. She'll follow your leadership."

Which makes me snort—a sharp bark of laughter. He doesn't know her. If I joined the polygamists, Emily would be even more determined to ruin them.

"Despite those feelings, unless you claim your rightful place as patriarch of your own family, she'll lead you astray faster than that prostitute you visited last winter."

Again, I wonder how he knows about that. I didn't proclaim it to him. Everybody knows intimate details of my life and everyone knows what I should do to solve my problems. Damn them all to hell.

"You feel it," he says. "You're going to die. You may never be with another woman other than a Nevada whore, who will not bear you children. You feel as if you're going to be erased from the earth. But." He waits a moment for emphasis. "God is not finished with you yet. He doesn't want you to dry up like a tumbleweed."

Of course I've felt what he described. In so many ways, I'm a simple machine, not even a brain, except for a reptile one. But to take up with those girls, force my aging and repulsive flesh on them? No. That's something I won't do. They deserve to love someone as young as they are.

Then I remember that as of this morning I have no income. "I could be talked into driving truck for you. But I'm not marrying your daughters."

He looks like he ate something rotten. "It's a package deal, I'm afraid. I need—God needs you in the family."

"Like the mob. The Family. Connection through marriage keeps everyone loyal."

"No, nothing like the mob. Their only goal is money and earthly power. Mine is heavenly manna." He pauses for effect.

You're lying to yourself, I think. *Or maybe only to me. Am I that susceptible?* He's offering what he thinks is an irresistible temptation in order to bind me to him. His idea that he's doing it because of God's will is absolute bunk.

"What is your goal?" Nephi asks. "You're at a crossroads. You can pursue God's plan for you, or you can join the Adversary's plan. God usually lets those who depart from his path fall into the ditch. They earn their own reward. But you are too important. If you stumble here, He will destroy you lest you disrupt his plan. It is better one man should perish than a whole nation stumble in disbelief."

It's not the first time his rhetoric has reminded me of that of the Dead Fathers. I remember that they wanted me to join him. It chills me to remember that the Dead Mothers said they are somehow in cahoots—both working in mysterious ways to accomplish unknowable ends. "I won't marry your daughters."

"Wrong choice, Christopher. Goodbye."

Something about the way he says it feels final. I don't think he'll come back.

"Goodbye, Nephi."

He eyes me as he walks sideways toward his truck. Spooky. When he opens the door, instead of getting inside, he pulls something out from behind his seat. "You're a loose cannon, Christopher," he shouts. "You're forcing God to use plan B. God told me he has a purpose for you. I don't know all, but He told me that if you aren't on His side, it would be better for you to be dead. I am His servant in this."

I am frozen for a second. *Plan B?* As he raises his rifle, I think that I'm not the one who's a loose cannon. Then my reptile brain kicks in, and I dive to the side as a bullet hits the trailer just behind where I stood. From the ground, I see him walking toward me. But he shakes as he walks. So does the earth. Then I realize that it's me who is shaking. He lifts the rifle again. "Please, no!" I scream. I roll under the edge of my trailer. On the other side, I crouch behind my wood pile. A second bullet tears through the trailer. Remarkably, I find myself wondering what book he's hit. I'm running, still crouched over. I make it around the edge of the hill and climb to the ridge—my heart pounding, my breath rasping. *You're too old for this*, I think, as another round whines past my ear.

Somehow, I keep going, even though I'm so winded I can hardly take another step. I see my own body lying with a hole in an essential organ—my brain or lungs or gut.

I reach the top of the ridge. I'm shaking with terror and exertion, but I am able to notice that I'm shaking with terror and exertion, so I know that I can do this. Adrenaline will keep me going for a while. I know he's following me because I haven't heard his truck leave and because he believes he was commanded of God to either bring me into the fold or eliminate me from upsetting what God hopes for this segment of the desert's history. The arrogant bastard thinks he actually has God's ear. The DFs said that God was holed up somewhere, and Nephi couldn't have a better connection than they do, could he? Things seem just as chaotic on the other side of the veil as on this side. And I really can't wrap my head around the fact that he said exactly what the Dead Fathers said—I have a purpose, a role in what is unfolding. He's in league with them somehow, along with Spencer. It's starting to feel like a universal conspiracy against me.

Then I think of what Thomas said about them being bad shots. Neither General Torrey nor Nephi seems a bad shot. They were both right on target. The General missed because it was dark, and Nephi missed because I jumped to one side at just the right moment.

I'm so angry still that I consider getting the .22 in my trailer and riding my bike down to shoot through his house. It would start a war. At that moment I think, *Let it come!* But the feeling dies pretty quickly. I'd probably hit a child, and if I start a war, I will lose. He's a better shot than I am and he certainly has better weapons. Just like everyone else arrayed against me.

It's uncomfortable sitting on the hill after the bastard made me flee. I haven't heard or seen him since hiding up here, and I hope he's gone home. I walk down to the brow of the ridge and crouch behind a juniper. I am far enough away that he could have started his truck, driven partway up the canyon, and circled behind me. I crawl into the middle of the juniper, which is one whose lower branches rest on the ground, so it's like a dark green cavern. I think of several things: my grandfather's story about shooting the coyote in the butt—the vomit of blood, which could happen to me; I also think about the Goshute who saw the soldiers killing his family and who had to run for his life and hide in the cave. I take breath after breath until I'm calmer. Then I think of Elijah when he hid in a cave after he offended Jezebel by mocking the priests of Baal when they couldn't light their altar, calling fire from heaven to light his own water-drenched altar, slaying the priests, and inviting black clouds heavy with rain that ended the drought. All that power and he also had to run and hide.

Finally, I think about Nephi Johnson's lie—that he isn't interested in money or earthly power. He has power over his children, his wives, and he wants power over the government, a secret, tick-like power, sucking its blood. He also wants money, which is power. If he didn't want money, he'd stick to ethanol, because he can bleed the government more by cheating with tax credits than he can by making moonshine whiskey. I believe he likes the idea of selling something worth hundreds of dollars a gallon. That desire was strong enough to bring him to violate his own principle—that alcohol is of the devil.

What do *I* want? That hasn't been clear for a long time. I wanted to be alone, peacefully alone—not hiding under a juniper because some fanatic believes God wants me dead.

Why did I want to be alone? Because most people are idiots. Including me. Consequently, being by myself, I'm attended by an idiot. I can't remember which Shakespearian fool said that.

What do I want for my life now? For most of my career as a journalist I felt that I was doing good, helping protect good people from conniving and corrupt ones. Then newspapers started to be replaced by websites, which is not bad in itself. But because any fool can create information on the web, standards declined. Evidence is no longer needed to make something newsworthy. Appearance matters more than substance. Lies are pronounced as truth, and truth is made a lie. By the end of my career, I no longer felt that I was doing much to combat the flood of lies.

I think about Emily returning with Nephi still on the rampage. She's the most competent, clever person I know, but he has a rifle. Worrying about her, I know one thing I want—her. I want her in my life again. She's so obsessed with her work that she can hardly sit with me, but she succeeded in creating a way to spend a few days with me. I love her. Love feeds on itself and so it blossoms with warmth inside me. I worry again that she won't come back. That she'll decide I'm not worth the effort.

After full darkness, the coyotes start calling to each other or to the moon or to their dead ancestors. Their yapping and wailing is always eerie, but tonight I am comforted by the familiar sound. I remain on the hill, watching and listening, but there's no sign of Nephi. I creep down to my trailer. It hits me again that it isn't mine. *Tomorrow I need to pack.*

When my lantern flares, of course they're there, waiting, cards already dealt—the last thing I want to see.

"He's gone," says my father.

"But you should listen to him," says Hugh. "He's right most of the time."

"Some of the time," says my father.

"If I'd done what he's doing," says Louis, "I could have saved my farm."

"The son of a bitch tried to kill me." I stand up and pace the small trailer.

They look at me like—duh!—of course he did.

"You were not thinking clearly," says Hugh, "when you rejected his offer."

"What if he comes back?"

"He won't," says Hugh. "He's given up on you."

"But we haven't," says my father.

Which only makes me more upset. I don't want them to see how angry I am; they'd just use it against me. So I try to find what Nephi's bullet hit. Of course it's another book. There's nothing else of value in the trailer. This time it's *The Second Sex*, a pre-second-wave feminist text by Simone de Beauvoir that Emily gave me on my twenty-fifth birthday—another clear message. But this one feels personal, because it's a book that Emily and I read early in our marriage and had long talks about—the ways she felt held down by the steel ceiling of patriarchy. A fundamental polygamist putting a hole in that spine feels significant.

"You're right," says Hugh. "That was no accident."

Which doesn't help my mood.

"Ironic," says Louis. "I agree—not an accidental penetration."

I'm furious, both at Nephi, who has ruined Emily's gift, but also at Louis, the misogynistic bastard.

"Get out!" I shout, but they don't move.

Hugh says, "Louis always goes too far. It was an unfortunate reference."

"It is typical, though. Typical of him. The three of you are unnatural, an aberration. People die for a reason. It allows the living to forget their parents' and grandparents' sins and remember their good qualities. You being here just reminds me of your imperfections. I want you all gone. I don't want to play cards, and I never want to see your faces again."

Louis looks at his cards, clearly chagrined. He's not embarrassed by what he said, I believe, but by doing something that caused my outburst that ruined the game. He says, "I'm sorry. Please sit down and look at your cards. Maybe this time you'll win."

Their faces are set, and I know I won't win, not at cards and not in my battle with them.

Then I remember that Nephi shot twice, so I look for another hole. This time it's *The Hero with a Thousand Faces*.

"Fitting," says my father.

"Or it could be if you started acting like one," says Hugh.

"Instead of a damned namby-pamby wimp," says Louis.

I sit down at the table.

"I don't feel like a hero," I say.

"Exactly my point," says Louis.

"The time demands a hero," says Hugh. "A general like Moroni. Maybe if you read about him, you would be inspired. He didn't hesitate to lay the sword to his enemies."

I try again. "I can't be a hero, especially if I don't know what's coming."

"War is coming," says Hugh. "How many times do we need to say it?"

"War? As with rifles and cannons? Drones maybe?"

Louis rolls his eyes at me.

"Of course, they must be spiritual cannons and drones," I say. "They can't actually destroy intelligence so what do they do?"

"Fool!" says Hugh.

My father puts his hand over his face.

"I know I'm wrong, so tell me!"

I have no confidence they will, but then Hugh says, "You're right. Nobody can destroy spiritual matter. But someone with a strong enough will can destroy identity. Reduce it to fragments of intelligence."

"Imagine it," says Louis. "Your soul could be blown into such small pieces that not even God could reassemble you."

"Spiritual war can be ugly," my father says. "Father protected our side in the first one and cast Lucifer and his followers out. But this will be much worse."

Hugh says, "You have to be careful about every step. This Dutch woman, beware of her!"

"That's ridiculous!"

"We're not talking about her tempting you with sex," says Louis. "If you bedded her that wouldn't hurt anything."

"Well, I wouldn't go that far," says Hugh. "But it's true that her head is what you have to worry about. Leading you astray with her ideas. It would be safer to eat poison than to talk to her. We've done our best with you, but you're intractable."

"Listen to us," says my father. "We're on your side."

"You tell me to be careful, which could be good advice, but it's damn vague. Give me specifics."

"We can't," says my father as they fade.

'What does that mean? You can't because you don't know yourselves? You can't because you don't want to? Or you can't because you're not allowed?" But there's no one to listen except for the mouse that comes out into the middle of my hallway, sniffing for food.

After they leave, I open the bullet-torn book about the hero's path. The prophet Elijah thought God was subtle. He didn't find God in the wind or the earthquake or fire but in the still small voice. Whichever divinity nudged Nephi's bullet toward this book is not subtle but certainly inscrutable. This sign is as obvious as a thunderclap, but what it portends is a mystery. I get angry enough to actually shake my fist toward the heavens.

"You're on!" I shout to whoever is inspiring Nephi Johnson. "I'm not taking this shit anymore!"

Then I regret my brave words and curl in my bed. I'm trying to remember how Elijah described the fire of God that consumed his sacrifice, so I grab my flashlight and pull down the Old Testament. It says, "Then the fire of the Lord fell, and consumed the burnt sacrifice, and the wood, and the stones, and the dust, and licked up the water that was in the trench." Then Elijah took the false priests who opposed him down to a brook and slew them all.

Harsh.

I wish I'd held my tongue. I'm not sure how Father God may react to my angry gestures. I trust Mother God more. I have no idea how to map His will onto the string of events that have happened in the past week and a half. I've thought of this image before, but it is a useful one to describe God's propensity to spring surprises on humans: His wrath may appear small at first, like the cloud that eventually brought the rain Elijah summoned, something small over the sea, like a man's hand. But the heavens can suddenly turn black with storm.

SEVEN

A Stranger Comes

I don't get out of bed the next day. It's not the safest place, because the walls of the trailer won't stop a bullet, but I can't make myself go outside and find a safer hole. Every little sound jolts me—the mice in the walls, the call of a raven outside, the rush of spring wind, the trickle of water running down the hill behind my trailer from melting snow. Even worse is my memory of the whine and thunk of the bullets. I imagine them slamming into my body.

I feel that the universe has betrayed me: the solitary desert is full of people. People I hardly know have shot at me, my ancestors from across the veil are nothing like I imagined and don't seem governed by anything but their own pleasure and interest. Certainly they don't obey any rules laid out in scripture. I haven't darkened the door of a church for a decade, but Father and Mother in Heaven are as reliable as rock and water. That they continue in one eternal round is cosmic bedrock. That they might be splitting up is incomprehensible. Maybe the worst fracture in my being is that Emily came back and is gone again. Maybe she'll return. Maybe not. As is my wont since I left my job and family, I nurse my grievances rather than doing anything about them.

All morning I don't even feel like eating, but by noon I'm hungry, so I fry myself some eggs and cheese and with them I eat canned peaches and bread toasted on the stovetop. Then, even though I'm supposed to be finding a way to move my books and belongings to another place, I go back to bed. I can't yet figure where I'll go, but somewhere close. I'm not finished here yet.

Despite my brave words the night before, I don't feel like standing up to anyone. I'm no warrior. Maybe I was an intellectual fighter when I could sit at my desk and write stories that uncovered what greedy officials and businessmen tried to do in secret. On paper I could be acerbic, incisive, fearless—I could call a spade a spade. Politicians and businessmen who I offended wanted to meet with me, explain their position or acts. I universally told them no. Also, I wasn't a great manager. I couldn't verbally rebuke those who needed to be rebuked. I had to fire someone once for publishing a story she had fabricated. I couldn't sleep for a week.

I'm warm and snug in bed, and I doze and wake, doze and wake, returning myself to equanimity. I wake in the afternoon, not knowing what woke me. When I turn over, a woman sits on the edge of the bed. She looks familiar, but I can't bring her name to mind. I'm not sure whether she's alive or dead. She's wearing a black dress that is plain enough that it could come from any of a number of decades. She also has gray hair, which is no clue either.

"You can't hide forever," she says with a light Welsh accent.

"I can hide for today. Who are you?"

She smiles, "You don't recognize me? Catherine Eubale."

Hugh's third wife—daughter of a friend of his first wife.

"Have you come to set me straight?"

"I wouldn't say it that way. I've come to help you see your potential."

"Potential?"

"As a tool in God's hand. As a bulwark against decay of the firmament."

"Me? A bulwark against decay?" I snort. "You must not know me."

"I'm not talking about coffee or not going to church or even visiting a lady of the night. I'm talking about your anti-social and anarchical tendencies." She looks around. "You're like a rat in a nest of disorder, and this trailer is just the outward manifestation of a worse, much more dangerous spiritual disorder." She leans forward. "Do you know what happened during the creation to material that wouldn't obey? It was sent back to the melting pot. Stripped of its particular nature."

"Spiritual disorder?" She's charming and I want to please her, but I can do little more than repeat what she's said. I don't really think she minds. She's come to give me a message and she won't brook any real disruption.

"Disrespecting the commandments that come down through the hierarchy from God."

"What commandments?" Now she's starting to irritate me. I mean I broke the one that says I shouldn't commit adultery, and I break the Word of Wisdom, and I've broken the Sabbath, but what else?"

"It's more that you have a propensity to disobedience. You lack trust in the system."

"This is the whole problem, you and your husband, my father and my grandfather—their warnings are so vague."

"The commandments are slippery to the wicked. It's clear enough to you what to do. Part of the problem is your maverick nature makes their words malleable, when they would be clear to someone with any backbone." She smiles in a way that communicates her sadness over my recalcitrant nature. "Will you be persuaded to help them maintain the universal order?"

"I'm frightened of the universal order," I say.

"That's a foolish fear. Who in their right mind fears order?"

"Well, we agree on one thing: I'm not in my right mind."

"In a way you are. You're in the mind you've chosen. You've always been stubborn and you're stubborn still. Like a hog you continue to wallow in your mire and like a dog you return to your vomit."

I don't have any answer to that. She's hit the nail on the head.

"I'm sorry." She stands and walks down the hall of my trailer. "I tried." Before she takes three steps, she's gone.

The next morning as I'm drinking my coffee and watching a trio of jackrabbits feeding, Spencer drives up in his truck. He doesn't wave as he passes. Instead he holds out one finger. At least it's his index finger. He's reminding me I have one day, which means today and maybe part of Saturday, to figure out where to live. I made zero progress yesterday because I was caught in a Slough of Despond.

I wasn't afflicted by lethargy my whole life; I was an aggressive journalist for many years. I think neither the Dead Fathers nor the Dead Mothers approve of my new mode of being. Thomas understands, I think. I drink the last of my cup. It's getting warmer at night, so I may be able to make a camp up by Goshute Spring. Or I could set up in one of the mines. Maybe there's nobody up the ladder in the thirteenth mine. Whether I know where I'm going or not, I need to pack my books and figure out how to transport them.

A figure appears from the side of the horse barn— probably the Dutch woman. She walks toward me—not hurrying, not dawdling either. I'm curious to meet this person the DF's warned me would corrupt me with her talk. She walks like a dancer or athlete, confident and controlled in every motion.

"Hello," she says. "I'm Alina Meijer." She reaches her hand toward me and I shake it. She certainly doesn't seem like a venomous snake. "The one who put you out of a job." She has no discernible accent, but she's working to say each word correctly, as if her tongue is too big for her mouth. She's almost as tall as I am, and she seems to be in her late twenties or early thirties. Her hair is shoulder length and auburn, nearly red, with rainbow streaks. Her eyebrows are darker brown than her hair. She's a lovely woman and not as young as the polygamous daughters. She reminds me powerfully of Karin, my granddaughter. Same slender face, thin lips. Same intent, intelligent expression.

"It's not your fault," I say.

"In a way, it is. I answered Spencer's advertisement." She shrugs. "He was persuaded by my industry and commitment as described in my resume." She gives me an ironic smile. "Also, he has the illusion that I might have sex with him. May I sit?"

"You have no accent," I say.

"And that surprises you?"

I shrug.

"It's only Americans who know only one language," she says.

"But I would assume that Dutch people would learn British English."

"We learn both. Actually I speak several dialects of both." She doesn't seem to be bragging, just stating the facts. "I even speak Scouse: 'We live in a world where we have to hide to make love, while violence is practiced in broad daylight.'"

If I had closed my eyes, I would have thought it was John Lennon sitting next to me. She even deepened her voice to sound like him.

"I also speak French, Spanish, and Polish. And I read Latin."

"Are you trying to make me feel stupid?"

"Are you stupid?" She smiles again in the same open manner.

"Sometimes I do stupid things."

"So you're human. So don't worry about it."

I don't know what to say. The step is narrow so I slide to one side. I'm reevaluating my judgment that she's a dancer or an athlete, but she may be a setter on the volleyball team, a genius linguist, and a chess master. Boomers are supposed to look down on the younger generations as slackers and prima donnas, but my experience on the newspaper is that they're strong, savvy, and ambitious. "Do you want some coffee?"

"I should take some, to be friendly, but I've already had two cups." She turns to look at me. Her face is calm and self-assured. "What will you do?"

"I haven't figured that out yet." I'm taken aback by her self-confidence. I could easily be angry because she is partly the reason I have to leave my home, and I should feel awkward about sitting so close to a lovely young woman, but I feel neither of those emotions. Nor do I find any reason to fear her ideas. She's just being friendly so far. "It seems—ah—unlikely that someone from the Netherlands would be perusing the want ads in Utah."

"I've always been interested in the Great Basin—Goshutes, Gold Rushers, Pony Express, Wells Fargo, Mormon Pioneers. Are you Mormon like Spencer?"

"My roots are Mormon."

"Hmm."

"That's quite an intense interest to make you move yourself across the world."

"I was finished with the university, with Amsterdam. Finished with the whole country." She's bitter about this expatriation, but I'm not sure I can ask her yet why. "I wanted a place as unlike the Netherlands as I could find on the map."

I laugh. "You've found it."

She smiles appreciatively. She points behind her. "You have no door."

"I don't."

"So creatures come and go as they please?"

"Yes." I tell her about the pack rat that built a nest of treasures on my bed, and it's her turn to laugh.

"Do you know the poet Gary Snyder?"

I nod, pleased that we have this connection.

"He has a house in the mountains—northern California. He leaves his door open so the creatures come and go. Unless he's too old now. He was still alive when I read that book a decade ago."

"When you were fifteen?"

She gives me a sour look. "When I was twenty-two. And how old are you?"

"Sixty-seven."

"Too old to be alone out in the desert."

I can't judge her tone—sympathetic or irritated with me because I underestimated her age. "*A Place in Space.*"

"Yes, that's the one. On being porous to the world. Like your trailer."

"My former trailer."

She shrugs. "As far as I'm concerned, stay as long as you want. I don't mind having a neighbor."

"Spencer gave me until tomorrow."

Alina looks chagrined. "He didn't tell me he was making you move out of your home."

"It's not your fault," I say to her again.

"Well, you don't look worried."

"I'm still not really facing it." I drain my cup. "He said you're fleeing the rising water."

She glares at me. "It is rising. Are you like Spencer? Don't you believe the climate is changing?"

"I do. But it hasn't risen much yet, and I would have thought that the Dutch would just build the walls higher."

"The land is also sinking—subsiding—in places where we've drained."

I think about what she's said.

"My decision isn't rational," she says. "I would be an old, old woman, maybe even older than you, before the water rose enough to be a serious problem."

"I still have the feeling you're holding something back." Instead of getting angry that a relative stranger is asking pushy questions, she smiles.

"Why I came to America?" she says. "I'm also puzzled by my decision. My reasons are insufficient. Taking a step is like falling and falling again. I could have fallen in any direction, but this is where I ended up." She looks out at the desert flat. "This is a strange and unusual landscape. It makes no sense, but I feel I belong here."

I still can't wrap my mind around the idea that a Dutch woman likes this arid landscape where little except for shadscale, halogeton, cheatgrass, and tumbleweed grow on the alkali soil. Very strange.

Then I see a dust trail—three vehicles arriving, one pulling a travel trailer, much newer than mine. At first I'm upset that I'll have more close neighbors to contend with, but then I see that the first truck is Emily's, and a stream of joy bubbles up. She came back.

One of the vehicles is a black van, its sides painted with dust. The truck pulling the trailer pulls off the road at a place ATV riders often use for camping—close to the O.K. Silver Mine road and about three hundred yards from my trailer. A man and a woman get out. It's too far to tell for sure, but I think I've met them before—other lawyers who work with Emily.

"Who are these people?" Alina asks.

"They work with my wife. She's a lawyer."

"Have they come to rescue you from Spencer's eviction?"

"Probably not. Emily will be overjoyed when she finds out Spencer has condemned the trailer."

The van stops on the road below my trailer, and Emily pulls into my lane. She jumps out, grinning. "I've brought the cavalry." She's happy, and I'm reminded again of the black wolf I saw wag its tail just before the kill. Her excitement is catching and I feel my own adrenaline rising. I would like to see Nephi's face when they put him in handcuffs.

She glances at Alina, then back at me, frowning slightly.

Alina and I stand. "Emily, this is—"

"Just a minute." She walks to the black van, and the driver, a woman wearing tactical gear, steps out. Emily points southwest toward the polygamist compound. The driver gets back in and the van leaves a dust trail in that direction.

"Where are they going?' asks Alina.

I explain to her that they are probably going to arrest Nephi and Frank Johnson.

"I would like to see that."

"There could be shooting," I say. "It could be dangerous, and they don't want civilians to get hurt."

"Oh," she says, disappointed. "What did they do?"

I tell her about their ethanol and moonshine business, about bleeding Lucifer, and about fundamentalist polygamy.

"Fascinating! The desert is everything I imagined and more." She's as excited as I would expect her to be if we were all movie stars. "Is your wife also police?"

"FBI. Federal Bureau of Investigation. And no, she's not. She's working with them to gather evidence. She's just told them where to drive and maybe what to expect."

Emily turns and walks closer to us.

I say, "I thought you wanted to watch Nephi's arrest."

"They won't let me go." She's staring at Alina's face.

"Emily," I say. "This is Alina. She's taking my place. Spencer fired me." I turn toward Alina. "This is Emily. We were—are married."

"Were are?" Alina smiles at Emily.

Emily steps closer. "You appeared in my dream, Alina. I'd recognize those eyebrows anywhere. And your hair. I'm glad to know you."

"As am I," says Alina. "Was it a pleasant dream or a nightmare?" She frowns and manages to make her eyebrows menacing. Then the frown disappears and she laughs.

"It was no nightmare," says Emily. "It was unsettling. Still is. But you weren't the fearful part. And here you are. In the flesh."

She reaches out her hand, and Alina clasps it as if they are already friends. As usual, things seem to be happening so fast I can't keep up.

I tell Emily about the General shooting at me, the prospectors setting off explosives, the state officials who came and made them stop, the trouble in the lek, and then Nephi shooting at me.

"My hell!" she says. "I leave you for a day and you get yourself in all kinds of trouble. I'm glad the arresting officers are going in locked and loaded."

Alina says, "The wild west." She gives me a funny look, and I wonder if she believes any of what I've said.

Emily is grim. "If people believe their own fictions, they come true." She turns toward me. "He actually shot at you? Was he trying to scare you or hit you?"

"He wasn't just trying to scare me." I describe my escapes from General Torrey and Nephi. "Between the two of them they shot up three of my books."

Alina's expressive eyebrows rise at that.

"That asshole," says Emily. I presume she's talking about Nephi. "I'm going to add that to the charges. If you are good with that."

I nod.

She says, "In lesser news: I got the injunction to stop Blythe, Blythe, and Smith from setting charges on the flat where the lek is."

"I saw them come—the wildlife officials," I say. "I'm grateful. But I'm not sure the birds will continue their dances. The blasts in the lower valley disrupted their mating. And the trucks driving up there didn't help anything. They may even leave the mating grounds."

Alina asks with her eyebrows, and I tell her about the mining company and the charges they set.

"Those bastards," she says. "Money is king for corporations, and they worship their king."

Emily nods. "There's so much going on that I've moved some of my team out here to the desert."

"That doesn't make sense," I say. "There's no internet, no phone reception. How will your team do their work?"

"We have a satellite connection."

I shake my head. "Are you really Emily, or someone else in her body? You never leave the city."

"I'm trying to adapt, not stay in a rut."

She looks from me to my trailer, as if she already knows what's up. To save time, I just say it: "Also in lesser news—I have to move out."

Emily walks to her truck and takes out boxes. "You can put your books in these. We should burn everything else."

That she had boxes ready for my books suggests she somehow knew I was getting kicked out. I've never believed in conspiracies. Still I can't imagine how both Nephi and she knew I was fired almost as soon as I knew it. It again seems that everyone around me is tuned into some channel that's not available to me. Of course, I'm tuned into a channel they don't seem to know about—speaking to the dead. That has proved to be little advantage because the dead, even the Dead Mothers, have difficulty translating their experience into language I can understand.

I look at my trailer and at the boxes. I don't want to leave this place. I don't want Emily or anybody else telling me what to do. But I've run out of options. I know it and she knows it. So it isn't as if she's making me do anything; she's providing a way out.

She watches my face as I mull all this over. I nod, she smiles and walks to her truck. She drives to where they parked the new trailer and the other truck. I think about sleeping on the ground, maybe in a mine. I hope I can move into the new trailer, but there's probably only room for her team.

Emily helps the other two guide their trailer into a spot next to a juniper tree.

"What did Emily mean—that she dreamed about me?" Alina asks. "Is she some kind of mystic?"

"She hasn't been. I never thought I'd hear those words coming from her mouth, 'You were in my dream.' It's earth shaking."

"There's more you're not telling me."

I can't lie to her. "She dreamed a man told her to come after me."

"Really? That's sweet." The eyebrows do their work again. "Come after you?"

"I've been living out here for almost four months."

"Oh," she says. "You don't have to tell me the whole story."

But I tell her anyway.

"You're frowning," she says after I finish.

I don't trust overly-friendly people. "Have you always made friends easily?"

"Usually," she says. "But this is different." She gestures between the two of us and nods toward Emily. "It seems I already knew you before we met."

"I feel the same."

The man and woman disconnect the trailer and put jacks under the corners to level it. Then another truck drives up, and Bennie Bullcreek gets out. I try to remember the names of the other two lawyers who work with Emily, but I can't. I wonder how long Emily means to keep them here. The trailer implies at least a week, maybe more.

I think about Emily's propensity to have many irons in the fire. I suspect there's even more going on than she's telling me. What does she think, that we're playing poker and she needs to hide her cards from me? Uselessly, I try to regain my composure. What she's keeping from me pertains to her work—her own business. I should feel complimented that she moved her office so she could be with me. I shouldn't feel pissy about her methods of bundling me with other work. *What do you want,* some female asks in my head, *to have no room in her head for anything but you? That would get old real fast.* It's my mother. I hope I get to see her soon.

I take the boxes inside my trailer, and Alina follows me. She takes an empty box and starts filling it with books from above my bed. I work on the shelves in the bathroom. She wrinkles her nose. "It smells the same as you."

"You don't have to help," I say.

My face probably shows how grumpy I am, not with her, but with Emily and myself.

"It's the least I can do. But I'll leave if you want me to."

I try to smile. "I am fine with your help."

"I won't make any more comments about your smell."

I shrug. "No big deal. I've gotten used to it."

She picks up another book, glances at the title, and puts it in the box. "Must be difficult to lose your home and your job at the same time."

"I guess it is. But this trailer was never a permanent plan. It's time to move on."

"You don't resent me for it?"

"Of course not."

"Wendel Berry. I've read everything he's written." She lifts a book—*The Long-Legged House.* "Ironic. You should have a house like Baba Yaga's that strides around on bird legs. Hopefully it would be better than this trailer."

"This desert plain, from here down to the river valley, is my home, not a ruined trailer."

"A refuge from civilization."

From more than that. From myself.

She turns and puts her little finger inside a bullet hole in the wall. "They really did shoot at you. I thought you made it up to impress your 'were-are' lover."

"I knew you didn't believe me." Her opinion would go even further south if I told her about the Dead Fathers—which I don't plan on doing. None of her concern.

She looks at me and catches me watching her. "What?"

"I'm just surprised that you're kind enough to help me."

"Because I'm Dutch. Or because I'm a millennial? Are you trying to classify me?"

I shake my head.

"My mother was religious. She told me to be kind to strangers because they might be angels in disguise." She grins. "Are you an angel in disguise?"

"Hardly."

We go back to work. She's not a good book packer. She pauses with every single one. Some of them she even caresses. "Have you read all of them?"

"The ones that were in that shelf—Berry, Abbey, Williams, Stegner—yes. The ones on this shelf, the ones you're packing now, are books I haven't read yet but want to."

She takes off a shelf three books and a stapled copy of an article and reads the titles, "*The Marriage of Heaven and*

Hell, Middlemarch, The Magician of Lublin, 'On the Electro-dynamics of Moving Bodies.'" She looks at me. "Such an odd assortment."

"Selected at random."

"Odd. I own all four of these. Many of these others. They're in storage in Amsterdam."

I stop shoving books into boxes. If this was the first coincidence of the recent past, I might have thought it just that. Now I'm getting *Twilight Zone* vibes. "Just before I came out here, I went to a used bookstore in Salt Lake and grabbed random books off the shelves as I walked through the store."

"Eerie." She picks three more books off the shelf. "I used all these for my thesis."

"Your thesis?"

"I didn't finish," she says. "The faculty in the Institute for Logic, Language, and Computation at the University of Amsterdam found my methods and results questionable. They rejected my prospectus and warned me several times to change my direction. Then they kicked me out for lack of progress toward my degree." She replaces the books. I have to reevaluate my first impression again. "Do you know what all these have in common?"

I shake my head.

"They were all influenced by Spinoza."

"I don't know anything about him."

"Jewish Portuguese philosopher who lived in Holland in the late 1600s. He believed that God is substance."

This surprises me. "Mormons believe God has a body."

Her brows go up. "I didn't know that. Spinoza believed that God is a self-conceiving substance and that the universe is a mode with specific of His attributes."

I turn around and sit on the useless toilet. "You've lost me. What is a mode?"

She sits on the end of the bed where we can face each other. I wonder if I should warn her about the bedbugs. Neither of us is paying any attention to our book packing.

"A mode depends from a substance." She looks at my face and I shake my head. "How can I say it?" She smiles. "God manifests the universe." She looks at my face again. "I've shocked you."

"It's just something someone said." I pick up another book and stick it in a box.

"Something someone said? That's pretty vague."

"My grandfather. He said it."

She frowns and her brows draw together. "Your grandfather. That's weird. Was he a philosopher?"

"Of sorts," I say. "Keep going. God manifests the universe. God gods."

"This led Spinoza to the idea that mind and matter are not separable or oppositional—a la Descartes. The whole universe is continuous. There is no unsubstantial substance." She stands and wraps her arms around herself. "It's cold in here." She moves her arms back and forth in rhythm, twists her body into what turns into a pirouette, stamps her feet. All this activity shakes the trailer.

"You're a dancer," I say.

"As an undergraduate. I blended forms."

"Of course you did," I say. "Are you warm now? The cold keeps me awake and helps me think."

"It's like an icebox in here."

I walk to turn up the heat. The blower goes on.

"Thank you," she says. "I'm not like you. I can't think when I'm cold."

"Mind and body, inseparable," I say. "But the same temperature makes you feel cold and me feel hot."

"Exactly, each person's attributes are like a bar code. Their attributes shine through them. Resonate through them. Manifesting their essence."

"Light," I say.

"Light?"

I have my old missionary scriptures somewhere. I go out into the kitchen, where I have some books stuck in next to the oil, salt, and pepper. I turn to what was once my favorite section—Doctrine and Covenants 88. "This is about the light of Christ, which is in the sun, moon, stars, and earth. It's also the power that made them."

I walk back toward her and sit on the toilet again.

"'And the light which shineth, which giveth you light, is through him who enlighteneth your eyes, which is the same light that quickeneth your understandings; which light proceedeth forth from the presence of God to fill the immensity of space.'"

"Are you saying that Spinoza influenced Mormonism?"

"No! That's highly unlikely. It's just a coincidence."

We sit silently for a minute. Meeting Alina has proved to be more unlikely even than seeing the Dead Fathers. "Joseph Smith said that there's no such thing as immaterial matter." I wonder if she might believe me if I tell her that I see and speak to dead people. "'All spirit is matter, but it is more fine or pure and can only be discerned by purer eyes.'"

She stares at me with a kind of bewildered wonderment. Her eyebrows are at high mast.

"Very strange. I think you might be a hookah-smoking caterpillar disguised as a street person."

"'Penny Lane' and 'White Rabbit.' Two of my favorite songs. Coincidences are everywhere, just like horse manure."

"Horse manure that I'll be shoveling for Spencer." She goes back to work removing books from the shelves. "You are a very odd man." She holds out my copy of *Thus Spoke Zarathustra*. "Have you read this?"

"No."

"Freedom and necessity. Right up my alley. Nietzsche said Spinoza was his precursor." She puts the book in the box. "I don't know about material spirit, but Spinoza might agree, if he could talk to us." She looks up at me. "God is nature naturing."

I almost fall out of my chair. What I don't understand: Why would the Dead Fathers warn me against this woman who is articulating one of the things they tried to teach me? "Fuckers fuck," I say.

"What?" Her eyebrows are like ascending flags.

"It's what my grandfather said. Badgers badger. Lawyers lawyer. God universes."

"Your grandfather wrote all this? I'd like to read what he wrote."

"He didn't write it. He told it to me."

"I have so many questions," she says. "This is so weird."

"I don't believe in coincidences."

"Neither do I."

"What does all this philosophy have to do with your thesis? How does Alina manifest herself? In a dance?"

She looks at me with just a suggestion of hesitancy, which surprises me. She doesn't seem like a person who hesitates.

"Go on. I'm fascinated."

"Don't be condescending."

I'm not. I'm too surprised by the coincidences in what she's said, which is maybe condescending because she's so young. I don't know how to express what I'm feeling, so I just wait. Finally she goes on.

"Spinoza was very deterministic. He believed that God could manifest the universe only the way it is. He manifests and predicts the universe. He patterns himself as he manifests the universe, so he couldn't pattern any other universe. It goes both ways. The universe is a template from God. By definition it can't be a template from anyone else."

I shake my head. "I hope for choice. I hope everything isn't determined."

"I'm agnostic anyway," she says, "I'm mostly interested in Spinoza's ideas as I've been able to distort them to meet my needs. He'd be appalled at what I've done. And I'm not a strict philosopher. I color outside the lines."

I thought I was beyond surprise, but this phrase from Thomas seems stranger than strange in her mouth.

"I apply Spinoza's and other people's ideas to language."

"Language is God?" I ask.

"You're missing the point."

"Humans do language."

"Yes, that's it. Bees do symbolic dance. But does the dance manifest them or do they manifest the dance? Do we manifest language or does language manifest us?" She turns to watch my face again. "'How can we know the dancer from the dance?' The words lead and the mind follows. But that's an ouroboros, a snake eating its own tail. A person says words out of who they are. If they're honest, anyway."

I feel almost as if I'm floating outside my own body. Surreal.

"Is that so strange? You were a journalist."

I cough and try to find words. "Not strange at all."

"For me, Spinoza and others—Heidegger, for example, or Aristotle, or Pablo Neruda, or Isabelle de Charrière, or William Blake." Her hands emphasize each name. "Or Maurice Sendak, or Dorothy Wordsworth, or Simone de Beauvoir, or anyone who uses language precisely—they all manifest themselves through what they write."

"People who don't write precisely also manifest themselves," I say. "Hacks hack."

She nods. "Using newspaper and literature databases, I tried to get at the connection between a person's writing and their essence—their essential nature. I also tried to determine what natural algorithms they use to manifest themselves."

"Damn," I say. "I think you're onto something."

"I wish you had been on my committee instead of those narrow-minded jackasses," she says. "But if they hadn't been jackasses, I wouldn't be here. As I said, very strange."

As I also said, I don't believe in coincidences, and I wonder what part Alina and I will play in the war that's chugging down the track—or up from the rabbit hole—toward us like a locomotive.

An hour later we finish packing the books and start carrying the boxes outside.

"What are you going to do now?" she asks.

I shrug. "I'm not sure. I may have to borrow a tarp from Spencer, make myself a tent."

"Where will you put all these books? Will your 'were-are' marriage partner help you?"

"Possibly."

"She brought you all these boxes."

"A good sign," I say.

"You and she have an interesting relationship."

"Interesting is one word for it." I turn toward the trailer. I lift my grandfather's .22 rifle from where it rests in the closet. It has baling wire tied around its broken stock. He once held it by the barrel and used it to hit a recalcitrant cow in the head. It's a wonder it didn't go off and shoot him in the stomach. I also grab my coffee mug, which has a picture of George Hayduke on it from Abbey's novel *The Monkey Wrench Gang*. I don't want to leave that behind. Outside I lay it against the boxes of books.

"Of course you would have a broken rifle," she says.

"It's a good thing I have a thick skin," I say.

She frowns. "Thick skin?"

"I don't take offense at much."

"Neither do I," she says. "We can be good friends." She smiles.

Emily drives over from where her trailer is parked. She stops next to the partial stack of books. I look at the trailer she brought out and I wonder again if she'll let me stay there. I can't leave the desert without finding the cave.

She stands next to the boxes. "I should have helped, but I've been getting my office set up." She lifts a box and puts it in the back of her truck. She's shoved her bedroll up toward the front of the bed.

"Are you sad?" Emily asks me.

"Not about that dump." I shake my head. "I'm ready to leave."

"A snake shedding its old skin," she says, which surprises me, because I'm the one who uses desert metaphors.

"I have something to show you." I go inside the trailer and from above a shelf of books I lift the rattler skin I found on the ridge.

"What's that?" says Alina, a box of books in her hands.

"A snake skin."

"Prime."

Outside, she loads her box into Emily's truck and reaches for the skin.

"It's delicate," I say.

She lays it along one forearm and holds the rest in her other hand. "Reticulated." She looks at me. "Does that word fit?"

"Yes. Perfectly."

"Like a skin," says Emily, which surprises me again. I'm the punster.

"Can I have it?" Alina says.

"Of course." I was going to give it to Emily, but Alina will enjoy it more.

"Put it on my dashboard," Emily says. "It will be safe there."

"Thank you," Alina says, smiling. "Both of you."

She returns inside for another box of books. I watch her for a moment.

"What happened?" Emily whispers. "Something's different—some tension between you."

"She told me about her research."

She snorts. "Come on. You're teasing me. What research?"

Alina puts another box in the truck. "What?" she says when she realizes we're talking about her.

"I was telling Emily about your remarkable research—Blake and algorithms and Spinoza and probably Winnie-the-Pooh."

Alina smiles. "The Pooh Bear books are in my database."

"Tell her about your thesis," I say.

But then the black van returns, so Emily goes down to talk to them.

"Another polygamist bites the dust," I say.

"The Netherlands has confusing laws about polygamists," Alina says. "It's against the law, but they let Muslims have more than one wife."

"Similar to here. Illegal but not prosecuted."

Soon Emily's back, frowning. "He cleaned it out," she says. "All that equipment—gone."

"You know that he doctored the records of his ethanol shipments," I say. "You don't need anything else to put him behind bars."

"I wanted to get him for distilling whiskey as well. Now there's no proof of that."

"There's 100 proof," I say.

Emily frowns at me. Alina smiles at Emily's response, even though she didn't seem to think my joke was funny.

"Are you going to be all right?" I ask.

Emily glares at me. "Of course. I'm just disappointed. If I hadn't gone with you to see him, we'd have him on this charge as well. It was a rookie mistake." She looks at me. "Are you finished here?"

All the books are in the truck, so I nod. "Probably."

I walk back inside the trailer to look around. There's nothing else I want, except for my sheepskin coat, which could be infested with bedbugs or other vermin. I start to put it in a plastic bag, but then I decide to just leave it behind. I think about what Emily said about all my stuff, that it should be burned. I want to be resentful. I will not burn my boots or my hat. Clearly, she expects something from me, just like the Dead Fathers. I should be upset, should rebel against her will. But the Dead Fathers assume they know what I want, and they don't make clear what they're offering in return. It's clear that what Emily offers is the chance to be with her again. But I won't get that chance smelling like a coyote and certainly not with bedbugs.

I walk back outside. "I don't have any clothing."

She takes from her truck a paper bag. Inside is a stack of pants, shirts, socks, and underwear, three of everything. Also there's a razor, a package of spray, and a bar of soap.

"The bed bugs are not on me now," I say. "They're just in my bed."

She puts the stack on the chair. "That's for lice. Spray your hair." She looks down. "Spray yourself everywhere." Then she walks toward her truck.

"I'm going to burn it now," I say.

Alina says, "You're going to burn your home?"

I nod.

"I thought Spencer was going to do it," Emily calls out.

"I'm going to do it."

"You'll start a range fire."

"It's spring and there won't be any danger," I say.

"I think you need a permit," says Emily, "so the county fire department knows about it."

Alina shrugs at Emily. "I don't think he'll change his mind." Then she turns to me. "Can I light the fire?"

I shake my head. "That's for me to do." She nods and walks down to Emily. Emily speaks to her and Alina's hands become animated, just as they did when she told me about her work. Together they get in her truck, drive it down the road fifty yards and get out again.

I step inside the trailer again. Now, everything seems filthy. The bedding. The floor. Even the washed dishes weren't washed carefully. Who was the man who lived in such filth?

From under the trailer I take an old gasoline jug that still has a quart or two in it. I crumple newspapers across the floor. Then I sprinkle gasoline across everything. After that, I walk outside and stare at the small propane tank for a minute. It might explode, which might be all right or might fire shards of metal in every direction. Or it might blow the top off and jet horizontally, cannon-balling through me or someone else or Spencer's barn. Finally, I decide not to risk it. I disconnect the tank and carry it down the road to where Emily and Alina stand. Then I wait for the propane in the lines to dissipate.

The trailer sits on a flat where nothing grows, but sparks or flaming debris could spread, so I pull an old shovel from under the trailer. I light the newspapers and walk outside and then lift the chair my new clothing is on and carry it toward the pond where I'll bathe. From there I see flames through the windows of the trailer, and smoke rises through the blanket on the doorway. The blanket looks as if a breeze is pulling it in—the fire sucking up air. Soon the inside is full of fire. I wish it was nighttime because the flames climbing into the sky would be spectacular. It feels good to burn it myself. It reminds me of fires my grandfather set to clear the land. It's also an act of rebellion against Spencer. I hope the Dead Fathers will be purged, but I worry that they'll follow wherever I go.

The big pickup drives over from where the new trailer is parked and three people get out. They stand next to Emily and Alina and watch my trailer burn. A window bursts, and flames and smoke erupt. Then flames burst through the roof near the bed. Soon the roof caves in and a flame leaps up, sparks streaming above that. Despite myself, I'm engaged in watching the flame—so powerful. The smoke smells horrible, not just wood but never-washed blankets, the old mattress, linoleum from the floor, old clothing. All of it burns. It's as if part of my life is wiped away—baptism by fire.

A truck comes from Simpson. It doesn't look like an official BLM truck, but I'm still worried. The truck stops and two men get out. They lean against their front bumper and watch the fire. Just tourists come to watch the fire.

A flaming paper lands in the brush fifty yards from the trailer, and I put it out with my shovel. More scraps of paper are swept up by the updraft of the fire; they drift above us and fall, so for a few minutes I'm busy stomping out small flames, shoveling dirt on flames that start in dry grass. Emily and Alina and the others join me in stamping out the flames. I begin to worry that I've made a bad decision.

But before long, even though the trailer continues to burn, scraps of flaming paper are no longer falling, so I relax a bit. I look toward the others and call "thank you!" They wave back. I notice that Bennie is talking with Alina and the woman from Emily's team, and Alina's arms and hands are flying. She must be telling them about her work on the algorithms of human speech. Words alone aren't enough for her; she dances her rhetoric.

I'm hypnotized by the various colors and sizes of flame coming from my home of the past four months. After an hour the flames die down, with just a few hotspots. The fire is spent. All that's left is a charred axle, the frame of the trailer, some smoldering wood. Alina walks down to the horse barn, and the others drive back to their camp. I look for the other truck, but it's gone as well.

I carry the clothing to the pond. I don't think Alina can see me; she's a quarter mile away. Even if she were to look, she'd get what she deserved, a glimpse of an old man's body. I take off my clothing and spray the chemical into my hair and onto my boots and my hat. I decide I don't need to spray my wallet. Then I wade through the mud into knee-deep water. I splash the murky water across myself, and strings of moss cover my belly and legs. I soap myself all over—ducking under the water to clean off the soap. The pond is so shallow I get my feet and butt muddy.

I find an old milk jug and fill it with water. Standing in the grass, I clean as much of the mud off as I can.

I had thought that the cleansing would feel like another baptism, but I'm not sure I was completely immersed. And, as I knew would happen, I don't smell better, just different. Like pond mud.

EIGHT

The Cavalry

After I dress, I walk toward Emily's encampment. Emily, Bennie, and the other two sit in camp chairs under the large juniper. The trailer, a little bigger than the one I just burned, is parked to the back of a small clearing, as far as they could get it from the dusty road. I wonder if there's room for me. Emily's face is blank as I walk up. I'm not sure she wants me there when they're clearly having a meeting, but I have nowhere else to go right now.

They're talking about Emily's lawyering projects here, and I definitely want to find out about all of them. I see another chair leaning against her truck, so I pull it out of its bag and unfold it. Nobody is widening the circle, but I'm not about to leave. Then Emily moves to make room for me. They have all stopped talking.

"Don't let me interrupt," I say.

"We're having a meeting," says Emily. "But you can stay."

"Is this wise?" asks Bennie.

"He's already part of at least two of these cases," says Emily. "Chris, you may remember Andrew." She points to a large man with a kind face.

"Andrew Foster," he says, shaking my hand.

She turns toward the woman, who has a shaved head, an elegant skull: "Lucía Chavez. You know Bennie." She turns toward me. "This is Christopher, my estranged husband."

"Strange husband," I say. No one smiles.

Finally Lucía does. "You look like a lost lamb," she says. But her smile is friendly now. Also, she's right—my home gone, my world skewed. "You've burned your bridges."

"Hopefully not all of them." I glance at Emily.

Everyone seems to take a breath, and their faces relax just a bit.

"So who will carry the ring to Mordor?" I say. This time both Lucía and Andrew smile.

"Don't make me regret this," says Emily.

"What is all this?" I point to the trailer and the table, the people. "Office vacation?"

"Not a vacation," says Andrew. "Emily wants our total focus on these cases. Every boot on the ground. She doesn't want us driving back and forth for three hours a day." He sounds like he's complaining but smiles as if glad to be here.

"I'm a real slave driver," Emily says.

"Anything to get out of the office," says Lucía.

Emily looks around. "So where are we now with the polygamists?"

"Nephi and Frank," I say. I counted them as friends before they became so ardent.

"And a whole slew of women whose names you don't know," says Emily.

I nod, conceding her point.

"We try to find where he moved his equipment to," says Andrew. "He had to hire a trucker to do it."

Emily looks at me. "Did you notice anything?"

I shake my head. "He wouldn't have driven it past here anyway. He would have used the county road." I point across the flat. "He could have taken it south to Delta or north to any number of towns."

Emily asks, "Which one, if you had to guess?"

"American Fork, maybe? He has relatives there. Not too far. When you all go away, he'll bring it back to where his pathetic cornfields are."

"Andrew, will you try to figure out by looking at past contacts what trucking company he might have hired?"

Andrew nods. "I'll get on that." He stands and walks to the trailer. There's a satellite dish on the ground.

"Wouldn't he use his own truck?" asks Bennie.

"His pickup isn't big enough," I say. "And his other truck is a tanker."

Just past the trailer, which is parked next to another juniper, I see a face. In the variegated shadow under the tree, Thomas sits on a low juniper branch. He notices me watching and raises his hand in a small wave.

I walk to the tree and put one hand on a branch near my head.

"The General," Thomas says.

"The General?" I whisper. I glance at Emily, who is, in turn, watching me. "What about him?"

Thomas grins and does the zipper motion with his finger on his lips.

I go back and sit down. "What if the General and Nephi are in cahoots?" I explain that General Torrey poached deer on my grandfather's ranch. "He might have a similar arrangement with Nephi. What if the General hauled the equipment away? If he did, I'll bet they didn't go over the mountains. And I'll also bet they didn't take the main road all the way to Skull Valley. If you look carefully, maybe you can see where he turned off." I point out into the testing grounds.

Emily frowns at me. "I thought you said you didn't see anything."

"I have gotten some new information."

The three of them look from me back to where I spoke to Thomas. He smiles at us, giving me another slight wave. Disconcerting.

Emily watches me. "I don't understand why he'd move it onto federal property. That doesn't make sense at all. But it won't hurt to take an hour and look into it." She turns her head slowly back to Bennie.

"Yes, boss." He gives her a flat, ironic smile.

Alina walks up the road that comes from the horse barn. Both Bennie and Lucía track her with their eyes.

"That woman is grace personified," says Lucía.

"She's a dancer, a linguist, a mathematician, and an AI engineer."

Bennie shakes his head. He seems unable to look away from her.

Lucía elbows him, but that's hardly a distraction.

"Time for dinner," says Emily. "And to get those books out of my truck."

"Where can I put them?" I ask.

"Under the trailer. For now."

When everyone stands, Andrew comes out of the trailer. He opens the tailgate of the double cab pickup and takes out a cooler and a folding table. He opens the table and starts spreading food.

While he's doing that, everyone else helps carry my boxes of books to the trailer and I stack them underneath. If it rains, they could still get wet from water draining off the slope next to the trailer, but it hasn't rained for some time and probably won't rain for weeks.

"Hey," says Alina. She takes the last box of books and hands it to me.

"You got here just in time," I say. "We're having dinner."

I look again toward Emily, who nods.

"I already ate," says Alina.

Lucía brings another camp chair from the back of the truck. Bennie widens the circle of chairs, and Lucía sets up the chair.

"Join us anyway," says Bennie.

"Thank you," Alina says. "I will." She sits in the chair, smiling at both of them.

We cluster around the table and make our sandwiches. Another cooler has sodas. Emily takes Alina by the sleeve and pulls her toward the trailer, near where Thomas sits. He fades out but his smile lasts for a minute longer—a neat trick. Cheshire Tomcat. For a moment Emily frowns at the branch where he sat. Soon she shakes her head and turns away, talking earnestly with Alina. I want to know if she saw him. If she did, it would confirm that I'm not crazy. Or maybe it would confirm no such thing.

By the time we finish eating it's dark. Bennie asks Alina if she wants a ride down to the horse barn.

"It's just right there," she says, arching one eyebrow. She turns toward the barn, and he watches her walk for a moment. Then he gets in his truck to drive back to the reservation, about fifteen miles away. Andrew and Lucía go inside, but Emily and I remain seated.

"There's a room in the trailer for you. It was going to be Bennie's, but he said he'd rather sleep in his own bed."

"Thank you. You?"

"I'll sleep in my truck."

"I can sleep there."

"I'm all set up." She stands from her chair, but I touch her on the arm and she sits back down.

"This seems like a lot of relocation for a few cases." I point to the trailer.

"Some of our work depends on us being on site—talking with the Goshute leaders and elders, making sure the mining company doesn't come back. Stuff like that." She taps a pencil against my knee. "And you're here. Without that, I would have had them drive back and forth. Bennie's our man in the desert anyway."

I nod. Put that way, it makes sense. "All of it's in your wheelhouse, environmental work, but not the polygamists."

"Off my normal path. But I worked with the Tooele County attorney on some other stuff, and he thought about me. At first, I was going to tell him no, but then I just said yes." She gives me a twisted smile, ironic. "Do you feel bad for your buddy Nephi?"

I shrug. "Not really my buddy. We'd talk every couple of weeks."

"When I saw that girl they wanted you to marry, I knew I'd made the right decision. That man should be in jail, but not all his offenses are easily prosecuted."

A pause where neither of us speaks. There's more to say, of course, but I'm all right taking it slow. I look at the trailer again. I see Andrew and Lucía moving inside what seems to be the main room. I wonder about not going inside and instead staying with Emily in the truck.

She touches my hand. "Mindful and careful."

Is she reading my mind like the Dead Fathers? She knows me better than they do. Is she asking me to stay in the truck with her but be mindful and careful about it? I say, "Slow and steady. Yes."

"Are we talking about the same thing?" she asks.

"Maybe not."

I lean away from her. From that perspective I can actually see her better. Her bluish hazel eyes, her perfect face, which is not harmed by being softer around the edges. Yes, for me, she's worth the work—something I haven't always known. Maybe fleeing for the past months has been a good thing. It's helped me see her again.

I lean to kiss her on the forehead. Afterward, she looks up at me—not puzzled, just unsettled, maybe not sure what I want from her, what she wants from me. I stand and go inside.

The main room of the trailer is fitted with desks and computer monitors. Lucía and Andrew stare at a screen. Down a short hall, I pass a counter with a sink, microwave, and coffee maker. Past that is a bathroom and two rooms with the doors open, both bedrooms.

Lucía calls out, "The last one."

"There are only two bedrooms. Where will you and Andrew sleep?"

"In the one next to the bathroom. There're bunkbeds in each room." She turns to Andrew. "I get the top. When I was a kid, my sister and I had bunkbeds, but she always had the top one."

He opens his hand and nods.

"So whose space have I taken?"

"Emily's," says Andrew.

"Bennie's," says Lucía. They both turn back to their work.

I check out the bathroom, and there's a damn shower in there. Emily could have told me but she let me bathe in that dank pond. I shower again. Put on clean underwear but the same clothes I had on. I look at my scraggly beard, but I don't use the razor Emily gave me. I leave it in the bag. I'm not going to go that far. Not yet.

I take the last room. It has space for only a bunkbed, a small dresser and a chair, but—a wonder!—everything is clean. The blankets are not grimy, and there are sheets, pillows, and pillowcases. Maybe I won't be comfortable enough to sleep when everything is so pristine. I undress, turn back the cover, and sit on the bed. My father appears, sitting next to me on the lower bunk. Louis is on my other side, right on my pillow.

"It's worse than we thought," says Hugh. "That young woman is a devil in disguise. Her work is blasphemous. Trying to find out the formulas that govern the universe. Talk about hubris."

"Much worse than a devil," says my father, his voice coming from the upper bunk.

"She's going to turn everything into a fucking mess," says Louis. "And you're not helping by listening to her. You believe every damn thing she says!"

"What were you thinking?" says my father. "Letting her pack your books, befriend you."

"She's seduced you!" says Louis. "At least your mind."

"And that was nothing like a baptism," says Hugh. "Not the burning or the bathing. You're secularizing the sacred."

Which I already knew, so I wonder why he's harping on it.

I don't know what to say. Of the many things that happened today, all seemed to happen *to* me, as if my own will is meaningless. So I don't have a clue what they're accusing me of doing. Well, they can accuse me of burning the trailer instead of leaving it for Spencer, and they can blame me for persevering in my dream of finding the hole the Goshute escaped into. Oh, and they can blame me for my revived love for Emily. I want to take credit for that. Maybe I'm moving out of my passive fatalism, which has become as much my habit as a nun's. "I don't understand why Alina's dangerous."

"It was fate that you two met," says Samuel. "But—"

I interrupt. "Alina said Spinoza was a fatalist. Are you the same, believing that everything is set, already mapped out?"

"Of course we don't," says Samuel.

"It isn't fated that you would be wooed by every word that comes out of her mouth," says Louis. "She's snookered you."

"Your will is the problem," says Hugh. "Your curiosity."

"Yes," says Louis. "You and the fucking cat. You're both going to end up dead."

"Language," says Hugh. "You have to show the boy some control."

Then Samuel climbs down from the upper bunk and pulls the chair from the end of the bed to face me. Louis puts the pillow on my lap and takes out a pack of cards, deals us cards onto the pillow. We don't have matches to play for, but they are fine playing with imaginary chips. One problem is that Louis and Hugh can see my cards, but I have the feeling they always know what they are anyway. The other problem is that they know how many chips I'm virtually pushing forward, but I can never tell what they're betting, so I'm at a disadvantage.

Some things change and some never do.

The next morning I go outside with not only my hat and boots on, but my pants and a shirt. I feel overdressed in my run to the porta-potty. Nobody else is awake yet, so I go back in and pour coffee into my mug—grateful that I don't have to strain stray grounds out with my teeth. I walk over to where my home was. Nothing remains but burned black earth and a few odd pieces of metal angling up.

I hear walking behind me—Emily. She's wearing a T-shirt that says, "I blame the patriarchy."

"Karin got it for my birthday. She went to one of those shops where they make any T-shirt you want." She turns around. It has a picture of Lizzo on the back. "It's Lizzo."

"I know. What was that song she likes so much?"

"Like a Girl."

"Yes. Do you think Karin will run for president?"

"She will do anything she wants."

Karin's bright face shines in my head and I feel loss. I haven't seen her for four months.

Emily looks at the blackened ground. "It looks like an explosion happened." She squints at me because the sun is in her eyes. "Whatcha thinking?"

"It was time to move on," I say. Last night after the Dead Fathers finally left, I pondered the future. "I propose that we take your trailer and take off. We could go anywhere across the entire West."

"Us and a couple hundred thousand others," she says. "The wide-open West is a memory." Still she smiles at me as we walk back to the new camp. "It's a rented trailer anyway."

"We could buy one, but you're not ready to retire."

"No," she says more sharply than seems necessary. "Not ready at all. Not for a while."

"Right. I was teasing. I was just a bit surprised when you let me sit in on your meeting yesterday."

"Because I'm generally territorial?"

I nod. "Especially when I complained about you being gone all the time. Ninety-plus hours a week means you always seemed tired at home. Like the man who comes home and buries his face in the newspaper. Distant."

"We both had the tendency to go all in on our careers. It just seemed fair, because earlier you had your whole being buried in the newspaper. You kept lawyer's hours back then." She stops in the road. "And whenever you start talking like that, it feels like you're trying to have a say in my career. Trying to make it like it was when I was home with the children all the time."

"Fair point." She's right in one sense. I am nostalgic for those early years, before I became obsessed with work, when we talked every evening about books we'd read, what the children were doing, what scandals I'd been writing about. But I'm not sure what good it will do to say that. Her career is so essential to her. Maybe that's what I'm jealous of. My career was essential for the first two decades. Then I had a decade and a half of dissatisfaction.

She looks toward Spencer's building. "Alina. Where did she come from?"

I know she doesn't mean the Netherlands. I also know she's through talking about us for now.

Emily says, "She's bright and well-educated."

"So what the hell is she doing out here?"

"Yes," she nods, happy that I understand the oddity of someone like that coming to this desolate place.

"I'm relatively intelligent and well-educated. And I came out here."

"But you are also obsessed and deranged. She seems to be neither of those."

It *is* odd that Alina came here. There's no denying that.

Just as we get to the camp Bennie drives up and parks next to the trailer. I get a second cup of coffee, he gets a first, and we sit next to each other at the table. "Chris, you were right. Tracks turn off on a road that goes out into the testing grounds. I followed as far as the boundary fence. They unfastened the wire and laid it down. Then they could just drive over it. With my binoculars I saw an old warehouse about two miles in. No soldiers there, but it's probably where they put the equipment." He peers sideways at me, uncomfortably close. "How did you know?"

I shrug. "Lucky guess."

"I don't believe that."

"If I tell you the truth, you won't believe it either."

"Try me."

"My dead great-grandfather told me."

Bennie nods. "So your ancestors are involved." He isn't asking a question, just stating a fact. "They ran sheep in this area, right?"

"Sheep and cattle."

"I didn't judge you to be a traditional visionary Mormon."

"I wasn't. Maybe I'm still not." I raise my cup. "I didn't peg you to be a traditional visionary Goshute."

"Touché," he says. "There are more things on heaven and earth, Horatio—"

"Ain't that the truth," I say.

During breakfast, Emily's team talks about what to do next. Emily sits next to me, which is nice.

"Tough to get a warrant for a military installation," says Andrew. He smiles as he looks at us all digging into the omelets he cooked.

"We could get help from one of Utah's senators," says Bennie.

"What good would that do?" asks Lucía, her coffee cup in her hand.

"Would apply pressure," says Emily.

"One of them's on the armed services committee," says Bennie. He looks toward the platter where there's a last omelet, and Andrew passes it to him.

"Good, good," says Emily.

Lucía turns to me. "Did you sleep all right?"

"Yes. Thank you."

"I wondered," says Lucía, "because we heard you talking." She asks Emily, "Does he talk in his sleep?"

"Didn't used to," says Emily.

"Maybe it's because it's a new bed," I say.

"I wondered if you might have trouble sleeping in clean sheets," says Emily.

"I got used to that pretty quick," I say.

Everyone takes their breakfast things inside, and I get ready to ride my bike up to the Valley of Mines. Just as I'm leaving, Alina shows up. She and Emily nod as if they have an understanding. About what? Again I'm in the dark—a state I should have gotten used to but haven't yet.

Bennie comes out of the trailer. "Hello, Alina."

"Hey," she says, smiling at him.

He stands awkwardly for a minute and then gets in his truck.

"You're going exploring?" Alina asks, "Can I come along?"

I look at Emily, who is busy giving instructions to Lucía and Andrew.

I nod.

"I don't have a bike," she says, "but I asked Spencer to bring me one next time he comes out."

"If you ask to use one of his horses, he'll get you one the next day." I park my bike again. "You need a hat."

"I don't generally wear hats," she says.

"In this country you need a hat to keep the sun off your head."

I go inside and ask the others if I can borrow a hat for Alina. Lucía goes back to her room and gets one that has "la Raza" across the bill.

Back outside I hand it to Alina. "La Raza," she says. "But I'm not. It's appropriation."

Lucía stands on the doorstep. "I don't mind. You can be an honorary Latina."

"Thank you," says Alina, and we start off walking. I glance back and Lucía is watching us closely. I don't think I'm the main target of her attention.

"Where are we going?" Alina breaks off a small branch of sagebrush and brings it to her nose.

"To look for a hole in the ground."

This doesn't surprise her in the least, but I tell her anyway about the murder of the Goshutes and the father's escape.

"In the Netherlands," she says, "we have race violence also. Nothing like that, but still some problems."

"Is there any place on earth free of it?" I ask.

"Probably not. We have Indonesians, Turks, people from the Caribbean and Africa. Black Lives Matter. So many protests."

"Were you involved? Are you political?"

"In my own way. I'm not much into marching and protests. But I agree with them. People are people. I'm not prejudiced, even against aging white American males."

"Why does Emily want you to keep an eye on me?"

"Because you're old."

"So's she."

"But she doesn't traipse across the landscape looking for a navel into the underworld."

"She told you that? I told you the story. It was a sanctuary for that Goshute."

"Maybe it can be both a navel and a sanctuary." She grins again, one side of her mouth pulling up more than the other and her eyebrows doing the same mismatched movement.

We walk through the Valley of the Mines, now empty of men and trucks, and I wonder if any of the shafts were caved in by the blasts. I see the willow staff I cut for Emily, which she left when we gathered watercress. I hand it to Alina.

"I'll look like a peripatetic saint," she says. "Or a wizard."

She looks like neither, but she seems pleased by her vision of herself, so I keep my mouth shut. We continue up and over the low pass into the next valley. I walk slowly toward where the lek was. "I wish you could have seen the sage grouse dance. But the explosions scattered them and disrupted their rituals."

Alina picks up a delicate piece of eggshell, left from the year before. I can see none of the birds and I wonder whether they'll come back or just create a new lek. How many of the birds actually mated after all the stress? It's bad if only a fraction of the females lay eggs this year. Alina takes out her phone and shoots pictures of the area, stray feathers, and tracks in the dirt, to show there was a lek there. I imagine Emily asked her to do this. Emily sweeps everyone up in her projects. She's even got me involved.

"Sad," I say.

"Also illegal," says Alina, "to endanger a lek. That's what Emily told me." She turns away from the lek and toward me. "Where do we look?"

I sweep my hand across the flat. "I've been over every foot already. I'm almost ready to give up hope."

"Don't do that," she says. "I think we'll find it today." She points to herself. "Young eyes."

"My eyes are perfectly good."

"I'm also lucky."

I think that what happened with her thesis was not good luck. But then maybe her graduate committee's decision had less to do with luck than with their own short-sightedness. I start along the bottom of a rock outcropping, systematically poking at the dirt underneath.

I glance back and she is not moving in any kind of orderly search pattern. Instead she pokes her stick at a rock, walks to a spot 25 yards away, then veers left. No rhyme or reason to her searching. She turns right, walks forward, turns left again, zags back a little. She sees me watching and waves.

I think about Emily's total lack of jealousy at me being alone with this young woman. For one thing, I'm happy she trusts me to keep my hands and eyes off Alina. I think of her as an older Karin, like a niece or daughter of a friend—which is apparently the way Emily thinks of her. This is remarkable because we've known her such a short time.

Later, we eat sandwiches sitting under a juniper. "What was your work?" she asks me.

"Guess."

"A university professor in Western American Literature."

"No."

"History?"

"I was a newspaper editor," I tell her. "Before that I did investigative reporting."

"What were some of your stories?"

"Oh, I've put that behind me. Now I look for a hole in the ground. Much less pressure."

"You must remember some. You're not senile."

"I'm only sixty-seven. Senility is a long way away."

Somehow her one lifted eyebrow messages her response to that.

"OK. I wrote about the health danger of particulate air pollution in Salt Lake, the theft of Native American pottery from reservations, the invisibility of Hispanic and other minority workers in Utah, the wage differential between men and women in Utah, Downwinders."

When she looks perplexed, I say, "Victims of drifting radiation from atomic testing."

"It seems that your work and Emily's intersect. Coincidence?"

"No coincidences anywhere. We have the same politics."

"Sticking it to the man," she says. "Like her T-shirt."

"What do you mean?"

"Capitalism is patriarchy. Raping the earth is patriarchy."

"Of course." It is bewildering to me that we have barely met. She reminds me a lot of Karin, that precocious girl. Alina is older, but in terms of worldview they could be twins. "You told me about your thesis, but I don't know what disciplines that could even fit in. I assume literature and philosophy."

"Linguistics and literature and computer science and artificial intelligence."

I shake my head. "Explain."

"The Institute for Logic, Language, and Computation is an interdisciplinary program. As I said before, part of my project was incidence studies. All the digitized books of literature and philosophy I could get access to."

"Ambitious."

She smiles. "I was ambitious. Obsessed even. And all the digitized newspapers in Europe." She grins. "We overlap in more than just our libraries, you and I."

"Overlapped," I say. "I'm retired."

"I'm also retired. Once I analyzed the algorithms of linguistic choice in human discourse. Now I watch over a horse barn."

"Such a remarkable transformation! Do you see your work with horse manure through the lens of Spinoza?"

"It was created when God thought of it." She grins. "You know he was a lens grinder by profession."

"God?"

"You know I meant Spinoza."

"No, I didn't know."

"And he *is* a good lens. He believed that thought composes the universe."

"And I believe it decomposes the universe as well."

"Heretic!" I think she wants to say something serious, so I keep my mouth shut. "I believe that both language and mathematics articulate the universe. The tension between particles of language and matter is the music of the spheres. The dance of the bees. My other lens is William Blake."

"The British poet."

"The same." She peers across the flat. "What's that?"

I can see a white rock next to a massive sagebrush. "A white rock."

"You're making fun of me." She gets up and walks toward the rock, which is about as big as a beach ball. She stands next to the rock, poking at it with her stick. She looks up at me, stamps her foot, jumps in the air and lands with both feet. Then she suddenly disappears as the earth swallows her whole.

NINE

Into the Umbilicus

I run toward the white boulder, wishing I was younger so I could get there faster. I imagine Alina crushed by rocks and dirt, blood flowing from a head wound. Even if she isn't dead, how will I get help for her? No vehicle, no phone, little expertise in first aid. Just before I get to the flat space between two juniper trees, her face appears, pale with dust. Closer, I see she's standing in a hole that is about a yard across. If she's standing on the bottom, it can't be more than five feet deep.

"Are you hurt?"

"Just startled." She looks at her arms. "A little scraped up. I slid down the side."

I step forward, but she holds her palm toward me. "Stop! It could cave in more." She's gone from my sight.

I poke the ground with my willow stick, and it seems solid enough. I step forward, probe with my stick, and step forward again. I put my hand on the boulder and peer into the hole. The hole is deeper than I first thought. A slope of rocks and dirt angles to the floor, which is probably ten feet down. If she had dropped straight into the deepest part, instead of sliding, she might have broken a leg. She must have clambered back up the side to stick her head out. She crouches on the floor and the light from her phone catches the shifting dust surrounding her. Through the haze I see small bones littered across the floor.

"A coyote den," I say.

"Do you think this is what you've been searching for?"

"I don't know. Possibly. Probably."

"And I found it," she says. "Prime."

"What does that mean?" I smile at her.

"Leave me alone. I like the word." She looks around her. "I don't see any coyotes now."

"Maybe they no longer use it."

"Would they attack me?"

"Maybe if you cornered one."

She moves forward a little. "I see an opening."

"Careful. More could cave in." She moves into the haze of dust, and all I can see is the reflection of her light. "Alina. We need better lights. We need helmets. Ropes."

She doesn't answer. I just hear her grunting and only see a flicker of her light.

I hope she's not going to get herself stuck in a passage too narrow for her.

Soon I can't see her light, can't hear her. "Alina," I shout into the hole. I remember a cave accident I covered for the newspaper. Nutty Putty Cave was on private ground but was a common place for teenagers and young adults to go. It had a lava tube they called the birth canal, a shaft so narrow that a Boy Scout once got stuck in it—all night, poor kid. They had to cut off his clothing and rub him with petroleum jelly before they could slide him out.

Later a guy got lost in an area called The Maze. He found a narrow hole that he thought would lead him out. The way became narrower and turned deeper and he got stuck, head down. Professional spelunkers tried to pull him out. They arranged a pulley system, but their pulley strained and then came loose, dropping him back into the hole. The pressure on his heart killed him. The owners sealed the cave off with cement, making it his tomb.

"Alina," I call again, panicked. I think of dropping into the hole to go after her, but I have no phone or flashlight.

Finally her face appears, climbing the side of the den. She reaches up, and I help her out of the hole.

"I didn't come to the end," she says. "It's really narrow at first but it's wider after that—at least as far as I went. Clay and rock. Weird. I thought caves were mostly rock."

Clay and rock, just like Nutty Putty.

It might not be the only cave in the area, but I have a strong feeling that it is the Goshute's cave. After all my searching, I'm unprepared for this moment. I probably didn't get any spelunking equipment because I didn't believe I would find the cave. I'm certainly not emotionally prepared.

"You found your umbilicus!" She laughs and does a spontaneous jig.

"No, you found it."

"We did."

I look around at the flat I've searched for four months and laugh out loud. I probably walked past this rock a dozen times.

"The Indian man crawled in there to save his life. Cool!"

"Goshute man. Yes, very cool. He went in this hole and resurfaced somewhere else. I want to see where he came out." I tip my head back and yip and howl like a coyote.

Her eyebrows arch. "You are off your wheels."

"Guilty as charged."

Then she grins and howls at the blue sky and her Irish quickstep turns into a dance around the juniper.

I find a branch that a cow rubbed off the juniper next to the boulder. I use it to cover the hole. Then I twist loose a few sagebrush branches.

"Is someone else looking for this hole?" she asks.

I shake my head. "The prospecting company is gone, but some rock hound might find it."

"Maybe there's another wacko desert man who had a vision of it." She smiles, and I do too. Finally.

She helps me finish covering the hole.

"I still can't believe it," I say. "I promise I'll never say another bad word against millennials."

She laughs.

As we leave, we startle a rattlesnake stretched out on a sunlit rock. It coils but doesn't rattle as we pass. Then it uncoils and slithers toward the hole we just found—disappearing under the juniper branches.

Alina's eyes widen, her brows arch. "I've never seen one before. We don't have that kind of snake in the Netherlands." She peers into the juniper branches. "Spencer warned me to be careful of them."

I catch her sleeve and pull her back. "He's right. Don't get too close."

"Why doesn't it rattle?"

"It's spring. It was out on the rock to warm up, but it's still sluggish. Probably overwintered in the cave." She seems satisfied, but to me the behavior of the snake seems strange.

But then the giddiness and wonder fade. I had built the cave up in my mind as a magical space, and as I looked down through the shifting dust, I mostly saw just a coyote den. I'm not sure what I hope to find when we explore further—the Goshute's bones? A cache of deerskins with writing on them? I was curious about the cave because of what Thomas wrote, and I thought finding it would mean or reveal something remarkable. Maybe finding it is sufficient to the act. Or the cave might be significant in a way I can't see yet. An umbilicus connects to some being inside the mother's womb. What creature will be down there? Maybe a monster, Lilith or Cain.

Back at camp, Emily asks, "Well did you find this magical cave?"

"Yes," says Alina.

Emily falls speechless, which makes me laugh. "Alina found it."

"Just lucky," she says. "I'm generally a lucky person."

I wonder. The coincidences just keep piling up. Again I feel that I'm a pawn, moved around on someone else's board in a game I don't comprehend. Alina showed up and immediately inveigled herself into my life—helped me pack my books, claimed she owns some of the same ones. I could be suspicious, but my bullshit sensor is well honed. I know Emily is always machinating behind the scenes, but she doesn't have an investment in the cave. That leaves the Dead Fathers as possible chess masters, but they seem almost as oblivious as I am. They issue all kinds of vague warnings, and maybe they aren't specific because they are guessing more than foreseeing. Thomas? That old coyote may be behind it all. The Dead Mothers? The universe?

It's not all about you, a voice says in my head. My grandmother's voice.

Good advice. I keep remembering what Emily said about even the stars seeming patterned to human eyes.

Alina transfers the pictures of the empty lek to Emily's phone. Then she shows the new pictures to Bennie and Lucía. I look at the three young people bent over the phone. I smile at Emily and she smiles back. I nearly say something stupid like *love is in the air*, but I don't want to interrupt the process. Lucía asks Alina if she wants to stay for lunch.

Alina says, "That would be nice."

We all sit at the table. I half listen and don't say anything. I think about how easily Alina saw the overlap between Emily's work and mine. I *am* invested in protecting the lek and in preventing radioactive waste from being dumped in the desert, but I find myself hesitating to intrude on Emily's business after she said I was jealous of her career. Part of my worry is that I'll just make her even more territorial.

Now they're talking about Nephi's case. Outflanked when he moved his distilling equipment onto the testing ground, they're trying to contact the senator from Utah who is on the armed services committee—Senator Gerald Clarke. The state Department of Historic Preservation may be able to help with the mines. The Wildlife Division or even the Nature Conservancy may help protect the lek permanently. The suit over the nerve gas spread is moving forward at worse than a snail's pace, but that still counts as progress. Soon the meeting breaks. Alina stands and jogs down to the horse barn. They all have their assignments and return to their phones and computers.

Emily stretches her wrists and hands. "I'm so tired of writing emails." Then she turns her chair toward mine. "What will you do now?"

I want to touch her hands, so I do, clasping them. They are soft as silk.

"Go down the hole. I need flashlights, a helmet, and rope."

"It's a den of snakes, probably," she says. "I'm worried about you." She removes her hands from mine.

"We'll be careful. I should be offended that you asked Alina to watch out for me. Do you think I'm that decrepit?" She doesn't answer—so, yes. She's firm that she doesn't want me to go. But I'm going. We're both obstinate, part of our difficulty.

I crouch down next to the stack of boxes under the trailer, but I can't find any of the books Alina says she also owns. I don't want to dump them all out, so I grab what's on top: Terry Tempest Williams's *Red: Passion and Patience in the Desert*. I glance back at Emily, still sitting at the table. I certainly want passion in the desert, which will take patience. I don't think the book will actually help me with my love life. It's about a whole different politics. Emily gets up and goes inside, and I follow.

She, Bennie, Andrew, and Lucía are working in the big room to the front end of the trailer. I lie on my bed and try to read. TTW talks about the politics of the red-rock desert, but there is just as much politics in the pastel gray desert, my homeland. She writes, "How are we to find our way toward conversation?" Yes, that is the million-dollar question. Not just in preservation of wilderness. Emily came to rescue me, but also to do her work. She wants to keep me safe, which I might think is sweet, but it borders on the parental. The cave is *my* business. She doesn't want me to question how she's managing *her* career, even if she has little time for me. She's being hypocritical.

It wasn't just as an editor that I hated face-to-face conflict. I was a middle child—mediating between my older siblings, two sisters, and my younger ones, a girl and a boy. I think that people are the same as adults as they were as children. Alina is right about identity and manifesting. Adults have the same blueprint as they did when they were a child. If they manage disagreements by deflection, they probably did the same when they were young. Same with aggressiveness, facing the person head-on, or passive manipulation—whining, always giving in, avoidance. I have come to think that time is so unfathomable that maybe the adult behavior causes the childhood behavior. Or neither causes either, but both behaviors and time are more like planets, crossing and recrossing orbits.

Still, when Emily uses her will on me or acts in a way I don't approve of, I retreat. It's a predictable cycle for us. When she had her affair and broke everything apart, she knew I would flee. I was a fierce and fearless writer, and if those I uncovered wanted a war of written words, I'd say let's go. But physical conflict is different for me. When Nephi shot up my books, I wanted to engage in the war.

But I'm no soldier and that desire quickly faded. Emily has always been like a general. Even though Nephi Johnson has outflanked her, she will be the one to figure out what to do next. I was good at sniffing out trouble, bringing it into the light, not at knowing how to deal with it on a personal level.

Tonight, when the Dead Fathers appear, there's no sign of cards. They stand in a row next to my bed and glare at me.

"You've really stepped in the shit now," says Louis.

"Actually, it was that girl," says Hugh. "She's the one who found the hole. Christopher would have never found it."

"Thanks for your confidence," I say.

"We told you she'd lead you astray," says Hugh. "You didn't listen."

"I'm getting so tired of this," I say. "You give me such limited information—generalities about a war. That I have a part to play. Vague warnings about Emily and Alina, who are not evil. You haven't been specific or honest with me."

"Lead you down a badger hole is what she's done," says Louis. "Down to hell."

"It was a coyote den, not a badger hole. Certainly not hell." I shake my head. "And you're obfuscating again." My voice is too loud. "Just tell me what you want from me. I wish you were done with me and would just leave me alone."

"Leave you alone?" My father frowns.

"Why don't you want me to go down into that hole?"

Now they're all frowning.

"The cave," says Hugh, "going into it or not going into it isn't the issue."

"Then what is the issue?" I shout. "You're not making sense!"

They look at me, perplexed.

"Little steps," says Louis. "Little steps down a slippery slope."

A knock sounds on the door. "Please," says a male voice, Andrew, "we're trying to sleep."

"What *is* the issue?" I whisper.

"Obedience," says Hugh. "That's always the issue."

"There are no other damn issues," says Louis.

"Obedience to what or whom?" When none of them answer, I ask, "Do you mean obedience to you or to God?"

"Obedience to Him," says Hugh. "Of course."

"Which requires obedience to us," says Louis, "because we're his damn representatives to you."

"God, the great Father in Heaven, sent you to me?"

Louis scratches the back of his head. I've shut them up again, but not for long.

Samuel says, "We believe he doesn't want you in that cave."

"Just on principle? Do you know why?"

"You're flirting with blasphemy," says Hugh.

"Not just flirting," says Louis. "You've gone all the way. You're having lewd intercourse with blasphemy."

I ask, "When did you talk to God last?"

Again, none of them answer. If there's anything the Old Testament teaches me, it's that there's a long history of people imagining they know His will. Usually they claim His will is to do whatever they wanted to do in the first place. Massacre children? Oh yes, God loves infanticide. I know history is more complex than this sweeping judgment implies, but it's true all too often.

They continue to try to persuade me to trust them and stay out of the cave. I hear birdsong before they finally leave. Alone, I lie on my bed and fall immediately asleep.

It is probably only a couple hours later when I hear Andrew and Lucía talking loudly, probably paying me back for my noise the night before. I look for my pants, but they aren't hung over the back of my chair, where I left them last night. The two extra pairs are gone from the shopping bag Emily gave me. At least my hat and boots are still there. If they really want to stop me from going down the cave, they should have taken my boots.

I clap on my hat and stick my feet into my boots. I wrap a towel around myself before going out into the larger room. I look for duct tape or twine to make a belt. Nobody else is up, but as I'm looking through the drawers next to the sink, Andrew comes out. He looks at me.

"You don't sleep much, do you?" he says.

"No, I generally need only five or six hours. I'm sorry I kept you awake."

"It sounded like you were talking to someone."

"Myself," I say. "I'm the only one who will listen."

"That's not true. Can I help you find something?"

"I—I've misplaced my pants," I say.

I look at his face and I realize how clever the Dead Fathers are. I'm completely discredited in Andrew's eyes, a doddering, senile old man.

"I have an extra pair." He's too courteous to ask how I lost my pants in such a small room. I don't tell him that I lost three pairs.

He brings them out. Seeing that he's turned his back to me, I drop the towel and put them on. The legs are too long and the waist is too wide, but they'll do.

"Thank you," I say, holding them up with one hand. He goes back into the room and brings out a short piece of nylon twine, newly cut. I take it and loop it around myself, tying it in front. "Thanks," I say again.

I get a shirt on, then grab a bagel and pour coffee and step outside. He's peeling potatoes. Lucía must be trying to go back to sleep.

Emily crawls out of the back of her truck. She looks like she didn't get enough sleep either. She walks right past me, intent on the trailer and either the toilet or the coffee pot or both. Soon she returns with a cup and joins me at the outside table. She takes a long draft of coffee, another, and then looks at my pants. "What happened to the ones I bought you?"

"I'm being visited by my dead ancestors." I watch her face. She'll think I'm crazy, but that seems less shameful than telling her that I can't locate my own pants.

She stares at me and takes another long drink.

"Your ancestors hid your pants?"

"They're devious bastards," I say.

She puts her hand on my arm and leans toward me. "What don't they want you to do?"

I should have known she'd drive straight to the core of the mess.

"They want and don't want many things, but none of them make sense."

"Name them."

"Last night they were angry that I found the cave. They don't want me to go back down into it."

"Seems sensible," she says.

"They were fine with me looking but they didn't want me to find it. Confusing."

"They want you to be occupied."

She's probably right. "They wanted me to marry Nephi's daughters, join his family. They want me to play poker with them. It seems to have significance more than a game to them. They weren't happy when I didn't let General Torrey shoot the pronghorn."

"Nephi has certainly been letting him poach on your grandfather's old farm."

"I think so." She's looking straight at me. I want to stay in her gaze, hold her in my gaze, but it's frightening. So again, I glance away, then back again. Her hazel eyes, blue or gray depending on the light and what she's wearing. The iris with a notch in it. Her. As if I'm looking into her soul. And she's new to me.

"You don't think I'm crazy." I'm still kind of shocked.

She opens her mouth, shuts it again, thinking. "I do believe you, as crazy as it seems." She leans back. "I also think you have to be crazy to see your dead ancestors."

I think at first that she's making a kind of play on words: *I believe you but I don't.* Then I know she's describing a kind of complex thinking that should be foreign to lawyers, who have to think in binaries—guilty or not guilty.

"You saw Thomas," I say.

"In a dream."

"A dream that you acted on."

"You want me to say that I'm as crazy as you? OK. I'm as crazy as you."

"Last night, they told me they want me to be obedient."

"Obedient? Obedient to what?"

"I guess to God, but He seems inscrutable."

She smiles. "The Ten Commandments don't fit what's going on here."

"Exactly. It's murky."

"Chris, murky is the new reality."

"Murky is our milieu."

"Put it on a T-shirt," she says. "Screw the patriarchy. Murky is our milieu."

That certainly fits the DFs. I start to tell her about the war between the Mother and Father, but it's too ridiculous. It's a balance between her believing I've seen something and believing I'm crazy. I don't want to tip the scale. "They warned me that Alina is a dangerous woman. You are also dangerous. They want me to leave you."

"You did leave me."

"You left—" I look at her. "We left each other.

"Yes, we did."

"They didn't want me to welcome you back. They wanted me to shut my door—blanket—in your face. Now they're upset." I glance at her but she doesn't respond. "They want me to drive you away."

"You keep saying what they want. What do you want?"

"I want you to stay. I'm glad you came. I'm frightened, though."

"Frightened?"

"In some ways four months was too long, in others it wasn't long enough. I keep thinking I'll just slide into our old ways of thinking."

"Old ways," she says. "Which were?"

I remember sitting in the living room; she's working on her computer. I put my book down and watch her. When she doesn't look back, I pick my book up again. I tell myself that I don't want to interrupt her, but it is also easier to read than to work through our problems. "Taking each other for granted. Not having any grace between us."

She nods.

"We let stuff get between us."

"But the stuff was important, so we need to find a way to balance."

"Right," I say. "We each need to make a space for the other in our minds. Not all the space in the world. Just a little dedicated space. A little cathouse in your soul."

She stares at me, then says, "Freudian slip. In the song it's a little birdhouse. But you knew that. Sometimes you drive—" She wipes her hands down across her face. "I think I do. Make space for you."

"Sometimes," I say. "Like now. You don't seem to be thinking about any of the projects you have going."

"Damn," she says, "that's lax of me."

She glances at the trailer. "I will work to make a little birdhouse in my soul just for you."

"Work?" I don't like her choice of words.

She stands. "Yes. Everything takes work."

"So we're finished."

"I can't do it all at once," she says. "I have to think about what you're saying. And I have a team to direct."

She's doing it again. She waits. I wait.

She says, "I'm trying, Chris. I want you too, but for much of our marriage, I had to place myself second to everyone else's desires."

"Not my fault." I think for a minute. "Not *only* my fault."

"Not your *only* fault. I blame the patriarchy."

"Me? The patriarchy? I'm the least patriarchal person I know."

"Yes. To your great credit. But—"

"But?"

"When your career took all your time, I was to just put up with it. But when the tables were turned, you didn't want to put up with it. Still don't."

"OK. Guilty as charged. I just hope you *want* to take time with me."

"I do. Want to take time. I'm trying, I really am. But there is all this weight surrounding our talk of my work."

"I can see what you're saying."

She's looking over my shoulder. Turning, I see Alina trotting up. She sits at the table with us. She and Emily trade smiles, and again I think they must have known each other before this week. They look like old friends reunited.

Alina says to me, "I can't come with you today. Spencer is driving out, and he invited me to ride horses with him and his friends to the top of Indian Peak. I've never been on a horse before." Her whole face is lit up with excitement. Her eyebrows are fairly quivering. She won't be so excited in the evening after riding a horse all day. She'll be too stiff and chafed to walk.

I don't want to wait a day to explore the cave but I also don't want to go alone. An old man climbing around in a tunnel alone is asking for injury or death.

"I'll wait until you can come," I say.

"I found a rope," she says. "And a couple of hand lights."

"Helmets," says Emily. "And head lamps."

Alina smiles again and pushes back from the table. We both watch her go. Instead of walking down to the barn, she dances. Full of pleasure in her own life. I'm jealous.

"Sweet girl," says Emily. "And so bright."

"I still find it remarkable that you dreamed about her."

Emily is quiet for a moment. "Yes. Like I said, she was there, and your ancestor, Thomas. We were in a desert plain, not sloped like this one." She points across the plain, which tilts down toward the riverbed five miles away. "I was anxious to get to some destination, but I couldn't form my mind around it. So I didn't know where to go." She hesitates. "I knew I was supposed to find you, but I didn't know where you were. I wanted to ask Thomas and the girl—Alina—but they were so engaged in conversation that I couldn't get their attention. Then in the next dream, Thomas finally talked to me. Said my name, like I told you. Then I bought a truck and came to the desert."

"You've never been a visionary woman," I say.

"And you've never been a visionary man, but here we are." She finishes her coffee. "I keep telling myself it was just a dream, but it feels like more than that."

"You and Alina are like old friends."

She nods slowly. "Strange, isn't it."

The trailer door opens and Andrew and Lucía come out, mugs and plates of potatoes and fried eggs in their hands. They sit at the table.

Lucía grins at me. "Who were you arguing with last night?" She glances at Emily.

"Not me." Emily holds out her hands in defense.

Lucía groans. "Andrew finally had to pound on your door."

"Actually, he knocked politely," I say. "I'm sorry. Bad dream."

"His ancestors visit him," says Emily.

I roll my eyes, but then realize that we can say the truth and nobody will believe it.

"Every damn night," I say. "Most argumentative men I've ever known."

"Talking to your ancestors? What is that code for? Talking in your sleep?" Andrew seems earnest, but there's no way to answer him without outright lying or telling a truth he won't hear.

Lucía says, "It takes two sides, both engaged, to have an argument. You can't have an argument with yourself."

I'm not sure what she means, but I don't want the conversation to continue down this path, so I keep my mouth shut.

She looks under the table. "Nice pants. Are you planning on gaining weight?" Andrew must have told her I lost my pants.

Bennie drives up in his pickup and walks over to the table. He looks around, probably for Alina, but he doesn't ask where she is.

"No joy," he says. "I can't even get past the senator's gatekeepers."

"Even if we could get in there," says Emily, "General Torrey can move the distilling equipment around."

"A shell game." Bennie turns toward me. "Nice pants. Maybe you'll grow into them."

"His *ancestors*,"—Lucía marks air quotes—"'stole' his."

He asks the same question Emily did. "What don't they want you to do?"

"Many things," I say. He waits for more but I feel too awkward to go on.

Andrew goes back inside and brings out bagels, cream cheese, and oranges.

They each report to Emily: Andrew's mediating between the Nature Conservancy and the BLM about buying the valley where the lek is—good. He can't find the trucking company Nephi might have used—bad. Lucía is trying to untangle the financial records seized from the refinery where someone is complicit with Nephi's scheme. Bennie talks about the nerve gas lawsuit being scheduled for a hearing in another month and the deadlock with his tribe about whether to accept or reject radioactive waste storage on the reservation.

I look across the flat at all the trailers parked—people who fled the city for the weekend. That's the only way I've tracked the cycle of days since I came out here. On the weekends there is an invasion. "Today's Sunday," I say. "Don't you guys ever take a break?"

Andrew and Lucía look at each other. "Not when there's such a flood of work as right now."

"They are very loyal," says Emily. "They don't take a break unless I do."

"Not even then sometimes," says Andrew.

"We're irreplaceable," says Lucía.

"More like no rest for the wicked," says Andrew. "It's the way it is. Junior partners are slaves to senior partners."

"No," says Emily. "Slaves don't question or make jokes. Or they get *flogged*!"

For some reason they all laugh. Even Emily. It doesn't seem funny to me.

Breakfast is over, and Bennie leaves in his truck. The three others go back inside the trailer. I'm still tired from arguing with the Dead Fathers most of the night, so I head back to my bedroom for a nap.

I wake for lunch and spend the afternoon reading my copy of William Blake's collected poems, which luckily was on top of one of the boxes. I'm reading from *The Marriage of Heaven and Hell*, which opens with fire and anger: "Rintrah roars & shakes his fires in the burden'd air / Hungry clouds swag on the deep." I skim the introduction: Blake was into revolution, both the American and the French and the threat of it in England. He ached for religious revolution because everyone in power, bishops and on up the hierarchy, had lost their way. Good had been made into evil and evil into good. So Blake chooses the Devil's Party, the party of freedom from religious hypocrisy and repression.

> *Prisons are built with stones of Law,*
> *Brothels with bricks of Religion.*
> *The pride of the peacock is the glory of God.*
> *The lust of the goat is the bounty of God.*

The wrath of the lion is the wisdom of God.
The nakedness of woman is the work of God.

I think I would have liked him. He could be describing my current state, where good and evil commingle. The desert was once a solitary place, good, but now everyone has come here, evil. Adultery is evil, but when Emily took up with Roger, it broke apart something that had become inflexible and dead. The Dead Fathers, who I've known all my life to be good men, now feel deceitful, manipulative, evasive, and nonsensical. If Blake came to my bedroom with the DFs, I would say that his faith in revolution is misplaced. Institutions will always manifest themselves as institutions. There can be no revolution that changes their basic nature.

I wonder how Alina used Blake in her work. Understanding that is probably beyond me. Is she also angry about institutions becoming brittle and unresponsive to human beings? I'll have to ask her. She doesn't seem like the angry type. She's the type who can get enough distance to see the issues clearly.

In the afternoon Spencer and his friends return. He doesn't even wave at me, even though I'm standing not far from the road. I think that Alina will walk up and tell me about her day, but she doesn't appear. After waiting a while longer, I walk down and climb the steps to the apartment. I knock on the door and finally it opens. She's in shorts and a T-shirt, and she leaves the door open as she hobbles back to the couch, where she has a pillow and blanket. "Why didn't you warn me? I thought you were my friend." She shows me her calves, which are bright red. Her thighs as well.

"I'm sorry. Would you have stayed back if I'd told you how much it would hurt to ride all day?"

"No. Spencer and his friends just laughed at me. I don't think I'll ever walk again."

"I'm sorry," I say. "I'll let you rest."

"It was glorious, though," she says. "I loved my horse. So much power! My mare went right up the steep parts. Scared me to death but so exciting. I loved being on top of the mountain. We could see all the way to Nevada, Spencer said."

"I haven't been up there yet this year. Too much snow."

"It's mostly melted but that was fun to see as well. We had a snowball fight."

That I would have liked to see. Alina from Amsterdam, a sophisticated world citizen, throwing snow at urban rednecks. I'm a snob. "Do you need anything?"

"I have pain killers and this horse salve Spencer gave me. It's helping."

"If you keep riding, it won't hurt like this every time. Just the first."

"I don't believe it," she says. "I may never walk again." But her eyebrows show she's joking.

I stand to leave.

"He's very angry with you for burning the trailer," she says.

"He told me he was going to burn it himself."

"He said you could have started a range fire." She seems undisturbed by the possibility, but Spencer's right.

I could have started a sagebrush fire that would have gone up the canyon toward the valley of the mines, maybe further.

"I was hasty."

"I think he's not that much worried," she says. "He just wanted to burn it himself." She lies back on the couch and winces when her legs rub together. "I won't make it tomorrow. Maybe Tuesday."

The next morning Emily says, "Could you come with me today?" At my look she says, "Salt Lake. I need to check in at the office to make sure everything's going smoothly." Which she could certainly do by satellite phone from the desert. What I want to do is to tamp down my fear and go to the hole without Alina, but Emily knows that, which is why she invited me—to keep me safe. Sweet, maybe. Controlling, certainly.

"I won't be any use to you."

"Not necessarily true. We can talk while we're driving. And the trip will distract you so you won't be tempted to go up to the cave and fall and injure yourself alone."

At least she's admitting straight up what she's doing. She's not always that transparent.

TEN

To my infant son, Thomas

For the first few miles, we don't speak. The hillsides are still yellow green. Soon they'll dry up.

"Her hardest hue to hold," I say.

"What?"

"Robert Frost, talking about the yellow in the green in early spring. Out here in the desert, that color is even more fleeting."

She doesn't say anything, probably mulling over what she has to do today. My hat sits on the seat between us, and she glances at it and frowns, probably because it's filthy. She'd better not try to mess with my hat. Some things are not negotiable.

But why? I'm not a rancher, just like I'm not a church-attending Mormon or a journalist. But all those identities are in my blood, even if the habits drawn from them seem affected and anachronistic. My grandfather Louis had that attitude toward his hat. "You don't touch a man's hat," he growled at me when I was small and had put his on my head and strutted around the cabin. But I didn't spend my life in the desert. Like the people I make fun of, I'm a kind of tourist—a committed one but still a tourist. My protectiveness of my own greasy felt hat has much to do with nostalgia.

Dust billows around us as Emily stops before turning right onto the main road, the old route for a century and a half. Pony Express riders and families in Studebakers going to California traveled this road. A few hundred yards after that, we pass Simpson Springs, where the soldiers were stationed that killed the Goshute's family. The military testing grounds spread to the north of us—white patches where bombs have exploded, a few Quonset huts in the distance, one close, its corrugated steel flashing in the sunlight.

Emily's eyeing that one as well. "I'd bet anything that the distilling equipment is hidden there."

I nod. "I could make sure. Follow the truck tracks on my bike."

"You wouldn't make it a mile past the fence before you were surrounded by soldiers in jeeps."

She's driving too fast and the truck fishtails a little on the gravel, but before I can say anything, she slows down. Once Louis rolled his truck on this very stretch of the road. He tumbled right down into a gulley. If we stopped, I could show Emily the rusted carcass.

"Bennie said he couldn't see vehicles at the building. I could go at night. I might make it to the building and get pictures before they come from the base at Skull Valley."

"They'd shoot at you," she says. "And they wouldn't miss."

"They wouldn't shoot at me." Probably they wouldn't. I'm wondering what possessed me to volunteer.

There's another silent space. We cross Johnson Pass and drop down into the next valley. We drive through a small Mormon town—Lombardy poplars pointing toward the sky and sprinkler lines watering alfalfa fields. I lean against the window and try to doze. When I open my eyes again, we're past Tooele, and the Great Salt Lake is to our left. I'm unable to bear the silence any longer.

I open my mouth, but she speaks first. "How can I be sure you won't run away again for four months?"

A rabbit lopes across the highway in front of us, but she doesn't swerve or slow. We miss it anyway.

I want to say that she can't be sure. *I* don't know I won't run away again.

"Chris, I feel unmoored." The truck drifts to the right.

"The road! Moor yourself on that." I turn sideways in my seat. "Exactly my words to myself while you were gone. Playing poker with my dead ancestors."

"I saw visions that prompted me to move my whole office to the desert."

"It made sense when you explained it to me."

"I was lawyering you. No. It doesn't make sense. It was impulse."

"Prompted by dreams. At Thanksgiving I just left. Total impulse."

"No, you had a reason. And checking out isn't entirely new for you." She looks at me and the truck drifts again. "Staying away, that was different."

"It felt different," I say. "Yes. It did. I didn't know how to come home."

"I used to be rational. Recently my life has become more and more foreign to me. What is my involvement in all this" —she swirls her hand above the steering wheel— "stuff in the desert if it isn't impulse, coincidence, accident?" She takes her lower lip in her teeth.

"It got us back together."

She looks at me and the truck drifts a little.

"The road."

She corrects. "Some people believe God has an individual plan for each of us, but if this is His doing, He's jumped the shark. One excuse to see you would have been enough. But five different cases and a vision? Nothing rational about that constellation."

We round the bend from Tooele Valley into the Salt Lake Valley and pass the Kennecott Copper smokestack. The lake is low, still wide before us, with Antelope Island rising out of the water, miles away.

I say, "I'm obstinate enough that all that might have pushed me the other way. I probably would have rebelled."

"Well, before this all happened, I found myself remembering your kindness, your gentleness. And I remembered what we were like before, before our—whatever. And—and then as I was gathering courage to—"

"You? Gathering courage? I don't believe it."

She bites her lip again. "I'll take that as a compliment. But it's true. I was frightened you wouldn't want to see me."

"You should have known."

"But I didn't. Now I do. Know. That you're happy to see me. Now." She swallows. The late morning sun slants gleaming on the white margin of the shrunken lake. "But what I was trying to say is that as I was gathering courage, all this started happening. Not just Nephi's case, but the mining, the nerve gas incidents, the atomic waste. Unbelievable as four cases dropping on me all at once was, I had those vivid dreams at the same time. Like—dream visions. Like my crazy sister says she sees. It was all just too weird."

I'm trying to process her view of what happened. It's clear that nothing is simple. Especially in terms of motives. Most are more complex than any of us recognize. For example, why do I run away from emotional tangles? Is it because I heard my parents arguing about my father's drinking? Was that so traumatizing that forever after I'm destined to run from conflict with those I love?

"I'm not running now," I say. "I'm trying not to run away emotionally."

"I know. Thank you."

We leave the freeway and soon drive past the Salt Lake Temple and the Church Office Building.

Emily brakes for a car in front of her and then drives around it. "I met your great-grandmother once."

"At the last Twist reunion, before they stopped having them. Just after we were married."

"Yes. She looked like a sphinx, sitting there with her cane. She looked at me as if she could perceive every atom in my body."

"Marie le Coultre."

"Yes."

"Thomas's first wife."

"She said to me, 'You.' As if it was an accusation. 'You have a part to play.' I thought, *She's senile*. Then she said, 'One day you'll know I'm right. One day you'll remember and know.'"

I don't know what to say, but what I feel is a settling, the feeling of proper proportion in the tensional web of Emily, me, the DFs, the DMs, Alina, the universe.

"There's a cliché about having an arresting gaze," Emily says, "but that fits her. She was an arresting woman."

"He left her to have relationships with men," I say. "Or they left each other. I guess it was congenial, or as congenial as it could be."

"Really? I never met Thomas, but I did see him in my dream. 'Arresting' isn't a word I'd use about him. He's like a joker or a Shakespearean fool."

"Or a coyote. He died before I was born. Dad said he was a teaser—had a nickname for everyone. Made up twisted lyrics for songs, told funny, embarrassing stories." I take a breath. "I mean I'd never met him until last week."

"I was going to say."

"He still seems to think of existence as a kind of joke. He has an ironic perspective."

"That fits what I saw of him in my dream." Emily stretches her forearm toward me. "I have goosebumps on my arms." She's right; I can see them. "My brain is telling me that you have absolutely lost it. That I should put you in a mental hospital."

"I don't feel crazy."

"Which doesn't mean you're not. But you don't seem crazy to me. And my dream. It wasn't much like a dream. It felt real."

"He certainly doesn't seem like a hallucination to me."

"Did people know at the time he was gay?"

"I've never read anything about it. I'm not sure how I would bring it up with him now."

"Maybe his wife and children swept it under the rug."

"If they hadn't, he could have been lynched."

We're almost to her law office.

"Ah, Emily, can I get some different pants?" I ask. "Before we go to your office?"

"Oh right," she says. "I wish you'd asked me before."

"I forgot."

"We *were* having a good talk." I recognize it as a summary statement, the kind of thing she says when she's done talking.

She takes a right turn and stops at a big box store on Fourth South. "Get a new hat as well," she says. "This one probably has diseases and parasites living in it." I grab my hat and run in. I find my pants size and put them on in the dressing room. I think about the cunning nature of the Dead Fathers and I get two more sets of pants, another shirt, and a few pairs of socks. I look at the hats but they don't have one I like, just bill caps. I think about getting another pair of boots, but good boots are expensive and this store doesn't really sell the kind of work boots I like. Anyway, the Dead Fathers wouldn't dare touch my boots or my hat. As I head back out, I think about our talk. Emily and I are coming to terms and it feels good. I'm so distracted that I almost pass the rows of cashiers, but then I see a cashier looking at me, her mouth open in dismay, and I double back and pay for my things.

When I come out, Emily smiles. "You look nice."

I haven't shaved or combed my hair, so I know it's not true. I'm probably developing an aroma again. "Adequate. I'm barely adequate."

"Who used to say that? Oh, your mother, as an old woman. If someone asked how she was doing, she'd say, 'I'm adequate.' So apt and funny."

"You two got along famously."

Emily glances at my bag of clothing. "Maybe you should leave most of that in my truck."

"I'm not sure that will prevent the Dead Fathers. They're pretty determined."

"Oh, it'll prevent them. Those bastards wouldn't dare."

I believe she's right.

Her office is in an old house on South Temple, between the Cathedral of the Madeleine and the Governor's Mansion. She stops the truck and I grab my hat. "Leave it here. You look disreputable with that on your head."

"Disreputable?"

"Yes."

I leave it on the seat and follow her inside. Even though she has two of her staff in the desert, her office is still a busy place. While she's meeting with her partners, she has the secretary, a young black man who talks with a slight British accent, record my story of Blythe, Blythe, and Smith blasting and disrupting the lek. Then I tell my stories of Nephi and the General shooting through my trailer.

After I finish, I wait in her office for a while, looking at her law books, her diploma, her pictures of me and of the kids. She has a picture of Carrie-Anne and Bruce and their children, one of Todd and Rhiannon and their baby, Joshua, one of Rebecca and Michael. I look at their luminous faces and something comes loose inside. I find tears in my eyes. *What am I doing?* I think. I just want to be with them.

Then I think about leaving the desert to the maniacs, alive and dead, and I know I can't do that either. At least not yet. I still have the strong and specific feeling I have unfinished business there.

After lunch at a small sandwich shop near her office, Emily announces that we're going to the church archives. "Your great-great-grandmother Alice Collins wrote a letter to her son Thomas when he was an infant."

"That's unusual."

"Yes, kind of a blessing but also a manifesto."

"I didn't know about this letter," I say. "How did you find out about it?"

"After I dreamed about Thomas and you told me who he was, I remembered that your mother told me about the letter. She found it in one of Marie le Coultre's journals."

"Why did Marie have it?"

"I don't know. Maybe Alice thought it would help Marie understand Thomas." She chews on her sandwich. "Anyway, your mother put the letter in the church archives with the rest of the Twist documents. I looked them up on the library website, but when I filed an online request, it was refused. I went down there, but they won't let me look at it. They may bring it out for you because you're their descendant."

I'm still stuck on the fact that I didn't know about this letter. "I wish Mom had told me."

"She told me. Women's matters." She sighs. "I should have told you."

"Women's matters? I'm going to have a word with her."

"You've seen her too? Damn. I want to talk to her."

We walk through the spacious lobby and main room of the Church Historical Library and enter a smaller reading room. Microfilm readers line one side. Emily fills out a request slip from memory, using my name. I hand it to the receptionist who has the power to request the item from the archives. She looks at the note. I'm sure she's going to say "no," so I keep talking. "My mother donated it, but she told me about my great-great-grandmother. I want to learn more about her and this is all that's left of her writing."

She smiles and nods. "Just have a seat."

Emily leans toward me and whispers. "Why are you so nervous?"

"I'm sure she knows I'm not orthodox Mormon."

"Don't be ridiculous," she says. "Do you think she can smell the coffee on your breath?" She smiles. "Now if you wore your hat in here, she'd know you're irregular."

"Ha, ha."

We wait a few minutes, and then the receptionist hands me a folder. Inside are photocopies of a document. "I thought we'd get the original," I say to her.

She shakes her head vigorously. "No. It's in the vault in the canyon."

"Why is it there?"

"I'm not sure. Maybe because it's especially valuable."

I take the folder back to the table and open it so that we both can read the letter. Then she stands over it and takes a picture of it with her phone. I watch the receptionist, but she doesn't seem to mind. Emily sits and slides the folder to me. The handwriting is elegant, perfect cursive, but also faded and difficult to read. Emily puts her hand on my shoulder and reads along with me.

July 24th 1858

To my infant son, Thomas,

I met with the Sisters today at Abigail Cannons, where the spirit of the Gods was pored out on us. Sister Eliza Young attended also. We met to celebrate both the anniversary of the day the Saints entered the Salt Lake Valley and also of our return from the south, where we were sent by Brother Brigham for protection from the envading army, sent by that fool of a President. I also made private memorial of the second month of your health after your [the word is blotted by a water stain] birth. Many times during our stay in Utah Valey, I thought I would lose you.

Sevral prayers were made by the sisters. Sister Snow prophesied that those in attendance would embrace resurected beings. Several others spoke in tongues, and others interpreted. From their words I know that our enemies will be defeated and end in disgrace.

I carried you with me and held you in my arms as I was blesed by Sister Rhoda, who is 79 and in good health, booth body and mind. She told me that my heart is as pure and as innocent as you are, my child. She said that you would be a mediator and heler of division in your life and afterward—that you would be endowed with the spirit from both our Mother and Father in Heaven, and partake of all their divine qualities. I was reminded of a blesing given you by your father Hugh, during your sickness that first month. You were borne in a Sibley tent about five miles from Utah Lake, and the air was damp, hot, and [another water stain—pestilent?]. It was all I could do from keeping you cool. He anointed you with oil and blessed you to live to ful adulthood and to see your own children playing at your feet. He said you have a mission, during your life or after, in helping the Saints join together as one, just as they did in the City of Enoch. The Holy Spirit confirmed to me that this is true. You are to be a peacemaker.

With love from your mother,
Alice Collins Twist

It feels as if Alice is standing before me, telling me herself about the blessings and her hope for her infant son. It's no secret that women at the beginning of the Church saw visions and gave blessings, but nobody talks about it at church. It affects me powerfully that Alice and Emily and Thomas and I are significantly linked. I also find myself thinking about Marie le Coultre, the woman who saved the letter. The woman Emily described as a sphinx. I wonder what she might tell me about her husband Thomas. Or what his second wife, Janet Cook, might say about him. She divorced him and married a younger man, my father told me. She'd have another view entirely.

The Dead Fathers have warned me about Thomas, but he seems harmless. He also seems supremely himself—at peace with who he is. I'm not sure my father or grandfather feel that way. Suddenly I hope that my grandchildren will meet their ancestors, both those who have come to see themselves clearly and those who are still discovering themselves, like me. Especially I'd like Karin to meet her Dead Mothers, Thomas, and my father. Karin would be happy that one of my ancestors was free from the traditional gender binary.

I take the folder back to the receptionist. After the wonder I felt reading the letter, she seems polite and efficient, not the sanctimonious gatekeeper I thought she was just a few minutes before. We leave through the light-filled entryway. "Do you want to go home for a minute?" Emily asks. "We could also stop in to see Carrie-Anne."

I shake my head. "Not yet."

"Maybe that's for the best. You're starting to have an aroma again."

"They won't care."

"Anyway, Karin's in school now."

I think about my reluctance to go home. Maybe I want Emily and I to be right first. I don't want to just slip unchanged back into my previous life. I also want to finish my "work" with the cave. After my mission to the Ojibway reserve, my mother wanted to drive up to Canada to get me, make a trip of my homecoming. My father insisted I fly home. He believed in the blessing of safety promised to all missionaries, and he didn't want me to be released and drive home without that protection. He was sure we'd have an accident. I'm both my father and myself in my current story. I want to finish my work before I return home.

Emily directs her truck west, back to the desert. Soon we pass the airport, where a jet takes off, going somewhere, maybe Los Angeles or Atlanta, London or Rio de Janeiro. Then the glistening sheet of the lake, the white, wide shore to our right, the Kennecott smokestack, impossibly tall, to our left. When I was a child and we were returning home after a few days with Grandpa in the desert, Dad sometimes parked and we would watch the rail cars dump fiery slag off the edge of a black plateau of cinders. It looked like a lava flow.

I think of Alice and the circle of women in the Cannon house. Had their husbands known what they were doing, these disciples of Eliza Snow? They may have known. Were they jealous that these women possessed spiritual gifts they didn't—the way I have been jealous of Emily's success? Not safe questions.

"It still feels remarkable that you sought out this letter."

She turns to look at me. "I told you. I was curious."

"You've always mocked your sister for having visions."

"I have. You have also. I still doubt her visions. I doubt my dreams. I certainly doubt yours."

"You haven't answered my question."

"I already did. I dreamed about Thomas and remembered that your mother told me about the letter."

I still don't know where these eddies and currents of space-time are taking us, but I'm beginning to have more confidence in the journey bringing me both danger— getting shot at—and unexpected pleasures—the Dead Fathers visiting, Emily coming to me, seeing my curious ancestor Thomas again, meeting Alina. Anything seems possible. For the first time in a long time, I feel the future opening up. Hope is the word.

I also realize that I can trust Emily's judgment. Her mixture of doubt and belief seems to fit the chaos we're experiencing.

"I didn't tell you everything that my father and Louis and Hugh told me."

She grins. "What are the old bastards telling you about me now?"

"Not much. They've moved on."

"To what?"

"The cave. Alina. They think Mother and Father God are in a trial separation."

"What?!"

I nod.

"Oh, my hell! You've got to be kidding." She frowns at me. "I wish you hadn't told me that. It makes me think that either you've completely lost it or the universe is coming apart at the seams. The first is much easier to believe."

I wait. It took a long while for me to even be able to think about the possibility.

She stops the truck at the edge of the road.

"My hands are shaking," she says. "You drive."

She stares out the other window.

We turn off the freeway after Grantsville and drive back to the desert through Skull Valley. We pass Iosepa, where Hawaiians who came to work on the Salt Lake Temple were forced to live because of the Saints' fear of leprosy. Like Eve, they traded paradise for a desert. We drive through the Eastern Goshute Reservation, Bennie's home, past the entrance to Skull Valley Testing Grounds and its guard station, General Torrey's domain. You can't go inside the gates unless you live in the town of Skull Valley and work on the base.

"It's a slippery slope," she says. "The cases, the dreams, you telling me that you've talked to your dead father. What I feel is shame. I'll never think of my sister the same, but now I'm no different than her. It was such a comfort to look down on her."

We come to the gravel road west toward Simpson Springs. A slippery slope. Good description of what I've felt—loss of control, increased momentum, the edge of the roof coming. Soon I'll be airborne. "It's either exciting or unnerving."

"Both. Definitely both."

A couple of ATV riders kick up dust on the right barrow pit. When they come to the desert, I wonder, do they see all these marks of history? Or is all the history invisible to them? Do they know they're driving on the Pony Express and Wells Fargo routes? Or that this road was later called the Lincoln Highway, the first road for cars that went all the way across the United States? Or would they be happy anywhere there was open space to roar across with the illusion of radical freedom from human bonds and traditions?

We turn off that road and continue south until we reach the trailer. After only three nights, the camp feels like home to me. Before, the decaying trailer felt like home and before that, the house in Salt Lake. Maybe it will again. The only thing sure is that change is on the horizon.

Before anything else tonight, I tell the Dead Fathers, "I want to talk to Marie again or Alice."

"Go ahead," says my father.

"We won't stop you," says Hugh.

"You must not know my mother well," says Louis.

"She does what she pleases," says my father. "She'd never do what any of us says."

"And talking to her will do you no good," says Hugh. "Believe me, I know."

I imagine the old Victorian trying to tell his daughter-in-law Marie how to comport herself. She would parry every comment with a quote with four citations. Or she'd ask him what kind of underwear he's wearing.

"What are you smiling about?" asks Louis. "You act as if you don't have a care in the world."

"I have many cares," I say.

"You think that going down a hole with that heathen is going to make you happy?" asks Louis.

"She's less of a heathen than I am!" My voice is too loud, but Andrew doesn't pound on the wall or the door.

"That may be true," says Louis, "but that doesn't mean you need to consort with her."

"We're not consorting!"

"You're talking," says my father. "Her ideas won't make you happy and befriending her won't help anything."

"And it's forbidden," says Hugh.

"By whom?"

"By us for starters," says Louis.

"Deal the cards," I say. "I'm feeling lucky."

Of course, I lose.

The next morning, my clothing has disappeared again and my boots too this time. Stealing my boots is crossing a line, but at least they left my hat. I try to think how this story might be told in scripture one day, a history of the dealings of beings from the other side with beings from the side of the living. It will be read as an implausible allegory. Christopher Twist, with barely a fig leaf to cover him, setting forth up the canyon on a quest. The story of Balaam's ass is much more plausible.

I clap my hat on my head and wrap the bed sheet around myself. I knock on the back of the truck and lift the upper door to the shell. Emily sits up in her sleeping bag.

"You look like a sheik," she says.

"I look like a sad old fool wrapped in a bedsheet."

"You kind of look like both. Is this a proposition or did they steal your clothes again?"

"Can it be both?" I say.

"It's broad daylight, so no, it can't be both." She hands me the bag that contains the extra set of clothing I bought. She also hands me a pair of running shoes. "We outfoxed them."

"Yes, you protecting this bag made it possible for me to cover my shame."

"Christopher," she says, "you have no shame."

ELEVEN

Compensation

After breakfast, Alina arrives on the bicycle Spencer bought for her after she asked if we could use his horses. It worked, just as I told her it would. She wears jeans and a long-sleeved shirt, also a backpack with two helmets and headlamps tied to it. "I got Spencer to get me some equipment."

"He sprang for these?"

"No. I paid."

"I need to pay my share."

"Doesn't matter," she says. "I have money I was going to use for tuition."

Everyone has some need for money, but I hated it when that need drove my decisions. Now my wants are reduced and I don't have to do anything. I stuff a hundred-dollar bill in the pocket of her backpack. Probably not even half the cost.

As we head up the canyon, it's chilly but not cold—normal for the desert just past the middle of March. The Valley of the Mines is empty except for a doe and a fawn, who look up and bound away into the willows. Three crows perch on top of the rusted tin building as if they're keeping watch. Alina reads the slogan about an unarmed man being a slave. "I should change it to, 'A man packing a pistol is compensating.'" I remember when Emily commented on the same sign.

"You'd have to get a gun to shoot the new holes."

"I'd just paint it over the old message." She faces me. "Do you have a gun in your backpack?"

"That's kind of an invasive question after what you said about compensating," I say. "You saw the rifle I own. My grandfather's single-shot .22 with a broken stock. He hit a cow on the head with it once."

She turns her bike and pedals across the stream.

"I shot rabbits with it."

"I knew you were a bunny killer when I first saw you."

"You knew no such thing."

"It was a safe guess." She glances over her shoulder, so I pedal harder to keep up. "There are more guns than people in the United States. In the Netherlands it's illegal to own a gun."

"Even for hunting?"

"You can get a permit, but you have to pass a year-long course and prove you have a place to hunt."

"I haven't shot my rifle for decades."

"You seem like a pacifist. I was joking about you being a bunny killer."

"Oh, I killed my share when I was young."

"So it's karma that you've been shot at. Now you know how it feels."

The morning is warm, too warm, and I start sweating as I push to keep up with her. She rides faster than I usually do up the canyon, through the Valley of the Mines, and up the road to the plateau. "Did you ride a bike in Amsterdam?"

"Everywhere."

We dismount at the hole and peer into the branches.

"I can't see that snake," I say. "Or any others."

She lifts off one branch, and I lift off another. Soon the hole is clear. I shine my light into the hole, but all I can see is the rubble from the cave-in.

"I'll go first," she says.

I nod. "Do Dutch philosophers know how to tie a bowline?"

"I'm sure they do, but I'm not a philosopher. I'm an analytic AI rhetorician." She unloads her pack.

"What does your project have to do with AI?"

"My original goal was to make AI that could converse like a human."

"Now?"

"I watch a horse barn."

"You know I'm not talking about that."

"Later I decided I could learn about humans from the patterns of AI. Now I want to know how the universe works." She lifts off the last branches.

"You want to codify the mind of God."

Her eyebrows shrug. "So you can see why they didn't let me finish. I'd overstepped the limits of my prospectus."

"God is plural for Mormons. Mother and Father."

"I read that somewhere. Maybe that's why my last calculations were off."

At first I think she's making a joke, but she seems serious. Even her eyebrows show nothing.

I take off my gloves, loop the rope around my waist, and tie the knot. Then I remove the loop, and she puts it around herself, under her armpits.

"Tighten it," I say, and she looks at the knot and tightens the loop so it fits her better. "You know knots."

"I used to go sailing," she says. "I've tied this knot before, but I forgot the English word for it."

I put on my gloves, pass the rest of the rope around the closer of the two junipers and around my butt. She steps backward toward the hole. Her feet are against the edge, and I'm carefully playing out the rope to lower her. Soon the rope is loose and I peer into the hole. Her white face looks up at me. "No snakes," she says.

"Not that you can see."

I take off my hat and place it under the tree. I secure it from wind with a couple of rocks on the brim. Then I don my helmet and turn on the headlamp. After looping the doubled rope around my butt, I walk backward into the hole. Once I'm halfway down the edge, I realize how difficult it is to hold to the rope and let out slack at the same time. I lose my grip and the rope slides too quickly. I drop about a yard, scraping my forearms against the side of the hole. I dangle for a minute, panicked.

Alina says, "Your feet are almost on the ground."

I let the rope slide through my hands and lower myself, but the ground is uneven and I trip, holding onto the rope and swinging around. She grabs my arm, and I'm finally able to stand.

"So far so good," I say.

"No, not so good. You were supposed to climb down there." She points to the slide of rocks that goes from the opening to the floor. You're going to injure yourself. Or me." She coils the rope and stows it in her backpack.

She's crouched because the ceiling is low, except where it's caved in. The room is the size of a Volkswagen bug, and the walls and ceiling are clay with rock embedded. Bones of small mammals litter the floor. There is no egress.

"This isn't the hole I'm looking for," I say. "This is just a coyote den."

She turns sideways and points. At the end, where the front bumper of the car would be, there's a tilted seam of rock and, under one end, a triangular space barely big enough for a child to push through.

"I slid under there before," she says. "It opens up again."

"I'm too big."

"No you're not. You're a skinny, wiry old man with no coordination." She smiles as she shimmies feet first under the rock. I see the glare of her headlamp as she looks up at me. "Come on."

"Are you sure this is a good idea?"

"Yes. You'll be fine once you get past this tight spot."

"That tight spot is what I'm worried about."

She slithers on through. I put my legs into the space and look at the small moon my headlamp makes on the rock a few inches from my eyes. I'm thinking about the Boy Scout who got stuck and the young man who died in Nutty Putty. I imagine that happening to me, sandwiched tight by a shelf of rock above and clay and rock below. Stuck in darkness. I'm positive I won't make it through.

"What should I do?" calls Alina.

But I'm not a corpulent Scout, and I have Alina to keep me from doing something stupid, like wedging myself headfirst into a dead end. I determine to go ahead. My helmet won't fit, so I take it off. My palms are sweating and my hands are coated with slippery, wet clay. I want to wipe them on my pants, but I can't reach my arms down. I take three deep breaths, fighting against my feeling of claustrophobia. Then I push against the rock and force myself deeper into the hole. I can't go sideways and I keep sliding on my back. I can't get leverage with my hands above my head, so I try shimmying like Alina did, but that doesn't work well. Then I feel her pulling on my feet. And finally I'm through. I'm breathing heavily and sweat runs down my face, mixing with the clay.

"Breech birth," Alina says.

I nod my head and force a smile. The Scout was trapped in a lava tube named the Birth Canal, so Alina's joke isn't funny at the moment.

At least I'm able to stand. The cave tunnel slopes downward, with a slab of limestone to the right and rock and clay on the left wall. It is much more comfortable here: the ceiling is about five feet above my head, and the walls are the same distance on either side. It's also cooler than it was outside. My sweat begins to dry, leaving me a little chilled. Walking will warm me up, I know.

"Clay doesn't seem structurally strong," I say.

She looks at the ceiling. "Seems stable."

"They may have loosened some of it with their blasting," I say.

"Do you want to go back?" she says.

I swallow. "No."

"Neither do I." She starts down an especially steep slope, where the floor is littered with flat slippery rocks of various sizes. She's halfway down when she slips and lands on her rear. She slides a little way, toward a jumble of boulders.

"Be careful!"

"I just bruised my pride," she says. "You be careful as well."

I inch my way down, wishing I had my staff. The gravel is flat like shale, and it slides under my feet. Finally I just sit down and slide to the bottom. I breathe for a minute, then we clamber over the boulders. On the other side is a relatively flat area. On one wall is a petroglyph of a human figure. It is a single line with stubs of feet and arms, hands splayed. The head is a set of mountain sheep horns with short lines across the top—hair or teeth. Next to it is a tiny creature with four legs and a pointed head, a lizard or salamander. It thrills me to think that the Goshute my great-grandfather wrote about might have seen these two images—carved by his ancestors or the people who lived here before that.

Alina takes a picture of the two carvings and then a closer picture of each one. "What do they mean?"

"Abandon all hope ye who enter."

She smiles. "Hope brought you here. Hope crawled down into the hole with you. You've been looking for this place a long time."

I point toward the carvings. "I wish I knew. Probably nobody alive can interpret them."

She leans close to a carving of the being with the curved horns. "Scientists study rock art."

"I know these are not Fremont. I think they are from what they call the Archaic period."

She says, "I wish I could figure out how to use art and symbolic images in my calculations about human will and choice."

"These are the essential formula for a life process."

She smiles at me. "That's a neat idea." She leads out again, striding down the cave with such vigor that I worry she'll trip over a boulder she doesn't see in the sporadic and dim light. I shuffle forward. Soon we come to a drop-off of about ten feet, but the face isn't sheer and we can climb down without needing to use the rope. The next variation is a split, with the main channel continuing downward and another shimmy hole to the right. On the wall near that hole is a squiggly line like a snake.

"Prime!" says Alina. She points. "Let's explore that way."

The hole is even smaller than the space under the rock shelf in the coyote den, but she's already sliding through, this time headfirst, dragging her pack behind her. I wait a moment, until I can't see her light from the hole, and follow. I put my arms above my head and push into the hole. It widens slightly and turns up. I grab onto a rock edge and pull myself forward. The tunnel levels off and I am able to continue pushing forward with my toes and pulling with my elbows. It widens again and I see Alina's light. The channel is smaller here, about three feet wide and four high. We have to crawl forward. My legs and arms shake with the effort, ready to give out. The pebbles dig into my knees and dust gets inside my gloves, making mud with my sweat.

I think about being outside, the sun above me and space wide around me—space enough that I could twirl without touching anything. I'm not frozen by fear but still quite unsettled at being so deep in the earth.

Fighting down my panic, I crawl forward through the clay. Ahead I see Alina's legs as she stands. They disappear as she crawls upward. I wait for a while because I don't want her falling on my head. I stand with difficulty in the space, just wide enough for my body. I step onto a jutting rock and push myself upward. Bracing my knees against one wall and my back against the opposite one, I inch higher. I see light, which makes me panic. I imagine myself stuck in the damn hole, seeing the brightness of the world but unable to get there. Fueled by adrenaline, I push myself out into another animal den and roll from under a rock shelf into the daylight. Alina is standing on the slope, grinning, her face and clothing smeared with gray clay. I'm breathing hard.

"You look like a ghost," she says.

"You look like a zombie." She laughs at that, a delightful sound.

Two hundred yards away, we see the cluster of cedars where we entered the cave.

I say, "This is where the Goshute must have come out. He could've gotten behind this rock outcropping where the soldiers couldn't see him. Then he could wait until they left."

Alina nods. "Do you think he made those cave pictures?"

"Those are probably older than his time."

She drops to her hands and knees, and I see she's going back down the hole. "We have more to explore."

I think about pushing myself into that constricted space again and my body rebels. "In a minute. I need to build up my courage."

She sits up and slides over to where she can lean against the cliff.

"You're breathing too hard. Are you claustrophobic? You should have told me."

"I didn't think I was. But that was frightening. I really just need to catch my breath." I look across the flat and feel the breeze on my face.

"We don't need to go back down there," she says.

"Yes, we do. I want to explore that other shaft."

She stands and finds a better seat on a boulder. "To the center of the earth. When I left home, I never imagined that this is what I would be doing." Her eyes shine and she grins at me. "We'll just keep going down to where there is another civilization."

I might be getting a Charlie horse, so I stretch my weary legs. "We'll descend into hell. Demons and sinners."

She takes a drink. "Do you really think that?"

"Of course not. Hell isn't a place you can go to. It's a state of mind."

She thinks about that. "You don't strike me as a religious person."

"I used to be. All my ancestors were. It's in my blood."

I lie down next to the shallow coyote den and slither feet first into the hole. "Let's do this." The first turn is hard and my clothing catches on the rock. I breathe for a minute and push through, catching myself with my feet and butt so I don't fall down the tube. Then I'm back in the tighter tunnel. I move to one side. "You go first."

"I am smaller," she says. "I can warn you if the way is too narrow."

"Strait and narrow."

"What?"

"Nothing."

"No. Tell me! You make me feel dumb when I don't get your joke because it's some American thing."

"It's what the Bible says about the way to heaven. It's tight and narrow."

"I thought heaven is supposed to be above the clouds," she says. "Not in a hole in the ground."

"Navajos believe heaven is downward. It's symbolic anyway. The way to heaven is tight as this cave. So we know this cave doesn't lead to hell, because the Bible says that the way is broad."

She nods, her face serious, as if I've said something important. In my younger days, right after my Mormon mission, I would have thought of this as an opportunity to tell her more about the church. I had so much unreliable certitude then.

We emerge into the other branch of the cave and continue down. The walls are still clay and rock. The air is warm and moist, not cold and clammy. I imagine a network of water and channels of rock spreading downward to magma. I trip over a rock and my light flashes around the cave.

"You all right?" Alina asks.

"Yes. I'm just tired." So tired that my legs are shaking again.

"Me too."

I doubt that she's as tired as I am. Climbing in a cave certainly uses different muscles than I generally use. As we continue, I'm grateful that the cave maintains its width and height. I have gotten used to being underground, and

I'm calmer than I was at first. Now I'm just worried about being strong enough to climb back out when I'm so weary.

We come to a cave-in with boulders blocking our way.

"Dead end," I say.

Alina climbs up them, but they fill the tunnel. "I can see through." She looks back at me, the glare of her head-lamp in my eyes. "Stand back." She pulls a head-sized boulder from the pile and it tumbles down, rolling a couple of times before it lodges again. She moves another, and another, before she climbs back down. "I don't think we're going to make it through here. At least not today."

"It looks fresh. Maybe the blasts loosened it."

She nods. "Let's move a few more rocks."

"I'm worried about this. If we move these rocks the ones above them will crash down."

"It's like Jenga," she says. "We won't move anything that isn't loose."

I don't like the image she's given me of all those inter-locking pieces tumbling on my head.

She climbs up again. I'm not going to let her do all the work, so I join on her right. The ceiling here looks solid enough. We pull small, loose boulders down and roll them behind us. I'm sweating again and stop to wipe my face with my shirt. We work for what seems like half an hour but probably is not that long. We still can't crawl through.

"Tomorrow," she says. "We'll bring some tools."

"Yes," I say, "a crowbar and a shovel."

We return through the cave and by the time we get back to the opening, I'm drenched in sweat, my shirt sopping. Alina somehow clambers up and ties the rope around the tree. I use the doubled rope to climb up.

The air is cool on my wet clothing, and I'm grateful to be out of the hole. I stretch my arms wide, which I couldn't have done in some parts of the cave. I'm free of the imagined weight of hundreds of tons of rocks above my head. Alina stretches also and then keeps moving, imitating the movement of a cat. I've never met anyone who has such pure pleasure in the motion of her own body. Kinetic pleasure.

About a quarter mile away a blue truck is parked, and two people stand in front of it, looking our direction. One has binoculars. "Your eyes are better than mine," I say. "Does either of them have a rifle?"

"I don't think so."

"Good. Everybody wants to take a potshot at me."

"Everyone?"

"Not everyone. Two people."

"A polygamist and a general. You are an odd man with odd enemies."

"Yes, I'm odd. But I'm not alone." I give her a wolf grin.

"I'm not odd."

"Right," I say. "You aren't a mystical mathematician who left her home where rain actually falls from the sky and moved to a desert where you followed a crazy man down into a hole in the ground."

"I led most of the way." She smiles back.

We both look at the truck.

"They don't seem like the kind who would shoot at you."

"Neither was Nephi. I think I'm right to be a little jumpy."

"Do you recognize the truck?"

"No." I climb on my bike. "Whoever they are, now they know where the hole is."

"What do you think they'll do? Dynamite it?"

"Probably nothing," I say. "But I want to talk to them."

I ride my bike toward the truck, but before we get there, they climb in and drive away.

"Probably just rock hunters," I say. "Either that or serial killers. Or both."

"You are a suspicious man," Alina says.

"I have reason to be suspicious."

I think about telling her about the Dead Fathers and their opaque warnings, but I don't want her to think I'm crazy, even if it's true.

When we ride into the camp, Lucía and Bennie look up from the table.

"What happened to you two?" Lucía asks. "You look like you've been rolling in mud."

"Crawling through mud," says Alina.

Emily comes out of the trailer.

"You're alive!" she says.

"O ye of little faith," I say. "We made it at least a couple hundred yards before we reached a cave-in."

"A cave-in!"

"But we can get past it with some tools."

That doesn't seem to comfort Emily. Alina takes out her camera and shows them the pictures of the petroglyphs. She looks at Bennie.

"What?" he asks. "I'm no expert on petroglyphs."

Alina says, "I thought maybe you'd seen something like them before."

"Do you read Old Frankish?"

She laughs. "Sorry. That was dumb of me."

"Not dumb." Bennie's looking straight at her face as if he wants to gaze at her forever.

Alina notices and gives him a smile back. She doesn't look away bashfully as some women might.

"Maybe I just didn't look at them closely enough," Bennie says. "I might have an idea or two."

"That would be fine." She sits next to him and Lucía leans across from her other side. They pass the camera around and look at all of them.

"These can help Emily," says Lucía.

Bennie nods.

Alina stands. "That trailer seems too small for all of you. There is a foldout couch in my apartment."

It's not clear whether she's talking to Bennie or Lucía. Bennie's not even staying in the trailer, but she may not know his home is only twenty minutes away. She may be talking to both of them.

Bennie and Lucía glance toward each other, and during that pause, Alina turns to go.

"Tomorrow?" I ask.

"Yes. Tomorrow. I'll borrow a shovel and a crowbar from Spencer's stuff."

"Spencer might not like that."

"Spencer's not here," she says over her shoulder as she rides her bike toward the horse barn.

Bennie watches her go, and Lucía pushes against his shoulder, grinning.

"I think I'm in love," says Bennie.

"Me too," says Lucía, also watching Alina.

Emily clears her throat.

"Not me!" I say. "She's a charming girl, but she's as young as our granddaughter."

"She's twice the age of our granddaughter," says Emily.

"Pervert!" says Lucía. "All men are perverts. You just said that to keep Emily from being suspicious."

"I'm always suspicious," says Emily, "but Alina can watch out for herself."

"Thanks for the confidence," I say. "She doesn't have to watch out for herself around me."

"Right," says Emily. "She's stronger and faster than you."

"I could beat her in an arm wrestle," I say. "Maybe."

Bennie says, "She's not much younger than I am."

Lucía says, "I take it back. Not every man is a pervert."

"I'm kind of in love with her too," says Emily. "I'm glad she kept you from injuring yourself."

Their teasing me and each other feels good. It's nice to have a circle of friends again. I came to the desert to be alone, but not being with people I loved just made me morose. I had once loved or even still love the Dead Fathers, but they have become such a pain in the ass that my love feels strained.

I take a shower in the trailer and put on the last set of clothes I bought in Salt Lake. After dinner, Bennie stands from the table and walks toward his truck.

"Let me know if it doesn't work out," says Lucía.

He grins, and then climbs in his truck and drives over to the horse barn.

We sit at the table and play poker, Andrew, Lucía, Emily, and me. I win steadily, not every hand, but my pile of beans grows through the evening.

Lucía says, "You must have sold your soul to the devil."

"My grandfather taught me to play."

"Close enough to the devil," says Emily.

Andrew and Lucía look at her but neither of us explain.

"He said it was the same as trading horses. You read the horse or the cards, and you read the faces of the seller or the other players. It was valuable to me as a journalist. I could discern bullshit."

Andrew throws down his cards. "You could be rich."

Emily says, "He doesn't care about money."

Lucía says, "Everyone cares about money."

"Flush," I say. "Clubs."

Then Emily is out of beans, and she stands. "I'm going to bed."

We play a couple more hands, but soon we all quit. I go to my room. When it's quiet, I head back outside again. The lights are on down the hallway—Andrew and Lucía still working.

Lucía smiles. "Good luck."

Andrew gives her a stern look.

"What? It's not a secret what he wants? It would be good for both of them."

Andrew bends lower over his computer. I'm with him. I don't like Lucía talking about my business. But she seems lighter and less confounded about sex than I am. Who's right? I think of turning and going back to my bedroom, but instead I shut the door behind me and knock on the back of Emily's truck. She doesn't respond so I knock harder.

"What?" she says finally. "What the hell? Is that you, Chris? Go away!"

"Sorry," I say quietly. "I thought we might—"

She's silent for a moment. "You want me to have sex with you." She's not whispering and I worry the others will hear her. "Are you all charged up after a day with your flashlight on Alina's behind?"

I open the rear hatch of the shell. Her face appears as she sits up.

"Emily."

"What?"

"That was offensive." I lower the tailgate and sit on it.

"Yes," she says. "I'm sorry. But that doesn't mean that your motives for having sex with me are clear."

She slides out, still in her sleeping bag, and sits on the tailgate.

"They seem clear to me," I say. "It's been almost a year." Immediately I wish I had said something different. Something about how much I like her and how pleasant looking at her is. Maybe even that would be too much.

"Mine aren't clear," she says.

"Do we have to be absolutely right before we touch each other?" Again, I know it's the wrong thing to say, but I don't know the right thing, so I blunder on. "I think all we need is to be basically right, and I think we are."

"I think we're moving toward each other," she says. "A kind of dance."

"Yes! That's it." I move closer to her and she doesn't move away.

"I want to keep dancing for a little longer or maybe a lot longer." She hesitates. "I'm just not ready, Chris."

"OK." I slide off the tailgate.

"Chris!"

"What?"

"I didn't say I want you to leave. I just don't want to have sex tonight."

"Oh." I'm disappointed, of course, but she said not *tonight*, which implies that some time she might want to. She said almost the same thing earlier when I was wearing only a sheet. And she definitely wants to be with me and talk. I sit again on the tailgate, as close to her as I can get without pushing her off the other side. Bennie's truck is still parked next to the horse barn, and I can see a light on in the apartment. Then the light goes out but the truck doesn't leave. Jealous is one word for what I feel. "Things seemed simpler when we were young."

"They weren't simple. You just thought they were."

"You're right. Looking backward doesn't help." We're face to face but I can't see her clearly. Symbolic.

"That's not what I said. I think we have to look all directions—forward, backward, at the present."

"Yes," I say.

She shifts on her seat on the tailgate. "Like you, I thought that when the kids were gone from the house more—all of them in school—we would reinvest in each other. I was disappointed when it didn't happen."

"You should have said something."

"I did. You looked straight at me and nodded, but you weren't really there. And when they all left home, I thought again that we'd have more time for each other. But nothing changed."

I do remember sitting in the kitchen, exhausted from work that wasn't fulfilling. I don't remember much about what she said that night. "You must have been very indirect."

"Me, indirect?" She doesn't speak for a minute.

I walk to the table and grab a chair.

"Chris!" she says. "Are we finished already? You're the one who complains about me not wanting to talk."

I put the chair in front of her. "No. I have trouble sitting with nothing to brace my back."

She shrugs the sleeping bag off her shoulders. Even though the sun is down, the earth is still warm. It will cool quickly, and I wish she'd let me join her in the shell.

"I remember us sitting and talking," I say. "I was always exhausted. You were talking and it felt like you were poking at me."

"Poking?"

"Telling me all the ways I was inadequate."

"Maybe I was poking. I guess I was. Like poking at a coyote in a cage. When I poked too hard, you got in your truck and drove west. I wouldn't see you for a few days."

"I didn't have enough margin to hear what you were saying. It felt like the city and the house and my job—everything was closing in on me."

"Every time I thought, 'This is it. He won't come back.' But then you always came back."

"To your disappointment."

"No! Stop talking like a teenaged boy."

I look toward the trailer. "Regret is worthless. Guilt is also. Unreliable emotions. Dishonest."

Just as I stand to go back in the trailer, she reaches and grabs my hand. I sit on the tailgate, and she leans against me. I can't move or she'll fall over. I stop and think for a moment. "I hurt you every time I ran away. What does it mean that we wanted to hurt each other?"

"I don't know."

"Maybe it means what we decide it will mean."

She puts her arm across my shoulders and pulls me even closer. "I want to stop hurting you. I want us to stop hurting each other. I'm good at shifting away from emotional intimacy, and you're good at running when conflict begins. We each know the snake we've picked up."

"Yes, we do. We've left bruises on each other."

"Everyone is a walking bruise," she says.

I touch her hand. "I don't believe that," I say. "Thomas isn't. We don't have to be."

"I can't believe you'd say that. A gay man in Victorian times?"

"Right." My father and mother hurt each other, or mostly he bruised her by his drinking, but did she ever understand his drinking? He was self-medicating for depression. I think about Louis and Sarah enduring a thirty-year separation. Tons of hurting, tons of bruising. I think about Thomas, Marie, and Janet, each with their head in a different kind of socially unacceptable cloud. Thomas wanted to love men, and Marie wanted to be able to think like a man. Janet entered polygamy, also unconventional, but that was her limit, and she left them. I'm not sure Hugh ever received a bruise that he was conscious of, but his wives certainly hurt each other. "Everyone bruises everyone."

"It does seem pretty universal," she says. "But Alina doesn't seem bruised."

"A clear soul. I don't think they hurt her permanently, even when they refused to approve her thesis and kicked her out of the university."

"She doesn't seem to hold a grudge. I think that's important." She takes my hand in both of hers. "We could learn from her."

For some reason I remember what Carrie-Anne said about Karin missing me. I hope I haven't bruised her. "I want to see the kids."

"Karin doesn't understand why you left."

Despite what I said about regret being useless, I feel it like a crashing wave.

"Carrie-Anne has been inviting me to dinner once a week," she says. "Put on hold while I'm out here. But I can call her."

"Yes. That would be good."

"A week from Sunday," she says.

"OK."

Andrew and Lucía step out of the trailer. "Is it safe?" asks Lucía.

Emily laughs. "Yes."

I wish they hadn't interrupted. I look at Emily, but the moment is gone. We relaxed with each other toward the end of our talk, and I want to keep going for a while longer. Our progress feels good—but incomplete. Maybe it will never feel complete, maybe it's good that I'm hungry for more talking.

"We need your input," says Andrew.

"You told me I was the slave driver," Emily says. "I'd gone to bed."

"But now you're up," says Andrew.

Emily leans over and kisses me. Her lips are warm and moist. She smells and tastes like Emily. No surprise there, I guess. The familiarity blindsides me. It has been so long.

She breaks away before I'm ready. I grin at her.

"Alleluia!" Lucía winks at Emily.

"Yes," I say. "Praise be."

"Oh, get a grip, you two romantics," says Emily.

Lucía raises her eyebrows.

"And keep your eyebrows quiet, Lucía," Emily says to her. "You're not nearly as good at that as Alina."

"Hmm," says Lucía, wriggling her eyebrows. "Maybe she'll give me lessons."

"In your dreams," says Andrew. He turns to Emily, "You are also a romantic. You are one to your core."

"I'm an idealist," Emily says. "I want to make things right in the world."

"A romantic idealist."

She's smiling with Andrew. We all are. Despite how much work I know Emily and I still have before us, I'm also infected by good cheer.

I don't turn on the light in my bedroom. I don't want the Dead Fathers to drive away my cheerfulness. I think about sleeping in my clothes, but I hate how they bind against me in bed. I could hide them, but where? I take my shirt and pants off in the dark and fold them under my pillow.

"Chris," says one of them, probably my father. "We need to talk."

"No, we don't!" I whisper.

"We sure do, you disobedient son of a bitch!" That's certainly Louis.

"It's just a cave!" I say. "You have lost your minds!" Maybe spirit brains are different from living human brains.

"And the tree of knowledge of good and evil was just a tree," says Hugh.

I think about saying that the original experiment in disobedience didn't turn out so bad, but I know it will just make the argument even more strident. Did Eve do the best thing? A debatable question, with the world so full of cruelty.

"Listen to what we say!" says my father. "We have a better perspective than you do. You're acting like a petulant teenager. Just do what we're telling you to do!"

"When you were alive, you weren't cryptic and authoritarian! Why are you this way now?"

"Because we care about you," says my father.

"I don't want to talk about it!" I say—too loud. Someone knocks on the wall. I cover my head with my pillow, my face in my trousers, holding tight to them with both hands. Maybe they won't be able to take them from me if I have a good grip. Or they'll just wait until I'm asleep. "Go away!"

I know that individual good people can be unreasonable when they join together under a banner. But it's not clear what the DFs' banner is. Maybe God the Father's but not God the Mother's? I'm not used to thinking about the earth being sustained by only a male God; they are the definition of unity. But the DFs are at enmity with the Dead Mothers. Doesn't make sense. Emily and I are familiar with enmity, so I know it's possible, but I thought the afterlife was more peaceable.

I don't move for what feels like ten minutes. My previous vision of these men was of caring, loving, even-minded people. Grandpa was stern and distant, but I knew he loved me. Once on my birthday he took me to look for moonstones on the foothills east of his fields. I still have the stones we found. I remember him older, sitting in his chair in his cabin, playing poker with Dad and me. I have good memories of my father: crossing a sunlit meadow with him in the Uintas, his beaming face when I show him my first high school news article, his stories about the desert at the dinner table.

Now they're always criticizing me. It's clear they are frightened. Fear can pinch anyone's vision. I wish I knew what they're frightened of. I'm reduced to guessing that they fear the women are taking over. Not just the women, but also Thomas. Another illusion burst. I thought it was just on earth that men felt fearful of the power of women and queer people. It also seems ironic that the women I've talked to who are dead don't fear the power of the men they love. Their attitude is, "Oh, those boys, what are they up to now?" But the Dead Fathers? They're petrified that their power structure might crumble.

Finally, I remove the pillow and sit up. I can't see them in the dark, but it doesn't mean they're gone. I hold my breath and listen. I can't hear them breathing, but that might not mean anything either. Finally, I lie down again and shut my eyes. It feels like a victory.

I've just drifted off when someone says, "Christopher." A hand touches my head, startling me, and my body clenches with fear that turns instantly to anger.

"Dammit! Leave me alone." I put the pillow over my head again. I wonder which of them touched me. Maybe it wasn't one of them and was instead Thomas. It could even have been Andrew, though I can't imagine why he'd come into my room. Or Emily. I hope it wasn't her. It would be disastrous if she came in and I told her to go away. I don't know who it was. The touch was just another undecipherable event. The universe is more inscrutable than I have ever imagined—inscrutable and a revelation of wonder.

Later, I remove the pillow—waiting. But the room is silent. Are they gone? What does gone even mean with them? Time is relative, so space must be the same. Space-time is flexible and relative. Which makes me feel again that I may never be rid of them. Eternity never before seemed so lengthy and torturous.

TWELVE

Vacuum of Power

The trailer is quiet as I leave my room this morning. I push a button and my cup fills with coffee without grounds in the bottom of the cup. I sit at the table outside and listen to birdsong. Emily's truck is still. I'm the only one awake. Even the birds aren't raucous, as they would be if the desert had huge trees. There is reason to hope. In my past life, before I came to live in the desert, hope was often anxious—its object something I should strive for but would probably not get. I felt pressure to do things, commit acts that would bring to pass what I desired. Like a story. The hero tries and battles and journeys but takes a mess of wrong directions before the one right act that turns the story around. I'm discovering that good also comes to those who wait.

Emily is the very definition of hope manifested as hustle, but I also know this is not what she wants from me in response to her "not yet." It certainly wasn't an invitation for me to strive or toil, endeavor or sweat, travail or moil or overexert, or any other number of ardent synonyms. Slow and relaxed, sometimes difficult or even painful, talking is the ticket to a future with her. I don't need to take extraordinary actions to reclaim her heart.

As if my grandmother, Sarah Quayle Twist, stands behind me, I hear the words, "Yes. Hope and be still," in her voice. I turn around, but nobody's there.

Then I hear another voice, slightly deeper but still feminine, "It doesn't mean you should do nothing at all with your life. Those also serve who get up off their derrière." The woman has a slight French accent, my great-grandmother Marie.

Before long, Emily opens the back of the shell and climbs out of her bed. She gets a cup of coffee and sits in the chair next to me, her shoulder touching my shoulder. When I turn to smile at her, my hat bumps her forehead.

"The sun isn't even up," she says. "Take it off so you don't put my eye out."

"This hat won't put your eye out." I take it off anyway.

"When you lived in the city, you didn't wear a cowboy hat."

"Yes, I compromised and wore a bill cap. I even wore it in the office, writing at my desk. People used to make fun of me. Out here I don't have to compromise my values."

She gives me a wry smile. "So it isn't just a practical decision. You do it because you idolize your grandfather."

I'll never admit she's right. I'm thinking about Grandpa Louis. The first thing he did in the morning was to reach for his hat and boots and stride out to the outhouse. When he came back he'd slip off his boots and put on his pants and shirt. At the old trailer I did the same. It pleased me to stride out in my underwear, free from propriety. "A cowboy hat is practical. This hat protects the back of my neck as well as my face. A bill cap wouldn't do that." I don't idolize him now: he's a pushy, cantankerous, stubborn man. But I feel the loss. He was my model for standing up to the man when I was a journalist.

A pair of sparrows fly down toward the horse barn, and we both look toward Bennie's truck parked there.

I say, "I wonder how long Alina will stay working for Spencer."

"Not your concern." She stands and stretches, a pleasant sight. "But I agree. He's a bastard and she'll soon get tired of him." She sits back down, shivering a little from the cold. "He's organized an ATV ride up a side road in Lost Canyon—Take Back Our Road Rally. The BLM closed the road because of a petroglyph panel there. He's invited every redneck rebel in the state. Some are coming in from out of state."

"He's like my grandfather," I say. "Doesn't like people telling him what to do and what not to do."

"Like someone else I know."

I reach to take her hand. "I always do what you say."

She smiles. "I wish."

"You told me to bathe and I did."

"After a week."

She's right. I'm as stubborn as my grandfather. But she is more stubborn than either of us. "We're bullheaded, both of us. That's why you love me."

"Whatever." But she smiles for a second before getting back to business. "Some of our people are coming out the night before the rally. Activists. We're going to camp on the road below the art rock panel and block it so nobody can ride past."

She's still fully in the world of striving, but that doesn't mean she wants me to go all Type A on her. Despite this, I still find myself wanting to hurry her up. How I proceed matters. Roses: no. Talking: yes. Saying romantic things: no. Saying kind things: Yes. Inserting myself into her business: no. Allowing myself to be interested in her work: yes.

"I'm going to explore a hole in the ground," I say. "I hope I never come to the end of it."

Bennie's truck drives toward us and stops next to Emily's truck. He and Alina get out.

"You two look cozy," says Alina.

Emily looks from her to Bennie. "I don't think we're the ones who've gotten cozy."

"You know that's not what I meant. Bennie and I, we weren't cozy."

"Far from it," says Bennie. "Cozy is not the word. Not at all." He looks at Alina. "Maybe someday."

Alina waggles her finger at him. "I like you, but you will be disappointed if you think that way. If you make plans for me."

His face turns sad. Alina watches and laughs. "You look like a little puppy. Makes me want to hit you with a newspaper." She taps one finger on his nose.

He shrugs and I realize another reason I like Alina: she refuses to let someone put her in a box. She stubbornly follows her own direction. When she felt that her committee in Amsterdam was trying to impose limits on her work, she ignored them, and when they used their authority to impose their will, she left not just the university, but the city, the country, and the continent.

"Spencer's coming tonight," she says. "He wants me to ride somewhere with him on his ATV. He's being secretive about it."

Alina sees Bennie frowning and gives him a shove. "Whether or not I jump into bed with him is not your business."

"Does he want you to?" asks Bennie. "That bastard."

Alina says, "Back off, Bennie."

Emily tells Alina, "Spencer's planning a rally near the rock art panel south of here. We're going to block the road with our bodies and keep them from going up that canyon. I just wanted to let you know."

"I won't be there." Alina turns from Bennie to Emily and her frown fades. "I'm apolitical."

"I don't believe that," Emily says.

"You caught me. But I'm going to be apolitical about this rally. I'm interested in seeing more of this place, so I'll go with him tomorrow, but I won't ride in the rally with them." She shrugs. "And it would be a bad idea for me to join you."

She doesn't seem happy about choosing sides. She's like me in this. Everyone in the world seems to be choosing sides and I want none of it.

After breakfast Emily and the others get in the van, and Emily tells me out the window that they'll spend the night in town because they have meetings today and tomorrow. Alina and I use Emily's truck to haul equipment up to the hole. There are footprints that are not ours, and not far away, truck tire tracks. I point them out to Alina.

She asks, "Do you think the people in the blue truck went down into the cave?"

I shrug. "We'll find out."

She ties our tools to a rope and lowers them, shakes them free. Then she ties a bowline around my waist and lowers me. She climbs down the rope, much more skillfully than I did the day before. I flash my headlamp around, but I can see only our tracks. I'm relieved that the strangers didn't enter the cave, but I don't like that they know where it is.

I follow Alina as we slide our equipment and then ourselves under the rock face. Carrying a shovel and pick, I think about one autumn in grade school, the fourth or fifth grade. We brought shovels and picks to school and dug tunnels in the hillside above the building. They weren't tunnels exactly, just deep ditches, but we covered the tops with boards and cardboard and dirt. When it was finished, we crawled around the passageways on our hands and knees. It was our maze, not belonging to anyone in particular. Ours. I realize that I think of the cave the same way, not as mine, not even as belonging to Alina and me, but as ours, humanity's, the Earth's. Emily might say I'm remembering my hippie days, even though that was a few years before our time, or that I've gone native. The Goshutes also once believed land and water and resources belong to everyone.

When we come to the rock fall, Alina pries the boulders loose with the crowbar and I roll them to the side of the tunnel. Then we trade places. I stick the bar behind a rock as big as a washtub but can't move it. I clear smaller rocks away from underneath it.

"Stand back!" I say. Then I shove hard against the pry bar. The massive boulder moves a little.

"Wait," she says. She joins me and we push together on the bar. The rock finally comes loose but rolls only a few feet.

"It's staying where it is," I say. "We'll have to work around it."

I climb to the top and flash my light up. I can see where the dirt and rock filling the tunnel came from, an irregular space about three yards wide and a little higher than that.

"More could fall any time," I say.

"Let me look."

I move out of the way, standing back on the floor of the tunnel. "Be careful."

Then she's standing up into the hole. All I can see are her calves and then not them.

"Alina!" I call. I hear her voice, muffled. Against my better judgment, I climb the fall of boulders and point my light up. I see her light flashing around. Then I see her face.

"It caved in because there's another room up here, another cavern."

"Does it go anywhere?"

"Not that I can see," she says. "It's just a cavity in the rock. Look out. I'm coming down."

I move back and soon she joins me.

"I think we can keep digging," she says. "Carefully."

We go back to her prying boulders loose and me rolling them back out of the way. She's working on top of the fall of rocks and dirt, and I'm below rolling boulders farther down. Then she disappears. "I'm through, but it needs to be wider for you."

I move more rocks back into the tunnel. It makes me nervous to work with that dark opening above me—I keep expecting a boulder to hit me. That would be bad enough, but it could as easily be tons of rock.

Alina works from the other side, and soon there is a space big enough for me to squeeze through. I climb down and we walk forward. It's comforting to have a solid ceiling above us again, even if it's an illusion. We could come to another place where the ceiling is weak.

The tunnel sometimes widens into a room, sometimes tightens so much that we have to crouch or even crawl to get through. We continue slightly downhill, clambering over boulders.

"Let's stop and eat," says Alina. "I'm starving."

I'm also hungry. I packed cheese sandwiches, apples, and sodas. She finishes one sandwich in about a minute and starts on the next.

"Do you miss being a newspaper editor?"

"No. I got out just in time. They're all dying now."

She takes another bite and a piece of crust drops on the ground. She picks it up and puts it in the wrapper of her first sandwich. "Not dying. Moving online."

"It's not the same," I say. "Small newspapers can't compete with social media for ads, so everything people read is national news, nothing local."

She finishes and puts the wrappers in her backpack. "That's why dinosaurs became extinct. They couldn't change."

I'm still on my first sandwich. "Or a meteor burned them up. Nothing they could do."

"The theory isn't that a meteor burned them but that the meteor changed the climate. Or that ash from volcanoes changed the climate. Or a disease killed them all."

"Sounds familiar," I say. "Maybe we'll go extinct from climate disruption." I offer her my other sandwich but she shakes her head.

"I took a climate seminar." She stands and puts on her backpack. "Before they kicked me out and I escaped to this place."

"We were both running from something."

"You were running from Emily? That seems—ah—not very smart."

I feel prickly at this line of conversation, but Alina is just herself, disarmingly friendly and honest. I finish my sandwich and take a long drink.

"I agree."

"You're lucky she came after you."

"Yes, I am." I put my trash in my backpack and stand. We start walking again.

"Bennie thinks she's remarkable. Every case she takes on has impact—social or environmental or political."

"She used to be in a legal firm that had mostly corporate clients. She decided she was generally arguing for the wrong side."

"I imagine that a person so driven might be difficult to live with."

I keep my face as blank as I can.

She laughs. "I know you two have had your difficulties, but it is sweet that you're focusing on each other again. I avoid making any long-term commitments. You keep taking vacations from yours. Which is worse?"

I stop walking. "What I did was worse. Losing touch with Emily, my children and grandchildren." She turns toward me, flashing her light in my eyes.

"Losing touch?"

"Distancing myself." She walks ahead and I follow her.

"But you're not distant from Emily now, are you?"

"Yes," I say. "There's still some distance between us."

"Some distance is good."

"You're right," I say. And she is. But I want to go home with Emily and to see Karin, and my other grandchildren. "Emily and I are finding the right proportion." We walk in companionable silence for a moment. "You remind me of my granddaughter—Karin."

"Childish?"

She turns, and I point my light at her feet so it doesn't flash in her eyes. "No! Frank and precise. Saying whatever she thinks and not caring what people think."

"Thank you."

I still find it remarkable how quickly I've relaxed around Alina when generally I have resented anyone who imposed on my space. I feel lucky she came to the desert.

The tunnel is a single continuous tunnel, which seems unusual to me. I would have thought a natural cave would have more branches. It's difficult to tell how long we've been underground.

"We should turn around," Alina says at the same time that I say, "We better go back."

Alina laughs. "Five more minutes."

We have only walked one minute when we come to a side branch, a small hole that leads to the left. I shine my light into it and the small tunnel opens up on the other side, but it doesn't look like the part of the cave we've gone through—more angled. I slither through and stand. I'm in a man-made tunnel. I can tell from the uniform arch to the ceiling and walls and from the scars of tools on the rocks. Alina stands next to me.

"*Ten* more minutes," she says, walking forward.

The passage is like all the tunnels in the Valley of the Mines that I explored before I started looking for the cave the Goshute hid in. Above ground, the cave entrance is only a half mile from the Valley of the Mines and we've been going downward for hours, so it would make sense if it intersected with one of the mines. Soon my suspicions are confirmed when we come out into a large room with many tunnels spreading out from it. It's the same mine I showed Emily, the one with the new ladder. The miners must have tunneled into the cave a century ago. I wonder how far they explored it. I'm grateful they didn't seem to damage anything.

It makes sense but at the same time it doesn't: we were in a strange cave that I had made into something mystical as I thought about it, and now we're in a mine. It's like the world has turned ninety degrees off true and nothing is the same. I think of the hundreds of yards of dirt and rock above us, none of it stable.

Suddenly I've had enough of being underground. "This way." I find the tracks and walk fast along them.

"Wait!" she says. "Where are we going?"

I don't know why I'm panicking but I can't focus enough to figure it out.

"Chris!" Her voice is from farther behind me. "Where are we going?"

"Look!" I say, pointing to the light ahead. I'm walking toward it and I hear Alina following again.

We're standing on the flat in front of the opening, and I point down at the tin building, the creek, and the road we walked along just hours before. "Here we are. It's good to see the sky again."

Alina grins, spreading her arms and turning to look at the valley and the ring of hills around it. Of course her motion continues in a whirling, leg-kicking dance.

I bend forward with my hands on my knees and breathe. "What?"

"I don't know. A panic attack or something."

"We're out now."

"Yes." Exploring the cave feels like my life, familiar and then strange, where I can't seem to get my feet under me.

"Chris, maybe you should sit down." Her hands are on my arm, pulling me toward an outcropping of rock where I can sit. She takes off my pack and hands me my water bottle. "Drink."

I feel foolish because nothing happened that would warrant feeling as I do.

"We were underground a long time," she says, pointing westward, where the sun sits just on the peak of Turkey Mountain. I'm surprised it's so late.

"I probably wore myself out moving all that rock," I say.

"I'm tired as well," she says. "But it was a good day. An adventure."

We walk down the mountain to the road, and soon we're back at the truck. I drive us down toward the camp. When we emerge from the cedars, I point to Spencer's horse barn—to his truck pulling a trailer, probably filled with his four-wheelers. "Maybe he'll fire you. Just like he fired me."

"Probably he won't fire me," says Alina. "Probably he'll forgive me."

"You may be right." I stop the truck on the road next to the camp.

"That was a good day, Chris," she says. "And we still didn't get to the end of the cave." She looks at me. "Will you go back in?"

I nod. "Tomorrow?"

"I can't. Remember, I'm riding ATVs with Spencer."

"Do you want me to drive you to your place?"

"No." I watch her walk toward the horse barn. A brilliant sunset spreads across the plain.

"Nice girl," says a voice. I turn and both Thomas and Marie sit at the table. I'm pleased they have come together. They are next to each other, and if there was once bitterness between them, it seems to have faded.

"She is unusual. She moves right past my barriers. I don't usually take to people so quickly." I sit opposite them. He's wearing a loose robe that looks like it's made of silk. I can't tell what color it is because it seems to be many colors at once. She's wearing a bright yellow blouse and white skirt. "I don't understand why someone so brilliant thinks she'll be satisfied just watching Spencer's buildings."

"She's doing the same job you were doing," says Thomas. "Why is it different with her?"

"I'm an old man. She'll get antsy soon."

"Why don't you tell her what you're thinking?" says Marie. "Maybe your wisdom will save her from herself." I think I could listen to her deep, French-accented voice all day.

They're both laughing at me.

I say, "She doesn't need me to advise her on her life choices."

"You're catching on," says Thomas. "A fledgling human."

"I'm glad she's here. It wouldn't be safe for me to go into the cave alone."

"She has a part to play," says Marie. "A difficult part that requires diplomacy and objectivity."

"And mathematical brilliance," says Thomas.

"Which she has in abundance," says Marie. "I may one day have the pleasure of sitting in on her conversation with Hypatia, Newton, Lovelace, Euclid and the others who are thinking about structure." It didn't take her long to get to name dropping.

"Explain." I hold my hand out. "Not about the mathematicians club. But about her part in all this." Maybe they'll be more forthright than the Dead Fathers.

"Patience," says Thomas. "You know what you need to know. In the absence of the Mother and Father, factions have developed. You don't need to dive in like a falcon."

"You are so pompous." Marie turns to me. "You are pleased with your day."

"Yes. We still have more of the cave to explore."

"What do you think you'll find?" asks Marie.

"I just wanted to find the cave Thomas wrote about. I like the idea of walking where the old Goshute walked. But. There is something in that cave. The Dead Fathers didn't want me going down there."

"I wonder if they're just underestimating the power of a good day," says Marie. "Or the beauty of a geologic formation."

"Don't you know what's there? You're the ones beyond the veil."

"Such a curious metaphor." Thomas stretches one hand flat in front of him—turns it over.

"More like a Möbius band that seems to have two sides but doesn't," says Marie. "A spatial anomaly."

I shake my head. "You're confusing me."

Thomas frowns, seeming genuinely pained. "I'm not trying to keep things from you. I don't know any secrets. There are petroglyphs at the end of the cave, but they're just petroglyphs. They don't contain a secret message. I know your other fathers are trying to make declarations. They want to make it seem that everything is at stake."

"It's what they do best," says Marie. "Try to steady the ark. Get their panties in a bunch." She chuckles. I think she really likes saying that about Hugh, Louis, and my father.

He leans forward. "Tell me about Emily."

"Emily?" I take a breath. "I think she may love me again."

"Again?"

I shake my head slowly. "Again and still. Old and new."

"That's so nice. I'm happy for you," he says.

"She has such interesting friends," says Marie.

"Her team?"

She nods. "I approve of their—ah—endeavors. In other words, I like their politics."

"Team," says Thomas, almost a question. "Endeavors. Politics. Words are so inadequate." He spreads his hands wide. "But they're what we have, right?" He's looking at me, not looking away. His face is familiar from the photographs I have of him, but also strange. To see his face change expression when I felt it was static forever. We have maybe half a dozen photos someone put in the archives. His face is similar to his father's face, and his son's, and grandson's, and mine. But also new, himself. It's like looking in a mirror and not, both at once. Surreal. Or superreal.

"Yes, you two are like twins," says Marie. "Doppelgangers."

"And Carrie-Anne?" asks Thomas.

"She wants me to come back to the city."

"What will you do?"

"I don't have a place here anymore," I say. "I'll have to go somewhere. I might as well go home."

"Does that disappoint you?"

I realize that it doesn't. "Soon. I'll go back. See my grandkids."

"That will be nice." Thomas stands. "It's good to see you again."

Marie smiles. "Thomas is such a tender man. He doesn't care much about ideas, but he listens to me out of courtesy."

They actually seem happy to converse with me. It feels like we are old friends. Which is bewildering, because I never knew Thomas in life, and I only met Marie a handful of times at big family reunions. The other bewildering thing is that the Dead Fathers implied that Thomas and Marie were acrimonious. They seem to get along fine. The DFs seem to say whatever serves their purpose, sometimes they say the truth, but sometimes they don't.

Marie nods and they're both gone. Or more accurately, I can't see them. Not with my eyes. But I know that he's still smiling, happy to see me, and that she still has an ironic twist to her mouth, something like what Alina does with her eyebrows but even more ironic, if that is possible.

As the sun sets, I look across the flat. It has been inhabited for thousands of years, ever since the lake shrank and went underground. The old people, the Goshutes, the Spanish and other explorers, pioneers going to California, the Wells Fargo wagons, Mormon pioneers (my ancestors and others), sheepherders (Anglos, Navajos, Mexicans, and Basques). Now new people, the rock hunters, four-wheelers, polygamists, army people, speculators—all following their desires or their desperate needs. A remarkable confusion. The confusion is more marvelous than I had imagined, a landscape where the living and dead pass each other, weaving a pattern as complex as the mind of God.

As dusk gathers, I go inside and heat up a can of chili. After eating, I sit on my bed. The wind whispers past the trailer, which makes it feel even emptier. I miss Lucía and Andrew. I wait for the Dead Fathers to show up with their cards. I wanted them to leave me alone, so I'm surprised that I miss them. I remember how it was when they first came—they seemed happy to see me. It was later that they became pushy and argumentative, but I miss even that.

Finally I undress and lie under my covers. Soon, I'm asleep and dreaming of the paths of animals crossing a hillside: the pronghorn follows a path of light, badgers and skunks on smaller lit paths, tiny paths of rodents, snakes and insects—adding their pathways to the human ones in a web of light. This light fills me also, and my soul brims with joy so full that I can hardly contain it.

Waking to the roar of Spencer's four-wheelers, I step out of the trailer and watch him and Alina head south to Lost Canyon, where the rock art panel is. They're probably planning the route for the rally in a week and a half. I hope Emily and her group will be all right when she tries to oppose Spencer's herd of four-wheeler riders.

I told both Alina and Emily I wouldn't go up to the cave alone. I clean the trailer instead, sweeping and mopping the floor, wiping down surfaces in the kitchenette, washing the windows, shaking out the rugs. I shower. I only have the one set of clothes, so I wrap myself in a towel, fill the sink, put my soiled clothes in it, pour in some dish soap, and scrub with my hands. I stretch a rope between two juniper trees and drape my laundry across the rope.

By lunchtime I'm still alone. I put my clothing back on and eat a sandwich by myself. I worry that the Dead Fathers have abandoned me forever because I refused to listen to them, that Emily's team will be harmed by the rallying rednecks, and that I soon may have to become a responsible human being again. Emily's mother Sondra sits across from me, and my first thought is that Emily has had an accident. My gut tightens.

She puts her hand on my arm. "Don't worry," she says. "Emily's fine."

"You scared me. I thought you had come with bad news."

"No, Christopher. I'm sorry I frightened you." Men are not supposed to get along with their mother-in-law, but she and I were friends.

"I've missed you," I say.

She seems puzzled at that.

"I'm glad you two have come to your senses," she says.

"Have we?"

"It seems that way."

I'm happy her mother thinks Emily and I will get together again. "What was Emily like as a child? She's told me her version—that you didn't know what to do with her."

"That's pretty much it. When Emily was little, she was such a determined child. I could never change her mind about anything. Sometimes she did what I said, but to keep the peace, not because I'd convinced her. She was that way at age two and I thought it was just the terrible twos, but she never changed. Not in that one respect. She had this tiny fury face when I crossed her. Then it was a larger fury face."

"I'm glad she's basically a good person."

"Yes." She frowns. "There is that. You'll survive."

"Yes, I think we will."

She touches my arm. "You're missing my point. They'll be back. Samuel and the others. They won't let up. Others will come. It's going to get ugly."

"They say there's a war coming, but they won't be specific."

"Get your binoculars," she says.

I get them and she shows me where to look—a building about two miles out into the testing grounds. There is a truck in front of the Quonset hut where we thought the distilling equipment was. Two men get out of the truck. They look like the General and Nephi, but from this distance I can't be sure.

"What are they going to do?"

"They'll soon move the equipment again. You better do something about that."

Then she is gone as well. I feel my journalistic curiosity itching. Why are these two men in league? That they are cooperating is all by itself a disquieting fact, but I feel strongly that what they're doing somehow connects to the battle that's coming. Once an investigative reporter, always one. I am determined to uncover everything that the Dead Fathers, Nephi, and the General are hiding.

Late that evening, Emily and the others come back—all except for Bennie. Their faces are somber.

Emily speaks first. "The company that wants to store radioactive waste on the rez gave a presentation on how much money every member of Bennie's tribe will make. About half of them were swayed, and we couldn't convince them of the dangers."

"That's frustrating," I say.

"It's part of the job," says Andrew.

"Where's Bennie?"

"He went to his house instead of driving back here," says Lucía. She looks at Andrew. "I'm starving."

"Leftovers," he said. "I'm bone weary."

They go inside.

"What are you going to do now?" I ask.

Emily looks at me. "Do something the bastards won't expect."

"What?"

"I don't know yet."

I tell her about the truck and what her mother said they planned to do.

"You saw my mother?" she says. "Why didn't she come to me?"

I shrug.

"She was—is—the most peaceable woman I've ever known. It surprises me that she'd get involved."

"Everyone seems to be choosing sides."

"So what does my work have to do with the concerns of the dea—of our, your, ancestors."

"I don't have a clue." It's funny to hear her try to talk about all this crazy business. I think she's thrown off kilter even more than I am.

"So what will you do?"

We hear Spencer's four-wheelers returning. Alina goes inside the apartment and Spencer climbs in his truck. He doesn't wave at us as he passes.

Emily glances toward Lucía and Andrew, who stand inside eating from plates on the counter. She lowers her voice. "Tonight at midnight we'll ride bicycles out there and take some pictures."

"You want me to come?"

"Only if you want."

"I want. But you don't have a bike." When she frowns, I say, "I'll bet you can borrow Alina's."

"I'll drive down to get it." She walks toward her truck. "I want to talk to her anyway."

"Do you want some food first?"

"No."

It's clear she means talk to her alone, so I go to my bedroom, hoping to sleep.

The Dead Fathers wait for me, sitting on my bed, so there's no room. Hugh is shuffling the cards, a sour look on his face. My father and Louis squeeze together and I join them, but we're so crowded that I pull the chair over. Again, it seems odd the way they're sitting—next to each other where they can easily see each other's cards. It would make the game less enjoyable, except that they seem to know all the hands anyway.

Hugh drops a pile of juniper twigs of different lengths on my lap. I go out to the kitchenette to get a cutting board and trim them with my pocketknife.

They smile at me. "Good idea, son," says my father.

I nod at each one, determined to control myself and my voice so I don't wake the others this time. But I also want to make them be straight with me. They owe it to me. I don't like all the tension between us.

Something about the smiles, a tightness at the corners, makes the affability forced. All of them look like my father did when once as a teen I was out talking until three o'clock in the morning to a girl who wanted to break up with me. She did. When I got home, Samuel came out of his room. "Hello, son, where have you been?" he said. He had the same tight, forced smile he's giving me now. I was so distraught over the girl that I couldn't talk to him but went straight to my bedroom.

At first I win a few twigs, but I know that won't last.

"In outer darkness," says Hugh conversationally, "every being is alone."

"That's funny," I say, "because that's just what I wanted when I first came out here. Then you showed up to keep me company."

"You're lucky that we wouldn't let that happen to you," says my father. "We would never leave you alone."

"I have mixed feelings about that," I say.

"The souls in outer darkness are frozen for eternity," says Hugh. "They can never commerce with another soul, so they are stuck."

"Dammed, as it were," says Louis.

"Emily has changed my mind about being alone. I want to be with my children, my grandchildren, my friends."

"What friends?" asks Louis. "We're the only damn friends you have."

I give him my sarcastic coyote grin.

"You and Emily have a strong bond," says my father.

"But she's like a snake in the garden," says Hugh. "The initiator of chaos."

I shrug irritably but say nothing.

"She's an aberration," says Louis. "And your marriage is a fucking travesty."

"That seems a bit harsh," says my father. "She's a good woman at heart."

"I wish you'd never left the ranch," Louis says. "You'd be a better person." I realize he's talking to me, not to my father, despite the fact that we both left the desert to have careers in the city. My father shifts uncomfortably, but my grandfather doesn't look at him. His hope, when I was a teenager and came out to work on the ranch every summer, was that I would take my father's place and be a rancher all my life. Instead, when he got old he couldn't keep it up and he lost it. According to him, we both broke his heart.

Hugh clears his throat. "What I was saying is that there is an order to things that is threatened now, since in the absence of our heavenly parents there's a vacuum of power. Many want to take advantage. But those who are determined to spread chaos will be cast into outer darkness, because that's where they belong, unmoored from the Father, abhorred by his children. Is that the state of being you want for yourself?"

I think of a poem by Stephen Crane that I read to Emily when we were courting, so I say it softly to the Dead Fathers:

> Should the wide world roll away
> Leaving black terror
> Limitless night,
> Nor God, nor man, nor place to stand
> Would be to me essential
> If thou and thy white arms were there
> And the fall to doom a long way.

"Well, that's depressing," says my father.

"Lacking the communion of the Saints," says Hugh. "So bleak and lonely."

"If it's a choice between Emily in hell and no Emily in heaven, I'll take hell."

"But that's the whole point," says Hugh. "In hell you're all alone."

"Are you three in hell? Or do you go back to your wives when you're not with me?"

That shuts them up.

"A few more questions," I say. "How is Emily spreading chaos?"

"She broke up your family with her adultery," says Hugh. "And she's disrupting what I came to this country to get. You know, in Wales my father didn't own the land he farmed? The lord of the estate rented it to him. My grandfather? Worked for wages. His father? Sharecropped on the lord's land. Out here was land for the taking. Every man could have whatever he could properly manage. That's the beauty of this country, economic opportunity, the freedom to make your own way. That woman—"

"Emily," I say.

"—is disrupting freedom for the mining company, for your friend the polygamist who needs to provide for his dependents, for the people who want freedom to ride their vehicles where they wish."

"That's a stretch," I say. "Freedom doesn't mean harming others or cheating the government or damaging public resources. That's small minded."

Hugh glares at me.

"I have another question. If Mother and Father are in a trial separation, why aren't the prophet and the apostles in Salt Lake talking about it?"

"From what I hear," says my father, "they don't want to cause an uproar among the members. Can you imagine what would happen if everyone knew what you know?"

"They're cowardly businessmen in suits," says Louis. "Their attention is more on the church's wealth than on salvation." When he was alive, he basically had the same attitude.

"I'm just a lowly Jack Mormon," I say, "but I don't think that's true."

"They're just not upset about it," says my father. "I'm as surprised as you. Really, it's inexplicable."

"Oh, it's explicable," I say. "You three are trying to steady an ark that's not toppling."

"Oh, it's not just us, everyone in this whole region is upset," says my father. "Everyone."

"The Mothers don't seem upset."

He scratches his head.

"War is definitely coming," says Hugh.

"What is my role?"

My father sighs, Louis paces. Hugh looks pained, constipated really.

"We've told you before," says my father. "We don't know exactly."

"We don't know all," says Hugh, "but we know that unless you start paying attention to our instruction—"

"We're all going to be in a world of hurt," says Louis.

I lose steadily until all my strong-smelling juniper twigs are gone, then I push past the Dead Fathers and slide under the half of the sheet and blanket they aren't sitting on. I pull the pillow over my head. When I take it off five minutes later, they have vanished. I never noticed when their weight left the bed.

THIRTEEN

Arrested!

At midnight, I come out of my room and stand next to Emily's truck. Her light is on and through the back window of her shell, I watch her loading a small backpack. I'm pleased that I find her beautiful. She looks up and smiles, even though she probably can't see me. Somehow, she knows I'm there. Probably from the sound of my walking or breathing. I like it that she seems to brighten when I'm there. That's old and new.

We load my bike in back on top of Emily's sleeping bag. Alina's bike is already tied to the roof of the shell. I climb in the passenger side, and Emily drives over the road to Simpson Springs campground, switches off her headlights, and creeps along a side dirt road down to some sheep corrals next to the border fence of the testing grounds. She parks and we unload our bikes. We swing them over the barbed wire and woven wire fence, built to keep sheep, cattle, and wild horses off the testing grounds. The signs warning that this is a testing ground, where they use live ammo and live bombs, should keep us out but don't. Her backpack has two handles sticking out the top, and when I check I discover she has a bolt cutter inside.

"Where did you get that?"

"Doesn't every lawyer carry a bolt cutter in their backpack?"

"Only law breakers."

"I got it from Alina."

"Resourceful."

"Here we go," she says, riding her bicycle across the flat. I follow and it's not too rough, mostly alkali soil, which won't grow anything except halogeton. It's easy to ride bikes over. We ride around occasional clumps of white sage. There is no moon, so it's difficult to see where we're going.

The crunch of our tires, the cool of the night, and the sight of Emily riding in front of me all make me feel like I could ride straight into the sky.

"We've never been on an adventure like this, have we?" I say.

"There was the time we cut a Christmas tree on Forest Service land without a permit," she says. "You were so frightened."

"It was my idea."

"You were still shaking in your boots."

I hear her breathing, maybe harder than I am. She'll never let on if it's too much for her.

In the distance to the northeast, I see the lights of the town of Skull Valley. I wonder about how much monitoring they do out in the deep of the testing ground. Is someone watching our progress through an image of our body heat? Probably. My greater worry is that we might ride through an area where nerve gas was tested.

When my father was a young man, he rode along the border fence, and a shell dropped not far from him inside the testing grounds. His horse jumped, but the real scare was when tan-colored gas boiled from the shell and the breeze took the cloud toward him. He said it was huge and kept getting bigger as smoke poured out of the shell. He rode the other direction as fast as he could but was soon enveloped by the gas. The cloud was odorless but thick, making it hard to breathe. He knew he was a dead man. He kept going and was soon out in the open air, heading for home. To his surprise, he and his horse were alive when they got there—never had any negative effects that he knew of. Of course he died of leukemia when he was six-ty-four.

Emily rides ahead and I think about the warning the Dead Fathers gave me; she doesn't seem like an agent of chaos to me—or no more an agent of chaos than anyone who takes action, hoping for a certain outcome. She's re-markably focused. Put together, as they say. I'm aiding her in breaking the law, but that's not the kind of chaos they're worried about.

We ride for about an hour and the desert's still quiet. When we arrive at the building, we can see no light. There is a padlock on the door, which Emily cuts with a quick motion, as if she's done it all her life. Inside, we turn on our flashlights and look around. I see bulbous boilers and copper tubing, similar but not identical to the ethanol dis-tilling equipment in Nephi's building.

"Eureka!" says Emily. She takes out a larger flashlight and starts a video on her phone, panning the room with her light and phone camera. It doesn't take her long. "Let's get out of here," she says. We climb on our bikes. She rides a short distance and then takes a few pictures of the building.

"They'll be too dark," I say.

We look at them, and they're just fine. The equipment shows up clearly. "I turned on the GPS, and the pictures are marked as to location."

We ride toward the fence. We're about halfway there when lights flash behind us. I turn and see two vehicles following. About the same time, I hear the growl of their engines. Soon they pass us and stop—jeeps full of armed soldiers.

"There's no reception here," says Emily quietly, "so the pictures are stuck on my phone."

"Try to upload them anyway," I say. "They'll go when they take us to Skull Valley and your phone gets into range."

I stand in front of her, hoping they won't see the light from her phone. I hold my hands up and the soldiers get out of the vehicle, their rifles pointed at us. It feels unreal, as if I'm in a movie that I'm also watching. Even as a reporter I was never in a situation like this. My heart is beating fast and I feel very much alive. I somehow keep myself from laughing out loud.

"Ma'am," one of the soldiers says. "Step out where we can see you."

She's silent and they take a step forward. I know they could actually shoot us, and I imagine myself draped across the hood of their vehicle like a deer carcass, blood draining out of my body.

"Emily," I say.

Finally, her bike drops and she steps out from behind me to my left, raising her hands. Two soldiers, a male and female, pat us down. The woman takes Emily's backpack and phone. They load our bikes and us into one of the jeeps and drive back past the building, continuing on toward the base. After a few minutes, we top a ridge and the lights of the military installation and the town spread wide ahead of us. We drive about a quarter hour more, nobody talking—which adds to my sense that this is all a dream. We're taken into a building and seated in a conference room. Two soldiers stay in the room with us, standing at attention, holding their rifles.

Before long, General Torrey comes in and sits at the head of the table. If they just woke him, it isn't evident because his hair is combed and his uniform impeccable. It doesn't look good for us. He shot a rifle at me. He won't hesitate to throw us in jail.

"Bring us coffee," he says. One of the soldiers returns with three paper cups. Then he stands next to the door. The General takes a long drink. He sets his cup down and glares at me. "What the hell, Christopher?"

"I couldn't sleep," I say. "So we went for a bike ride."

"What are you doing with whiskey distilling equipment?" Emily asks.

He turns to her, clearly puzzled, and I realize he doesn't know who she is. I wonder if we can keep that a secret, but they're probably going through her backpack, where she keeps her wallet. Even if she had taken it out, they would figure out her identity.

"This is my wife," I say. "Emily Ransome."

His eyes widen. "Emily Ransome? You're married to Emily Ransome?" Now I see lines of weariness around his eyes. He's older than me, but I should be wary: even an old coyote can bite.

She smiles at him, and he wipes his hands down his face. He turns to the soldier who served us coffee. "Bring us the phone."

The soldier lays the phone on the table, and the General slides it toward Emily. "Unlock it. It will save time. Delete the pictures, then we can talk."

She smiles again but doesn't touch the phone.

"You will have a criminal trespass on government property leveled against you. You'll lose your license to practice law."

She still just looks at him, the slightest smile on her lips.

"Pictures taken illegally will not be useful in court."

The General turns from her to me—as if I could be any help. I just shrug.

Emily asks, "Why do you have Nephi Johnson's distilling equipment in a shed on government property?"

"I don't—" It seems to sink in who he's talking to, and he shuts his mouth. The silence stretches. I'm used to silence, but this tactical silence makes me anxious. I clear my throat, but neither one looks at me. They're like two mountain sheep ready to butt heads.

He finally turns to me. "It has always been my policy to try to get along with the ranchers in this valley."

Right, I think. When Louis let army officers spotlight deer in his fields, he was both giving them recreation and getting rid of vermin. Win-win.

Before he can go on, Emily says, "Except when you let the wind blow nerve gas across their sheep herds."

"My predecessor was in charge when the Goshutes say that happened." He purses his lips but doesn't look at her. "Like I said, your family has been in this area of the desert for many generations, and I want to give you some slack, but I need control over those pictures."

Emily clears her throat, and he looks back toward her, frowning. She says, "You can talk about your old boys' club with the ranchers all you want, but you can't just ignore the fact that you have illegal distilling equipment stored in a building on government property." She doesn't know whether the pictures went to the cloud or not, so she's bluffing. "What I don't understand is your motivation."

I say, "He's shooting deer at night on Nephi's place."

The General taps a pencil on the table and then shifts his eyes away from me. My semi-dormant journalistic spidey sense says I'm right.

"That's not enough," says Emily. "There's something else." Her eyes widen, and she turns to me. "Where do you think Nephi sells his whiskey?"

"You numbskull!" I say to the General.

"Call the FBI," he says to the soldier next to the door. "Get them to authorize the county sheriff to arrest these two." He stands. "Then call the county sheriff." The soldier leaves.

Emily's face doesn't change.

The cell phone lies between them, but she doesn't look at it. Finally, he takes it and gives it to his assistant. "Open it, see if the pictures were uploaded to a cloud."

The General leaves the room. I'm surprised that they leave us alone, but then we're in a room in the middle of a military compound, and even at this ungodly hour, there's probably an armed soldier outside the door.

I lean toward her. "You were—"

She stops me with a small shake of her head. Does she think the room is bugged?

"—marvelous." I fold my hands in front of me. "I wouldn't have been able to keep from checking the phone."

She smiles slightly, pleased with herself.

"We may go to jail," I say.

She puts her hands behind her neck and stretches in her chair. "We're not done having new experiences." She puts her hand on mine. "We'll have to post bail."

"They'll put us in different cells." I look at her and am again moved again by her beauty. "I love you."

"We're already—still—in different cells." She smiles. "But maybe we're breaking out of them," she says softly. "Your attraction is attractive."

"Those words are attractive," I say.

She strokes my hand, and I hope the soldiers never come back.

I say, "What will the others do without you there?"

"I'll have to phone them. Lucía will take charge. And we won't be in jail long."

We look at each other, and neither one of us looks away. Her beauty seems consistent with her life. It's not the overwhelming but untried beauty of her youth when seeing her and touching her was like a drug, but a beauty that comes from making her face her own. Her intelligence shines like the light of the moon, her energy like something brighter.

As the sun comes up, a couple of soldiers throw our bikes in the back of a double cab pickup truck and drive us to Tooele. We go into the police station and are booked. The charges are registered, a bail bondsman meets with us, and we're done. As Emily predicted, the sheriff impounded our bikes as evidence. She borrows the bondsman's phone and calls Bennie to pick us up, and we walk to a café for breakfast while we wait for him.

We both order hotcakes, bacon, sausage, fried eggs, coffee, and orange juice—the whole shebang.

"Thanks," she says.

"For what?"

She looks down at her bacon. "For coming with me last night. For committing a crime with me. For being happy to see me."

"Let's sleep at home tonight," I say.

She looks at me.

"You said they could do without you for a while," I say.

"I lied," she says. "They'll fall apart without me. We have too much to do."

The server brings our drinks. I pour creamer in my coffee and take a long draft. It's a good moment because I know the caffeine will kick in soon.

"But I can join you in your room," she says.

My heart smiles. Then I think about the Dead Fathers standing over us. "Or in your truck."

"It's a single mattress."

"Same in my room," I say.

"But more vertical room."

I grin and it feels like my birthday all over again: Emily is willing.

They bring our food, and I dig in. I'm famished.

"You have butter on your face," she says. She wipes it off with her finger, and I take her finger in my mouth.

"You're acting like a teenager," she says. She removes her finger and frowns.

"Yes, I am. Isn't it fun?" My heart jumps again, but it's half anxiety this time.

"It is. But it feels premature. Also, not sustainable. That's what we learned."

I don't want to get mired in the past again. But that's both impossible and unhelpful. "You're right. But we also learned that we need a little spice, a little adventure."

"Like getting arrested?" She finally smiles.

"Now that's not sustainable. But yes. Maybe not that drastic, but having some order of adventure together."

"Good argument, counselor. But I still think we need to move slowly."

I smile at the idea of moving slowly, and she tries to glare at me, but ends up giggling like a teenager.

Not long after we finish eating, Bennie pulls up. As we climb in, he looks at our faces and shakes his head without a hint of a smile—which makes me laugh.

"Are you two drunk?"

Emily laughs as well.

"Drunk on life," I say.

"I disapprove," he says. He's wearing jeans and a Bob Marley T-shirt.

"Of life?" Emily asks.

"Of sneaking onto the testing grounds and getting yourselves arrested."

"Yes," says Emily, frowning. "It could cause us problems."

"We didn't even see the inside of a cell," I say.

"You sound disappointed," he says. "I want to never see the inside of a jail cell."

I don't know what to say to that because he and I would probably have a very different experience inside a Utah jail.

We drive south and up over Johnson's Pass. From the top, I see the desert spread before me, the volcanic peak of Turkey Mountain, the malformed hills and bluffs—white and gray and a little green—mostly cheatgrass. It feels like home, what Stegner or somebody called the proper edge of the sky.

We turn off near Simpson and retrieve Emily's truck. When we pull into the camp, everyone comes out to greet us, Alina as well.

"I told you," says Lucía. "She has no comprehension of the damage she's done."

"I wasn't arguing," says Andrew.

Lucía turns to me. "No sense of self-preservation."

"Right," I say happily.

Emily goes inside.

"You want to go to jail?" asks Alina.

"No," I say.

"That's not a reason to be so happy." Lucía catches my arm and examines my face. "How can you be such a good poker player with such a bad poker face."

Alina smiles and raises one eyebrow.

Bennie says, "This just means more work for us."

Andrew sighs and walks inside the trailer. I follow, anxious to find out if the pictures are secure. At a computer, Emily opens her cloud account and the photos are there, showing all Frank's distilling equipment. "Good. This will cause a stir."

"Or not," says Bennie. "These pictures have zero legal value."

"They have news value," says Emily. "The fact that the head of a military base has equipment that was used to make illegal alcohol."

"I question," says Lucía, "whether that's worth losing your license."

"It's not automatic."

"But it could happen," says Lucía. "The state law board could take it right away."

"We've already been arrested," I say.

Emily leans back. "But the General could drop charges if we give him these pictures."

"He's such an asshole," I say. "He might refuse to drop charges."

She turns toward me. "Still, we need to decide what we do—which I can't do until I get some sleep." She looks around. "Carry on."

"You should have talked to us," says Bennie. "We could have talked some sense into you."

"Maybe," says Lucía, looking from her to me. "Maybe not. She's always taking chances like this."

"Stop lecturing me, you two." Emily leaves the trailer, headed toward her truck. "I'll wake up for lunch."

I'm still too wired to sleep, so I turn to Alina. "You ready?"

"Yes," she says.

We don't have our bikes and Emily needs her truck, so we grab our helmets, rope, and headlamps and start toward the Valley of the Mines.

We walk next to each other on the road. A magpie flies along the dry streambed to our left. Every time I see one, I remember what my grandfather Louis said about them when I was little—that he hated seeing them because it meant a dead animal was close, and it might be a cow. I see another magpie join the first and they're tearing at a dead rabbit.

"The cycle of nature," Alina says.

"Red in tooth and claw."

"Tennyson."

"You surprise me all the time," I say. "You're a computer scientist."

"I can read. You're a journalist, but you know Tennyson. Just as surprising."

"Touché."

"I was surprised when Bennie told me that you and Emily trespassed on the testing ground."

"It surprised me," I say. "It was her idea."

"That makes sense."

"What does that mean?"

She smiles across at me. "That Emily's more adventurous."

"I was arrested also. I'm adventurous."

"If you say so."

"Going into a cave isn't adventurous?"

"I'm not trying to insult you."

"I know." We walk farther. "But why are you helping me? Just because Emily asked you to watch out for me?"

"Helping you?" She stops in the road, frowning. "You were looking for the cave long before I came here, but I am the one who actually found it. I'm not as invested as you but I am invested. We help each other."

"Sorry. You're right. I guess I have thought of it as my cave. It's not my cave or yours."

"It's the world's."

"Yes," I say. "I told myself that already, but it's easy to slip back into thinking mine, mine, mine!" I'm pleased at my pun but Alina doesn't respond, so I smile and start to explain.

"I get your lame joke!" We walk for a moment. "I help you be safe because Emily asked me to." She glances at me. "But who is to keep her from making careless decisions?"

"Not me!"

"Mm-huh."

"You don't really disapprove of what we did."

"I wouldn't have the confidence to question anything Emily does." Her eyebrows take an ironic slant.

We walk in silence for a moment. "It's interesting to me why we do things. Why anybody does what they do. Part of why I'm so curious about this cave is my great-grand-father's story, and you don't have that reason. But you're still pulled to it."

"I watched a documentary about caves in France with pictographs inside. It was so exciting. Now you and I have discovered some." She starts walking again. "With you, it's more than curiosity. You are obsessed."

"Yes, I'm pulled like a magnet to that cave."

"Yes. And I was pulled to this place. Why did I want to go to the Great Basin? My reasons don't add up to what I feel. I'm also pulled to this place and to this cave."

"Do you think I'm insane?"

"I'm no longer certain what that means."

"It means someone perceives a universe that nobody else does," I say, testing the idea. "Like Blake did."

She looks as if she has a bad taste in her mouth. "That's basically what my graduate committee said. They questioned my objectivity, especially concerning Blake." She walks ahead but turns back, and her face seems open or vulnerable. "Do you believe you're insane? You're certainly different from most people I've met."

How I answer is important to her.

"Of course I don't." Maybe I should tell her everything, but I remember that she says she's agnostic and I lose my courage. It's silly because of how briefly I've known her, but I don't want to lose my friendship with her. "Do you think you're insane?"

"No."

"Maybe insanity is not just being different from everyone, it's being unable to function with any level of happiness." I think as we walk. "And that kind of difference is often destructive—doing harm to yourself or others. Neither of us fits that definition."

"Yes. That's a better definition."

We walk steadily and without talking. I'm turning over what she said. In the past four months, I've had experiences that I would have said only mentally ill people have. But

I feel more sane and happier than I have for years. We walk in silence after that, but it's a companionable silence.

After another half an hour, we come to where the canyon narrows as it enters the Valley of the Mines. This time, instead of going in through the cave entrance up on the plateau, we enter through the thirteenth mineshaft—where we emerged before. We walk into darkness along the track but soon we have to switch on our headlamps. From the big central room, we retrace our steps along the shaft that leads to the cave.

"I'm excited to see what's down the other branch," Alina says as she steps through the hole between the mine and the cave. I nod and my light strafes up and down the wall. Inside, we turn left down the tunnel we haven't explored yet. Before fifteen minutes of walking, with a little scrambling over boulders, the cave opens up.

We both flash our lights around the room. On one side is a broad limestone wall. Petroglyphs cover the space, carvings over carvings, dozens and dozens of them. In the middle is a rectangular figure with splayed hands and stubs of feet. Its back is covered with lines that form small shapes. I try to decide whether it looks more like a spotted animal, a puzzle, or a map of garden plots. From the top extends one line, a narrow neck, and the head has mountain sheep horns and a jutting jaw.

Other figures overlap: a circle with a stem and a bar across the stem, a human or maybe a lizard figure with stick-like legs and rays extending around its head, a thick-bodied figure with arms raised and a penis dangling. Curved lines like a stream or pathway, a human hand, a curved line with rays coming out—maybe the sun. A crude mountain sheep or deer, both with huge bodies—full of meat. There are a couple of concentric circles, which I read somewhere might be springs. More small salamander or horned toad figures like the one we saw earlier.

Also, more thin figures topped by mountain sheep horns. A strange mal-shaped figure with elephantine arms and legs but a thin waist and big hips and thighs; its neck, a single line, snakes to one side so that the head and body seem disconnected. A lizard crawls up the wall, big as a human, with a line for a body, a small circle head, and lines for legs and toes. A big boulder has lines crosshatched across it as if someone laid a net over the rock. Another boulder has humanoid and salamander figures crawling across its surface. A whole wall of rock art.

I can't stop grinning. I've never seen this many petroglyphs in one place, at least not in my part of the Utah desert. It feels overwhelming, and I want to sit and examine each one.

Alina's light flashes toward me. "You don't seem surprised."

I want to tell her that Thomas told me the art would be here, but I'm still worried about what she'd think. "Because there were those others, I thought there might be more."

"Hmm." She seems to know I'm holding something back. She walks across the room where the tunnel, much narrower, continues. She crawls through but soon stops. All I can see are her feet. "It narrows to nothing." I think of the man in Nutty Putty with his head wedged into a crack that he thought was a tunnel that would widen out.

"Alina! Come back out!"

She slides back out. "It's too narrow for a person." She shines her light on my face, and I close my eyes. "What has you so worried?"

I tell her about the man buried in Nutty Putty.

"Oh," she says. "That's horrible."

"I'm glad you came back out."

We turn toward the panel again. I sit on a boulder on the opposite side of the room. Alina traces her finger along a wavy line.

"Don't touch," I say. "Fingers have oil on them."

She nods. "They're beautiful." She walks across the cave. "Here are some that look like charcoal drawings."

A cluster of humans rides horses, their feet extending below the animals' bellies. They are more realistic than the others.

"It looks much more modern," I say. "Maybe a Goshute drew it."

"Maybe these are the soldiers who attacked the man's family in your great-grandfather's story."

I look at the sketches. There are some figures lying on the ground. "Could be."

"Who made the older ones?"

"Maybe, like those others, these are Archaic or even Paleoindian."

I pass my eyes over the carvings again and again. Beautiful carvings, more of them than I've seen in this part of the desert. I wonder why the Dead Fathers thought it so important that I not go into the cave and not see this artwork. Like Thomas said, there is nothing revolutionary or epic about them. In the grand scheme of things, they are not going to magically change the earth, take humanity in a new direction. They especially won't turn us toward a wrong direction, which is what the DFs implied. They're just lovely and I like looking at them. It's like looking at a sunset or the edge between the hills and the sky to the west of my trailer. I try to figure out my feelings, but I'm not sure why the petroglyphs give me such pleasure. They're right, fitting, proportional, evocative. They embody essential things—people, gods, water, food, and maps of landscape. They are a link to people who lived many thousands of years ago.

"What do they mean?" asks Alina.

"They mean that artists spent hundreds of hours here. It means that these were important."

"They're very old."

"I'm grateful the blasts didn't crack the wall or bring down the ceiling in the room," I say. "These will help in Emily's work to stop the mining, even in the lower valley. Which would be very good."

Alina also sits on a boulder. "You knew about the petroglyphs before you saw them. When you saw them, you smiled and nodded."

"My great-grandfather told me about them."

"He did?"

I nod and my light flashes on the floor.

"You didn't talk about them when we first went in the cave."

"He told me yesterday."

"Yesterday."

I nod again.

"He's dead, isn't he?"

I feel like a bobblehead.

"And the petroglyphs were here." She doesn't stumble over what she's just found out about me. She just rolls with it. Or at least that's what she seems to be doing. "Cool."

"I have come to believe there is no such thing as insubstantial substance. The universe is continuous, matter and spirit."

She grins. "Yeah, you're definitely crazy as Blake."

"Yes."

She lifts her phone and takes pictures of each carving and several of the whole wall. The act reminds me of what Emily did the night before, and I hope jeeps aren't waiting for us when we come out of the mineshaft—jeeps or divine strikes of lightning. The Dead Fathers believe they know God's mind, but when I asked them if they've talked to the Father, they were silent. It seems they really don't have a clue what God thinks.

Soon Alina stands in the middle of the room. She curves her back in imitation of one of the human figures, then another, moving around the cavern. Her arms move like jags of lightening. It's partly in imitation of the carvings but more like a kinetic conversation with them. When she's finished, she sits on the floor of the cave. She shines her headlamp on the ground and draws in the dirt with a rock, long and pointed like a finger. I take a small electric lantern out of my backpack and put it on a boulder. Then I sit on another boulder and watch. At first, she imitates the art on the wall, but then she makes her own drawings in the dirt—a snake, large and small birds, a portrait apt enough that I recognize Emily's face. Then she starts writing numbers in patterns, a complex formula maybe.

"Is that one of your algorithms?" I ask, shining my light across her work.

"*My* algorithms? If I discover how you choose words, is it my algorithm or yours?"

"You invent the formulas which do or don't predict with accuracy."

She angles her head in acceptance. "So if it's wrong, it's mine, and if it's accurate it's yours?"

"Exactly," I say.

"Also, when I say 'algorithm,' it's a shortcut for several kinds of operations. I was trying to determine the algorithms and the matrices and specific formulas that predict how people make choices in language. And maybe in other matters."

"Could you do the same with the people who made these carvings?"

"Possibly. I assume these carvings manifest the people who made them."

I stand over the drawings she made. "You said 'and in other matters.' So you could predict other kinds of human behavior than just speech patterns."

"Possibly." Her mouth and her eyebrows both seem to smile. "Keats again: how can we know the dancer from the dance? Bees dance to communicate. These people drew their dance."

"Do you believe that choice is determined? Like Spinoza? Us discovering the cave and this art were fated to happen?" Thomas predicted that the General would come at night and try to shoot a pronghorn. That happened. Emily dreamed about Alina and then met her. The Dead Fathers predicted that Emily and Alina would corrupt me.

Has that happened? The universe just doesn't seem linear. It seems chaotic and predictable at the same time.

"Hmmm." She lays back on a slab of rock, and her light makes a moon on the ceiling. "No short answer to that. I believe that choice is complex. A mathematician with all the data might predict with very little error."

I think about the forces internal and external that led to Emily and me splitting up and returning to each other. For a time I thought it was simple: I left because of her adultery. Now I know it was much more like a recursive matrix of action and response, a tangle, not anything like a simple line of cause and effect.

"Some people in my church believe that God knows everything that is going to happen."

"I'm agnostic about God, heaven, and all that shit." She draws her finger along a seam of clay from the wall opposite the panel and marks her face, a line on each cheek. "Could there be a dimension, something like heaven, where the math is different than it is here? I would guess that the math is the same."

I drifted away from the church, partly because I had tired of trying to figure out what was in God's head. Now I'm curious again—curious and fearful.

She says, "My main concern is psychological—how people perceive their universe and how that affects their choices. If they believe only in things that can be seen or shown with experiment, they make different choices than if they believe that some of the universe is transcendent or magical. Or people might believe that the unseen universe is just an extension of this one, like William Blake did. He had a complete tensional map of the universe that included the natural and the supernatural in one system—continuous. Just like what you believe. Do you make paintings of gods and angels?"

"No," I say. "All this is too much for me." It's warm in this section of the cave and I realize how sleepy I am. "Do you want to stay here a while or go back?"

"Stay."

"Then I'm going to look at the art horizontally."

"It's a good way to view art."

When I lie down on the floor of the cave with my backpack for a pillow, she smiles.

"Old people like naps," I say, switching off my light.

"I'll watch over you," she says.

I wonder what made her say that, but it was nice, and soon I feel my thoughts drift away from rationality, which isn't that far these days.

When I wake, I wonder how long I've been asleep. It's darker than dark. I turn my light on and see Alina sleeping. Her face seems happy, peaceful, so I wait for her to wake.

Before long, she sits up and turns on her light. "I'm ravenous." She looks at her phone. "Good. It's about an hour until dinner. We'll be back in plenty of time." She turns her headlamp toward the squarish animal on the wall and scoots closer to it. "That looks thicker than any deer I've seen in pictures."

"Maybe they drew what they wanted to find," I say. "An animal that would last them all winter."

"Let's go find one. I could eat the whole beast tonight."

Soon we emerge from the mine. Below us next to the tin building sits the blue truck we saw before when emerging. The same two people stand in front of it. One points up to us, and they both look through binoculars at us.

"Creepy," says Alina.

"Let's find out who they are and why they're spying on us." I shout, "Hey!" I wave both arms above my head and scurry down the slope as fast as I can without slipping. I'm ready to tell them to get the hell out of here. Which I have no right to do. When they start to get in their truck, I shout and wave again. "Wait, dammit!"

Instead of getting in their truck and driving away, they shut the doors without getting inside and walk to the front, leaning on the hood and watching me as I trot toward them.

FOURTEEN

The Night Terror

They seem to be talking. Then I can't see them as I shove my way through the brush at the bottom of the slope. I hear Alina scrambling down behind me.

When I burst out of the brush, they are only a hundred yards away. Walking toward them, I can't tell whether they are women or men. They have short hair like men, but their faces are slender and feminine. My granddaughter would say, "What difference does it make? Stop putting people into categories!" She's right, but I'm old and, although I try to see the world like she does, I keep slipping into traditional binary ways of thinking. These two are wearing slacks and button-down shirts, one with blue checks and one solid russet.

"Hello," I say. "I saw you the other day up on the flat, and I'm curious. You seemed to be watching us. And here you are again."

"We saw you crawl out of the ground like marmots," says one, the one with the blue-checked shirt. "That made *us* curious."

"We found a cave," says Alina. "Actually, I found it by falling into it."

I want to stop her from revealing any more information about the cave, but I realize that she's just doing with them what she's done with me, being open and friendly.

"An effective method of discovery," says Russet Shirt, "one we've used many times."

"We fall into the most remarkable discoveries," says Blue Checks.

"Well put," says Russet. "Well put."

Alina says, "We found these wonderful petroglyphs inside."

It bothers me that she keeps giving away our secrets.

"It seems more than coincidence," says Russet, "that we are here again to witness you coming out of a hole in the earth. This time a mine. We assume that it's connected to the cave."

"Yes," says Alina. "The miners broke through into the cave."

"Why are you here?" I ask.

"You're so suspicious," says Alina.

"As he should be," says Blue Checks. "We could be anybody."

"We could be dangerous people."

"It's not easy to tell whether people you meet are friend or foe."

I fold my arms, which is about as threatening a gesture as I can manage.

The two glance at each other. "This will sound silly," Russet says, "but every few days, we play a game."

"We get in our truck," says Blue, "and we roll dice to see which direction we'll drive." Russet gets a wooden box from the cab of the truck. In it are several colors of dice—many-sided dice. "Some are for direction. This one, the yellow one, is for distance."

"And we go where the dice lead us."

"An idle game."

"But one which helps us fall into discoveries."

"I love games like that," says Alina. "But it's improbable that chance took you here again so soon."

They look sheepishly at each other. "We cheated," says Russet.

"We were so curious about what you were doing," says Blue, "that we didn't roll the dice today. We just came back."

"Why did you leave last time in such a rush?" I ask. "What are you really up to here?"

Alina gives me a dual frown, eyebrows and mouth. "Don't be so paranoid. It's time for names. I'm Alina Meijer."

"I'm Delta," says Russet. "They/them."

"I'm Marion," says Blue. "He/she/they/them, sometimes it."

I wonder if they have last names, or if like Madonna, Sting, or Lizzo, they only need the one.

They both turn toward me.

"Christopher Twist."

"He/him," says Alina, and then for some reason she laughs.

"Twist?" says Marion. "That's an interesting name."

"Welsh," I say.

"What does Welsh Christopher do?" says Delta.

"He twists," says Alina, grinning, and she shows us with her dance what twisting might be like. Nothing like the hip-gyrating dance from before my time.

Suddenly Marion is gone. I didn't see them go, but they are definitely gone—just like the Dead Fathers.

"Well, that's not something you see every day," says Alina. She looks around for Marion, but she's still gone.

"Oh," says Delta, "that's unfortunate. Marion let the cat out of the bag."

"Who are you?" I ask. "What are you?" I wonder if I could try to shake their hand.

"I'm so glad you asked," says Delta. "We bridge. What's supposed to happen is that at every moment, one of us is alive, one—ah—not alive. One body and spirit unified and one only spirit matter. They usually have more self-control."

"Prime," says Alina. "I can't really see any difference between you. At least I couldn't until they disappeared."

"Well, the transition is supposed to be too fast for your eye to perceive." Delta glances at me. "We left last time because we ought to maintain distance. Stay objective." She—or they—turn to Alina. "But it seems that we have more to talk about."

"We do?" Alina says. Her eyebrows seem quizzical.

"We certainly do," Delta says, glancing back at me. "Thomas and all the others. The War. Challenging times require innovation in our methods." She—or they—glances at the truck. "But not right now. Marion and I have work to do."

"So we'll see you again?" Alina asks.

"Soon." They turn to Alina. "We are very pleased with your work as a mathematician and a dancer, and we have a job for you. If you want it."

Alina's eyes widen and her eyebrows go very high. I've never before seen her surprised, not even when Marion disappeared. "A job? Doing what?"

"Mathematical dancing." Delta moves her own body in a jerky kind of dance. She smiles. "What you do best—making sense out of complex data, convoluted patterns."

"We'll get back to you with details." Delta smiles. "It will be prime."

Alina's eyes crinkle. "As in prime numbers."

"It's a good word for you to use. Unpredictable and random but patterned."

Alina is as pleased as I've seen her in our short time knowing each other.

Delta climbs into their truck, and Marion is sitting in the passenger seat.

"Do you want a ride?" Delta asks.

"We can ride in the back." I use the back tire as a step and sit with my back against the cab. Alina joins me, and Delta puts the truck in gear.

"What could they want me to do for them?" Alina whispers, frowning. "They talk as if they know me."

"The world is full of surprises," I say. "I'm just as bewildered as you are. But I can no longer say my life is boring."

"I'm very curious."

At the main road they let us out.

I smile and wave.

Alina opens her mouth to say something.

"See you soon," says Delta.

"Very soon," says Marion.

The truck heads north, and Alina stares at their dust. "Curiouser and curiouser."

"Yes." I feel enlightened, buoyant, by the petroglyphs and the pleasant conversation with Alina and now with Marion and Delta. The world seems full of mystery.

Alina and I walk toward camp and Spencer's horse barn. We're each lost in our own thoughts—mine on the pleasure it will be to tell Emily about our day. It may happen tonight that we move from conversation to touch.

My good mood bleeds away at the sight of a black Hummer with army insignia parked next to Emily's truck. Nothing good can come from such an official vehicle. Emily sits at the table talking to a man in a dark blue uniform. I want to strangle him, but that's not something I could actually do, so I do what is more natural. I sit next to Emily and listen.

"The General won't wait forever. You need to decide by tomorrow noon."

"This is blackmail." She says it flat, with no particular emotion.

"Federal trespassing."

"Which is much less serious than having private alcohol distilling equipment on a military installation."

"Which might have many military uses, if there were such equipment."

"We—" Emily gathers herself to stand. "This trading of threats has no purpose."

The man in the suit, who has a wide, fleshy face, doesn't respond. Finally he unfolds his hands and says, "Tomorrow."

Emily looks down at him. "OK. I'll let you know by then if I change my mind."

The man nods. He glances toward me and leaves in his Hummer. His dust follows that of the color couple, Russet and Blue, which I like better than Delta and Marion. But I will call them by their true names if/when we meet again. Bennie comes out of the trailer, followed by Lucía and Andrew. From their faces I can tell that they are, so to speak, loaded for bear.

We all sit in silence. Finally, Bennie says, "Emily, the pictures are useless in the investigation or prosecution of a case."

"As you told me several times already." Her words are louder and her tone angrier than seems necessary.

Bennie doesn't back down. He's either foolish or courageous, maybe both. "You're more important than this one case. Important to my community."

Alina sits on the step to the trailer. Unlike usual, she's perfectly silent. I am as well. I don't want to increase the tension. It looks like we won't be telling the group about our discovery tonight. Disappointing.

Lucía opens her mouth to say something but stops herself.

"You talk as if your license isn't important to you," says Bennie. "This is not like you to take such a risk, and for what? So you can say you beat a polygamist and a general?"

I want to ease the tension with a joke about a lawyer, a polygamist, and a general going into a bar. But for once I follow Lucía's example and keep my mouth shut. Emily looks at each of us and her jaw clenches. A line appears across her jaw, a sign that she will never change her mind. I'm immediately angry in response to her anger. I read somewhere that anger is merely a sign of having something to lose. I know that's true in my case. But I feel that I've already lost it. I want this wrangling with the General to just go away. At the petroglyph panel, I was full of—what?—joy. Looking forward to maybe sleeping with Emily tonight. I felt invincible. Now she's dug her heels in. She will never let herself be beat by anyone. She'll never give in to the General's demand, and this pissing fight with him will take so much energy.

Emily says, "Stop ganging up on me!"

Nobody but Bennie says a word, and I worry that Lucía will break out laughing. Andrew looks at me and at Emily. "We have work to do." He stands and tugs at Lucía's sleeve until she stands and walks with him toward the trailer. Alina moves out of their way, and she and Bennie join them inside.

I know it's foolish to try to talk to her when she's in this mood, but I blunder ahead anyway. "You should just give him the pictures. Nephi's going to jail anyway."

"Maybe. Nothing is certain. Not even that I'll have my license taken away if I don't give him the pictures. It's all unsure. I want to know what his relationship to Senator Clarke is. What political damage would the General suffer? We don't know. I want to know but I can't find out before tomorrow. It's frustrating."

"You get so stubborn."

"Chris."

"It's true. You're like a mule sometimes." I fold my arms. "Just like your mother says."

"Stay out of this, Chris." She faces me, hands on hips. "Back off. It's not your problem."

"But it is. I'm in it whether I like it or not. I will have a criminal record as well."

"Possibly. And do you really care anyway? What difference will it make? It's not like it matters when you're out here in the desert."

"Emily, when you leave the desert, I want to come home too."

"Maybe you will. Maybe running away is a habit you can't break."

"Give him the pictures!"

"Leave me alone!" she shouts. "I can't think with you badgering me!" Andrew stands at the window but doesn't come out.

I go around behind the trailer where nobody can see me. I should know better than to push her. I don't really care if I have a felony or not. Won't change my life. I mean it will cost some money, but it won't affect me once it's over. We used to argue this way. One argument was over whether I should retire or not. She wanted me to keep working. I did for a couple of years only to keep us from arguing. Other things, moving or not moving, going to church, not going to church. We argued a lot. But that wasn't even the problem. The problem was we argued but didn't resolve. I don't like conflict and when we'd argue it felt horrible, so I'd back off. I'd capitulate or occasionally she would, but we'd never work through things. Soon all those unresolved issues just became a part of the fabric of our marriage, and then we let work get in the way and became distant from each other. Living in the same house but not really seeing each other. We didn't argue anymore, but the bland sameness was both easy and horrible. Then she tried to blow things up. I shake my head to clear out the old patterns of thinking about us. The old story is too predictable. I'm tired of it. Finally my hands stop shaking.

I smell food, so I return to the group. Everyone, including Alina, is sitting at the table—buns and barbecue, coleslaw. Emily looks at me, but her face is blank. I want to tell her that anger is worlds better than apathy. She doesn't give me an apologetic look, and I don't want her to.

She says, "I don't want to destroy the pictures on the cloud."

I go inside and fill a plate. I stand over the food for a minute before going back outside.

"But I can't afford to lose my license. I hate that bastard getting away with this. Both those bastards."

"OK," I say. "Emily. It affects you more than me. But it does affect me. Both of us were charged with trespassing on federal property. I want us to decide together."

She nods. "Let's go for a drive after dinner."

Dinner is painfully silent. Finally, we finish. I walk toward Emily's truck and sit in the passenger seat. Soon she follows. She turns left at the main road, so we're headed south toward Lost Canyon, where the BLM closed the road to protect the panel of petroglyphs.

"I think it's not your decision," she says. "Despite what you say, I don't think you really care about having a police record."

"But it does affect me. I don't want to go through the effort and expense of a trial when it won't do any good." I take a breath. "You want to put us both through this just because—"

"I don't want to let him beat me. That's why I'm a good lawyer."

I nod.

"But what?" she says.

"Lose a battle, win the war."

"Losing this battle won't help me win the war. It drives me crazy that they might get away with it."

She stops the truck at the art. Another vehicle is parked there.

I look at it and know she's driven here to meet someone. I thought we were going on a drive to talk, but she was combining that with part of her business. "You could have told me you had a meeting," I say. "I've always respected your boundaries, but you have made assumptions about me. Like now."

"Now?"

"You said, 'Let's go for a drive,' and let me assume we were going on a drive to talk, to work through this, but you had another purpose. You have business, so you were doing two things at once. Which means I am only half important. I have half your attention."

"No," she says. "You have all my attention."

"It doesn't work," I say. "We're here in the truck and right there," I point out the window, "is someone you want to talk to. So it's like there's a clock ticking on our talking. It's already hard enough for me to talk, so this just makes it impossible. So just don't talk to him."

"I can't do that," she says. "This will just take a minute, then we'll finish talking."

"I'm walking home," I say.

"Don't be adolescent," she says. The line is in her jaw again and I know she won't give in.

I open the door and start northward along the road. What gripes me is that it is such a petty thing. Not the decision about the General's offer, that's not petty. It has never worked to try making decisions for her. And it's not my way. So why am I digging in my heels now? I don't want to go to jail, but that's not why I'm pressuring her to give the pictures to General Torrey. She and I have generally been either an irritant to each other or we keep our distance, avoid the abrasion.

It's half an hour before I hear her truck behind me. She stops next to me, rolls down her window. "Get in." She takes a breath. "Please get in."

"You had your meeting with him after all, even though I asked you not to."

"It was efficient. I can multitask."

"You just proved you can't."

I start walking again.

She stops the truck and gets out. She walks fast to catch up to me. We walk for a couple hundred yards without talking.

"This is like fifteen years ago," she says.

I nod. "It just makes me tired."

"We haven't learned anything in all those years. When I talk with people, anyone, I give them all my attention. It's one of my superpowers."

"I don't want it to be a technique with me. Your superpower is an illusion. You give me all your attention inside certain parameters."

After a pause she says, "You want all my attention all the time?"

I sound sulky even to myself. "No! Of course not." Even though I don't like how I'm acting, I feel that I have a legitimate claim—that I want her attention sometimes. Not all the time, which would be horrible. But some of the time. Which is what has been happening in the desert. She gives me a lot of attention and she has her work—perfect. Why am I angry now? I realize it's because she misled me. "Emily, if you had just said, 'I have a meeting with a guy over at the petroglyph panel. Can you come with me and we can talk on the way?' Then I could deal with it. Or I could say, 'No. I'll wait until you come back, and then we can talk.' But what happened is you said, 'Let's go for a drive.'"

"Oh," she says. "Is that all we're fighting about?"

I shrug. "Probably. I feel foolish and petty." Then I stop. "No. It's important to me that you are clear and straight with me. If I'm involved, you can just tell me your plan."

She nods. "I will. I don't want to go back to when there was nothing between us because we backed away from argument. It would be better to divorce."

"It feels today like we're regressing. But it's because we haven't argued for so long."

"We've argued," she says.

"About things. Decisions. Not about us."

"There's also what to do about the General. We do have to make a decision."

For once I keep my mouth shut.

She chews her lip. "Let's talk to him."

"And say what?"

"I'm not sure. Right now it seems that we're stuck. Either we hurt him and he hurts us, or you and I back down and he wins. I know he's not going to back down."

"But if we turn it around, make him see the problem another way—"

"Right. He still might refuse to back down." She reaches for my hand, but hesitates. "You care about me. About my career."

"I do. I care about many of the same issues that you do. And in this one thing, we acted together. We can decide together."

"I agree."

We're standing in the middle of the road. I watch her face.

"What?"

"I want to tell you about my day."

"Yes."

I tell her about the petroglyph panel. "Such strange and wonderful figures. Like maps of their souls."

"Like that Picasso we saw in London."

I grin at her. "Of the girl holding a dove. That's exactly what they remind me of."

"That was a good trip."

"Yes."

"I can't even remember why we went. Some event you were covering."

"Yes. The Royal Geographic Society convention."

We hold hands as we walk back to her truck.

We drive past Spencer's place, the black skeleton of my old trailer, which stands as a testament against Spencer for making me move out. At the camp, she goes in the trailer to call the General. I just sit at the outside table. She comes right back out. "He doesn't want to wait until morning. He wants to meet with us tonight.

We get back in the truck and drive to Simpson. Not long after that, we pass the fence where we climbed over and took the pictures. Emily seems distracted, her mind turning over possibilities. Both she and the General need a way out, but right now I can't imagine how they might compromise.

I see something in the road ahead. "Slow down!"

She sees them too, horses crossing the road, dozens of them. The truck spooks them, and they gallop into the darkness, running away from us until they crowd into the fence, which extends parallel to the road.

"Wow!" Emily says. "I love seeing them."

"If the fence was gone and the people with it," I say.

She mocks surprise. "A rancher's grandson speaking against fences? What is the world coming to?"

"It's going to hell, but you're trying to slow the descent."

We continue to the east gate of the town of Skull Valley. The soldier in the booth won't let us through at first but finally talks to General Torrey's secretary, gives us an address, and waves us on. We drive slowly through the town, which looks like many other little Mormon towns—a lot of trees, even though it's the desert, a small high school, three churches. We are let through another gate by another guard, and then we're on the base. After parking in front of the administration building, we walk inside. It's hurry up and wait. For fifteen or twenty minutes, we sit outside his office.

"A power move," says Emily.

Finally, the door opens and we're invited in. His huge desk between us and him.

"Have you made up your mind?" he asks.

"No," I say, "we haven't."

Emily says, "Neither of us wants this disruption. You don't want the pictures out, but I want Nephi Johnson's ass in prison."

"The pictures won't help you prosecute him."

Emily nods. "But you don't want it known that you have hidden illegal distilling equipment in one of your military warehouses. You really don't want it to get out that you've been buying illegal whiskey from him."

"You can't prove that!"

"Probably not in a court of law, but if I publish the pictures of his equipment in your building, people will find it easy to believe that it was quid pro quo."

"I've dealt with worse problems," he says. But I can see that he doesn't want to have to deal with this one. "I can blame a lieutenant, and he and the problem will just go away."

"Maybe," says Emily. "Maybe not."

"I'm retiring soon anyway," he says. "Even if I didn't blame someone else, it won't hurt me."

"What if I send the pictures to Senator Clarke?" says Emily. "He will take quick action. You might even lose your pension."

The General glares at her. "No, I won't."

They're working toward another impasse, trading threats, just like she did with the lawyer. She probably knows what she's doing but she can't turn away. I have authority issues, but she has the same issues in spades.

"Give the equipment back to Nephi," I say. "Make him solve his own problems."

Emily turns toward me and her eyes widen and she smiles. We both watch the General's face as he mulls this over. It's clear he doesn't want to back down.

"Let me shoot the pronghorn," he says to me.

Apparently, he doesn't know I'm no longer living next to the pond where the pronghorn drinks. "No," I say.

"Take yourself off the nerve gas case," he says to Emily.

"These are completely different issues," says Emily. "Let's not mix them together."

"Then no," he says. "I won't be pushed around by you two."

Emily stands.

The secretary, a young man around thirty, whispers something to the General.

I stand and follow Emily to the door.

"Wait!" The General's face is red. "I'll haul Nephi's equipment back to him." He levels his finger at us as if it's a pistol. "But—"

The secretary whispers again. The General is furious, but he nods. "You have to take my word on this."

"I'll not make any use of the pictures," says Emily. "You have to take my word on it."

"Yes," says the General. "Get out of here before I change my mind again."

Emily's smiling as we walk down the hall.

"You won't see that equipment again," I say.

"Maybe not," she says. "But we have a better chance than when it was in the building on the testing grounds."

"I'd still like to see the senator nail him for buying bootleg whiskey for his officer's club. Or whatever he was using it for."

"Me too," she says. "But that won't really change anything. The military will still be the military."

Outside, a subordinate has loaded Emily's bike in the back of her truck. As before, both bikes won't fit inside the shell, so I help the soldier tie mine to the roof. She makes us sign a receipt for them, and we drive back across the desert toward the camp.

When we get back to the trailer, Emily says she's tired and climbs in her truck. Sitting on my bed, I work through my disappointment that she didn't come to my room.

"She'll keep teasing you," says Louis.

"She's not teasing me," I say. "We still have a lot to work through."

"If you had taken Nephi up on his offer," says Hugh, "you wouldn't be in this position."

"No woman should have a monopoly over you," says Louis.

"Leave him alone," says my father. "He's made his decision."

"A decision with consequences," says Hugh.

"As he's finding out," says Louis.

"You went into the cave," says Hugh. "Again."

"The rock art is wonderful," I say.

"I've never seen it," says my father. This surprises me.

"It's impressive," I say.

"Enough about the art," says Louis, glaring at me. "You disobeyed us."

"So what?" I sound like a belligerent teenager even to myself.

Hugh says, "You have no idea what it will be like if there's another war in heaven."

"What will happen to the damned infrastructure," says Louis. "This whole planet will wobble like a flailing top."

"I thought it was self-sustaining," I say.

"Do you believe in perpetual motion?" says Louis. "Do you think the laws of entropy just gave up in this pocket of the universe?"

"I thought that it balanced out," I say. "In some places in the universe entropy makes things fall apart but in other areas life happens, things fall together."

"You have a kindergartner's view of physics," says Louis.

"Instead of trusting us," says my father, "you went into that cave."

"Again, so what?"

"In the beginning the Gods organized the earth," says Hugh. "'And the Gods watched those things which they had ordered until they obeyed.' Even rocks and dirt and water obeyed. Why can't you obey?"

"I can think of three reasons." I hold up one finger. "You're not God."

"But we speak for Him," says Hugh.

"Do you?"

None of them will answer that question. I hold up a second finger. "Second, you haven't given me any reason to obey you. Going into a cave? Why is that wrong?"

"God's ways are inscrutable to the disobedient," says Hugh.

"Damn right," says Louis. "Inscrutable. God created this earth, created rules for his own purpose."

"What's your third reason?" asks my father.

"I was curious and the mine is interesting. The rock art panel is wonderful. It made me feel close to the divine."

"The question is which divine," says Hugh. "Certainly not the Father."

"You're barking up the wrong tree," says Louis.

My father says, "I can understand why you reject blind obedience, but sometimes you just have to trust people who know more than you do."

"So much is at stake," says Hugh.

"The rock art may be beautiful, just as you said," my father continues. "Significant to the people who made it. But its significance to you is out of proportion. You care so much about it that you will let it influence you."

"Again, so what? So what if it does influence me?"

"He's listening but not hearing," says Hugh.

"You think we're hard on you," says Louis. "We've been like wet nurses."

"We know you and love you anyway," says my father. "We have tried to use persuasion."

"Well, that didn't work," says Hugh. "You won't like who's coming next."

"Oh, is it the Ghost of Christmas Present?"

"Joke away!" says Louis. "Neither one of them follows the rules."

"Not like us," says my father. "We usually don't have much to do with them."

"Damned important beings!" says Louis. "Highest rank!"

"Like a visiting general authority," says my father.

"They're coming to straighten you out," says Louis.

"See if you can be saved," says Hugh.

"Deal the damn cards," I say. "Let's get this over with. I'm sick of you. It's a curse to be visited by the dead."

Instead of playing cards, they leave, shaking their heads sadly. Maybe the Dead Fathers are like traditional ghosts who perseverate on the same track until they finally fade away. The thought makes me sad.

I lie down but the bed is hard as metal. I sit up again, and I'm not in the new trailer but back in my nest of filthy blankets in my old trailer. The door blanket shifts as if by the wind and a woman enters, growing more solid as she draws closer. I wonder why she used the door when the DFs never do. But it's a dream so maybe it's symbolic of her entering my domain. Another woman enters behind her and stands above me, frowning. The most beautiful woman I have ever seen, she has a thin face and full lips, dark hair bound in a knot at her neck. She sits on the edge of my bed, her hip pressed against my thigh. She's still frowning, glaring really, and I wish she'd relax and smile at me.

"So much wasted potential," she says. The woman behind her paces back and forth along my short hallway. She carries an axe. The first woman's disappointment and the other woman's anger both hit me like blasts of frigid and overheated air, which should average out but don't, cold and hot at once. I am a failure, a filthy man lying in my own filth. Even if I bathed and shaved, combed my hair, and put on a suit, my soul would still be filthy. I'd still feel inadequate before these two. I want to please the first woman and get as far away from the second as I can.

"He will never measure up!" says the woman with the axe. She tries to crowd around the first woman. "Let me past." Her knuckles are white on the handle of the axe.

"Have patience," the first woman says. "He sorrows for his sins and wants to do right." Her voice lilts like the song of a meadowlark, and I want her to never stop talking. "He wants to be a better man." She finally smiles, but then her smile fades. She frowns at me. I want to never displease her again.

The other woman gestures with her axe. "His will is unsteady. Like a wave tossed by the wind." She grips the axe, and I know that if the other woman lets her, she will kill me, or worse, destroy my very being.

The first woman touches my face, and looks into my eyes. I feel naked and vulnerable.

"I don't know what you want me to do."

"Of course you do."

I should stop being a cog in the smooth machine of the hierarchy. Then she might smile at me again. I could do exactly what the Dead Fathers have told me to do. I realize that Emily is a rebellious and selfish woman and a tease. She will never come to my bed. I should crawl on my hands and knees to Nephi and beg to marry his daughters.

"You want to do better, don't you?" She smiles.

The other woman says, "But your flesh is weak." Her hands slide down the handle as if she's getting ready for a swing. "Let me give him a taste!"

The beautiful woman holds my face between her hands and turns my head flat on my bed. The other woman places the axe blade against my temple and I feel its sharpness. She increases the pressure. The pain is unendurable.

It isn't just physical pain, and the pressure makes me feel that my eternal soul could be pierced and wounded.

Both of them turn as the door blanket opens again—my grandmother Sarah. "You go too far!" she says to them. "You're violating the formulas."

"As we must do," says the beautiful woman. "You're also intervening."

"As *I* must do."

One woman releases my head and the other lifts her axe. Then they are both gone. My grandmother sits next to me on the bed. I'm grateful that she drove the fearsome woman away, but I wish the other had stayed.

"You're on your own now," my grandmother says. She touches me on the temple. The pain stops, but then she leaves and I feel bereft. With the beautiful woman also gone, I feel that I can't hold myself together anymore. My identity was a joke, and without her my soul will fragment into spiritual atoms. The gravity that holds my being together has weakened and every piece of me is repellant to every other piece. I feel my identity dissipating like a scent in the breeze.

When I was young and had a high fever, I had a nightmare. The details were different, but the feeling was the same. A mountain of rocks, maybe the whole earth, turned like the gears of a clock, smashing me. It doesn't make sense that something could be like a clock gear and also like a mountain of rock, but that's what I remember. If it wheeled across me once more, I would be crushed. Oblivion would be a release from that pain and pressure, but oblivion was also terrifying, the loss of all sensation and human contact. The two visitors made me feel I was back in my fever dream.

Andrew and Lucía stand in the doorway.

"Are you OK?" Lucía asks.

Andrew looks worried. "You were screaming."

I can hear their words but they are far away, separated from me by a barrier of gauze. I struggle out of bed and push past them. I leave the trailer and go to the back of Emily's camper shell. I lift the back window.

"What's going on?" She sits up in her sleeping bag. "Christopher?"

I open the tailgate. "I need—" I can't finish, but I crawl into the back of the truck.

"You're sweating." She puts her hand on my forehead. "Do you have a fever?"

I lie on the edge of her sleeping bag, curled like a fetus. She puts her arms around me. "A nightmare," I say. "It was awful."

"Will it help to tell me about it?"

"I don't want to talk."

Her arms are around me, spooning me, and her hands grasp my arms. After a while my body unclenches. People are frightened of ghosts, but I've never been frightened of the Dead Fathers, just angry. Those two predatory spirits showed me that there may be something to people's fear of the dead. They could have been demons. They made my will into a candle with a wick so short that there was room for only a tiny flame, easily extinguished. I wonder who they are. They seemed higher in the hierarchy than the Dead Fathers, but maybe my ancestors know the identities of those two women.

Every time I feel myself slipping toward irrationality and sleep, I jerk myself awake. Emily's holding me, but I may never feel safe again.

FIFTEEN

The Matriarch
Takes the Reins

I stay close to the trailer the next morning. The sun is bright, the coffee strong, and Emily and the others are close by. Alina is working in the horse barn, so I shouldn't go up to the cave anyway. It's a pleasant morning and I sit at the table with the book of Blake's poems in my hand, but I'm not reading. I'm letting the spring sun warm me to my bones. Emily is busy, but she finds time to come out periodically to sit with me for a few minutes. Midmorning, I tell her about my nightmare, and she listens, her arm around me.

"Was it a nightmare or a vision?" she asks when I finish.

"I don't know. I don't know the difference." She sits a while longer and goes back to work.

It felt real, but I wasn't in the new trailer. I was in the old, burnt one. I hate to think what a mess I'd be in if Grandma Sarah hadn't shown up. I've always read the Book of Job as a parable. No way would God give Satan that much control over one of his children. Now I wonder.

I couldn't muster any will in the presence of those women. Was that how it was in the Garden of Eden when Adam and Eve heard the voice of God? If so, Eve is even more a hero than I thought. She made it so we could exercise our own wills. I doze in the sun and it seems that not just Sarah but also Thomas, my mother, and others are comforting me. That they're watching out for me makes me feel a little safer, but I also feel like a thin reed, bowing whichever way the wind blows.

Toward afternoon, I have lunch with the others. Emily tells me she received a phone call from the Tooele County prosecutor; the county sheriff and the FBI raided the polygamist compound already that morning and found the distilling equipment back in the building. They seized it, charged Nephi with tax fraud and distilling without a license, and put him behind bars with bail set at half a million. They also charged Frank for lesser crimes and released him on $10,000 bail. Not as guilty by lack of initiative. By nighttime I feel brave enough to sleep in my own room in my own bed. Or what feels like mine even though it's a rented trailer. Nobody bothers me that night, not the Dead Fathers, not the unbalanced women.

After breakfast the next day, one of the polygamist boys drives to the camp and says his mother, Betty Sharp Johnson, wants to talk to Emily. Emily asks me if I want to go with her down to the polygamy compound. I still don't want to be alone, and I'm interested in what Betty might have to say, so I'm glad to go with her. Alina wants to ride along.

"Why?" asks Emily. Maybe she's worried about having someone with so few filters on her mouth coming along on a potentially uncomfortable situation. She should also worry about me.

"I want to observe it all—cowboys, ranchers, Indians, polygamists. I want to understand why Western Europeans adopted polygamy."

I say, "Oscar Wilde said, 'Everything in the world is about sex—except sex. Sex is about power.'"

This quote makes Alina smile. "Oscar Wilde said that? So did Janelle Monáe." One eyebrow goes up. "Did he copy her, do you think?" Then she laughs at her own joke.

"That's unfair, Chris," says Emily. "Polygamy is a very complex practice. You should know that."

"It is complex. It's also about power."

Alina turns to Emily. "Can I come, Mommy?"

Emily nods. "But don't call me your mother."

Alina grins. "Grandmother, then?"

Emily just frowns, as if she's either angry or nonplussed. Maybe a little of both. It's tough to stay irritated with Alina, and Emily's face is overtaken by a smile. "We'll drive the double cab truck then."

Once we're moving, Alina says to me, "Your ancestors were all polygamists."

"Except for one branch of my mother's family," I say.

"But you're not polygamist?"

"No, it was outlawed by the orthodox church more than a century ago. These are fundamentalists that cling to the practice."

"And you are a member of the orthodox church?" says Alina. "I thought Mormons didn't drink coffee or swear."

"Or trespass on government property," I say.

"Or never go to church," says Emily.

Or visit prostitutes, I think, but for once I'm smart enough not to say it.

"I gather you're not orthodox orthodox," says Alina with her wry smile. "But you know all about the scriptures and the doctrines."

"He does," Emily says. "Not me."

"People who don't believe don't study so much."

"I am a paradox," I say.

"Me too," says Emily.

"If there are two of us paradoxes, that means—"

"Christopher!" Emily says. "Don't say it. It's not even funny."

"It's kind of funny," says Alina. "But we're a trio of doxes."

Emily drives down into the valley. When we get close to the farm, I see the sprinklers running but the tractor is idle. The door to the building that held the distilling equipment hangs open. We pull up to the house and knock on the door.

The door opens, and a young boy looks at us. Then he calls, "Aunt Betty." She comes, face pulled down in a frown, which makes her look a bit like a bulldog. She leads us to the dining room and we sit at the table. Alina and I sit to Emily's right. "Thanks, William. Tell the other Aunties that we are not to be disturbed." He leaves and she turns to Emily, lays her hands flat on the table. Alina and I could be invisible for all she notices us.

"You helped the FBI put Nephi and Frank in jail?"

"I was assisting the county attorney, and yes, we worked with the FBI."

"This will ruin our family," says Betty. She looks at Emily. "Not just financial ruin. Without Nephi at the head of our family, we'll fall apart. Social Services is already investigating us—with no real cause. The children are safe and happy, and I won't allow marriage before the girls are eighteen. We don't drive our boys away like some polygamists do." She sighs. "Frank thinks he can lead our community, but the two brothers are very different. Nephi is focused and a good organizer."

"And a criminal," says Emily.

"He was making up for what the government takes away."

"You mean taxes," says Emily, "that pay for schools and police."

"We don't send our children to public school and the police have never been our friends. We'd do just fine without the government."

Emily's eyes widen, as if this is a perspective she's not thought of before. "At this point there's not much I can do."

"Really? I had my sister in AF look you up. It seems you can do about whatever you set your mind to."

Again, it appears that this woman has surprised Emily. I'm really loving this conversation.

"You work for underdogs everywhere."

"Do you have a plan, a suggestion?" Emily asks.

"What if he saves everyone time and expense and confesses to distilling whiskey and cheating on the ethanol credits?"

Emily looks at the tabletop, thinking. I glance at Alina, who is focused on the two women.

"If you know about all that and helped him, then you're guilty too," she says.

Betty stands from the table. "I thought it may be a mistake asking for your help. We want to get out. We want to join the communities in Colonia Juárez. We'll be left alone there."

"Mexico has a government too," says Emily. "They'll expect you to pay taxes."

"So we're no worse off. I've spoken to my sister there. In terms of community and economics, we'll be better off. Anyway, we're going."

Emily frowns. "What are you asking me to do?"

Betty speaks quickly and firmly. "Talk to the county attorney, get him to talk to Nephi's lawyer, work out a plea bargain. It will save everyone money and time."

Emily looks at me, but I just shrug, nothing to say.

"I have five sister wives and twenty-four children to take care of. Frank's no help. I'm also committed to making sure his wives and children are safe and happy. What will happen to us?"

"Do you think Nephi would accept a plea bargain?"

"I do," says Betty. Then her voice and face both become even firmer. "He'd better." She opens the swinging door into another room. A woman comes through, followed by her children, then another, and another. They must have been waiting for her signal. The girls all wear pastel dresses, ankle length. The boys wear white shirts and trousers. I see Betty's daughters, the three Nephi offered me, move behind their mother. Soon the room is full. We are surrounded by women and children.

Betty gestures toward her sister wives and the children. Finally she looks back at Emily. She bends and takes Emily's hand. "Please."

Emily removes her hand, staring at Betty's face. Finally she nods.

"Thank you," says Betty. "Thank you." She shakes each of our hands.

We walk out to her truck, and Emily drives back through the farm.

Alina leans forward between the two front seats. "Wow! What a woman!"

"Yes," says Emily. "Canny. I've read about the network of polygamous women. They all help each other out. It is common opinion that they have no power, but if the man steps out of line, they join together to correct him. At least in some groups."

"The rhetoric of that conversation was remarkable," I say.

Alina mimics me and nails my tone and rhythm of speech, my facial expression, even the motions of my arms. Emily breaks into laughter, and Alina laughs along.

"The rhetoric?" Emily can hardly drive, she's laughing so hard. "Oh, the rhetoric."

"Yes," I say. "She took control of the story."

"I know," says Emily. "It just struck me funny. The rhetoric."

"I don't see what's so funny," I say. "And it's very rude of you, Alina, a rhetorician, to mock me about making a comment about physical rhetoric. All those children constituted an argument. She made it cruelty on our part to disagree with her."

They both stop laughing and are listening.

"It wouldn't work with judges in court," says Emily. "Or maybe it would."

"Human will and choice," I say.

"I can visualize a graph of that function," says Alina. "A dance of kinetic volition."

"Now that's funny," I say.

Alina smiles.

We see a pair of pronghorns, mother and fawn. Emily stops the truck and we watch them. Alina is grinning so wide her face could split. Emily's also happy to see them. Me? I'm happy about more things than I can number, the main one being that Emily came back and we're working through the troubles. Slower than I want, possibly, but we are making progress.

"You are both helping me become human again," I say. Emily takes my hand. Alina puts her hand on my shoulder. I realize that I haven't felt this happy for a long, long time.

"Friendship," says Alina, "is stronger than polygamy." She gives us her wry smile with one eyebrow raised and Emily laughs again.

Emily leaves immediately for the city; she's set up an emergency meeting with Nephi's lawyer and the FBI prosecutor. It's a sign of their respect for her will and ability that they both make time for her. She plans to come back tonight. Alina and I stand on the verge of the road. She's still grinning. "A mother and her little one."

"You've seen both polygamists and pronghorns in one day."

She gives me a look. "Both interest me, so don't make fun of me."

"Only a little."

She has barely started to walk down to the horse barn to get her bike when we see dust coming, and Delta drives up with Marion in the passenger's seat. They stop next to us.

"Hop in," says Delta.

"We want you to show us the cave," says Marion, leaning across her partner. Alina and I climb in the back seat, and Delta makes a U-turn and soon turns onto the road to the Valley of the Mines.

As we pass between the junipers, Alina tells them about her life in Amsterdam. "I have undergraduate degrees in poetry and coding." It feels like a job interview. "A minor in dance."

"A good balance," says Delta.

"We're very much into balance," says Marion. "Balance, bridge, arch, tie, span. *Equilibrate, evenwicht, equipoise*, etcetera." Alina does this thing with her arms, her head lolling, and the configuration of her body somehow manifests balance.

"We span," says Delta. She points at me. "But you're the one putting a spanner in the works." They laugh.

"I am?" I ask. "What exactly am I doing?"

"'I am,' he said," says Marion. "Iamb a lamb."

Delta says, "Madam. I am Adam." They laugh.

I look at the two of them and they both seem as corporeal as the truck and the rocks and trees we're passing. "I want to know which one of you is dead and which alive."

"We are both both," says Delta, "in such rapid sequence that nobody can tell. Not even us. Like the Heisenberg uncertainty principle."

"Are we wave or particle? Difficult to tell at any instance."

"We flickerbridge."

"More like Schrödinger's cat," says Alina. "Are you each alive or dead?"

"Or it's more like Christopher's raven." Delta points out the window at the bird that flies ahead of us and settles in a tree.

"My raven?" I ask.

They both laugh.

"But with us," says Marion, "you can't open a box to determine which it is. So it's forever indeterminate."

I shake my head. "I don't understand."

"But you do," says Delta. She takes both hands off the wheel, but the truck still tracks, so I don't say anything—even though I wish she'd pay more attention to the road, which has descended into the gully and is very rocky.

"The two of you," says Marion, "spanners in the works." She pauses. They pause. "But we're sidetracked about us."

"We could talk about us all day," says Delta. "Alina?"

"I studied the connection between the poetry of Blake as a prime text and non-binary coding as a way to explore probable human choices. Possible futures determined by possible actions," says Alina.

"Bingo," says Marion. "That's the stuff that will either unravel the fractal order of the universe or knit it up again."

"We can't decide which we'd like better," says Delta.

"Maybe both." Marion grins. "A knitting up that unravels."

"An unravelling that knits." Delta interlocks her fingers as the truck somehow misses a boulder that her right front tire was going to hit.

"A balance," says Alina. "A relative balance. Prime!"

"*Exactamente*," says Delta. "Might I say you have a way with words?"

Alina shrugs. "But then I gave up."

"You didn't just give up," I say.

"They kicked me out," she says.

"Which resulted in our good fortune to meet you," says Delta, "although we knew *about* you."

"We certainly did," says Marion.

"You say I will also have a role," I say.

"Pivotal," says Marion, turning good-naturedly toward me.

"I wish I could understand what this role is. So I can prepare myself." We're passing through the canyon into the valley. The stream is to our right. I shouldn't worry about Delta's driving, but I'm sure we're going to drop into the streambed.

"But that would endanger the balance," says Delta.

"Not-knowing is key," says Marion.

"You know, '*One step enough for me*,'" says Delta. "Like that."

"But I can't even see one step ahead," I say.

"Of course you can," says Marion. "You enjoyed the petroglyphs."

I wonder what enjoying the petroglyphs has to do with anything. "So doesn't my knowing I have a role endanger the balance?"

"No. It ensures the balance. It's the difference between being on your toes and having your choices handed to you. The cave is a prime example."

"Actually I found the cave," says Alina.

"That's right," says Delta. "I always get the two of you confused. Except one of you dances and the other one doesn't."

"I dance," I say. "But it's all in my head."

"It took both of you," says Marion. "Alone, neither one of you would have found it."

"But why the cave?" I ask. "Is there some secret message for the world in those petroglyphs?"

"Not secret," says Marion.

"No secrets," says Delta. "Simple stuff."

"Like everything we need to know we learned in kindergarten," says Marion. "That kind of stuff. I am human. This is a pronghorn. There is a spring with clear water in this valley. A stream runs from the spring. Essential stuff. Important stuff." They level a finger at Alina. "Not complex and abstract like Spinoza."

"But not secret," says Delta. The truck finally does hit a boulder, bouncing all of us. "That was surprising."

"So if it's not secret, why does it have to be discovered?" I ask.

They both seem puzzled by my question.

"He's like a child," says Delta to Marion.

"A baby. It's actually quite cute."

"A little lamb. Iamb a lamb."

"It's not the cave," says Marion.

"And it's not you."

"It's the act."

"The enactment of the act."

"Just like we bridge. A verb."

"The act is like moving a pawn."

"Christopher and Alina open. Like that. Christopher and Alina cave-discover. Christopher and Alina disobey and open to discovery. Eve apples and Newton apples."

"Précisément."

"Clear as smog," I say.

"I get it," says Alina. "So elegant."

"Use your imagination, Christopher," says Marion. "You're not nearly as dumb as you pretend to be."

Alina laughs and slugs me softly on my shoulder.

We enter the Valley of the Mines, and Delta turns left toward the tin building. Nine crows sit on the roof of the rusted tin building. Marion and Delta look at the crows and at each other. The smiles fade from their faces.

"It's come to that," says Marion.

"Well, it always was in the cards."

We cross the valley, climb the steep slope to the spill of dirt, and enter the mouth of the mine.

Marion and Delta put their arms across each other's shoulders as if they are winning a three-legged race. They walk fast and steady, their steps exactly hitting the railroad ties. We stumble along behind them.

"I knew someone like them in Amsterdam."

"I don't believe it," I say. "There is nobody else like them in the world."

"A little like them. Funny like them. Gender fluid and funny."

"Irrepressible."

"Yes."

We soon come to the big room. Alina and I flash our lights around. Of course, Marion and Delta see fine without lights. I point to the new ladder. "Somebody's been up there recently."

Marion sniffs the air. They do this with their mouth open and their tongues extended a little. Maybe they can taste whatever scent is in the air. "Three somebodies."

"Recently and anciently."

"Millennians," says Marion, "like Alina."

"That's millennials," says Alina.

"So different from you," says Delta. "These are true millennians."

I start laughing.

"What?" asks Alina.

"It's just too much. God is playing with my head."

"Not God," says Marion. "They have other things on their minds right now."

Marion and Delta smile into my light.

"The Three," Delta says.

"The Three Nephites," I say to Alina. "The Book of Mormon says that Christ visited the people on this continent, and when he left, three of his disciples wanted to—"

"Tarry," says Delta.

"Like John the Beloved."

I say, "They don't taste death, pain, or suffering."

"Except for the sins of mankind," says Delta.

I step toward the ladder. "Can we meet them?"

"Probably." Marion listens and tastes the air again. "But they're not in now."

"OK," I say, "I want to know their names."

"Now *that* is secret," says Delta. "Still secret."

"We call them Thing Number One, Two, and Three," says Marion.

"Take a guess," says Delta. "Their names could be Nephi, Timothy, Jonas, Mathoni, Mathonihah, Kumen, Kumenonhi, Jeremiah, Shemnon, another Jonas, Zedekiah, or Isaiah."

"You have a twenty-five percent chance of naming one."

"Thirty-three if you name Jonas."

"Kumenonhi," I say.

"Oh, we can't tell you if you're right."

We turn and continue down the shaft toward the entrance to the cave. "Do they eat and sleep?" Alina asks.

"They're still human," says Marion. "Except they can't die if they don't eat."

"Thing Number Two went on a food and sleep fast in 1964," says Delta. "After forty days she went kind of crazy. It was pretty catastrophic."

"The other two had to pour a mixture of raw eggs and olive oil down her throat to get some calories in her. To bring her back to sanity and halt the destruction."

"The Alaska Earthquake," I say.

Delta nods.

We crawl through the opening into the cave and turn left toward the petroglyphs, which we reach in a few minutes. Delta and Marion stand shoulder to shoulder looking at them.

I am moved again by the elegance of the lines. A circle, self maybe, water maybe, a pronghorn, a wavy line, again for a stream. Water is life in the desert. Jagged lines. Lightning? The people who made these glyphs and their Goshute descendants wandered in a twenty-mile circuit, moving with the seasons, eating greens, berries, tubers, nuts, meat from insects, rodents, and mammals, small and large. They circled through time as well as through space. Or, more precisely, time was not merely linear for them. The seasons cycled but individuals were born, matured, and died. But they thought of even a person's stages as a cycle, this life and the next.

Delta turns to me. "You see it."

"Persuasive physical rhetoric," says Marion, gesturing toward the wall. "Not much room for the will to power."

"Just enough room," says Delta. "Power is organization. They were organized."

"Diffused power," says Marion.

"Opposition in all things."

"A balance."

"Like us."

"They had a society that was stable for thousands of years."

"Then ownership happened."

Delta faces me and puts her hands on my shoulders. Normally I'm not a touchy person, but I don't mind her gesture. I can feel her hands there and can't sense the vacillation across the veil. "Commerce tips the scale."

"When people have enough to trade, they also have enough to say, 'This is mine,' and others want to take it. Make it theirs."

"Excess creates a whole different algorithm." Delta takes her hands away.

"The fractals of human behavior."

What Emily would say comes into my mind. "So many women died from childbirth. Without some excess, there isn't enough to go around. Those people were always hungry despite working all day to gather food."

Alina nods. "Babies died. Old people died sooner than they do now."

"I guess you have a point," says Marion. "Every system has problems."

"Every system is imperfect but theirs worked for them."

"Death is not the worst that can happen."

I sit on a boulder, hoping to stare at the panel for an hour, study each one.

They move away from the panel. "Well, that was fun," Delta says.

"We'll let ourselves out," says Marion. "Oh," she turns back, "speaking of the will to power, you learned what it was like in the Garden of Eden. Luckily your grandmother is a formidable woman."

"Who were they?" I ask.

"You already know."

"Great-Aunt Sula," I say.

"You got it in one."

"It's a bad sign when she shows up with an axe."

"Time to run for cover."

"And her sister wife, Agnes." I feel both fever and chill remembering her.

"Lovely woman."

I wouldn't use the word lovely. She used her beauty as a weapon. She inspired longing yes, but also terror and the threat of oblivion.

They both touch me, one hand on each shoulder. It's clear they understand my fear of Sula and my desire for Agnes. Even now I would do whatever they asked.

"Sula loved her husband but she also loved Agnes."

"See you later, Christopher."

They are already walking up the slope of the cave and away.

"Wait," says Alina, but they don't turn back. We hear them still talking, laughing occasionally. Alina turns her light in my face. When I hold my hand to stop the glare, she points it at my feet. "Sorry, Chris. I keep forgetting." She looks up the tunnel. "I wanted to ask them more."

"Their answers would twist in the air."

"They make some sense," she says. "Who are Sula and Agnes?"

I tell her the story of the murder with the axe.

"They were survivors," Alina says. "It kind of proves the point that capitalism makes us selfish and greedy."

"Maybe that's what it shows. That poor old miner might not have survived the winter if he had shared. Maybe it was a practical decision that would have happened even when subsistence was the norm." I sit back on the boulder. "I used to idealize my ancestors."

"You idealized Sula and Agnes?"

I shrug. "Even them. As you said, they were survivors. But especially my male ancestors. But now that I'm talking to them, they don't seem so perfect."

"You said 'them.' You've only told me about talking to your great-grandfather."

"I—ah—play poker with my father, grandfather, and great-great-grandfather."

"Poker! Why didn't you tell me this before? That's significant."

"Significant?"

"I have a whole chapter in my thesis on the resonance between games of chance and the algorithms of the universe."

"So God does play dice?"

She makes a face at me. "Do they cheat?"

"I'm sure of it, but I never figured out how. When they play, they're petty, bossy, argumentative, and condescending."

"Sounds like my thesis committee. They acted that way because they didn't want to deal with the implications of my research. Before I got to know them well, I admired them also."

I point at the carvings. "I'm probably doing the same for these ancestors of the Goshutes. If they were here, they might be just as unpleasant as my ancestors. Still I admire them for having a stable culture for so long. I know they had a difficult time of it, but Delta and Marion didn't think it a huge problem that they had subsistence-level lives."

"They had time to represent their lives in art. Just like us, they used language and symbols to portray the complex balance between survival and procreation."

I gesture toward the whole panel. "Can you put all this in a mathematical formula?"

She smiles. "Yes. The answer is always 42." She makes this weird shape with her arms, and somehow that's also the number 42.

I laugh.

"But I don't have the right kind of data."

I look at the petroglyphs. "If the balance is off, so that everyone makes the predictable choice, then there's no room for growth. It's the devil's plan."

Alina shines her light at my face and moves it to my feet again. "The devil's plan? You're speaking Greek."

"The Mormon idea is that Jesus designed the Plan of Progression, which would give Adam and Eve incompatible commandments. On the one hand they were to progress, but on the other they couldn't progress because he told them not to eat of the tree of knowledge. Jesus told Father and Mother God the plan—that sin was inevitable and even desirable, because it only happens when choice is available."

"Did they know all the consequences?"

I shrug. "Possibly. Anyway, Lucifer said, 'I offer a better plan. Make them never sin.' He wanted to establish a system that would cause everyone to make 'correct choices.' He didn't want an algorithm that approached balance of will between God and Man."

"I thought you were a journalist," Alina says. "You sound like a professor in lecture mode."

I frown at her. "One more thing, then I'll stop. I think that Lucifer didn't like chaos. He didn't like it when he couldn't predict where water would flow when dripped on a perfectly smooth plane."

Alina laughs.

"What?"

"Pretend I'm Delta. What kind of music does the inventor of the internet dance to?"

I smile. "Al Gore rhythm. He didn't invent the internet. By the way."

"Of course he didn't," she says. "I hope Delta and Marion are not gone forever. I miss them already."

We make our way out of the cave and out of the mine. Again, as every time I emerge, I'm surprised by the light, the spring-greening valley, the blue, blue sky. The flat-bottomed sun sitting on the western hills. I can't remember the poet who invented that image—the flat-bottomed sun. Probably a Greek. Every time I think of that I also think of the Queen song 'Fat Bottomed Girls,' so it's a confusion of images. They make the world go round.

We don't talk much as we walk back to the camp. I'm so full of what I've seen and learned that I don't have words yet. So many questions that I can't articulate the first one.

SIXTEEN

Triangulation

Bennie, Lucía, Alina, and I gather for dinner. Andrew left earlier for a meeting with state officials about establishing a historical preservation site for the plateau of the cave. The difficulty is weighing the value of the cave and the lek. Both should be protected, but the preservation needs of each are different, making the situation complex.

"How was your day?" Alina asks Bennie.

He shrugs. "Not much progress. My people were probably showered with nerve gas and other poisons in the sixties, but the government lawyers fight us all the way."

Lucía says, "It will happen. Emily doesn't give up."

"The problem isn't her. We're divided as a tribe—not over this lawsuit necessarily, but over the company that wants to store atomic waste on our land. On one side are those who want the money, on the other those who don't want to poison our land with radioactive waste. It's both physical and spiritual damage to have it there."

"Both the nerve gas accident and the atomic waste dump come from the idea that desert is wasteland," I say. "Not habitable."

"Exactly. And the two cases influence each other because the disunity on the nuclear waste diverts time and energy we need for the battle over reparations for the nerve gas. Very difficult."

Alina puts her hand on his arm. "If anybody can pull them together, it's you."

"Thanks." He looks at her hand and his face struggles between a smile and a frown.

Lucía says, "Will you help me with something inside, Chris?"

"What?" I look at her, and she angles her head toward Alina and Bennie. "Oh. Sure." I get to my feet.

Inside, she leans against the kitchenette counter. "He's a good guy. She doesn't seem like the type to make a long-term commitment, but I think he is that type. I hope she doesn't hurt him."

"Maybe guys just want to have fun too."

She frowns at me.

"Not me!" I say. "I was talking about Bennie."

"So you're a proponent of long-term commitment?"

A loaded question. I nod. "Yes. I'm not great at it, but I'm learning." I serve one back at her. "What did you mean when you said earlier that you're in love with Alina?"

She shakes her head. "I just said it to be funny. Because Bennie said it. Even Emily said it."

"So you're just watching out for Bennie?" I smile. "No conflict of interest?"

She steps back, and I think she's offended, but she laughs. "I have so much more experience than Bennie. I'm not the one who will get hurt."

I lift my eyebrows.

"I'm teasing. Also, I couldn't take up with her after she dumps him. It would hurt him twice."

I shrug. "If anybody could make a triangle work, it's Alina."

"Triangles never work," she says. "You of all people should know that."

Is she talking about Roger and Emily and me? I'm surprised she knows about that. Emily does treat Andrew and Lucía like co-equals if not family.

I don't say anything for a minute.

"I've offended you," says Lucía. "Emily and that prosecuting attorney, Roger Finley, didn't hide what was going on."

"I didn't know it was so public."

"I don't believe secrets are healthy. When you left, she was torn up. She dropped Roger like a—a toad."

"She did? I thought that was later. Around Christmas."

"No."

"She used him to shake things up," I say.

"Maybe."

I can tell she has more to impart. "Go on. Tell me."

"I've never understood why your people thought polygamy would work."

"Sometimes it kind of worked," I say. "Two of my great-great-grandfather's wives got along. Two of my great-aunts murdered a man and lived together not far from here."

She snorts.

"But," I say, "it was usually a fiasco."

"A disaster," she says. "All those love triangles and quadrangles and octagons. None of them stable."

I can't keep a grin off my face. "The geometry of love. You and Alina think alike—the mathematics of human intercourse."

She smiles. "Points of intersection."

"Give me a fulcrum and I can make the earth move." I laugh at my own joke.

Now she snorts again. "You know, you're not nearly as funny as you think you are." But she says it with a kind voice.

Emily comes back after dinner. "Nephi agreed," she says. "We have to wait for a judge, but his plea bargain will go through." Despite this success she's peevish.

I know better than to say something useless like, "Do you want to talk about it?" If she wants to talk, she will.

We sit still for a moment. Alina uses her eyebrows to signal Bennie, and they stand and drive down to her apartment in the horse barn. Andrew brings out the cards, and the rest of us play poker using a stack of chips that Lucía brought from her last trip to town. As before, I win steadily, which could be because I'm playing with people limited by their bodies and perceptual capacities, or it could mean something else entirely. Anyway, it feels good to win, but it's a temporary feeling. I know that I'll soon feel unsettled again. One by-product of all the chaos of the last two-and-a-half weeks is that my traditional ways of assigning meaning through rationality, empiricism, guilt, or desire have been upset, come unmoored, and I can no longer interpret my life. I'm not comfortable in my own skin, which could be a good thing, a sign of growth. Like a snake I'm ready to shed the past. At least that's what I tell myself.

Emily keeps glancing at me, even when it's not my turn to bet or ask for cards, and I have trouble reading her face. Not really happy or sad, maybe curious. Curious is good; I can work with that.

After I clean them out, I say, "I think I'll have a shower and turn in."

I'm lying on top of the covers, waiting for a knock. I blink and they're standing around my bed.

I shut my eyes, open them, hopeful, but they haven't left.

"Please, not tonight," I say. "I have a headache."

"Ha, ha," says Louis.

"You've been abridged," says my father.

"Spanned, tuned up, balanced," says Louis.

"What the hell does that mean?"

"Basically it means you've been measured and found wanting," says Hugh.

"By Marion and Delta? They didn't judge me, not like you do."

"They are good at their job," says my father.

"And they don't really judge," says Hugh.

"You said I was measured and found wanting."

"Measuring doesn't always imply judgment," says Hugh. "If I said you're six feet tall—"

"You'd be lying," says my father. "He's five-eleven."

"That's what Marion and Delta do, measure how balanced things are," says Hugh. "They don't judge what it means."

"What it means is up to us," says Louis. "They measured you, and we've found you wanting."

"In obedience," says Hugh.

"I don't think so," I say. "If the rocks obey, that means they are true to their nature. I'm true to my nature. I'm true to the light shining through me."

"Faulty comparison," says Hugh.

"Rocks aren't carnal," says Louis. "You're damn carnal."

"You'll couple with that woman who is fighting for the other side," says my father.

"It's complex. What she's doing provides more freedom for some and less freedom for others. Like every human act."

"She's opposed to the kind of freedom the West was founded on," Louis says.

"The freedom to do whatever you damn well please even if it hurts someone else." I glare at him and he glares back. I wonder what would happen if he punched me. I think I'd get knocked to the ground. Maybe I'd have part of my identity scattered like stardust.

"We've warned you enough," says Hugh.

"Stay out of that fucking cave," says Louis.

"You'll be sorry if you don't," says my father. I look at his face and he really seems concerned.

"What are you going to do? Make it collapse on me?"

There is a quiet knock. As the door opens, they are gone. Emily peeks around, her hair draping over one shoulder. She shuts the door behind her and leans against it. She's wearing a T-shirt that's too big for her—a picture of Bob Dylan when he was young. "Who were you talking to?"

"My father, grandfather, great-great-grandfather."

She swallows. She seems as nervous as a teenager, and I feel about the same. Dylan's forehead looks stretched out because it's a t-shirt made for a man. She's also not wearing a bra and I try to focus on her face but my gaze keeps drifting down.

"It's like your dream," I say. "You've never been a dreamer. Before I came to the desert four months ago, I'd never seen spirits. Now you've dreamed dreams and I've seen spirits."

"Like the crazy people in our families. It makes me feel a little ashamed I doubted them."

I can't stop my own babbling. "What used to be crazy is normal now." She steps forward and stands in front of me. I move to one side of the bed. "I've felt disrupted, turned every which way."

She sits on the bed. "I've been thinking about what you said about multi-tasking."

I move my hand in a dismissing motion. "No big deal." I don't want to get back into that argument.

"It was a big deal to you at the time. It's not a big deal now because you want to have sex instead of talking."

"We talked about it a little." I soften my voice. "We made progress."

She puts her hand on my foot, and the sensation goes up my thigh.

"I'm very much a type A personality," she says.

I wait but she doesn't continue. "I used to be."

"No. You just loved uncovering stuff. Opening diseased things to the light. Even a natural type B person can focus on what they love. You just had trouble switching that focus to me. I was jealous."

"Jealous of my work?"

She thinks a moment. "No. That's not it. I knew this about you when we married. At the beginning you were also focused on me, but then you drifted. I guess I was jealous of what we had earlier."

It's my own argument. "You—" I begin.

"I blamed you for what you're blaming me for now. We drifted. Yes, both of us."

She's moving her thumb in a circle on the inside of my thigh, and I can hardly think about anything else.

"I promise," she says, "I will make time for you."

I want to touch her back, but I don't. Fool that I am, I open my mouth again. "Time—" I close my eyes and lose the words I was going to say.

"Time out?" Her hand stills.

"No, don't stop! Time is funny. Circular. The same thing happens—"

She puts her finger on my lips. I want to take it into my mouth, but I hesitate, and she takes it away. "Please stop talking." She leans back against the wall. "Let me talk for a minute. You're right about me multitasking." It's like the words are dragged out of her. "My second commitment is that I will tell you when I'm multitasking if you're around so you know how to respond. I'll be more transparent about my agenda."

I can't see her face clearly when she's back under the bunk.

"This is really difficult." She leans forward and with both hands pushes her hair behind her ears. I'm frightened she's going to stand and leave the room.

"Don't go," I say. "Please."

"I wasn't leaving." She smiles, both wry and sad. "Have we ruined the mood?"

"No," I say. "I needed to feel that you heard me."

Her mouth twists like she wants to make a joke. Then she stops. "I do. Hear you. When we were first married, focus on each other came naturally."

"Was it really focus on the other? I'm not sure we knew each other."

"Maybe. But it was nice. When you held me, I melted. My being paid attention."

In the light I see the blue of her eyes. "As does mine. You are still striking."

She laughs. "Striking?"

"Your eyes—sometimes gray sometimes blue. Your face—it's a fine face." I touch her cheek.

"Yours as well. I like looking at your face. Now that you've bathed, I can get closer." She puts her hand over mine and leans forward to kiss me lightly.

"I didn't have any reason to bathe. Now I do."

"Do you have hope that we can change? Be more mindful of each other?"

Her hand drifts back to my thigh, and my body sings Hallelujah.

"Mindful? I can't think when you're doing that. But it certainly makes me feel hopeful."

She laughs and pushes me back on the bed, kisses me again. I feel the pull of her through my whole body—strong as electric current.

Then it's as if the Dead Fathers are peering at us. I can't see in the darkness whether or not they really are standing at the foot of the bed. "Dammit to hell!"

She rolls off and lies next to me. "What happened?"

"I'm worried they're watching."

"Who?"

"My ancestors."

She's silent for a minute and I don't know what she's thinking.

My body's still humming with desire. "So frustrating. I wish they'd leave me alone."

"Are they here now?"

"No."

"Don't you think they have other things to do? Is the afterlife constant window peeping?"

I think about them. They told me to avoid reconnecting with Emily, but I think they'd have enough empathy for me to stay away now. I hope so.

"No, I don't think it's constant spying."

She leans toward me. Kisses me again. Moist lips, warm, probing tongue.

I turn my head and break the kiss. "When I was young, it wouldn't have mattered that they were watching."

"When you were young, you finished in twenty seconds. I don't mind taking time for this."

"All those years, I thought the goal was efficiency, but that has been our undoing."

"A pox on both your efficiency and my multitasking."

We hold each other, her head on my chest. I stroke her hair. "This is nice. Do you know that I like you?"

"Ah, yes," she says. "I believe it again. Do you?"

"Believe it? Ah, yes." I sing, "I believe in miracles," and she joins me: "Since you came along, you sexy thing."

I tug at her shirt and she lets me pull it over her head. I sing again, "I believe in nakedness. Where's your bra, you sexy thang?"

She snorts "Oh, my hell, Chris. I have missed you so much. Your wretched singing. Your bizarre humor."

She helps me out of my clothing and we move together for a long, long while. Afterward she holds me as if she'll never let me go again.

"Compartmentalize that!" I say.

She laughs again, a sound I've always loved. "I can't. It was all in all."

We lie in silence and it's like my whole being is smiling. I think about the petroglyphs and wonder which one or ones describe this—maybe the widening spiral. The elementals: water, food, sleep, love. Repeat. Life cycles.

SEVENTEEN

Spelucking with Peter

The next morning when we dress and walk out of our room, it's late. I keep thinking about it being our room, not my room. Everyone's heads turn toward us as we come out of the trailer; even Bennie and Alina are there. They're finishing breakfast, and Andrew smiles at us. Lucía grins. Then she leans her head back and whoops. Soon everyone is cheering, and I join in.

Emily, red-faced, says, "I hope this is not the usual reaction from the peanut gallery."

"Was there an earthquake in this region last night?" says Andrew.

"Don't you know it's rude to talk about someone's private life," says Emily, but she doesn't have a vestige of anger on her face, and she's struggling to keep from smiling.

"I think nothing is private in a small trailer," Alina says.

"It's right to celebrate," says Lucía, "after such a long dry spell."

"How long was it?" asks Alina. "The dry spell."

Emily shrugs.

I calculate in my head. "Ten months, twenty days. Ah—and two hours."

They all laugh.

Emily looks at me. "You are seriously obsessed." Finally a smile blooms on her face.

"How?" Alina says, puzzled. She looks from me to Emily. "How and why did you go that long? What is the use of that kind of self-deprivation?"

"That," says Bennie, "is not a safe question."

"Back off guys," says Emily. "Not your business."

"Right," says Andrew. "This whole conversation is making me very uncomfortable."

"Go to hell, Andrew," says Emily.

After breakfast, they gather around the outside table to bring each other up to speed. Alina and I join them. Bennie says he's got a meeting that afternoon with the paralegals who have interviewed older Goshutes about their experience with the nerve gas. Andrew says he met with not only the state history people, but with the hunters and the BLM. They just argued, even though both sides accepted him as a mediator. He had also met with the Nature Conservancy and Cannon-Sharp. Lucía would get an archeologist to write descriptions of the petroglyphs in Lost Canyon and also the petroglyphs in the cave, based on the pictures Alina took. Emily had worked out the final details with Nephi Johnson's plea bargain, and she also had met with Bennie and the state about the proposal to store radioactive waste on the reservation. So she had finished her assignments to herself. Alina was going to muck manure out of the horse barn.

"What's next?" I ask Emily.

"I have a surprise for you."

"I don't like surprises."

"You will this one."

She won't tell me anything else. We make far too many sandwiches and load them into a cooler. So it's not just the two of us. "What is your plan?"

She looks toward the road as a vehicle drives up. When it stops next to Emily's truck, I see it's Carrie-Anne and Bruce with their children in back. Carrie-Anne gets out and unstraps Erica. Karin and Peter hug Emily. Even though the number of sandwiches warned me, I wasn't prepared. I fill my eyes with them, and I can't speak.

Emily smiles at me. "I told you you'd like this."

"I do. I'm also frightened," I say softly.

"That's silly," she says.

Carrie-Anne hugs me. "The teachers had an in-service day, so we decided to take advantage of it."

"Thank you." Tears well in my eyes.

Carrie-Anne hugs me again. "You're welcome. If you can't get Muhammad to come to the mountain—"

I turn to Karin. She looks taller. She has rainbow streaks in her hair. She frowns at me but finally walks into my embrace.

"I missed you, Grandpa."

"I missed *you*," I say.

"You should have come home," she says. "I was lonely for you."

I hug her again, precious child. "I had some things to think about."

"Will you come home now?" she asks.

"Soon. I promise. Soon."

Peter is pulling at his mother's hand. "I want to go now!"

"Go where?" I ask.

"I don't understand why you ran away," Karin says. Clearly, she thinks it was selfish of me. I agree. She frowns at me again, and I see I'm not going to get by without saying something more.

"Your grandmother and I weren't getting along."

"So you ran away?"

"Not very good of me, is it? It felt like my only option." It sounds silly to say out loud. "What I know for sure. I'm glad to see you. I've missed you."

She gives me only a flat smile, apparently not ready to forgive yet.

I bend over Peter, who hugs me stiffly and then returns to his grandmother. I hug the baby in Carrie-Anne's arms, and she immediately starts to cry. I shake hands with Bruce, who pulls me into an embrace. "Glad to see you, Christopher."

"Same here," I say.

"Are you ready to go spelunking?" asks Emily.

Peter tips his face up to her. "What's spelucking?"

"It's looking for luck in all the wrong places." I feel giddy to see them.

Carrie-Anne groans. "Bad grandpa."

Karin says, "We're going into a cave. Grandpa discovered a cave."

"Are you sure it's safe?" asks Carrie-Anne.

"I've been down there several times." And several times the Dead Fathers warned me against it, but nothing happened. "It's safe." I wonder if I've told the truth. It was difficult for Alina and me. We had to crawl under a ledge. And there's the place where the ceiling caved in. I want to show them the cave, especially Karin. If we go in through the mine, we can look at the petroglyph panel and it will be easier. "I don't have enough helmets for everyone."

"I rented helmets and lights for us."

"Good. We'll be safe."

"OK," says Emily. "Jump back in your car."

"It's not a car," says Peter. "It's a SUV."

Emily and I climb into her truck.

I sob once, surprising myself. "You should have warned me." The longing for them is like nostalgia, but for the present, not the past. Or the longing is for a future. "What the hell was I thinking?"

"Hmm," she says. "You did what you felt you had to do."

"That's what I told Karin."

She starts the engine. "Now you'll appreciate them."

"I lost so much time." I lean against her shoulder, awkward across the gearshift. "You. You came after me."

"I did." She nods. "Yes, I did come after you. I did that one thing right after—after my other mistakes."

We go first and the others follow, up along the dirt road that leads to the mines and the cave. I've passed these cedars so many times, walking and on my bike. It's nice to be going past the familiar turns and dips with my people. My family.

Emily drives into the Valley of the Mines.

I ask, "How do you want to go into the cave? We can climb down into the mouth in the next valley or we can walk into the cave through the mine, up there." I point to the thirteenth mine. "I think we should go through the mine."

Emily asks, "Will it be more of an adventure if we go through the top? Will we see more of the cave?"

I nod. "It's just easier to go in the bottom. Much of it is through the mine, where you've been, and that's very open. And the petroglyph panel is closer to the bottom. We'd have to lower people with a rope if we go in from the top."

"I think it will be fun for the kids to climb down."

I think again about the tight spots and fallen rock. They're all smaller than I am, and Alina and I cleared the way through the cave-in. "More difficult, but yes, more fun." I look back at the other vehicle. "I'm glad they came to see me. And the cave." I look across at her. The morning sun makes her face glow. "I'm glad you will get to see the petroglyphs. I think the kids will love them."

I direct her to park her truck next to the tin building. "We can leave your truck here so when we come out, we can ferry Bruce or Carrie-Anne up on top to get their SUV. That way we won't have to walk back up to the opening." I walk to the other vehicle and explain the same to them. We move the bag that has my helmet and the rope from Emily's pickup into the SUV, and I point to show the children where we'll come out of the mine. Then we crowd in with them and Bruce drives up and over the pass. As he navigates the bad road, I look to the left and seem to see something move on the skirt before the thirteenth mine, which is where we'll come out. When I look more closely, I see nothing. We park at the juniper near the mouth of the cave, and everyone gathers around the hole. Peter runs right to the edge and peers down.

"Stand back," says Carrie-Anne. Karin pulls Peter back a little.

"Stop it!" he says. "Stop it, Karin."

"The ground isn't stable," I tell him. "You could fall in and hurt yourself. That's how we discovered it. The ground caved in and my friend fell down inside."

He still shrugs out of Karin's hands and steps forward again. Carrie-Anne reaches as if to stop him, but he doesn't get as close to the edge as he was before. She smiles at me, apparently counting that as a win, or at least a truce, in her constant battle to keep her adventurous and impulsive son safe. "You're sure this is safe?"

I nod. Her battle with me is similar to her struggle with her five-year-old son. As she helps Bruce and me put the rope around the tree, I think the Dead Fathers' warning seemed even more firm and desperate than their usual vague rants. I look at the happy faces of my grandchildren. Emily, Carrie-Anne, and Bruce are excited too. I think about what they'd say if I tell them that my dead ancestors warned me not to go down in the cave. Carrie-Anne and Bruce are firmly rooted in this world and have made clear what they think about their visionary aunt, Emily's sister, dreaming dreams. I could tell them it's too dangerous, and we could do something else, but I want them to see the cave Alina and I discovered. Bruce hands out the helmets and headlamps. I'll just have to be vigilant for any danger.

Peter says, "I'm smiling and scared, both at the same time."

We sling the rope around the tree, and Carrie-Anne climbs down into the hole first. She uses the rope to steady herself as she climbs down the fall of rock to the side of the hole. Then Bruce lowers Peter down to her while I hold Erica's hand. "Hello," I say, "I'm your grandfather."

"Hole." She strains forward to see where Carrie-Anne stands below her. "Mama."

"How old are you?"

She holds up two fingers.

"Smart kid!"

Karin goes next. I show Bruce how to tie a bowline and he lowers Erica. I'm worried about how to get Emily down the five-foot drop, but while I'm thinking she holds the rope and clambers down. Then it's my turn. Bruce makes me tie a bowline around myself. As I make my way down the slope of boulders, I slip and fall about a foot before Bruce catches me. Soon we're standing together in the cave. The light shines on us from the opening, but I have them turn on their lamps.

I point to where we have to go, under the ledge that made me claustrophobic the first time.

"Through there?" Carrie-Anne says, holding Erica.

"Maybe we should have entered through the bottom," Emily says.

"There's another way?" asks Carrie-Anne.

"We'll be fine," says Bruce.

I take my helmet off and slither through head first. From the other side, I call back, "See? Nothing to it."

Karin comes next, then Emily and Peter.

Carrie-Anne comes last. When she emerges from under the rock slab, she says, "You should have warned us, Dad! I pictured something more like Timpanogos Cave. Much more open inside."

"It's more open the rest of the way," I say. "Except for one spot." The only light now is from our lamps. "Here we are, Peter. Spelunking."

He runs ahead of me and Bruce calls him back.

"I want to be first," says Peter.

"Grandpa is our guide," says Carrie-Anne. "He needs to go first."

Bruce grab's Peter's hand, but Peter pulls against him, trying to get ahead of me.

We stop at the rockfall where Alina and I had to move boulders to make a way. Carrie-Anne balks again, but Karin climbs through, then I do. Karin helps bring Peter and Erica across. By the time we're all on the other side, we're covered with clay dust.

"That was way sketchy," says Carrie-Anne. "I was frightened more rocks would fall on us."

I don't know what to say to her. As we continue down the tunnel, Erica wants to walk so we go slow.

"How did you find this cave?" asks Karin.

I clamber over a boulder and offer my hand to Emily, but she pushes it away. "I'm younger than you are."

"Three months don't make any difference." I turn back to Karin. "I've been looking for it ever since I came to the desert." Peter tries to run past but Karin snags him.

"My great-grandfather wrote about it," I say, "about a Goshute man who hid from soldiers in this cave."

We have to walk single file past some rubble.

"Were they trying to kill him?"

"Yes. But this cave saved his life. He hid from the soldiers in here. Also, I didn't actually find the cave. My friend Alina found it. She was standing where the hole is now and it caved in. I was watching and she just disappeared."

Karin frowns. "Alina. Who's she?"

"She's my friend, too," says Emily. "She's from the Netherlands, and she takes care of the horse barn that's not far from our camp. She probably kept your grandpa from killing himself in this cave."

"Oh," says Karin.

"I think you'll like her," I say.

"I'm glad she watched out for you," she says.

"And I watched out for her."

"Lucky you're both still alive," says Carrie-Anne.

"We're safer down here than you were as you drove your car to get here."

Carrie-Anne snorts. "Doesn't feel safer."

"Safer than my school," says Karin.

"It is?" says Bruce.

"Really?" says Carrie-Anne.

But Karin says nothing else. What is she talking about? Gangs, guns, drugs? Probably homophobia.

Walking with one hand on the moist wall, I worry about all of them, the troubles they will all face. "The world's a scary place," I say.

"Dad!" says Carrie-Anne.

"I'm glad I have my light," says Peter. "I'd be scared without it."

"Your mom and I are here," says Bruce. "You're safe."

"Safe," says Erica.

"I know I'm safe," says Peter. "With my light I can be first. I can be the guide."

Suddenly, I don't feel safe. I feel beset by fear. What Karin said about school being dangerous has penetrated my psyche like an arrow. So it's not the cave that frightens me. It's everything outside the cave, all the deceit, hatred, and violence in the world. I wish I could hide in the cave with the people I love, protect them. It would be very odd to have a panic attack about the state of the world when I'm far from the world, deep in the earth.

"Are you all right?" Emily asks.

I nod and walk ahead. Soon I'm calm again. We stop several times to rest, sitting on boulders. The kids have snacks. Peter gobbles his and runs ahead with his light. When his parents both call him back, he starts climbing on a wall. I worry he's going to fall, so I move closer to him.

I ask Karin, "Do you have friends at school?"

She smiles at me. "Of course I have friends, Grandpa. School is good. It just sometimes doesn't feel safe."

"I could come and beat them up."

She rolls her eyes at me. "They'd beat you up."

I cast around for another question. "What is your favorite class?"

"Math. It's like a puzzle. A game."

"I'm in the first grade," says Peter.

"What do you like?" I ask.

"Reading."

"They're both good students," says Bruce.

"Look at me," Peter says. "I'm climbing." He steps up on a rock sticking out from the side of the cave. He finds another rock, slightly higher, and steps up onto it.

"Be careful," says Carrie-Anne.

"Someday, you'll be a great climber," says Bruce.

"I'm already a great climber."

Karin lifts him off the wall, and he calls, "Karin! Stop it!"

Emily and Carrie-Anne look toward me, questioning. I stand and we continue down the tunnel.

After a while, Peter says, "This is a long cave. I think this is the longest cave in the world."

"It's long," I say. "But we'll come to the end soon."

After a half hour of slow walking and climbing, we pass the side tunnel that leads up to the surface and about the same amount of time later the side tunnel that leads down to the mine. "That's where we'll go out."

"I want to go out now," says Peter. "I'm bored of this cave."

"We're almost to the petroglyph panel," I say.

"What's a petroglyph?"

Karin takes his hand. "It's art carved into the rock."

"You've done such a good job with them," I say to Carrie-Anne. I hope I don't sound patronizing.

She smiles, looks at Bruce. "We try." She lays her hand on my arm. "Mostly we try not to run away."

I think about saying nothing because she's trying to start, or continue, her fight with me. But then I think about all the not-talking that lay between Emily and me.

"You don't trust me not to run away again."

She shakes her head. "I love you, Dad. That's why I'm so worried." Then she puts her arms around me.

Peter shouts, "Hurry up, Mommy!" She turns away and walks forward.

The hurt is not lessened by the hug. I wish I hadn't run away. I want to explain that it was hardly conscious. Or maybe I just didn't have the tools to know how to stay. Maybe I do now, or maybe I will run away again, just as before. I hope not.

Finally we come to the petroglyph room. I sit on a boulder, back from the others. Peter touches a concentric circle carved in the wall.

Bruce says, "Don't touch. Just look."

I stand and point to the art—the snakes, salamanders, pronghorns, strangely formed people, the wavy lines and circles for water.

"There's a sun," says Peter.

"So primitive," says Bruce. "Like children's drawings." He says it as a positive thing, but it makes me cringe, even though it was my first reaction. Why does it feel different when he says it?

"They carved about the essentials," I say.

I can't help thinking that his attraction to the primitive, and my own, is a fog, a romance of our own creation, that keeps us from seeing the objects. After all, we take water and food for granted in a way the carvers couldn't.

"They're wonderful," says Carrie-Anne.

"They'll be protected," says Emily. "We're trying to get them protected, anyway."

"Look at me," says Peter.

We turn and he's halfway up the wall behind us, hanging onto a small outcrop of rock.

"No, Peter," calls Carrie-Anne.

I see that Peter has also taken off his helmet. Bruce, who came in last, rushes toward him. I can only hold out my hands as if to grab the child as he falls, landing on his feet but toppling over and banging his head on the floor. He immediately wails. Carrie-Anne and Bruce bend over him and he gets up and hugs first Carrie-Anne and then Bruce. We all gather around them.

"Peter," says Carrie-Anne, "you have to be more careful." She flashes her light on his forehead and I see a bump as big as a small chicken egg. She turns to Emily. "It may be safe for adults but maybe not for him."

He stops crying. "I was being careful. You scared me and I let go."

Bruce looks at me and Emily. "He's always getting hurt. He doesn't have a strong sense of self-preservation."

Bruce tries to put Peter's helmet back on, but it rubs against the bump.

"I can't wear it!" he howls. He runs back down the tunnel, his headlamp flashing on the cave walls.

Bruce trots after him. "We're going out a different way. You need to wait for Grandpa."

Then the light stops flashing.

"You need to put your helmet back on, Peter."

Carrie-Anne sighs. She, Erica, and Karin follow. I had wanted to spend more time with the petroglyphs. I glance at Emily and she takes my hand.

"They'll remember this," she says.

We follow the others. When we catch up, I reach out to Peter. "Can we be co-guides?"

He takes my hand. "What does that mean?"

"It means we both lead."

He nods but soon lets go and runs ahead of me. When he passes the turn, I call him back. "This way, Peter."

We walk down the chiseled tunnel and into the big room with the ladder leaning against the wall.

"What's up there?" asks Karin.

I tell her, "I've not explored it yet."

She stands at the foot of the ladder. "Maybe there's a whole other branch of mines up there."

The others are already across the room.

"I guess we'll have to climb up it a different time," I say.

She nods and we catch up to the others. We walk along the railroad. Peter makes a game of jumping from tie to tie. Soon we see daylight, and Peter's still leading everyone. I realize I'm no longer apprehensive. The Fathers were wrong. We went in the mine. Peter got a bump, but he's fine. Carrie-Anne was unhappy it was not a clean and open cave, but nothing happened.

Peter is first to step into the sun; I'm last. Again I'm astonished by the gray rocks, blue sky, green trees and grass. It happens every time.

Peter grins. "I like spelucking." Everyone laughs. The egg on his head has not gone down any.

"We're lucky he didn't get hurt worse," says Carrie-Anne.

Peter runs to the edge of the small flat that extends out from the mouth of the mine. "There's Grandma's truck." He points down the hill to the tin building. He's standing above a four-foot drop-off.

"Get back from the edge!" Carrie-Anne calls.

Then I hear a snake and step toward him. It's not close to Peter. It's coiled under a bush at the corner of the flat, warning him to stay away.

"Peter!" Bruce shouts and runs. Peter turns and slips, reaching for his father's hand. I hear the thunk of his head against the rock. When I get to the edge, Bruce is already bent over him. Peter lies still. Carrie-Anne slides down and reaches to pick him up.

"Don't move him!" commands Bruce.

Instead of going down the four-foot cliff, I try to walk down the tailings. I slip and land on my butt, sliding on the rocks and dirt. I get to my feet and walk toward Bruce. Peter's chest doesn't seem to move.

"Is he breathing?" Carrie-Anne says. "I can't see his chest moving."

Then there's the slightest rise and fall. "He's breathing. He is." But it's unsteady. His chest is still, and then it rises again. Then it's still for a time. Rises again. I try to find his pulse under his neck, but I can't find it. I look at Carrie-Anne's face, already streaked with tears.

"I'll call for a helicopter," Bruce says. He plunges down the hill. The truck is half a mile away at the foot of the rocky slope. Getting to it will take too much time and even more time to drive to cellphone reception.

Carrie-Anne puts her hand lightly on Peter's chest. I glance up and see Karin holding Erica, who watches with wide eyes.

"It's irregular," I say.

I take off my sweatshirt and cover him with it. "I'll be back in a minute." I run into the tunnel. I start too fast and stumble and fall over a railroad tie, banging my hip. When I can get up again, I go slower. Step and step and step. Frustrating and slow. Finally I cross the big room. With one hand on the ladder, I catch my breath. Then I start up. I'm about halfway up. I glance toward the top and three faces appear.

"Help! Please help! My grandson." I see a man start down the ladder, so I climb down and step off to make way for him. "My grandson fell and is unconscious. We don't dare move him."

I see another man come down the ladder. When he reaches the ground, I see he's taller than the first. A woman also comes down the ladder and joins us. I don't know what I expected exactly, maybe robes and sandals, but they're all dressed in T-shirts and jeans and wearing cross trainers.

"I'm sorry, Christopher," the first man says. "We'll do what we can."

They all have dark hair. Two men, one shorter than the other, and a woman, even shorter.

"Follow me!" I run through the big room and into the tunnel that leads outside. I hear their steps, but they're not keeping up with me. "Please, quickly."

"It never pays to rush," says the woman. "That leads to mistakes."

"Yes," says the taller man.

"Please hurry." They continue after me with infuriating slowness. I flash my light back to illuminate the floor for them so they won't trip over a boulder. I'm not sure they need the light, but I keep flashing it back and forward.

Soon I hear voices and hurry out of the mine; I step to the edge. The snake is still coiled about two yards from me, still under its bush. It starts to rattle again. I don't have time for it now, but I intend to smash its head with a rock.

Emily and Carrie-Anne are kneeling next to Peter with their hands clasped across his body. Emily speaks in a soft voice. As I get closer, they let go of each other's hands.

Peter opens his eyes and sits up. "Was I asleep?"

Carrie-Anne kneels again and touches his head with her fingertips. "How is your head?"

"My head?" He touches the goose egg on his forehead. "It's good. I slipped off that rock." He points to the ledge.

Carrie-Anne stands and cups her hands around her mouth. "Bruce!" He is almost to the truck, but when he hears her, he looks up. When she waves for him to come, he starts back toward us.

Emily looks up at me and the three others.

"It seems as if everything turned out all right," says the taller of the two men.

"We weren't needed after all." The first man who spoke to me puts his hand on my shoulder.

The taller man walks toward the bush where the snake is still coiled. He bends over it. It rattles, but then the rattle sputters and stops. It slithers off the ledge into deeper brush.

"Good luck, Christopher," says the woman. "So far you're being spectacular."

Then they turn and disappear down the shaft.

EIGHTEEN

The Propensity of Twist Men

Carrie-Anne and Emily both look toward the dark mouth of the mine. Karin sniffles as she holds Erica, who has had enough of it. "Let me go!" she wails.

"What the hell?" says Carrie-Anne. Her voice shakes, as do her hands.

"Who are they?" Emily takes my arm.

"Who do you think?"

She shakes her head. "Clearly, anything is possible."

Carrie-Anne carries Peter back up to the flat. Karin comes close, still holding Erica. Carrie-Anne sits on a boulder, her arms around her children. "Too close. You shouldn't have taken us down there, Dad." Her voice is still unsteady.

"It was my idea," says Emily.

"But you hadn't been down there before. Dad's the one who knows how dangerous it is." She's talking calmly, but then she almost never raises her voice. It's difficult to tell how angry she really is. I did know the danger, and I was warned by the Dead Fathers.

"I'm sorry," I say.

Bruce joins us, breathing hard. He peers into his son's eyes, gently touches his head. He looks toward Carrie-Anne; now his face is angry. "I thought it was too late, and that's why you called me back.

Carrie-Anne bursts into tears. "I'm sorry."

Bruce wraps his arms around her and she has her arms around the children.

"I'm so sorry you were frightened," she says. "I was too upset to think."

Bruce says, "I'm just glad he seems all right. We can take him to emergency on our way home."

"Yes," says Carrie-Anne.

"You're holding me too tight," says Peter. "You're squishing me." Bruce and Karin back off, and Peter wiggles out of Carrie-Anne's arms.

Carrie-Anne won't look at me. Bruce slowly leads them down the mountain. Emily and I follow them.

"Careful, Chris," says Emily. "I saw you slip. You could have banged your head just like Peter."

I say, "We're all so fragile."

"I'm grateful our own children were more careful than Peter is."

"It's a wonder he's alive. Two serious head bumps in one outing. He should be locked in a padded room." Two falls and a snake. It seems excessive. I watch Carrie-Anne's back. This outing was zero steps forward and a hundred steps back with her.

We have our picnic next to the tin building on a grassy patch near the stream. Carrie-Anne still avoids looking at me. Karin has also stiffened up again. Peter finishes his food and is soon up and running around. He sticks close to us. Maybe he's a little more careful.

Karin keeps her eyes on him. Then she glances at her mother.

"Are you all right?" Carrie-Anne asks her.

"He wasn't moving and then he did," Karin says.

"That about sums it up," says Emily.

"The desert is a dangerous place," says Carrie-Anne. "I prefer the city."

Everywhere is dangerous, but I don't say anything to contradict her. She's still too angry with me. I sit on the edge of the group on a half-rotten log. The kids are chattering, but Bruce and Carrie-Anne are still grim around their mouths and eyes.

"He's all right," says Emily.

"Luckily," says Carrie-Anne. "You two allowed us to run free when we were kids. So much happened that you never knew about."

"And you survived."

Carrie-Anne nods and seems slightly less tight and angry.

But they still eat fast and then encourage their children to finish so they can leave. I hug the children, but Carrie-Anne ignores me as she gets in the vehicle. Emily and I drive behind them. At the main road, they turn right and we turn left. Emily passes the camp and parks near where my trailer was. "I want to look across the desert," she says, which surprises me. Maybe she's trying to imagine how I see it. We walk to the hill above my grandfather's homestead and watch the trail of their dust.

"I didn't tell you that the fathers warned me not to go down in the mine."

"They did?"

"They also warned me to stay away from you and to marry Nephi's daughters. So they haven't given me reliable advice in the past. But then Peter fell. Twice. Once is a coincidence, twice is a sign."

"I think he has accidents many times every day," says Emily, "so two isn't even a coincidence." She breaks off a dry juniper twig and taps her shoe with it. "He's all right. The children will remember this—especially Karin. How fragile and precious life is. They know we love them and want to share beautiful things with them."

"Well that turns the whole experience into an epigram."

"Sorry. We'll be unpacking this for a long time."

"Carrie-Anne—"

"Still loves us."

"She won't trust me again to take the kids on an adventure."

"She'll relax again."

"Maybe she shouldn't." I feel tears in my eyes, and she takes my hand. I can't speak. "Peter," I finally say. "You brought him back from the edge."

She smiles. "Carrie-Anne and I did."

I think about the warning of the Dead Fathers. "I wish they'd be clear with me for once."

"Who?"

"My father, his father, old Hugh."

"Oh, them." She frowns in a manner I can only think of as bitter. "I don't trust dead people."

"I don't understand their motives. I trust my mother and yours, my grandmother, and Marie."

"Maybe the message is we shouldn't trust controlling, dead male relatives."

"I trust Thomas. But I should be able to trust the others. Especially my father. So I'm anxious."

She takes my hand again. "You're doing fine. Isn't that what that woman said?"

"Yes. She did. Yes, she did." I kiss Emily's hand. "But I think there is more trouble coming."

We share a bed again, but this time we hold each other for comfort, not for sex, even though I would have been happy to go ahead and burn our candles at both ends—a problematic metaphor in this context. She falls asleep first, and I worry the Dead Fathers will come and harangue me. But I wait and they don't and soon I'm under as well.

They invade my dreams. We're in my grandfather's cabin near where my old trailer stood. The cabin was torn down when I was a young man. There's no deck of cards, and my father points his finger at me as I sit at the table. "Your grandson could have died."

"Whose fault would that be?" I say.

"Not ours," he says. "We're messengers, not influencers."

"Messengers are influencers."

"We're worried," says Louis, "because you're fucking up the balance."

"You shouldn't have left him," says Hugh. "You should have blessed him yourself instead of letting the women do it."

"I didn't think of it," I say. "I don't have God's ear."

"Who does?" says my father. "We all do the best we can."

Which lets me know, again, that they are about as distant from God's presence as I am.

"We warned you not to go into the cave again," says Louis. "Another principle violated."

"What principle?" I ask. "Is there an eleventh commandment: Thou shalt not enter caves?"

Hugh stands and looks down at me as if I'm a bad dog. Clearly, there's no hope for me. "This child wants reasons. With faith there are no reasons."

I shake my head.

"We want you to learn faith," says Hugh. "Faith and order. When there's no order, anything can happen. Like today. You're the man. You should have blessed him. You shouldn't have run for help."

"Disorder sounds great," I say. "Let it happen. Now leave me alone." They don't seem to care much about Peter, just that their concept of order was violated. I want to argue that Emily, who they think is an agent of chaos, has the most ordered mind of anyone I've ever known. But they're talking about a strait and narrow kind of order—top-down order—the Patriarchy. She has never accepted it as legitimate.

"You're pushing him too hard," says my father. "That doesn't work with him." It seems hypocritical because he also pushes me.

"That woman is a real problem," says Hugh, reading my mind again. "You have abrogated your responsibility with her."

"Go away!" I shout and find myself sitting up in bed.

Emily is standing next to the bed. "What's wrong? You were thrashing around and I thought you'd hit me."

"Horrible dream. The Dead Fathers."

"Those bastards should leave you alone," she says. "If they ever visit me, I'll tell them a thing or two."

"They're frightened of you."

"Of *moi*?" she says. "Those silly men."

She climbs back into bed, and this time we move beyond comfort to pleasure.

At breakfast the next morning, we talk about our protest of Spencer's rally up the closed road, which will happen tomorrow. As we're finishing, a local BLM officer, Carl Peterson, stops in front of our trailer.

"Hello, Carl," I say. We met before and talked about the petroglyph panel.

He nods. "Chris."

"Normally I have more important things to worry about." He's a pot-bellied man with hair so light I can't tell if it's blonde or gray; his smile is amiable. "But I'm getting pressure from above to make sure you move your trailer. There's a regulation against camping for more than two weeks in one spot."

"I wonder which of our many enemies it is," says Lucía.

"Spencer?" asks Alina.

"Probably him," says Emily.

"Hard to tell." Carl grins. "You have more enemies than I have friends, and I have a lot of friends." As he climbs into his truck, he turns. "If I knew who it was, I would tell you." He waves his hand in a circle. "There are more bastards around than you can shake a stick at."

Once he's gone, Alina asks, "Where will you go?"

Emily turns to me.

I say, "There's a nice spot under some cottonwoods on a dry streambed south of here."

"How far?" asks Alina.

"Four or five miles," I say.

"I can still ride my bicycle over," says Alina. "It will just take me longer."

"You're going to get fired like I did," I tell her.

Her eyebrows contradict me. "We get along all right. You loved irritating Spencer."

I smile. "Yes, I did."

We pack up the table and chairs, hook the trailer up to the double cab truck, pull it over to the spring near the mouth of Coyote Canyon, and park it under the cottonwoods, which provide better shade than the short junipers near Spencer's building. From here we can see the smokestack at the Intermountain Power Plant forty miles to the south. We also have a good view of Keg Mountain, which looks less like a keg than a grave mound. Another sign? I hope not.

Even though the canyon where we parked the trailer is close to the pictograph panel, Emily wants us to sleep in tents across the closed road. "We don't know when they'll show up. Maybe before dawn. We want to be there when they come." Late that afternoon, we drive our two vehicles about a mile farther south to the mouth of Lost Canyon, where a side road goes up the canyon. Or used to. Now it's blocked by a BLM sign that announces the road is closed. Lucía and Emily park the trucks in the middle of the side road next to the sign. Andrew gets out and looks at the ground to the side of the road, which has a thick crust of crypto growing across it.

"We shouldn't put our tents up here," he says through Emily's window. Emily looks at me and I nod. Twenty-five yards farther, closer to the rock art panel, is a dry watering trough. Cows don't use it anymore, but they've walked there and chewed their cud there. It's flat and free of crypto.

I point to the place. Emily frowns. "Cow pies."

"Choose your poison." I point to a ridge to our right. It ends in a low rocky cliff. To our left is the spot mashed down by cows, the dry trough, and junipers growing close together. "The rally will have a difficult time driving past us here." I get out and start kicking the cow pies toward the dry tank. The others watch from the road.

"I've always wondered where the term 'shitkicker' comes from," says Lucía. "Now I know."

I spin a wide, dry pie toward her like a Frisbee. "Catch!"

She ducks and it flies to the other side of the road.

We're all kicking and tossing disks of dry shit, and soon our campsite is clear enough. We carry our tents and set up some in the road and others between the road and the trough. More counterprotestors will arrive early in the morning, hopefully before the ATV riders get to us. We walk back to the trucks, and Andrew hands us camp chairs and tin containers with food. He carries a small folding table, and Lucía carries a camp stove and a griddle. Andrew sets up the stove on the table and puts a couple of the tin containers on the griddle. He smiles at us.

"Brown-sugar beans, corn, and pulled pork." The rest of us put camp chairs in a half circle near the table.

Emily and I walk up the old road to look at the panel, which is about 200 yards from the tents. There is a range of petroglyphs similar to those in the cave—older than Fremont and Ancestral Puebloan rock art. The cave humanoids are narrow-waisted and broad-shouldered, its animals huge and rectangular, and its intricate drawings of god-like creatures have roots deep in the ground and fingers reaching like lightning toward the sky. These drawings are—what? Less idealized, more internal than the petroglyphs in the cave. But they are similarly schematic, like maps of consciousness. We stand, shoulders touching, and look at the figures of humans and animals, the circles large and small—sun and moon. More snakes, concentric circles, and lines like the meandering of streams. More drawings that look like nets or maps. I see a tall humanoid followed by a shorter one, and a shorter, and finally a shorter. It's like those stickers people put in the back window of their minivans to show how many children they have.

"They lived on this land without technology," I say. My story of the desert: the Twists are newcomers.

"I know you long for an easier time," Emily says. "Less hectic. But you also say they had to work eighteen hours a day to find food."

"You sometimes work eighteen hours a day," I say.

"No doctors. Always hungry except for a few times when there are pine nuts or when they killed a pronghorn or deer. But I see the virtue in cutting back."

"To twelve hours a day?"

She smiles. "Maybe even below that."

We walk back toward the tents. Everyone sits in the camp chairs. I think about building a fire to look at instead of the stove with the trays of food on it, but this group would not want to create a pit where there was none before.

"Almost hot," says Andrew. "Just a few more minutes."

Bennie arrives, Alina with him. Andrew calls for them to get chairs from the truck, which they do. They sit next to each other. I pull my chair over to theirs.

"I quit my job," she says. "I've got all my stuff in Bennie's truck." While still sitting, she does a short heel-toe tap dance in the dust.

"I told you something would happen. At least you didn't get fired like I did. What will you do?"

"I'll figure something out."

"What happened?"

"Spencer decided he wanted to talk about his political opinions. We were fine as long as he didn't talk silliness, but I couldn't stand having to listen to him."

Bennie says nothing. Smart man. I notice Lucía is paying close attention to our conversation. When she sees me watching her, she grins and turns away. Who knows what bends the road ahead may take? Maybe she'll get her chance. Not my business.

Andrew puts large spoons in the food tins and drinks and rolls next to the stove. I smile because the small table is completely full of good things to eat. He places tin plates on a chair, and the six of us file past and fill them. We also have tin cups and hot water for hot chocolate.

"You are a wonder, Andrew," Emily says. "Thank you."

We lift our spoons and tap our cups. Nobody talks for a while because we're all hungry. We each compliment Andrew again, and then Lucía looks toward Emily.

"What?" says Emily. "I don't want to talk business for a minute."

While we're still eating, a BLM truck drives up and stops on the main road. Three men get out and walk toward us. They each have guns on their hips. One is Carl. This time his face is much more serious. The other two stand to either side of him, their arms folded. We all have plates on our laps so none of us gets up.

"Hello again," I say. "What's up?"

"We'd like you to disband," Carl says. "We don't want violence. Go back to your trailer."

Lucía sets her plate on the ground as if she's ready to stand and argue.

Emily says, "Unless we're doing something illegal, we'd like to stay."

The three men frown at each other. One of them rests his hand on his weapon.

"We're not fighters," says Lucía. Which is an abject lie. "We have no weapons." Except for their mouths and brains, which are formidable.

"The other side does," says Carl. "We don't have the manpower to deal with a group that large—to keep them from doing whatever they want to do. They may have a hundred ATVs coming tomorrow."

"Are you going to make us go?" I ask. The man with his hand on his gun nods. But Carl says "no."

"You'll be facing a hundred guys with guns. Talk about loose cannons. You can't fight for protection of the petroglyph panel if you're dead."

"That's a little dramatic," I say. "Spencer's in charge."

"You trust him not to do something stupid? And even if he doesn't, there are hotheads who will. Hotheads everywhere." He glances at Emily.

"We'll talk about it," says Emily. "Thanks for the warning."

The three of them walk back to their truck and drive away. Lucía picks up her plate, and everyone looks toward Emily.

"Raise your hand if you want to leave." Nobody raises their hand. "Who wants to stay?" Everyone raises their hand, even me, even Alina.

Alina grins. "Will there be a shootout?"

Bennie opens his mouth.

She pushes his shoulder. "I was joking. There can't be a shootout if only one side has guns. I'm not stupid."

"I would never think you're stupid," Bennie says. "How do you know I don't have a gun?"

"Do you?"

"No."

"So why are we arguing?"

He doesn't know what to say to that.

"Should we worry?" Andrew asks Emily.

"I don't know." She looks at me.

"Spencer is careful with his weapons," I say. "He'll probably keep the other riders in order."

"Probably," says Andrew. "Not much of a comfort."

He has made apple cobbler and whipped cream for dessert. We line up again and fill smaller plates, except for Alina who gets a large plate and two pieces of pie. We all sit back down. We're not as hungry so now we eat more slowly.

Bennie and Alina speak quietly. Lucía looks at them. She finishes her pie quickly, then puts her plate in the trash and returns to her chair. She stands behind the chair as if she's going to move it, maybe next to Bennie and Alina, but then she just sits down. She seems more unsettled than usual. Alina certainly is easy to love. Lucía looks around at everyone's faces, clustered around a non-existent fire. I can't see the Dead Fathers or Mothers, but they may be watching also. I think about absence and presence.

"Why here?" Lucía asks me. "Why did you escape to this desert?"

"So Emily would come out and rescue me."

"So sweet of you." Lucía's tone is definitely ironic.

"Not the whole story," says Emily. "His father had a ranch out here."

"Two places," I say. "Where my trailer was and where Spencer's barn is. He had a shack and a couple hundred acres. In the thirties. And right down there." I point to the river valley to the west. "His ranch is where the polygamists farm now. Farmed. Soon they'll head to Mexico, I guess."

Bennie looks across at me. "My father worked for him. This was when my father was a young man, before he married my mother."

"I might have met him. I used to come out here every summer and work when I was a kid and a teenager. But I don't remember him. Maybe it was after I left for college."

Everyone is silent, listening.

"My grandfather got titles to a string of homesteads in the early fifties. About thirteen hundred acres."

Bennie levels his index finger at me as if it's my fault. "Two sections of land, two square miles." Bennie doesn't like ranchers.

"Blame Thomas Jefferson," I say. "He was the one who established the grid system, so every part of the U.S. could be owned. Whole different system than your ancestors had."

Bennie nods. "The land wasn't ownable."

"I didn't know there was homesteading in the twentieth century," says Andrew. "And I thought you could only homestead 160 acres."

"It was 320 for Desert Entry homesteads, 640 for a couple. Grandpa had his sons and his sons' wives homestead for him. My father thought he was going to get the part he homesteaded, but when he got married, Grandpa made sure he knew it wasn't his. Like the seagulls in that movie, 'mine, mine, mine.' Grandpa thought he would become a wealthy rancher, but it's so difficult out here. Seven inches of rain a year. He pumped water from underground, but that got expensive in the seventies."

"He was a little senile when I met him," says Bennie.

I nod.

"He died poor. I wonder who will try there next. Who will fail next. Everybody thinks they can make it work in the desert, but it's just too hard. Someone will buy it, though. Someone always has the illusion they can transcend the limits of climate. More likely it will be someone crazier than Nephi. Maybe survivalists will decide to make it their new Eden."

"Your grandfather told me about a coyote that he shot in the bunghole," says Bennie.

"He told that story to everybody. At least everybody who would listen."

"The bullet forced the—ah—what fruit was it?"

"Red currants."

"Up through its body in a red vomit."

"Gross," says Alina.

"Why did *that* story stick in his head instead of memories of his children?" asks Emily. "He was a violent man."

"Some coyote was always trying to steal his resources," I say.

"Or he was the coyote stealing other people's resources," says Bennie. "No offense."

"You're right about that. He took his own children's homesteads."

"Which was a blessing to every one of them," says Emily.

"Probably so," I say. "It moved my father to the city and kept me out of poverty. But I still love the place down there. Love it here as well."

"Loves it beyond all reason," says Emily, but she's smiling.

"I see why he loves it," says Alina.

Emily just nods.

"My father said Grandpa let General Torrey poach deer and pronghorns in his fields," I say. "Of course he wasn't a general back then. Just some officer. His rationalization was that the deer and pronghorns ate his alfalfa. And the rabbits. He was getting some of his own back."

Bennie says, "He had my father butcher them for the General. Animals that my ancestors hunted."

"He would have done that," I say. "He was a strong-willed man. Racist. His heroes were the Vikings, the trappers, and the pioneers. He died a lonely man. His wife and he lived apart for twenty years before he died."

Emily says, "It's the propensity of Twist men to move west and escape civilization."

"Not my father. He moved east."

"The exception that proves the rule," says Emily.

"You've done both," says Alina. "Moved east then west. Now you're going to move east again."

"Probably," I say.

Emily says, "You've been thwarted in your efforts to die a lonely man."

I think about my father now—his new priorities. He certainly was a lonely man when he was alive.

Bennie says, "My father told me that when your grandpa was old, he thought the wind whining through the boulders above his cabin was Marilyn Monroe and her sirens singing to him. My father thought he might get his cane and hobble up there."

"His second favorite story."

"Have you heard the sirens?" Lucía asks me.

"I tried when I was fifteen, but all I could hear was the wind. I was very disappointed."

"He died out here, didn't he?" says Bennie.

"The creosote built up in his stove pipe and it exploded one winter," I say. "He couldn't hobble out in time."

"Poor old guy," says Andrew.

"He was eighty-five."

"Is he—" Emily stops. "Did he ever get over his bitterness?"

"No. He never did." What surprises me is that when he died he was an agnostic. Now he thinks of himself as one of God's servants.

"Elder abuse," says Emily. "Your father and uncles left him out here."

"Where he wanted to be. We took him food. My father and I tried to bathe him in the hot springs to the south."

"There are hot springs?" asks Alina. "We should go."

Bennie nods.

Lucía lifts her brows. "You can come too," Bennie says.

"He thought we were trying to drown him," I say. "He howled and howled that he was being scalded."

"Strange people live in the desert," says Emily.

"I live here," says Bennie.

Emily smiles at him. "And?"

"People are strange," I say. "Everywhere."

"From what Chris has told me," Emily says, "Louis wasn't the strangest."

"There was one guy whose wife died, and he just set up with his daughters. He lived over in Six-mile Canyon, south of here. And there was a woman who traded sex for sheep. She lived southeast of here around the end of the Indian Mountains. She had the biggest herd around." I think about telling them about Sula and Agnes, but that story no longer seems odd and funny. I don't know that I'll ever tell the story again because it brings up memories of their terrifying visit.

"Sex and power," says Alina.

"The Goshutes and their ancestors lived here in balance for a thousand years. Perfect balance." Bennie looks at me. "Perfect poverty. If my tribe brings in nuclear waste, they'll never be poor again."

"I admire their old way," I say.

"I know you do," says Bennie.

"You keep forgetting about the women who died in childbirth," says Emily. "I'd be dead with Carrie-Anne."

"You left that out of your equation," says Alina to me.

"It's a conundrum," I say.

"Not much of a conundrum," says Lucía. "Women are better off now. Everyone is."

Bennie pays no attention. "They wove wide flat baskets they'd use to scoop up anthills, and they'd spin them, and the gravel would fly off and the ants would stay in the bowl. They herded grasshoppers into ditches and drowned them. They managed the pronghorns, never eating all of a herd."

"They ate anything they could get their hands on," I say.

"White men wanted to remake them or kill them off. Nobody let them find their own way into the future."

"My great-grandfather knew of a man whose family was slaughtered by US soldiers," I say.

"I hate this story," says Emily. "You don't have to tell it over and over." I guess I'm getting like the DFs, garrulous old men talking too long.

"The man who found the cave," says Alina.

"Yes." Despite what Emily said, I tell Lucía and Andrew and Bennie the story. "So he avenged his family's murder."

"I've heard of that man," says Bennie. "My grandmother told me."

"It's time for a happy story," says Lucía. "Like the woman who got rich on her sheep-for-sex enterprise."

"My grandpa had a hired hand who took his wife out here to live with him. They went around all day in the nude."

"Sunburned themselves into the hospital," says Emily.

"Really?" asks Alina.

"I don't know," says Emily. "But that's probably what happened."

"Yes, nudity," says Lucía. "Let's hear about that, not murder of girls."

"Someone should start a colony on the old property," says Emily.

Andrew wears a slight, sly smile. "A nudist colony."

"Andrew," says Lucía, "you pervert."

"They wanted to be like Adam and Eve," I say.

"Doesn't anybody else have a story?" asks Emily. "He'll go on all day."

I continue anyway. "Before they became ashamed. When I was young, my cousins and I would take off our clothes and find a clayey part of the ditch. We'd cover ourselves with mud and dance around."

Lucía raises one eyebrow.

"Just my boy cousins," I say, "at least when we were older. Once they drove out here late on a winter night. I was already out here. It was a cold, full moon, and when they got to where I was sleeping in an old railroad car adapted to be a bunker, they woke me up. It was bright as day outside. We took off all our clothes and ran around in the snow."

Didn't you freeze your—toes?" asks Lucía.

"Too much adrenaline. Grandpa came out and told us to get the hell back inside and go to bed."

"Ah, to be young and naked," says Lucía.

"Some of my best times," I say, "were when I was naked."

Lucía and Alina laugh. Andrew smiles, and Emily tries not to but does anyway.

Maybe she's right that I'm boring them. But I admit it; I like having people listen to me, especially after having only Spencer and Nephi to talk to for so many months. They like talking about themselves even more than I do. Then I realize something else. Last fall I talked myself into the idea that I wanted to be alone, that solitude best fit my nature. I've learned, primarily from Emily but also the others, how mistaken I was. We fool ourselves when we think we know what we want.

Emily shakes her head and won't look at me. "As a journalist, you told good stories. Stories that had an end."

So I finally stop. We sit and watch the stars. Lucía moves her chair close to Alina and Bennie. Emily and Andrew talk while I hold Emily's hand, massaging her palm with the fingertips of my other hand. Unfortunately, it doesn't seem to distract her from her conversation.

"We better try to get some sleep," she says finally. The others start toward their tents. Emily walks down to her truck and I follow. "There's not room," she says. "Sorry."

There would be room if she had the will, but it would be crowded. "Me too."

I lay my sleeping bag out on the ground under a juniper next to the tents where there is a carpet of duff.

Soon the whole camp is silent. I roll over in my bag, and a yard away my father, grandfather, and great-great-grandfather sit on their haunches.

"Damn, you startled me," I say softly.

"He's never going to stop being recalcitrant," says Hugh.

"Not while he's having sex with Bathsheba," says Louis.

"She's my wife," I whisper, even though he's made me angry enough to shout. "I'm grateful she's come back to me."

"I know you are," says my father. "It's just that she's getting you all tangled up in her business. If she would just accept you the way you are, it would be fine." I wonder if he's really talking about his own tangles with my mother.

"Those officers are right," says Hugh. "Anything could happen tomorrow."

"If you die," says Louis, "you'll abandon the real field of battle."

"Which is imminent!" says Hugh. "We've warned and warned you. And you haven't listened. It will be like stumbling into battle in your skivvies. You'll be cut to pieces."

"If you're dead, you'll join us," says my father. "There is that."

I look at him. He's not stupid, so he certainly knows that that is the last thing I want. I was frightened when Peter almost died and even more frightened when Sula and Agnes appeared in my dreams. I'm not ready for death.

"You have reason to be afraid," my father says quietly.

"I know I do, but I can't think with all this pressure." Their pressure is nothing like the pressure I felt in my dream of my two great-aunts. Between my desire to please and fear of death, those two women gave me no room for choice. And that makes me angry. Anyone who robs people of volition is evil. But then I quail again. I can't match them in any kind of mind-to-mind conflict. As Hugh said, I feel completely unequipped to face what is coming. The Dead Fathers have no real information, just impassioned warnings about indefinite possibilities.

"You should by now know that we don't have unlimited vision," says Hugh.

"But we are trying to help you," says my father.

"Help you avoid being a damned fool," says Louis.

"Go away!" This time I don't control my voice well enough, and I hear voices from the tent that's between me and Emily's truck; I've waked or at least disturbed Alina and Bennie with my midnight shouting. I pull the sleeping bag over my head, and after five minutes I look out and the Dead Fathers are gone.

NINETEEN

Peaceful Resistance

The sun is not yet up when the other counterprotestors arrive: a carload of college students with signs, a van of Goshutes, a few archeologists, and a couple of students from the environmental club at the U. Eighteen more people, with us twenty-four total—not many against the hundred, armed ATV riders Carl predicted. Andrew has a griddle set up and I flip pancakes. Lucía, Alina, and Emily cut up fruit, and Andrew does everything else, boiling water, setting out plasticware and plates, arranging the condiments.

After breakfast Bennie walks around to the far side of the rock and soon appears on top, the zoom lens on his camera.

"From a distance it could be mistaken for a gun," says Emily. "Someone will think you're shooting at them and they'll shoot back."

He puts on a shorter lens. "I'll wait until they get closer." He also has a drone that he flies above our heads and back to the rock.

"You can't manage both," says Emily.

"You may be right," he says as the drone runs into a juniper tree. Alina extracts it from the branches and carries it up on the rock. He hands her the control and she experiments with takeoff, maneuvering, and landing. As with everything I've seen her try, she's good at it.

A car appears below us. A young woman gets out carrying a camera. She walks toward us. "Hello," she says. "I'm Lisa Christensen from the *Tooele Transcript Bulletin*."

Emily steps forward and shakes her hand. "I'm Emily Ransome, thanks for coming. I was just going to talk to the group."

"Fly on the wall," says Lisa.

Emily calls the group closer around her. A few stragglers walk back from the pictograph panel. "Thank you for coming to join our counterprotest to the illegal ATV ride that's going to happen a little later. We'll stand for protection of these artifacts and against ATV riders breaking the law and driving wherever they want."

"We'll stop the bastards," shouts Lucía, watching the reporter.

"Probably not," says Emily. "We'll link arms across the road. Remember, we don't fight back. We just let our bodies go limp if they try to move us. We're not trying to resist them with physical force. We're just showing our opposition."

Emily nods toward one of the Goshute women, who then speaks to the group about the sacred nature of the drawings.

The reporter, Lisa, touches Emily on the elbow and they stand to one side talking. Lisa takes her picture.

Emily points to the outcropping of rock. Bennie and Alina join them, and they show Lisa the way up. Emily comes back and stands next to me.

"I sent press releases to every news outlet in Salt Lake," she says. "I guess this kind of trespassing is commonplace now."

"Disappointing."

Around ten, we hear the rumble, as if a thunderstorm is coming, and the first ATVs appear where the road crosses the top of a ridge to the north of us. The first men and women drive three abreast on the road, with some renegades from this group of renegades driving below the road on the flat. When the leaders see us, they stop in the road next to our trucks, and within a minute there is a crowd of about fifty of them, only half of what Carl predicted. Maybe by the end of the day I'll only be half dead. We can hear the sound of them talking loudly to each other over the sound of their engines. Many of the vehicles have flags—Trump, Thin Blue Line, Don't Tread on Me. A couple pull next to the road-closed sign and hook chains to their four-wheelers and pull it down. They turn off the main road and roll toward us.

We spread in a line across the road the BLM closed. To our right are the tents. To our left are boulders at the foot of the small outcropping where Bennie, Alina, and Lisa stand. They take pictures as the four-wheelers rumble forward. Spencer rides the one in the middle front. He glances toward Alina. His frown deepens.

Spencer stops about ten yards from us. "This is a legal road," shouts Spencer over the rumble of the machines. "Move your asses out of the way."

"If we move our asses," shouts Lucía. "Can the rest of us stay here?"

Spencer grins and says something to the rider next to him, but then Lucía laughs at him and that pisses him off. He rolls his vehicle forward until it's about an inch from Emily. My whole body is tight, but I don't have any idea what to do. I'm breathing too fast and I feel lightheaded. Other vehicles roll forward. They spread wider than the road, rolling across the cryptobiotic soil between the brush and junipers. Someone on the right edge of the group takes a rifle out of a boot he has attached to his four-wheeler.

Emily sits down in the road. I join her and the others do as well. The only sound is the growl of the idling motors. I can't hear the buzz of the drone Alina is operating.

"You don't have the authority to open this road," shouts Emily.

"Run over them," shouts someone from the back.

"Don't be an idiot," shouts Spencer.

"There's not room to drive around them," shouts someone else.

"That's why we chose this place." Lucía grins at Spencer.

He looks to the left. He motions for the rider on that side to drive forward. He does, and one tent lists toward him as he drives across the edge of it. The next rider, a woman with a boy behind her, is not so careful and the pole bends on that side. The tent folds over on itself. Spencer walks over and speaks to the next riders, and they take the stakes out of the tent, drag it to one side, and stake it in its new place. One refastens the pole, which isn't even broken.

Emily, Lucía, Andrew, and I walk over and try to get in their way, but the vehicles are moving bumper to bumper and a couple dozen of them pass through. Bennie is still taking pictures. One rider, the one with his rifle out, points it up at Bennie and Alina. Lisa has ducked out of sight.

"Slate, you damn fool!" Spencer shouts. "Put your weapon away!"

"They're taking pictures of us."

"So what? What we're doing isn't illegal or secret." Spencer looks up at Alina, who smiles and waves at him. He glares at her for a moment and walks to his vehicle. He may think of what she's doing as a betrayal, but he probably wouldn't think of firing me as a betrayal. Neither do I, now. So much good has happened to me as a direct result of him firing me and kicking me out of the trailer.

"It's not illegal to destroy government property?" Lucía points back at the downed sign. Trespass on a closed road?"

She stands in front of Spencer's vehicle. Spencer glares at her but backs up and drives around through the gap she left when she stood in front of him.

Our line is broken and all of us are milling around. Soon all the vehicles are across. They proceed along the road and up the canyon. They will probably go over the pass and down the other side. Emily looks after them. "Dammit to hell!"

Lisa comes off the rock and walks down toward the intersection. She talks to several of the people who joined our group that morning, then she drives back northward.

Emily looks like she'll bite the head off the next person to talk to her, so I walk up the road toward the petroglyphs. Lucía and a few others join me, including Bennie and Alina. The drawings are covered with dust.

"They don't think of this as art," says Bennie.

Alina bends over and blows on the rock, clearing a small patch of dust. "It can be cleaned up."

I walk back down to the rest of the group, and the others follow. Emily is tight-lipped and furious. Even though they broke the law, most of the riders will not be prosecuted—maybe not even Spencer, who organized the rally.

Everyone works together to take down the tents and stow them in the back of Emily's pickup. Emily climbs onto a boulder. She looks much more composed now. "Thank you for showing up. This is not the end. We will not give up until we protect this sacred and valuable petroglyph site. First, we will publicize what they've done, and then we will pressure legislators and BLM officials to respond to this crime. But that isn't all we need to worry about." She talks about the efforts to keep radioactive waste off the reservation and the efforts to get compensation for the nerve gas and other accidents.

"The state is with us," says a middle-aged woman, dressed in a T-shirt and slacks. "They haven't backed down on their rejection of atomic waste—not just on the reservation but anywhere."

"They still can dump contaminated stuff under a certain level of radioactivity," says Bennie.

"Right," says the woman. "We have to monitor it to make sure the waste disposal company isn't cheating."

They talk more, but I lose track of the conversation. I'm thinking about how Emily and Spencer went nose-to-nose over a road. I remember the white line of her mouth, the anger inscribed on his face.

Their eyes, those of Emily and Spencer and everyone else here, receive light reflected from the rocks, dirt, and junipers of this part of the desert, but they see different landscapes. And because of my experiences here and the stories I know about this place, I see another one. The man who was husband to his daughters, Nephi and Frank, my ancestors Hugh and Thomas herding their sheep. All color the place. I see it differently than I did a year ago, especially since the night visits of the Dead Fathers and Mothers, Sula and Agnes, Delta and Marion.

Other people don't even see landscapes. They see potential that can be developed. To the white businessman, it seems logical to put atomic waste where there are so few people. That is, if the company is thinking about anything beyond profit. To the Goshutes, like this woman and Bennie, the natural order and balance of the land is disrupted by the poison. All of us, the businessmen and Bennie and Alina and Emily and I, see order and disorder in our own version of the place. Maybe "universe" is a better word, more inclusive of all the ways we see. We perceive different universes. How can we even communicate?

Hugh sees patriarchal hierarchy in a manner that is very different from the way I see it. His version of order seems authoritarian to me, and my version of order seems chaotic to him. The Dead Mothers seem to embrace an order that is diffuse, less focused on a chain of authority. I am like my grandfather, at least when he was alive, a maverick. I like the fractal order of the natural world. But to the pioneers, the natural wilderness was frightening and disorganized—a place where a soul could get lost. I guess chaos is any order you can't perceive, any pattern you can't see. Or maybe it's all chaos and our perceptions create the illusion of order.

We walk toward the vehicles, and those who joined us for the protest head north. I ride with Emily, and Andrew drives the van back to the trailer. Everyone is still buzzed, still wanting to talk. We unload the camp chairs and put them up in a circle. Alina sits alone at the table, so I sit across from her.

"You had an adventure in the cave," she says. "Emily told me a little."

I tell her the rest, including what happened with the Three. I tell her what I know about Emily's prayer over Peter.

"You're fortunate to be married to such a woman."

I nod. "Yes. I am. She's a force of nature. Unconventional."

"Screw convention. Convention kicked me out of the university."

I look back at the circle of chairs, the team talking animatedly.

"Emily gave me a job," she says.

"Good."

"Part-time. I'll build a database of all the decisions of all the judges on environmental matters. So she can be scientific about predicting how they'll react to new cases." She smiles. "I'll also be interning with Marion and Delta."

"Interning? With Marion and Delta?"

"Yes. Working with them."

I have trouble wrapping my mind around the word "work" in connection with those two. Work implies focus of effort, and Marion and Delta are as erratic and spontaneous as particles of gas.

"What will you be doing?"

"Apparently I'll help them maintain the universal algorithms and formulas for human choice."

"Human choice needs enabling?" I shake my head. "I thought all that was metaphorical." Or delusional. "You will actually be helping to manage human choice?"

"Helping to enable it. They think that my algorithms will help them maintain balance. "They say mine are even better—ah—more elegant than the system they've been using."

I struggle to understand. Even better? That's so confusing. For one thing, I am still blown away by the whole idea that the universe isn't inherently balanced. That balance needs maintenance. And for another, the idea that they have been using an inferior system scares me. "I guess I didn't think they really did anything."

Alina's eyebrows go up, but it's true. I thought they were just funny and a bit delusional. Or even more delusional than I am. I shake my head again. I had thought I was used to cognitive dissonance, but I'm not able to grapple with the picture of Alina doing projective mathematics and choice-enabling with Delta and Marion.

"If I thought about their work at all, I guess I thought they've always been balancers and they just do it by instinct or some divine power."

"Always?" asks Alina. "That's a long time. Someone else balanced before them. Someday they'll retire. And they're always looking for better ways to protect human and animal and plant and geological will. It's a constant process of adjustment, especially since so many beings want to destroy the balance for their own gain."

I think about the two women who invaded my dream and controlled me. The Dead Fathers said Agnes and Sula don't follow the rules, but how are the rules enforced, if at all? Was my grandmother showing up part of the balancing?

Alina says, "It's not magic."

I smile.

"What? You think it's funny that cosmic power isn't magic?"

"No, not that at all. What came to my mind is pretty dumb. I just wonder how you get paid for working for such beings. They're probably not practical financially."

She shrugs. "Probably not. They talked about showing me where to dig for a gold nugget the size of my head. I couldn't tell if they were joking. Anyway, I don't care if they pay me or not. I'll be working with the primary formulas of the universe. I am very excited. In fact I'm meeting with them now."

"Now?"

She nods toward the farthest cottonwood, and I see Delta and Marion sitting on a downed log.

We get up and walk toward them.

They stand when we come close. "Christopher," they say simultaneously. They look at each other and laugh. "How good to see you."

I sit on the log but everyone else remains standing so I stand again. I don't like being seen as the old man who has to sit every chance he gets.

"Are you ready for what's next?"

"What's next?" I ask. "I'd like to know what's next."

"What will knowing change? You'll make the same decisions."

"So you can see the future?"

"No," says Delta.

"Only probabilities."

"Nothing specific. But we know you."

I wish I could say I know them. I look closely at their faces. I can't see the flickering as they exchange places across the veil. It must happen as fast as alternating current.

"We have work to do," says Delta, turning to Alina. Marion moves also, so our circle of four is broken into three of them with me shunted out. A not-so-subtle sign that they are anxious to get going.

Alina nods. "I'm ready."

"But first," says Marion, "we see that Christopher is unsettled about something."

"That simply won't do," says Delta. "We can't have our Christopher unsettled." She puts her hand on my arm. They laugh again, and I can't tell for sure whether their laughter is friendly or if they're mocking me. Probably both.

I remember the feeling I had when Sula and Agnes visited me. I wanted to please Agnes. "I have always thought that no one could force me to think a certain way. That I'd see through all sophistic rhetoric, but—"

"Then you met those untamable sister wives. Aren't they awesome?" They each take an arm and seat me on the log. Then Delta sits to my left and Marion to my right.

I nod "They scared me—"

"Shit—"

"—less."

"Yes. I was petrified of Sula and would have done whatever she told me to. But I *wanted* to do what Agnes wanted me to do. It was as if the impulse to please her was my own idea. She is horrible."

"That's one word for her. Another is wild splendor. She has her place. But that's not exactly what's bothering you," says Marion. "You've gotten over your fear."

"Not really. I'm frightened but also unsettled." I consider what to say next. "I thought agency was innate—ah—self-generated. Not—not outside." I feel flustered that I can't explain what I'm thinking. "It doesn't make sense that agency needs to be maintained if it's innate. But their will—I say 'will' because it was as if they were one person, but one pulled and one pushed—I can't describe it. They manifested their will in me, directly, without persuasion or argument or physical force. My own will meant nothing." I'm glad to be sitting down and feel the comfort of them to either side of me.

"She cheated a universal law," says Marion. "Dictated by the Gods."

"But not a natural law?"

From my left: "What is natural?"

From my right: "What does that even mean?"

They might as well be saying that the earth is flat or that the moon is a disc painted on the surface of the sky. "You're saying that agency needs to be legislated? It's not part of my natural being, an aspect of intelligence? That's frightening."

"You say that as if balance is in opposition to agency." Delta puts her two fists together. Then she clasps her hands. "Opposition and unity. Volition, just human volition, can only happen when the universe is balanced."

Marion continues for her. "Volition and balance are not opposites. But there is opposition of will. Opposition creates balance, which creates agency."

Alina paces back and forth in front of us. "Blake understood the principle of contraries."

"Don't you want to sit down?" Marion says. "You're making me nervous."

"Opposition in all things," says Delta.

Marion says, "Without which all things must be a compound of one."

"If the universe is singular, it must remain as dead."

"Neither sense nor sensibility," says Marion.

"No, that's Jane Austen," says Delta. "Neither sensibility nor insensibility."

I'm so worked up that I stand and pace across from Alina. Delta and Marion stand and pace in a comical way, and Alina starts imitating their imitation, and it's suddenly like a skit from the Marx Brothers. "Stop!" I step toward the three, and Delta and Marion step toward me until I can feel their breath on my face with complete disregard for how uncomfortable that makes me. I sit on the log again, and they join me again. This time Alina does as well. "You're not helping. If it has to be maintained, it can't be innate."

"How can a citizen of the United States say that?" asks Delta. "You are thrown. Thrown into a situation. Will is not platonic."

I do feel thrown, as in the rider was thrown off the spinning bull.

"Are there lesser and greater choices here in this world?" asks Marion.

"You're talking like Spencer," says Alina to me. "He wants freedom to drive his four-wheeler anywhere. Freedom of choice is not absolute."

Delta puts her hand on my shoulder. "Spencer's idea of freedom depends on someone else's lack of freedom. He is unable to imagine someone else's light and circumference."

Marion says, "Can a child in a ghetto become president of the United States as easily as a graduate of Columbia, Harvard, Princeton?"

"Of course there are varying degrees of choice in human institutions," I say. "People want power so they rig the system to limit other people's choices."

"You think the universe is any different?" asks Marion.

"You talk as if we inhabit an ideal universe," says Delta.

"Or as if there are corners of space-time that are ideal," says Marion. "No. Not even on Kolob."

"We're stuck," they both say. "Heidegger et al. Here and now."

"Everyone's stuck?" I feel like weeping. "God's stuck?"

"Mother and Father, both stuck."

"Everyone's choice is limited," says Marion. "Even the ducks and the salamanders."

"But I still feel in my soul that the ability to choose is innate. That's the point of the story of the Garden of Eden."

"Not the point of that story at all," says Delta.

Marion also shakes her head. "The point of that story is that in Eden the algorithms and formulas were very different than they are in this world. The Voice of God was so loud that they couldn't hear anything else. Loud as the voice of Agnes."

"But Eve could hear something else," I say. "She listened to another voice. Despite the omnipresence of the voice of God."

"Eve was—"

"Unusual."

"You remind me of her," says Delta to Alina.

I shake my head. "She was able to choose even though there wasn't much option for choice." I feel exhausted. My brain is worn out from trying to comprehend what they're saying. I still don't feel the truth of it in my body. "Sula. I think if she shows up again, my grandmother might also." I stop until both of them are focused on me. "Did you send her?"

"Send?" Delta frowns.

"That's not the word for it," says Marion.

I list the synonyms. "Facilitate, enable, nudge, clear the way for, aid, oil the gears, expedite."

"It has to do with light. The light of the sun, moon, stars, and earth. Light of the Son."

"Yes, that light. It fills the immensity of space."

"The law by which all things are governed."

"We calculate, the light communicates, and your grandmother, who was watching, knew what to do."

"Moved to act. She moved and was moved."

I remember how I felt when my grandmother showed up. She got between me and them and she gave me hope. I was still frightened, but I wasn't frozen with fear. I knew I would survive. I feel tears beading in my eyes. No one speaks for a minute. Alina sits next to me. Delta smiles and Marion pats me on the head as if I'm a child, which oddly does comfort me. I wipe the tears out of my eyes.

Delta and Marion stand and Alina does as well. They seem ready to leave.

"You still have a question," Delta says.

"My Dead Fathers told me that Mother and Father have separated."

They look at each other. "We don't know that."

"Your Dead Fathers are speculating," says Marion. "Speculation runs up and down their hierarchy like a virus."

"Mother and Father aren't around right now," says Delta. "That's all we know."

"And in this apparent vacuum of power," says Marion. "It's even more urgent that we recalibrate the algorithms."

"Rebalance the pull toward order and the pull toward disorder."

"It needed to be done anyway."

"At least once a millennium."

"Hence, Alina."

"Alina, the millennial."

"A wild card. This Alina."

Alina smiles and takes each of them by the hand. I wonder if she can feel the current of their switching and balancing.

It feels like I'm finally getting some answers. I remember they're not talking about the war or my role in it. "The Dead Fathers keep telling me something is coming down and that I have a part to play. But I don't understand what is happening or what my part is."

"Of course you know your part," says Delta. "The petroglyphs show you. Everything shows you."

"The porcupines and pronghorns and rattlesnakes show you," says Marion. "Alina showed you. Peter showed you."

Peter? "Peter showed me what?"

They look at me sadly. "We'd love to talk all day."

"All eternity."

"But we and Alina have work to do."

"Living, dead, and wild card," says Alina. "We're a team. Prime."

They each put an arm across her shoulders and walk around a juniper next to the cottonwood. When I follow, they are gone. I feel the loss of them. I still have so many questions. But my primary emotion is loss. I wonder if I'll ever see Alina again. I hope I do.

"Of course you'll see her again," my grandmother Sarah says. She plucks a juniper berry and uses her front teeth to bite away the covering of the nut, which she puts in her mouth. She didn't grow up in the desert, so she must have learned that from Grandpa Louis, who taught me that when you don't have water, you suck on a juniper berry. She walks back to the log and we sit there.

"I have so many questions," I say.

"And I have so few answers." When she talks, she moves her hands with every phrase, as if she's signing.

"That's the beauty of it. There is no end to questions. William Wines should have put that in his repetitive lyrics. Questions multiply before us like the spread of a sound wave."

I smile. "There is no end to being. There is no end to light."

"Exactly. 'There is no end to space-time' is another line he should have written." She watches a pair of wrens darting through the yellow-green cottonwood leaves. They look like they're playing hide-and-seek. "You know he and Einstein are doing fine work together. One day Alina may collaborate with them."

"Alina?"

"She has a depth that you looked past."

"I hope I perceived it a little. She seems—ah—organized in her being. Sorted out. I envy her. I just feel tangled."

"You have your virtues," she says. "I'm very proud of you."

I move to sit next to her. "Proud of me? What have I done?"

She pats my hand. "You love."

"I left."

She nods. "You did. But it's working out, isn't it? Your love was dormant but you let it rebloom when it had the chance."

I notice a cottontail sitting under a sagebrush. I wonder how long it's been close enough for me to reach down and touch it. "I wish I knew what I'm supposed to do."

"Don't we all."

"Louis and the others are constantly pushing at me."

"Oh, Louis. He became a bitter man, alone in the desert." Her smile is gone, her eyes sad.

"I would like to be rid of them."

She seems pained by my statement. "You don't really want that, do you?"

"I guess not. I've loved them and admired them my whole life. But they never leave me alone."

"Things will shift and balance," she says. "You can afford to be patient."

"Have Father and Mother God separated?"

"I don't know. If they have, the universe will become much more herky-jerky." Her hands play tug of war with the air between them.

"Sounds frightening."

"But we'll survive even that. You'll survive."

I'm thinking about the battle that the DFs are always warning me about.

She says, "Christopher, you're ready."

I sigh. When I look up, she's gone.

When I return to the trailer, Emily, Bennie, Lucía, and Andrew are all busy inside, working on computers or talking on phones. Emily looks up and smiles but turns back to her screen, so I go outside.

I wish I had as clear a picture of my role as everyone else seems to have of theirs. Emily and her team members have an articulated plan and well-defined objectives. They know when they succeed and when they fail, a standard to measure success against. It's not my mode, although I worked that way as a journalist. I had less a plan than a procedure—a personal algorithm: I followed a bad smell in government or business until I uncovered the rotting thing. I was pulled toward answers. I guess I'm still like that, even if I'm no longer frantic with striving.

My grandmother seems to be fine in a state of not knowing. I decide that there's a difference between not knowing and apathy. When I left Emily, I didn't know why she'd taken up with Roger, but I didn't care. The less I knew the better. I didn't want to try to figure out what had happened or what we could do. I moved myself toward a state of passivity and embraced my own stolid inertia. Then I acted, but it was to run away. Now I care but worry that I'll make a mistake and mess things up worse than they were before. I don't yet have my grandmother's confidence in flux. She seemed unconcerned that Mother and Father God might be splitting up. Herky-jerky indeed. I'm jerked around enough by tensions in my own being let alone by tensions with other people. Despite my flirtation with anarchy, I don't look forward to the universe becoming even more unstable.

I hike back up to the petroglyphs. What draws me here? The will of some being I can't see? The pull of the land, which according to Joseph Smith can express will? Or is it just the esthetic pleasure of looking at art. This time I don't see lines that need to be translated; I see lightning, springs, streams, people, and food animals. It's true I don't need an interpretation.

I step closer to examine a circle with a dot in the middle, and I see a rattlesnake stretched out on a ledge a foot from my face. It lifts its head, testing the air with its tongue. I slowly move back. It coils and rattles and the sound spells terror, sends chills through me. I'm far enough away, now, that it can't strike me. I watch as it re-laxes again and stretches out in the sun. Snakes are in the petroglyph panels and a snake startled Peter, causing him to fall. But the same snake obeyed the Three.

I think about the Garden of Eden story, that a snake represented Lucifer as he cultivated disobedience. I've always thought that Lucifer introduced disorder—things falling apart. But now I don't think Lucifer introduced dis-order, just a different kind of order. A more absolute order where everyone obeyed. True disorder would be much more disastrous. Or maybe Eve kept it from being disas-trous. I believe that she wanted to experience the non-ide-al world. Empiricism is learning through experience, and the doorway to that way of living, to self-discovery, was disobedience to authority.

I look at the snake again. He and his race are perfect-ly consistent. He felt threatened, so he coiled and rattled. Before that, he wanted to warm his cold blood, so he lay in the sun. He eats mice and other small mammals, di-gests them, shits out the bones and skin. Owls, hawks, eagles, coyotes, deer, pronghorns, jackrabbits, kangaroo rats, shrews, scorpions, ants, and grasshoppers: all crea-tures fulfill the measure of their existence. And the Gods watched the creation until it obeyed. A paradoxical kind of obedience—becoming one's own self as fully as possible. Will and entropy, order and chaos, obedience and experi-ence, constant rebalancing of oppositions.

The snake is still stretched out, absorbing the sun. My grandmother Sarah is right to hope. I catch hope from her like an infection: Delta, Alina, and Marion will achieve an imperfect or approximate balance. It's inevitable. Or at least I hope it is. If it were perfect, the universe would become dead, a compound of one. Delta and Marion, with Alina's help, will enable the oscillation of an imperfect cosmos.

Back at the camp during dinner, we watch Andrew's computer screen for news about the confrontation. He's tuned into a Salt Lake City station. "Nothing on the national news," he says. Bennie sent the AP and all the local news stations his stills and the video Alina shot from the drone. He finds a Salt Lake channel that shows the line of us sitting in front of the swarm of ATVs.

"You did good work," Emily says to Bennie. "*We* did good work."

"Stirring up the libertarian hornets," says Lucía. "We need to be careful. Who knows what those rednecks might do."

"Some of my best friends are rednecks," I say, but everyone ignores me.

Bennie says, "My tribe members set a date for a protest at the proposed site for the radioactive waste dump. At least most set a date. Some still want the money." He looks around. "Where's Alina?"

"I don't know," says Emily.

Lucía and the others shrug.

I say, "She has a part-time job."

"Another one?" asks Emily.

I nod.

"That's one resourceful girl," says Lucía.

"Who hired her?" asks Bennie.

"Their names are Marion and Delta." Everyone looks at me. "They're doing work in the area." I look around. "Something to do with universal algorithms. I don't understand it."

Bennie says, "She didn't tell me. I've got her suitcase and a box of other stuff of hers." He seems to know I'm not telling him everything, but if I say she's involved with eternal beings, he'll probably become alarmed. Or maybe he'd take it in stride. Also, how can I explain what they're doing when I don't understand it myself?

"You can put her suitcase in the back of my pickup," says Emily.

Bennie shakes his head. "I'll keep them. I'm going to sleep in the back of my truck."

I can see he wonders whether she'll come back for the night. Lucía was right about Alina, that free spirit, probably hurting him.

Emily moves her clothing and other things into my bedroom in the trailer—a good sign. That night—how did Hemingway and Carole King put it?—I feel the earth move.

Afterward, as I drift toward sleep, I think that maybe Emily and I have found a way to keep the Dead Fathers away. Win-win.

In the morning, I'm sitting on a camp chair, drinking my coffee. Bennie's truck is gone, so maybe he decided to go home to sleep. Before the sun reaches me, a vehicle pulls up. Frank Johnson gets out. He's wearing Levis and a bright blue shirt. He bends back inside and takes his rifle from the rack behind the seat. He stomps toward me "Where is she?" he shouts.

Every muscle in my body tightens. "Who?" I finally manage to rasp. Before this stint in the desert, I'd gone my whole life without getting shot at. Now it's an every-other-day occurrence.

"You know damn well who. Your demonic wife." He seems to spit the last word. "I want to look her in the face and tell her she's destroyed us. Uprooted and broken our family."

I see Emily peering out the window, and I motion for her to get back. I don't want him facing her. She'll certainly say something to rile him up even more. "You don't need a gun to say that to her. How did she ruin your life? She worked out a plea bargain with your brother. He won't spend decades in prison."

"Plea bargain?" This time he actually spits on the ground. "My brother gave up everything. We'll be impoverished. We were finally making good money and now we'll be dirt poor. And we're forced to move to Mexico." He steps toward me. "Where is she? I want to talk to her."

I hear a noise behind me, and Frank raises his gun as the door opens.

It's Lucía. "What's all the shouting about?"

"Maybe you should go back in the trailer," I say.

"That trailer wall won't stop a bullet," she says. "Who's your friend?"

"This is Frank Johnson," I say. "Frank, this is Lucía Chavez."

"Glad to meet you, Frank," says Lucía, walking forward with her hand extended.

He doesn't know what to do at this greeting, but he lowers his rifle to shake her hand. That's what Mormons do instinctively, shake hands, so she's effectively disarmed him.

"We had it perfect out here," Frank says. "Nobody to bother us. Making good money. Now we have to leave our home."

"As part of the plea bargain?" Lucía asks. "I don't think so."

Frank is talking, maybe calming down.

My body unclenches slightly. I feel gratitude welling up for Lucía's intelligence and courage. I still don't want Emily to come out. "You could stay on. Actually make ethanol. Or if they are concerned about buying your ethanol, you could raise alfalfa and cattle, like my grandfather did."

He looks at me. "You think I'm stupid. That land with the piddling amount of water we pump won't make us a living."

"You think Mexico will be worse?" I ask.

"Probably not. I just don't want to leave my home. But they're all set on going, so I either have to leave the community or go with them. I don't want to live in that country. Surrounded by Mexicans."

He seems oblivious to the fact that Lucía is Latina.

She laughs at him. "*Pobrecito. ¿Cómo sobrevivirás?*"

He glares at her.

I believe that while Nephi would actually shoot to kill, Frank just has the rifle to boost his confidence.

I say, "I'll give Emily your message."

He glares at me for a moment. Then his rifle droops. "Don't bother. I just needed to let off some steam. My own wives won't listen to me. I have no choice in this whole mess." He climbs into his truck but calls out the window. "That's what government does. Takes our freedoms." Instead of leaving, he sits in his truck, as if he doesn't want to go home again.

Lucía looks at me. "Crazy people live in the desert."

I wipe my hands down my face, but that just spreads the sweat around. I should be used to it—being scared shitless by another idiot with a rifle. I'm dead tired of it. I take a drink of my coffee but now it's cold. "Don't I know it. I'm one of them." Even when I was an editor, I didn't think of myself as belonging in the city. If there was ever a story away from Salt Lake, I leapt at it.

"The other night it sounded like you were having an argument with yourself in your sleeping bag." She searches my face, probably looking for signs of senility. "Were you asleep or awake?"

I sigh. "Sometimes it's difficult to tell."

She leans forward, a concerned look on her face. "Maybe you ought to get tested." She pauses. "A complete psych profile."

I watch Frank who is still just sitting in his truck. "I don't need to get tested to know I'm off my rails."

Frank finally starts his truck and drives back toward the dry river valley.

"It couldn't hurt. Gathering more information about yourself."

I nod but don't commit to seeing a psychiatrist or whoever.

Emily appears. "That damn fool."

"He probably wouldn't have used that rifle," I say, "but I'm glad you didn't stick your head out. His brother shot through my old trailer."

She joins us at the table. "What a way to wake up."

Bennie comes in time for breakfast. He looks at me and I shake my head. "Haven't seen her. But I know she's all right. These people she's working for are—trustworthy." At least I think they are. They operate under different rules. At breakfast, Emily tells the group that they'll finish up within a few days. "Probably by Tuesday. It's been nice to get out of the office. And it's been productive to be close to the action."

"It's been wonderful here," says Andrew. "I mean I've never been in this kind of desert before. When I wanted to get outside, I've always gone to red-rock country."

"But now we go back to the city," says Lucía. "I feel the same as Andrew. I'm going to miss this place."

"The work's not all done," says Bennie.

"The work will never be done." Emily stands and stretches her arms toward the sun. She turns to face the group and smiles. She raises one finger. "The ethanol/whiskey case is on track to be resolved."

Lucía cheers.

I wonder if Frank will find the courage to tell his brother that he doesn't want to leave the U.S.

Emily holds up another finger. "The Nature Conservancy is weighing whether to buy the flat; they probably will. Possibly the mining valley as well."

This time Andrew, Bennie, and I join Lucía in cheering.

Three fingers. "And the state history people are starting the process to protect the cave and petroglyph panels. And the panel in Lost Canyon."

More cheering.

"The case against the U.S. military for killing Goshute farmers is moving forward," says Emily.

The others cheer again, but I'm tired of her rhetorical game.

"At a glacial pace," says Bennie. "It looks as if the state will support the slim Goshute majority in keeping radioactive material off their land."

Emily says, "We've done good. Now we need to be closer to the legislature and the courts."

"Back to the hive of madness," says Bennie. "It's been nice to have you in my part of the world." He looks at me. "Mine and yours."

"Neither of us owns it," I say.

"You won't have that much farther to drive," says Emily. "The north end of Skull Valley is close to I-80."

Bennie shrugs. "It's still been nice."

Emily turns to me. "Are you finished here as well, now that you've found the cave?"

I stand next to her and take her hand. "I'll head back with you, if that's all right." I say it but something still feels unfinished.

Emily smiles and puts her arm across my shoulders. "It's just what I hoped."

Lucía says, "Chris, you've gotten soft sleeping in this nice trailer." She and the others stand.

"That I have. Soft in the head as well. Soft and old."

"I was teasing." Lucía looks at me for a minute. "But you know that. You're all right for an over-privileged but still depressed white guy who shouts at the voices in his head." Before I can think of anything to say back, she opens the door and steps inside. I have to admit, what she said is pretty effective as the last word.

TWENTY

Walking into a Trap

They get back to work, and I am lost about what to do with the morning. What I'd like to do is talk to Emily about what happened with Peter. Or talk about anything, her work or her thoughts about how it will be living in our own house again with all its memories. Or talk with Thomas or Sarah or Marie. Or bike or walk up to the cave with Alina and ask her more about her work with Delta and Marion. But Emily is busy, Thomas, Sarah, and Marie are not showing up, and Alina is probably also too busy. I'm glad to have discovered that extended solitude makes me morose. It goes against the grain of what I thought I knew about myself. Short periods are healthy, but I don't want to spend eternity alone.

At noon the Nature Conservancy people, and state history people, and representatives from both the Wildlife Division and the Bureau of Land Management are going to meet me for a glimpse of the former lek and a tour of the cave and petroglyph panel. Andrew, the best negotiator of the group, has arranged the meeting. Afterward,

I'll show them the panel we tried to protect. The Nature Conservancy may buy all three parcels of land, then give them back to the state to manage. With a state legislature hungry to escape the authority of the feds over state land, it could be a dangerous move, but the state history folks will have responsibility and authority to protect the parcels. And federal employees are spread far too thin, as evidenced by what happened with Spencer's group.

The snow has melted from the hillsides. I feel like walking to the meeting at the cave even though Emily would loan me her truck. Hugh was a great walker. Sometimes he took a horse and buggy to Salt Lake City from his home west of the Jordan River, but often he walked. Every month or so he walked between his main homestead in the Salt Lake Valley and his ranching operations overseen by his secondary wives in Rush Valley—at least a forty-mile distance one way. Our old camp was only a couple of miles from the Valley of the Mines, but the new camp is at least six miles if I take the road. But if I cut across the foothills, the hypotenuse of a triangle, I estimate I'd have to walk only about four and a half miles. I tell Andrew where I'm going and he nods.

I walk up a ridge, then turn north. The desert spreads to the west, flat except for the bluffs and small mountains that thrust up between them. The river valley winds five miles to the west. Again, I imagine the Goshute and his ancestors walking here. I find a network of deer trails, above the foothills and below where the mountain rises more steeply. By selecting carefully I can wind through the junipers and oak brush, following the contours of the ridges and canyons. When I round a bend, I see two people walking ahead of me. I lose sight of them as the path curves inward at a canyon. I walk faster but when I finally catch up, there is just one person—Thomas, walking with a cane. He turns and smiles.

"Hello, Christopher."

"Hello. Who was with you?"

He turns forward and walks on. We're about halfway to the valley. Ahead and below, I see Spencer's horse barn, a group of trucks and trailers parked around it—probably some of the people who drove on the closed road yesterday morning.

"Thomas?"

He finally turns and faces me. "One of the artists who worked on the two sets of panels. A thousand years ago." Then he walks on.

"I would love to talk to him."

"There would be a translation problem." He whacks juniper and piñon branches with his cane as he passes.

"Because he doesn't speak English?"

"That, of course, but you two don't see the same world."

"I've wondered before how they saw this landscape. Maybe we think about water the same way."

"Well, no. You've never watched a family member die of thirst. And your attitude toward water is still utilitarian. He thinks of it as—" He takes off his hat and scratches his head. "It doesn't translate—a blood miracle." He stares at the ground for a moment. "No, that's not right either. Semen. Holy semen."

We walk in silence. Ahead there is a piñon with something high in its branches—a clump of mistletoe? Closer,

I see it's a porcupine gnawing bark. We stop and watch the motions of its front paws and head as it strips bark.

"Do you know how porcupines make love?" asks Thomas.

"I've never thought about that. No."

"Very carefully." He smiles at me.

I snort, caught off guard. Although nothing he does or says should surprise me. I look around for this porcupine's mate but don't see any other brownish clumps in the trees.

"No," says Thomas. "They couple high in a tree, and when the male climaxes, he leans back in ecstasy and shrieks as he falls to the ground." He's not smiling. "This is why porcupines have become so rare."

"You know I believe everything you say."

"Of course you don't. Only a fool would believe everything anyone says."

"Holy semen," I say, chuckling.

"Oh, that's real. It's in the traditional stories. Father sky, mother earth. Engendering growth."

The porcupine is still eating, small motions of mouth and paws, a creature both fat and delicate.

"How do humans make love?" he asks as we turn to walk on.

I shrug—having no idea where this conversation will go now.

"You know this," he says. "Humans make love in every way imaginable. Exuberantly, reluctantly, chaotically, tenderly, savagely. Like eagles and shrews. Like lynxes and snails. Snails spread their semen through the water and the lady snail catches the little swimmers like a net. On land they throw semen like love darts. Did you know some species of snails are male during the first part of their life and female during the last part? Fluid. Humans, having imagination, borrow from all the animals. Glorious and chaotic entanglement."

Like many males, me included, he has an obsession with semen. "Why are you telling me this?"

He looks at me sharply. "I am expressing. Baring my soul to you. Does what I say have to have a purpose? I'm not like your other fathers."

"I thought of you as a heavenly messenger," I say.

"I am. Not heavenly exactly. I wouldn't speak for everyone. But I do have a message."

I wait.

"Prepare yourself. Gird up your loins. Brace up. Buck up. Get ready."

I try to keep from rolling my eyes. He sounds just like the DFs. "I've been told that before."

"But now it's imminent."

He used the same word the other Dead Fathers used. I wonder if imminent means in a thousand years or in one hour.

"I'm not in charge of anything," says Thomas. "And time is different for me and you. But I estimate your second guess is closer than your first."

At his words I panic, despite the smile on his face. I look down at the uneven trail to keep from stumbling, and when I look back, he's gone. I wonder what the challenge will be. He hasn't given me a specific message. If I stop thinking and just feel, work past my panic, I realize that his stories about porcupines and Goshute ancestors and sex and love conjure the same emotional response in me as looking at the ancient petroglyphs.

As if on cue, I hear gunfire and dive flat against the ground, banging my hip on a rock. The shots sound again, but they are some distance away. None are whining past my head. I look down and see that Spencer and his friends are lined up and taking turns firing into the hillside where my trailer used to be. I assume they're target practicing. The hill they're firing into is far below me, but I worry that a stray bullet will find its way toward me. I start jogging, as fast as my old body will let me.

As soon as I'm out of sight of the shooters, I slow down, but I still feel uneasy. Soon I cross the last ridge and drop into the canyon just below the Valley of the Mines. After a few minutes I pass the last bend and see a single truck parked next to the tin building. There's no logo, but I assume it's the people I'm supposed to meet. When I'm almost to the truck, two men and a woman get out—the same mining company officials who talked to me three weeks earlier. The woman carries a pistol holstered at her waist. They stand at the back of their truck, and I stop about ten yards away. I don't want to get too close to them because they're glaring at me, mad as hell.

"You have really screwed us over," one of the men says. He wears the same yellow overcoat as before. I wish I could remember their names. It would make talking to them easier.

"All our investment is lost if this deal with the Conservancy goes through," says the woman, still wearing slacks and her expensive hiking boots. "Cannon-Sharp is selling the land, so all the money we spent on sonic mapping is wasted."

"A lot of money," says the other man, leaning against the fender of their truck. He's the only one wearing different clothing, a nice leather jacket, dyed dark brown.

I start to tell them that it wasn't really me, I didn't contact the Conservancy people, I didn't actually find the cave, Alina did. But I say none of that because it was my will that they fail. I refused to help them. I didn't even contact the mine exploring club like I told them I would. But I did talk to Emily. Even though she already knew, I am responsible.

I'm not sure what to say. "You didn't drive all the way out here to complain. What do you want?"

"You could get them all to back off," says Yellow Overcoat.

"We've already put two hundred thousand into this project," says Leather Jacket.

"To say nothing of the loss of our future profits," says Boots.

Their faces are so contorted by their loss that they seem to be in physical pain.

"I can't help you."

I'm reminded again of *The Monkey Wrench Gang*. Which of the characters am I? Certainly Seldom Seen Smith, the Jack Mormon. Not Hayduke. I'm not wild and violent. I just want them not to change this area of the earth that I love.

Leather Jacket shows me a paper. "We will make you a partner, guarantee you one percent of the profits."

"One percent could be anywhere between a thousand and a hundred thousand," says the woman.

"This won't do any good. It's out of my hands. Never was in my hands." I can see they don't believe me.

"Man, you drive a hard bargain. Two percent. Not a penny more."

"No." I walk past the truck. The trail to the mine is just on the other side of the tin building.

"You son of a bitch!" says the woman.

I glance back and she has her handgun out. Not really pointing it at me.

"Chrissy," says one of the men. "No." Part of my brain, the part that stands to the side and watches, says dispassionately, *Today you might die*.

"He needs to know we're serious about this," Chrissy says. "I don't want to lose all that money."

My hands are shaking and I don't know if it's more from being frightened or being furious. I continue to walk away from her. I guess anger won. I'm almost to the back corner of the building when she fires her gun, and it thunders like doom. I flinch and realize that she's shot into the metal walls of the building. I duck behind the corner.

"You need to listen," she shouts.

I hear their voices again, too low to understand. I hear another truck engine, and I creep through the back door of the tin building. It no longer has a floor, just dust and wild animal manure. I peer through where one of the front windows was, and the two men gesture at Chrissy as they all stand next to their truck. Past them, I see motion, two SUVs creeping into the valley. The people from the various agencies are here to look at the cave. Not the cavalry but close enough. Their engines shut off, and I walk back around the building. They've parked on the other side of the mining company truck and everyone gets out—seven or eight of them, including Andrew—a good number of witnesses. One of them is Carl, the BLM manager, and he has a badge and authority to arrest someone but probably only on BLM land. We're on Cannon-Sharp land.

"What was that sound?" Carl says.

Nobody speaks.

"Target practice," says Chrissy.

I walk out, and she opens the back door to their truck. "This is not over," she says quietly.

My arms and legs are still shaking. I believe her. The two men climb in their truck. As they pull away, I hear their angry voices.

Andrew and the others stand next to me as the dust settles.

"Were they threatening you?" asks a woman who has blonde hair tied in a bun.

I nod.

Andrew asks, "Are you all right?"

I nod again. I could hug him, hug them all.

"Well it's not in your control," says a man with gray streaked through his hair.

"So I told them."

"The idiots," says the woman.

"Christopher, thanks for meeting us." The man with gray streaks shakes my hand.

"This is Sam Roberts," Andrew says. "He's director of state history." He introduces the others, but I only remember a few names.

"Are you all right?" says another woman, black hair cropped at her neck. Harriet, I think.

Carl comes closer and listens.

"When that bullet hit the building, I thought I was dead."

"I'm going to retire early," says Carl. "Every idiot out here has a gun."

They all nod and frown. I feel myself putting on the persona of the old desert philosopher. And why shouldn't I? I'll give them their money's worth. The desert philosophers I've known were all bullshitters, so I've had good role models.

Andrew says, "Chris's people have lived here for five generations." I have the feeling he sees right through me but accepts me anyway, or at least accepts what I can do for his project. Our project.

"Let's go photograph some petroglyphs," the blonde-haired woman says.

"And then the place where the lek was," says someone. Her uniform has a Department of Natural Resources insignia on the shirt pocket—Alicia Freeze.

"If you feel up to it," someone else says to me.

"I'm fine now. I'm just glad you came when you did."

"You should press charges."

"You should hire a lawyer," Andrew says, smiling his slight, wry smile.

Someone hands out helmets, and several people shoulder their cameras.

Sam says, "Lead on!"

I climb through the sage and rabbit brush and up the slide of rocks at the end. We put on our helmets and walk into the mineshaft. I turn on my headlamp, and I take giant steps along the ties.

One of the women makes a sound, "Pip!" and laughs at the echoes.

"How does a mineshaft have petroglyphs?" asks Alicia.

"The petroglyphs are in a cave that links to this mine," I say.

"Didn't you read the material?" asks a man I think is named Brian.

"Whoops!" she says. "I'll fail the quiz."

"No quizzes," says Andrew. I watch him as he talks to one person, then another, another, as we walk. He's the grease that makes this whole thing work—all these people with different agendas.

We pass through the large room. I flash my light up at the ladder, but there's no sign of the Three.

"We have to work out whether to protect this whole mine," says the blonde woman, "or just the cave."

"Or all the mines in the valley," says someone else.

Hearing footsteps, I turn my light toward the sound. Marion and Delta appear as if they are ghosts, just manifested. The group becomes even quieter. "Oh," someone from our group says to them. "You startled me."

"Hello," I say.

"Hello, Christopher," says Marion. "It's good to see you."

"Especially good to see you unpunctured," says Delta.

"Well put, Delta. Well put."

"We see that support arrived just in time," says Delta.

"You arranged that?" I ask as all the officials crowd around me.

"Who are your friends?" asks Sam.

"Arranged? That's not what we do. That implies that we're purposive."

Everyone stares at them. "These are, ah, peripatetic spelunkers," I say. "I've met them down here several times."

Andrew frowns. I suspect he doesn't believe me.

"I like that," says Marion. "Peripatetic spelunkers."

"We should introduce ourselves that way."

"Hello, I'm Marion. I'm a peripatetic spelunker and I balance."

I walk back toward the middle of the big room and gesture for Marion and Delta to follow. I lower my voice. "You must have intervened again. I thought I was going to get shot."

"Yes, somebody cheated again. It was no coincidence that those three were there when you showed up alone."

"We had to allow a rebalance."

"Who cheated? Not those three from the mining company. They must have been compelled by someone."

"Now that, we aren't allowed to say."

"Who doesn't allow you?"

"The universe. Reality."

I can see they're not going to tell me. "How is Alina?"

"Great!" They both say at once. "She's a revelation."

They proceed deeper into the mine, disappearing into the darkness. I turn back to the others.

"Who were those guys?" Brian asks, touching my arm to get my attention. "What were they talking about?"

How can I begin to explain? "A spelunking game. They were complaining that someone was cheating."

"But they don't have lights or helmets," says Alicia, looking toward where they disappeared.

"Must be part of the game," says someone else, whose name I can't remember. They're all clustered around, ready to move on.

"Yes, like free climbing," I say. "Like rock climbing without ropes. They spelunk without lights or helmets." I feel odd lying to these people, but the idea is still funny. That Marion and Delta spelunk in the dark. It's metonymic of what they actually do.

The officials chatter as we walk down the mine shaft but become quiet as we move into the cave. "We're lucky the miners didn't damage the petroglyph panels," I say. "These mines are a hundred years old, and the people working here wouldn't have known how precious they are." Before long, we enter the petroglyph room, and everyone is silent again. The photographer sets up a tripod for her camera and several lights that shine from different angles. I sit to one side on a boulder and watch as the others examine the panels.

"Wonderful," says Harriet.

"We don't know what they mean for sure," says Alicia, "but these spirals probably represent springs." She looks at me.

"There is a spring here in this valley," I say, "and a couple more to the south of here. I can't tell the scale of the map."

"Right," she says. "That's difficult."

I look again at the elemental drawings. I could look at them for hours and never get bored.

They are slow going out, and one short man keeps tripping over the railroad ties because he can't get his steps right. When we finally emerge, they blink in the sunlight. I look down and see a small herd of deer in the meadow. I point them out to the others as we stand on the lip. When we make noise coming down the slide of rocks, the deer lift their heads to watch us, and they continue watching until we're almost to the floor. They bound into the willows and disappear.

The three ravens sit on the top of the tin building and watch us. A man takes a picture of them with his phone. Someone else says, "Ravens seem so ominous."

"Nevermore," says the man who took the picture.

Some of the others grin or groan.

"The three fates," says the historian, smiling.

I think about telling them that he has the wrong three, but Delta, Alina, and Marion are not weaving our fates. Instead they are trying to keep the forces that tug at us in balance. "They're just ravens," I say. "Carrion eaters. They're watching to see if one of us stops moving." It could be my grandfather talking—the best bullshitter I've known.

The historian doesn't seem to know what to say to that. And that's inaccurate anyway. Of course they are carrion eaters, but no creature has a singular role in the complex fabrics of the universe. I don't intend to dismiss any creature's role in what is. Andrew smiles. He's done his job and I've done mine. The mine and petroglyphs will be preserved.

TWENTY-ONE

Badgers Never Back Down

Nothing unusual happens when I show them the cave entrance and the remains of the lek up on the flat to the east, nor when I show them the petroglyph panel in Lost Canyon. They drop me off at the camp. I'm tired and everyone else is still busy, so I go inside to nap in my bedroom. At first, I can't sleep, thinking about Chrissy, who shot into the tin building. She could have shot at me instead of giving me a warning. I hope that was the danger Thomas and the others have said was coming. If so, it's over and I'm unscathed. Finally, I drift off.

In the evening, Emily and I drive to Salt Lake to have dinner at Carrie-Anne and Bruce's house. Dust rises behind us as Emily drives toward Simpson Springs past Spencer's building and the burnt spot where my trailer stood.

"It's an olive branch from her," says Emily. "After we took her and her children down in the cave."

"Should I talk to her about it? Let her vent at me?" It's the end of the weekend, so the campground is only half full.

She frowns as she considers. "Probably not."

"She keeps forgetting that it was your idea."

"And you keep forgetting that you embraced it and were our guide." She turns onto the main road. "You knew what we were getting into better than I did. You are as foolhardy as Peter."

I want to tell her that she's as foolhardy as I am. We trespassed on army land together. Soldiers had rifles pointed at us. It will do no good to say it so I don't. And I haven't told her about the mining speculator who shot near me into the tin building. I am going to be leaving the desert in a few days and will hopefully never see that woman again. Emily would go after her like a bulldog, and she has better things to do with her time.

When we arrive, Karin and Peter are sitting on the bench swing on their porch.

"We waited a long time for you," says Peter.

Karin smiles. "Ten minutes."

"It was a long time," he says firmly. "Maybe six hours."

I glance next door at the house where I will soon move back in with Emily. It's red brick, a conventional house, and it seems both familiar and strange after my stint in the desert.

Inside the air smells of oregano, fresh vegetables, and pepperoni. We are having pizza, and ingredients are spread across the kitchen counter. Carrie-Anne says to me, "You put on your pizza whatever you want." Bruce has made ten-inch circles of dough, one for each of us.

"What are you putting on yours?" I ask Peter.

"Everything!" He raises his arms in triumph. He looks a little like the figure with raised arms on the petroglyph panel in the cave.

"Even pineapple and hot peppers?" Bruce points to those two items in small bowls on the counter.

"Everything except pineapple and hot peppers!" Peter's arms go up again. He kneels on a stool as Bruce paints red sauce across Peter's dough. Then the child puts each item in a small pile on his dough.

"You're supposed to cover it all with cheese," says Karin.

He ignores her and places a small pile of cheese between the pepperoni and the olives.

"What should I put on my pizza?" I ask Peter.

"Everything!" we say together, our arms raised.

"I'm even going to put pineapple and hot peppers on mine."

"Yuck," says Karin.

While we're waiting for the first set to bake, we sit on their deck in the warm spring sun. I peer across the backyard fence at our house, the place we raised our children. Emily sees me looking and puts her hand on my arm. *You are a treasure to me*, I think. I want to make love carefully with her until my body gives out and then we will just hold on to each other even after our minds are gone. Then we will undertake another adventure. Death, I suppose, will still be an adventure.

Peter looks at me, a worried expression on his face. I catch Karin watching him as well. Instead of saying what he's thinking about, he gets a piece of paper and a pencil and fills out a ten-by-ten multiplication chart. Carrie-Anne talks about the difficulty of teaching toward a standardized test, which her high school requires her to do, checking her lesson plans and curriculum. She seems a little jumpy. I wish I could put her at ease. I know Emily's right about just letting us heal. I am glad, despite the danger, for being able to let them see the cave and the mine. I hope she'll mellow. Time is on our side, I hope. Love and time. Not every tangle needs to be untangled immediately.

Karin tells us about her girlfriend, her first. I think about my first girlfriend, and I know I wouldn't have been as open about the relationship as Karin. When I had my first date, it was before I could legally drive, so the only way I could get to the dance was to ask my mother to drive me. I had my date meet me at the high school so I wouldn't have to have my mother and that girl in the same car at the same time—too embarrassing. Emily tells Bruce about Alina working for her part time, creating a database of judges' past judgments and a program that will respond to people on social media about environmental issues.

"She seems to know what she's doing."

"Alina?"

"Yes. Chris, what's her last name?"

"Meijer."

"Alina Meijer!" he says. "Alina Meijer is in the desert! She was doing research at the University of Amsterdam, but they didn't approve her thesis because it involved some material—literature, I think—that they decided wasn't scientific." Bruce works as an AI architect.

"The poetry of William Blake," I say. "The philosophy of Spinoza. To mention just two. She wanted to include all human discourse in her study."

"Such a coincidence!" Bruce says. "I read an article of hers in *IEEE Transactions on Pattern Analysis* and—" He looks at our blank faces. "An artificial intelligence journal."

Emily laughs. "She was mucking out Spencer Murdock's horse barns or something when you came out before. That's why you didn't meet her."

"Remarkable!" Bruce is grinning like a fool. "She's famous! I can hardly believe the coincidence."

Coincidences everywhere, just like horse shit or daisies. The smell of the baking crust mingles with the smell of the ingredients, and my mouth waters. Finally, the pizzas are ready, and we sit at the table. I look around at the others: Peter carefully cutting his pizza into small pieces with one topping on each; Karin watching him and laughing; Emily and Bruce talking about the implications of artificial intelligence. Carrie-Anne cuts thin slices for Erica. I think about what I've missed in the last half a year. So much life. But then I think about what I've seen and experienced—the Dead Fathers, the Mothers, Marion and Delta, Alina, Thomas. The pronghorn, who would be dead now if not for me. All of it has awakened me, sharpened my sense of awe.

It's almost time for Peter to go to bed and for us to head back to the desert when he tugs on my sleeve. When I look down, he says nothing, watching me.

"Just tell him," Karin says to Peter.

"I dreamed that you were in a movie, Grandpa," he says. "There were robber cowboys, but instead of horses they were riding bicycles. Everybody was shooting their rifles at everyone else. You were in the middle and you didn't have a rifle, but you didn't hide. All around were all these animals—deer and birds and rabbits trying to help you, but they couldn't get to you. So you got shot in the leg."

"What a scary dream!" says Carrie-Anne. "Good thing it was just a dream."

He's not comforted and neither am I. The dream was much too specific to dismiss. He says, "Be careful, Grandpa."

He turns toward bed, holding Karin's hand. It seems that I'm not out of the woods yet.

Before heading back, we stop at our house because Emily needs to get a few things. She walks ahead through the rooms, and I follow more slowly. The spears of the agave and mother-in-law's tongue in our entryway have dried up. The blue couches, the brick fireplace, the kitchen table and chairs, seem so right, as if they've been present in my subconscious mind in the desert. Of course they have. It's logical that the rooms are both familiar and strange, both at once. Walking through the rooms evokes deep emotions—pleasant and difficult memories. I'm both observer and subject—a disembodied spirit traversing time. It's a chilling feeling. I get a pitcher from the sink and water the plants.

"I asked Karin to tend them," says Emily, coming out of the back of the house, "but she apparently hasn't been as regular as I wanted."

As we leave, I think about Peter's dream. Whatever happens, soon I'll move back to this house and Emily and I will vacuum and dust. We'll cook a few meals and it will smell familiar. I'll live here until I die and after that, I resolve, I'll stay away. I will not do what the Dead Fathers are doing and haunt Emily and Carrie-Anne. Especially not Karin or Peter.

As we pull into the camp, Andrew and Lucía are getting out of the truck.

"Alina's going to cook us breakfast tomorrow," Lucía says. "We've been to Tooele shopping."

"A Dutch breakfast!" says Andrew.

"To celebrate our time in the desert," says Lucía.

"Where is she?" I ask.

"At Bennie's place," Lucía says. "They took all the food we bought. Apparently, he has a real stove with an oven."

The two of them stand near the table in front of the trailer.

I look at Emily and smile. "Good night," she says to them.

"Sleep well," says Andrew.

Lucía opens her mouth to say a joke or something, but then she just smiles and says nothing.

The Dead Fathers visit my dreams as I'm sleeping next to Emily in the trailer. They are more solemn than I've ever seen them. They don't speak at first. Seeing my family shifted something for me. I'm still upset with the DFs, but I also recognize the bond we have. I remember good times with them—well not Hugh, who died long before I was born, but I've read about his life. They each loved their wives in their own way and loved their children. They had hard lives and lived according to the knowledge available to them. My father and grandfathers' love with their wives broke down, but that happened to me too. If it weren't for Emily, I'd still be alone in the desert, trying to decide what to do.

My father frowns at me. He's ready to issue another warning, I'm sure.

"I know, I know," I say. "Whatever else I do, I shouldn't go to the cave tomorrow."

"Smart ass!" says Louis.

"Actually," says my father, "the cave would be fine, except that you can't get there without going through the mining valley. That's where you shouldn't go."

"We implore you," says Hugh. "We hoped you would champion our cause, but everyone agrees that you have traitorous blood pumping through your veins."

"So we've changed our tack completely," says Louis.

"I don't agree with your decision," my father says to the other two.

"It's not time to get soft," says Louis to him.

Hugh faces me. "Because you're useless to us, everyone agrees that our best chance is for you to stay out of it."

"But if we can't persuade you," says Hugh, "she will take action."

"Who?"

"Never you mind," says Louis.

"Sula?"

They look at each other.

"She's—they're going to get real firm with you," says Louis. "They've lost patience. You won't even make it into the valley."

"Stay in bed all day," says Louis.

"Talk to Emily," says my father.

"Get rambunctious with her," says Louis. "An all-day orgy."

"Do anything but go into the canyon," says Hugh. "We want you to have time to repent."

Even in my dream, I think. Why do they do this if they don't want me to go? They must know I won't listen to them—that I'll probably do the opposite of what they want? Have they learned nothing about me?

"You've been warned," Hugh says. "We love you and want to protect you."

"But if you won't listen—" says Louis.

"You will probably join us," says my father.

"It all depends on who shoots first," says Louis.

"Who gives into their impulse first," says Hugh.

Which is terrifying.

"Peter said he dreamed I was shot in the leg."

"Only if you're lucky," says Louis.

"Death is not the worst thing that can happen," says Hugh. "You've been so lukewarm in this life that God will spew you out of his mouth."

Then they are gone. Still dreaming, I'm wandering alone on the flat below the Simpson Mountains. In dreams I've read about in the Book of Mormon, wanderers feel lost in the wilderness when they are on a dark plain. But that's not what happens with me. I feel joy walking across the land I love. I sing and laugh as I walk. Then I'm at the bottom of a desert canyon and as I walk up, I see women standing on both sides above me on the sloping walls of the canyon. I recognize my mother Lucy, my grandmother Sarah, the other wives of the Dead Fathers. Marie is there and another woman, whom I finally recognize as Janet Cook. She's standing with a man, and they're both smiling. Hundreds of my Dead Mothers. Their love for me emanates from them like waves of perfume or light filling my head, my body. "I love you," say my mother, my grandmothers. It's like a murmuring chorus. Then I see that Thomas is there, standing next to another man. Other men stand next to their wives, many whom I don't recognize. They're singing also—a song rich with love.

I open my eyes, touch Emily's shoulder. She puts her hand on mine. The feeling of being loved, being recognized, is just as strong as in the dream.

A knock comes on the door the next morning. "You don't want to sleep through this breakfast," Andrew says.

Emily, who is on the outside of the narrow bed, swings her legs to the floor. "We're getting up."

We dress quickly and I clap my hat on my head. Outside, the table is full of food: cheese, sliced meat, sliced bread, also jam, honey, hazelnut spread, strawberries, cream, a dark syrup that smells like apples, sprinkles, the kind that go on cupcakes. Alina has also made a cake that smells like Christmas—cinnamon, cloves, nutmeg, and something else.

She and Bennie must have stayed up all night. Neither of them look it, though; Alina seems pleased with her work and her gift. Bennie is as happy as I've ever seen him. Alina turns toward the spread. "You just put the bread on a plate and put on whatever you want, sweet or savory."

Andrew brings out a pot of coffee, and everyone's talking as we pass around the food. I feel a smile spreading across my face. It reminds me of the communion I had with my family the day before.

Emily sees my smile and returns it. "Thank you, Alina. Such a sendoff."

"It's only a small way of showing my gratitude." Alina smiles, but there is a sadder current underneath. "A way of saying goodbye."

"Hopefully not goodbye," says Lucía.

"So long," says Andrew.

"You have welcomed me into your lives."

"How could we not?" says Emily. It's my feeling exactly—Alina is a marvel of friendliness.

I put down a token piece of toast on my plate and smother it with jam and fruit and cheese and meat.

"That's not how you do it," says Alina. "You are the most disorderly person I have ever met."

Bennie sits next to Alina with a sad face. He's looking at the trailer. I see a suitcase and a box sitting next to my boxes of books.

"I've almost forgotten what my normal life is like," says Andrew. "I can hardly hope that the person I hired to water my plants will have done it right."

"My plants were dry yesterday evening," says Emily.

"I'm going to take a long, long bath," says Lucía.

"I'm going to cook splendid food for my friends," says Andrew. "Eggs Benedict, jambalaya, and falafel."

"I'll get an old trailer and put it in my backyard," I say.

Emily waggles her finger at me. "No, no, no."

"I was joking."

"It will be nice to be home," says Emily, "and sleep in my own king-sized bed."

Alina folds her arms across her chest. "Not nice for me. I'm staying here."

Both Bennie and Lucía look toward her.

"You know there's room in my place," says Bennie. "It's not a king-sized bed, but it serves."

"Yes, it does," says Alina.

"We'll be only a couple of hours away," says Lucía. "I have room in my apartment if you ever want to do the city. Like I said, no goodbyes."

Alina looks from one to the other. "It's good for a girl to have options."

At that Bennie and Lucía look at each other. Bennie shrugs. Lucía smiles as if to say, *Let the games begin*. Apparently, she's changed her mind about letting Bennie have the field without competition.

"Where will you live, Alina?" asks Emily.

"This is a rented trailer," says Andrew. "We have to return it."

Alina says, "Actually I have a place to stay. I'm saying that I'll miss you."

Bennie frowns, but he's not stupid. He keeps his mouth shut. He must know that Alina won't be crowded. I wonder where she's going to stay. Hopefully not back in Spencer's apartment. Bennie might be hoping the same thing.

Soon we're just picking. I've eaten so much I feel like going back to bed. But Bennie, the true food warrior, filled his plate three times when I only managed two.

Andrew says, "I'm glad you brought us out here, Emily. I've hardly been outside Salt Lake City since I moved here. Just a couple of trips south."

Lucía raises her coffee cup. "To Christopher in his natural element."

"You mean squalor?" I ask.

"No! This landscape." She moves her hand across the horizon.

"Beautiful," says Andrew, "in its own arid way."

"If you had seen the inside of his trailer," says Emily, "you wouldn't have such romantic ideas about him as a man of the desert."

"Squalor is the right word," says Alina. "Except for the books. They were just disorderly."

"It's been good to be with people who love this area," says Andrew, politely ignoring my detractors. "You've helped me see it through your eyes." He raises his cup to me and Bennie.

Bennie clinks his cup against Andrew's. "To people who can see and hear. I mean who take care in seeing and hearing."

Alina raises her cup. "My eyes have been opened. To the Great Basin."

Everyone smiles and raises their cups.

"While we're toasting our gratitudes," I say, "to showers." I look at Emily. "Much better than a pond."

"Oh, yes," says Emily, raising her cup with everyone else.

"To Andrew's cooking." I say. They raise their cups again.

Emily smiles at him. "You have been wonderful—doing your work and getting us food, both." She drains her cup and then sits for a moment. She's on the edge of her chair as if ready to pounce on some prey or run a race. It's only a few seconds before she claps her hands together. "Enough of this talk. We have work to do."

Bennie gets in his truck and the others step inside the trailer.

Alina turns to me. "I'm going up to the mine valley. Marion and Delta are waiting for me," she says. "Do you want to come? You could drive Emily's truck back. She said I could borrow it."

I think about what the Dead Fathers said. I may be stumbling into trouble, but that means Alina might also be in danger.

"Yes. I'll come."

Bennie is still parked, watching us. He leans out the window and we walk over to talk with him. "What if you two took a day off? Stayed close to camp."

Alina smiles at him, but her smile is twisted a little. "Has it come to where you want to tell me what to do?"

Bennie says, "Of course not. It's just that I noticed a group of people congregated at Spencer's barn. I'm worried about what they might do.

"Maybe they'll just try to ride through the mining valley before it gets closed to ATV traffic," Alina says.

"Maybe," says Bennie. "I don't like the look of them. One is the guy from Spencer's group who pointed a rifle at me and Alina."

"Thanks for the warning," I say. The third I've received against going to the valley.

"I'm going," says Alina. "I have work to do."

"Work?" he says.

"Yes, work."

He's still puzzled. If he knew as much as I do about her work, he might be even more puzzled.

"We'll be fine," she says and turns away. He looks as if he's going to say something more, but it would be to her back, so he rolls up his window and drives away.

"You should stay here in camp," she says to me. "I can return Emily's truck this evening."

"Has it come to where you want to tell me what to do?"

"No, it's long past that point," she says. "You disobedient man. Oh, that's an oxymoron."

"I'm coming."

We borrow Emily's truck and drive along the Six-mile Road, far enough behind Bennie that his dust doesn't coat our windshield. We pass the black spot where my trailer once sat. I look toward the horse barn, but there are no vehicles parked there.

"They must be gone," says Alina.

I no longer see Bennie's dust, but neither do I see his vehicle parked along the road. We turn off onto the side road that leads to the mines. As we pass along the familiar track up through the junipers, I wonder if this will be the last time Alina and I will go to the valley of the mines together. "I wish I could understand better what you're doing with Marion and Delta. I believe rationally that laws aren't different in the heavens, but I've never believed it in my gut. I've felt that earthly matters are earthly and heavenly matters are different, or at least beyond our understanding. I can't get rid of that narrative."

"Math is universal," says Alina. "Well that's a simplification, because mathematicians still have a lot to learn."

"I think I get that part of it as well as I can. What I don't understand is the process—the practical methodology."

"It's like writing code but with sounds—the sounds of all the animal and human phonic systems, the sounds of the earth like wind and quakes—and images, like the carvings. I'm not working with just open and closed circuits in a binary. It is a lot like complex music, Bach multiplied by Beethoven squared."

I think about the singing I heard last night from my ancestors. "A heavenly choir. Music of the spheres."

"Yes, like that," says Alina. "But with motion, opera or ballet. Mozart to the tenth power 3-D and tactile. I dance, manifesting balance."

"OK, say I have a glimmer of understanding about the language or code, but you've said nothing about the interface. A computer keyboard and a computer give access to the Internet. How do you get access to the music of the spheres?"

She laughs, and the sound is also music. "That's the most elegant part of it. You think of interface as a conduit and a barrier. There is no conduit, no barrier. It's right here." She holds her hands out.

"A spiritual interface? Transcendental?"

She shakes her head. "You're still thinking of a keyboard. There's no secret interface. No conduit between my body and the universe." She does a kind of windmill dance where one leg and two arms point toward me. She turns and moves her arms and fingers and it's still a dance, but also as if she's conducting music with her movements.

All this still leaves me puzzled.

We pass three magpies sitting in a juniper tree. Then we pass three ravens, and just beyond that, three bald eagles. Three sets of three carrion birds.

Alina points out the window at the eagles. "Not a coincidence."

"I think you're right."

"You should turn back," she says.

"Only if you do."

"I won't be intimidated," she says. "And Marion and Delta are relying on me."

I can't let her go alone. Foolish. What could I do to protect her that she wouldn't do better herself? Still I have the urge to watch out for her.

We ride forward again. We are about a hundred yards into the narrow part of the canyon when we turn a corner, and fifty feet ahead, I see figures with rifles lined up across the road. My reptile brain kicks in: *get away, get away!* I fumble putting the truck in reverse. My heart thumps and then races. All I want is to get the hell out of there. Two guns fire and the steering wobbles. They've shot out Emily's tires. Part of me comments, *You will regret that!* Emily will not let it go.

"Get out," General Torrey shouts. He carries his issue revolver with a barrel as big as a culvert.

This can't be happening, can't be. But it is. The damnable DFs warned me. Even Peter warned me.

"We should stay in the truck," I say to Alina.

"They can shoot us just as easily through the window. But they're not going to do that. They're just going to threaten us."

There are five of them; the General is in the middle, with Nephi on his left and Chrissy, the woman from the mining company, still wearing her slacks and boots, on his right. He carries his deer rifle and she, her small .22 pistol. There are a couple of men from Spencer's group. One has an assault rifle and another his hunting gun, big enough to bring down a bear. For a split second I wonder, *What influences in heaven or hell bring all of them together?* But at this instant the logistics seem less important than the fact that we have five guns pointing at us—four rifles and a pistol.

"It's like a Western movie," says Alina. "*The Magnificent Seven.* This is something I couldn't have imagined happening before I left the Netherlands."

I remember deer I've shot, what a rifle does to the meat. I imagine a bullet hitting me or Alina, what would happen to our bodies.

"We should get down on the floor," I say.

"There's not enough room."

My legs feel weak, as if they'll give out any second.

"Christopher Twist," calls the General. "Get out of the truck."

"They just want me." I reach for the handle. "I'll go talk to them."

"No," she says. "Don't."

"I'm back," shouts Chrissy.

I should respond, but I can't make my mouth form words, can't make my body move to obey him.

He says, "You have caused all of us tremendous trouble."

"That's an understatement," says Chrissy. I will never, even in my senility, forget her name again and have to call her Boots.

My hands tremble, but I still wonder why Alina said seven. They are not the Magnificent Seven. They are the Frustrated Five. But then I see that there are seven—a woman on one end and a man on the other. The woman is Sula, but the man is a stranger. At least neither of them has a gun. But they may not need them. If I thought I was frightened before, I was wrong. The terror I felt during my dream, terror and impotency, flood back into my body. I can hardly breathe.

"Oh, no," I croak. I want to get out and run back down the canyon, but my arms still won't work to open the door and I'm sure my legs won't work to run. I'm trapped by forces I can't hope to combat.

"On three," says Alina quietly. "Get behind the truck."

I remember what the Dead Fathers said, that the outcome would depend on who gives in to their impulse first, but I'm not sure what difference that will make in terms of our action. "No," I say. "Just leave. They won't do anything to you and you can go for help." This time I succeed in opening the door and stepping out. Legs shaking, voice shaking, I stand behind the door, which is only an illusion of protection, and say, "She's leaving. Your beef isn't with her." I feel the waves of will coming from the man and the woman. All I want to do is turn and run. *You've run before*, I say to myself. *And it always worked out. Turn and run. Now!* Instead I step to the side of the useless door. I can no longer force myself forward, not even one more step, but I'm not running.

I hear the other door open and turn my head to see Alina standing on the other side of the truck.

Chrissy points her pistol at Alina and barks, "Stay where you are. You're involved!"

"She and your wife," says the General, his voice shaking with anger. "A threesome."

"Where is Emily?" calls Nephi. "That woman ruined my life."

"She's in town," I say, but my voice is unsteady and squeaks.

"She'll be here soon," says Sula.

I believe her. Emily will have heard the shots and may come with Lucía and Andrew. *You should have listened to the warnings.* "How will shooting me help anything? I have zero influence on all your troubles." I wince at how ineffective my argument seems, even to me.

Alina whispers. "They're watching you. I'll go for help."

"Wait!" I whisper. "I was wrong. They *will* shoot you."

"Do not leave," says Sula, with a voice as harsh as that of a smoker. "Either of you."

I'm too frightened to move anyway, so the command doesn't change anything.

"Fucking environmentalists," says one of Spencer's friends.

"You refused to listen to warnings," says the man on the other end from Sula.

I am a coward and I want to tell them that it wasn't me. It was Emily. She's the source of their problems. "I was incidental, inconsequential."

Sula shows her teeth like a wolf. "Emily's machinations are not the whole story. Neither of you are inconsequential."

"But I'm the weaker link."

She smiles. "It's good to have a clear picture of yourself."

Run, I say, to myself, *that's the only way out of this.* "Her machinations, as you call them, won't stop if I'm gone. Tell me what you want from me!"

"Your death will change the flavor of it all." Sula smiles. She reminds me of a mountain lion I once saw. I had been tracking it, but then I found my own tracks and its tracks doubled and realized that it was now tracking me. The thought of the similarity nearly makes me pee myself.

The man on the other end of the line says, "And all it took to get you here was to tell your ancestors to warn you not to come."

"Emily, on the other hand," says Sula, "is much less tractable."

"Now," says Alina quietly.

"Not yet. They'll shoot you."

"Move!" she says. I hear her scrambling on the other side of the truck. I still can't move for a second, but then my brain starts working and I turn and take a step toward the back of the truck.

"No!" shouts the General.

I hear a shot and then it's like someone rapped me on the thigh with a stick. I look down and there's a hole in my pants and in my leg toward the outer edge of my thigh. I reach down and my fingers are wet. I find another hole in the back of my leg. The two holes are close to each other. The bullet passed through the outer part of my thigh, in one hole and out the other. In the scramble, my hat comes off. I reach for it and don't get it, but I nearly fall.

Chrissy still has her pistol raised. I should get around the truck, out of her line of fire, but now that I'm actually shot, paradoxically I feel calm. I'm not afraid of her anymore. Instead of doing the smart thing, I hobble to a boulder at the side of the road and sit. Now it's starting to hurt like hell. I press the cloth against my leg and blood oozes out. Luckily, it's not pumping, so the bullet probably didn't sever a major artery.

"Are you all right?" asks Alina from behind the truck.

"They hit my leg. It's not bleeding bad. It didn't hit the bone."

She swears steadily in Dutch, but ends with, "Those fuckers."

"Stay behind the truck." My thigh is throbbing with pain now.

"Bennie," says Alina, pointing up.

I hear a whirring sound and the drone flies above our heads. General Torrey has his hand on Chrissy's arm. He's forcing her gun hand down.

The drone flies fast toward the seven in the road. It sweeps across in front of them and then rises straight up. One of the men from the ATV rally shoots but doesn't hit it. He'd need a shotgun to hit a small thing like that. The drone swoops toward them again, passing not far above their heads.

"Fuck it," says one of Spencer's group. "This whole thing is a really bad idea."

The two men dash to their vehicle and jump in. Their truck roars past us. Soon the others head toward General Torrey's vehicle. I worry that Chrissy is going to shoot me again, but Alina moves between her and me. I say, "You should have stayed behind the truck."

As their vehicle drives past, I hear them shouting above the sound of the engines. Sula has disappeared, but I'm sure she and the man who came with her are still close, intent.

Seated on the boulder, I let myself relax a little. I was shot, and it hurts bad, but the wound isn't life threatening. I've lived through worse pain, kidney stones and a few times a migraine headache. I take down my pants, letting them droop around my ankles, and bend forward to examine the bullet holes. Neither the entry wound nor the exit has more than a trickle of blood. But I feel the adrenaline waning and the wound hurts even worse. I feel dizzy. Alina points behind me at where the bullet went through the door. She rummages in the truck and returns with a first aid kit. She gives me a couple of pain killers and finds a bottle of water. She puts antibiotic on the wounds, then gauze pads. She wraps my leg with tape and then an elastic bandage.

I gently pull my pants back up. "Good for now."

"I think you're in shock," says Alina. "You're not acting like a person who's just been shot. You need a hospital."

"I do need an antibiotic to keep it from infecting."

She looks up, but the drone is gone. "Oh, Bennie. I'm going to kiss him when I see him next."

"But you'd kiss him anyway."

"There are kisses and then there are other kisses," she says. "This will be one of the others." She takes my hand and pulls me up. "Can you walk?"

"Yes." I show her by walking to the truck and back. "I'm not going to be running a marathon soon. Or dancing a jig, but I can walk."

The truck can't be driven, so we walk down toward the main road. We turn the corner, and Marion and Delta block our way.

"We need you," Delta says to Alina.

Marion says, "He's essential also, but we have to give him space."

"Emily will be here soon," says Delta, pointing back along the road. "And Bennie."

"He can sit and wait for her. She can help him."

Delta smiles, "Up or down. Whichever you choose, Christopher."

Alina still seems reluctant to leave me.

"Go," I say to her. "Emily and Bennie will take care of me."

They walk up the road toward the Valley of the Mines. The air above the valley looks odd—wavery, as if heat is rising. But I see no smoke. I look back at the road where Emily will soon come to help me. My leg doesn't seem to be bleeding now. It hurts, but I feel like following them up to the valley. I tell myself that would be a stupid thing to do, but I also want to see what's happening there. I decide to walk as far as the truck. At least I'll be able to sit inside instead of on a boulder. My leg hurts worse when I walk, and I have to limp. I weigh my curiosity against my pain and the possibility of more pain. For once in my life, I'm determined to do the sensible thing. *You won't be of any use anyway—a weak, fallible human.* As soon as I'm around the bend, I see Emily's truck. There is someone sitting on the hood—Thomas.

I limp toward him, wincing at the pain.

"Take a load off," he says.

I step onto the bumper with my good leg and sit next to him. The hood of the truck is slanted where I'm sitting, and I put my palms flat to keep from sliding.

Thomas says, "Having difficulty making up your mind?" He points up and then back down the road. "Seeing a once-in-a-lifetime cosmic event or finding safety. Which will you choose?"

I glance at him. "What cosmic event?"

He just smiles. "You won't find out if you choose safety."

"You're as pushy as the other Dead Fathers."

"You'll make a good choice."

"They said I'm lukewarm. Which I took to mean that I waver. That I'm not consistent in my choices. Which is absolutely true."

"We all waver," says Thomas. "This shaking keeps me steady."

My hands slip an inch against the hood. I'm in a precarious position in more ways than one. "I love that poem."

He smiles and touches my arm. "We think by feeling." He smiles as if the core of his selfhood rejoices.

I say, "I wake to sleep—"

"And take my waking slow." He rotates his hand, but I don't go on.

"I can't remember it. But that's how I feel, a slow awakening."

Thomas says, "I love the part where he says, 'I hear my being dance from ear to ear.'" He seems to be the happiest I've seen him. Not that his face has ever shown sadness, just that he looks like he's brimming with joy. "My other favorite part: 'I learn by going where I have to go.'"

The big, double-cab truck pulls up behind me, and Emily gets out, runs toward me. Bennie is close behind her. Thomas is gone. I realize that my fear of Sula, the mountain lion woman, has faded. Maybe Thomas is doing his own balancing, leaving space for my agency to expand.

"You got shot," she says. "Andrew called the police and an ambulance, but it will take an hour for them to get here."

"Where's Alina?" Bennie asks.

I point up the canyon.

He starts back toward his truck.

"Wait!" I slide off the hood and stumble as my weight falls on my bad leg. Bennie walks back, and he and Emily face me. Emily looks ready to ask Bennie to force me into the truck. "The people who shot me are gone. And anyway, it was a .22 and didn't hit anything important." I know she won't be satisfied with that, so I pull my pants below my knees and show her and Bennie Alina's work. No blood shows on the bandage.

"Is Alina safe?" asks Bennie.

"As safe as anybody could be."

"What do you mean?" he says.

"You need an antibiotic," Emily says.

I nod. "But not this instant." I point ahead at the shimmering air.

"Chris, what the hell is going on?" Bennie asks.

"One answer is I don't know. But I want to find out." The Dead Fathers said war was imminent, and maybe that confrontation was what they meant. I think not. I take another step toward the shimmering.

Emily grabs my arm. "No!"

"Will someone please tell me what's going on? Who were those five people?" Bennie stares up canyon. The sky over the valley looks like wavering heat rising from a cauldron. "I recognized Nephi, but not the others."

"People who think that Emily and I have wronged them. A woman from the company that wants to mine here. The general who tried to put Emily and me in jail."

"You can't even walk," says Emily. She looks from me back to the sky above the valley. "You're crazy if you want to go up there."

Bennie's still watching the sky. "Is Alina there?"

I nod.

He starts trotting up the canyon.

I have only a vague idea of what's happening, but he's absolutely clueless about what he's running toward. I walk back toward the truck and get in the passenger side. Emily climbs in the driver side and starts the engine. But she doesn't move. She's looking toward the valley.

"Just a look," I say.

"I don't know who's the greater fool," she says, putting the truck in gear and pulling forward. She stops when she reaches Bennie and he climbs in.

After a few hundred yards, we emerge from the canyon and enter the Valley of the Mines. Emily stops the truck a couple hundred yards from the tin building and we get out.

"What the fuck?" Bennie says.

The sky looks like a mirage, shimmering with light. But it's the whole sky, not just a rim on the edge of the horizon.

I start forward. "Chris!" says Emily. "Stop and think."

I glance back at her. Bennie seems frozen, still standing next to the truck. His face is hard to read. Sure he looks frightened, but his eyes are open wide with what seems like wonder. He says something in Goshute, but he still doesn't move.

I walk through the willows next to the creek, only limping a little. It'll be worse when it swells up. One of my willow sticks lies next to the stream. Using that as a cane, I find it easier to walk. It isn't just the gunshot that's making me unsteady, it's my body nearing collapse after a massive dose of terror and adrenaline. The voices have come back into my head, and if I didn't know better, I'd think they were straight from my own soul. *I'm going to regret this. Danger, danger, danger!* Exactly as if I'm hearing the rattle of snakes all around me. Driving back down the canyon seems the best thing I can possibly do.

Emily, who has come up behind me, takes my arm. With her on one side and my staff on the other, I'm able to walk fine, despite the swelling in my thigh. As we emerge from the thin screen of willows before us, I see nothing unusual. But then, I see someone standing on the hillside. A woman wearing a dress made of some thick material. It looks like the Goshute clothing I've seen in the natural history museum in Salt Lake, woven from the blossoms of rabbitbrush. Then she's joined by a man dressed in a waistcoat and trousers. A woman in a Victorian dress, a man in an army uniform. Then it's like evening when you see one star, then another, then a dozen. Soon I'm seeing the valley filled with people. Some are dressed like cattlemen, with boots on their feet and hats held respectfully in their hands. Some wear only a breechclout. Others wear clothing weaved from rabbit fur, and maybe cedar bark. Most faces are sun and wind weathered, so those that are Goshute and those that are European have similar skin color. Some faces are darker, and some are pale, looking as if they didn't spend all their days in the sun. Some with long hair, some with short, blonde and brown and black. Many wear somber or pastel clothing, but others wear colorful shirts, a patchwork of all the colors in the spectrum. Some of them talk to each other, some are silent. They stand next to the tin building, on the aprons of every mine, on the pathways, meadows, and sagebrush slopes. There are probably ten thousand men and women.

The hillsides are full not just of people but animals as well. The animals are as diverse as the humans: badgers of every size and stripe, kangaroo rats, jackrabbits, cottontails, rattlesnakes, porcupines, pronghorns, mule deer, elk, hawks, eagles, even bears and wolves, creatures that disappeared from this area a hundred years ago. I glance back at Bennie, and he stands where we left him. Frozen, maybe, but watching everything. I face forward again. Every step is difficult but also a revelation. Like walking the edge of a thousand-foot cliff. I want to be there but I don't. I am pulled to see and maybe understand and pulled to run in terror.

"Oh my God," says Emily. She's stopped, still holding my arm. Her grip is not the only force that keeps me from walking forward; fear has completely frozen me. "You've led me into a hallucination."

"You see them too?"

She nods.

"Maybe it's not a hallucination."

"More likely we've both lost it," she says.

Every being faces the center of the valley, an empty patch of meadow twenty yards in diameter. There doesn't seem to be any hierarchy in the placement of people or animals, but maybe there is a pattern I'm not seeing. Stranger than the sight is the total lack of sound. Not the crack of a twig or the shifting of a foot.

Every hormonal and neuronal warning goes off as I step forward, walking toward the tin building, but Emily pulls harder, still holding me back. "Are you crazy?" She's whispering and glancing around.

"I thought we already established that," I say.

She seems even more frightened than I am, a surprise because I thought nothing scared her. "Let's just stand here on the edge and watch—see what is going to happen before we do anything."

"That is so unlike you," I say. "We are part of this. Everyone has told me so."

"Dead people have told you so," she says. "Please. Who knows what—" she moves her hand in the air "—all these—entities—will do to you."

I stop and think seriously about what she says. I feel Emily's hand on my arm, and I feel both invited to walk forward and warned not to. Both at once. Barbarians, some of them certainly my ancestors, killed some enemies by tying horses to their legs and arms and pulling them apart. I'm not yet physically or spiritually dismembered, but I can imagine them both happening.

The Dead Fathers said my intelligence could be dissolved, all the material that gives me identity atomized and scattered. That would be worse than death, which I narrowly escaped. As they predicted, I was shot—but the bad shot pulled the trigger first, the one with a low-caliber gun. Maybe she aimed for my thigh and not my heart or head. Or maybe she did want to kill me but was too angry to shoot straight and missed. For sure if one of Spencer's buddies had shot at me, I'd not be standing. I know in my bones that I have a part to play, and I really, really, really want to find out what that part is, but I also want to back away and leave this gathering. Maybe the Dead Fathers will stop pestering me if I push through. Or maybe I'll fragment to atoms of intelligence. Worse than that, Emily could also be destroyed. I hope she'll stay behind.

I take one step along the pathway. "No," she says, but her heart isn't in the word. She walks forward and takes my hand. I don't want her to be in danger, and I don't want myself to be in danger either. But I'm supremely grateful she's holding my hand. It makes it all a bit less terrifying.

We make our way toward the building and the open space next to it, where no one stands. I see the Dead Fathers waiting near the Dead Mothers, all close to that empty circle. Seeing them, my fear wanes enough that I can feel something else—the tension between them. In fact the air seems to hum with energy, something like opposing magnetic fields. But it isn't just two sides pulling at each other. It's more of a constellation of individual tensions. We move past a couple of skunks, breathing their sharp odor. We continue through the sagebrush and then meadow grass. People and animals make way for us. A bull elk moves aside, and I smell his musk as I pass. A man and a woman wearing doe skin also move to one side, and I smell woodsmoke and the musk of their bodies, which is not as strong as the elk. Two skunks step aside, a woman in a pioneer blouse and skirt. Snakes, a fawn, and a bobcat make a path. Even a badger moves out of our way, something I've never seen before. Badgers never back down.

TWENTY-TWO

Anticlimactic

I look back at the tin building, and on the peak stand Delta, Marion, and Alina. Maybe they were there all along and I just didn't notice them. They watch Emily and me, but not even Alina smiles. Their faces are blank, impartial, the faces of referees—which gives me hope and further quiets my fear. They'll make sure everyone follows the rules, whatever the rules are. Alina's knees are bent, her feet shoulder-width apart, and her hands out, as if she's an athlete, a fighter, a dancer, or all three, ready to leap in any direction.

I look more closely at the faces of the people I'm hobbling past, supported by Emily. My grandmother Sarah's face shimmers, and I can't tell what age she is. Her visage reminds me of an artwork I once saw by Maddison Colvin—photographs of the altar of every church in central London, all overlaid, on paper-thin, acrylic sheets. The blended image was both particular and universal, many and one. That's how Sarah's face looks, as if every moment of her existence shows at once. I look from face to face, and they all look like that. Even the snakes and pronghorns shimmer. If this is what eternity looks like, it's wonderful. Thomas is between Marie and two men. He has his arm around one of the men. Their faces waver also, even though when I saw him earlier, he seemed singular in time. The Dead Fathers shimmer too. I wonder if they appeared to me in their simplest aspect so I wouldn't be overwhelmed.

The buck's antlers are there and not there, in the velvet and in their prime, dull and pointed, all at once. The white and tan of the kangaroo rat ripples in time, small and large at the same instant. Badgers, cottontail rabbits, pronghorns, skunks, porcupines—all shimmering with power.

I also can feel the tension building, individual and communal wills manifesting themselves. "War is coming," the Dead Fathers told me. And now Hugh and Louis are right before me, glaring at me as if I am one devil and at Emily as if she's another. They're so focused in their rage that they become singular, just as they appeared when visiting me in my trailer. My father's face just seems sad. I'm sad as well. People I love may soon try to destroy each other. I think about the oblivion I felt in my dream, no sensation, not even pain. I don't want any of these shimmering entities to be lost, their atoms scattered. What will happen to the earth because of this battle? Will tectonic plates shift? Will the jet stream slow to a halt? Will there be earthquakes and hurricanes all over the world? Or will souls of living entities dissipate, as if they never existed?

I step to the edge of the circle with Emily, and we turn and look at the ranks of people and animals surrounding us. It's quiet, but the feeling is like before lightning strikes and your hair stands on end. I want to do something to prevent this impending battle. I want my dead ancestors, my mothers and fathers, to get along. That seems a faint hope, not nearly as strong as the anger I see on many of their faces. I want my predecessors to return to each other, like Emily did with me, an imperfect couple, striving and wrangling, but not giving up. Have Mother and Father God given up on each other? The people I trust most say they don't know.

Hearing the Dead Fathers talk, I would have thought these beings would be arrayed against each other, enemies on either side, but there are not two sides, no clear division of forces. As I stand at the edge of the empty circle and pull Emily closer to me, I hear what the multitude is saying, but it's not clear who is saying it.

"Entropy." A voice that shakes with intensity, maybe anger.

"Agency." A quieter voice.

"Progression." Firm.

"Negentropy." I can't tell the tone. And there's a pause after that one. The voices continue, powered by a variety of emotions.

"Order."

"Fractal growth."

"Obedience."

"Freedom." A shout.

"Balance."

"Fragile existence."

"Certitude."

"Rebellion." Another shout.

"Chaos."

"Civilization."

"Imprisonment."

"Doubt."

"Flexibility."

"Conditions and consequences."

Ripples and echoes of these and other words and other symbolic acts pass through the crowd like wind through a field of grass. It's as if they have argued for so long from so many angles that they don't need to state the logical chain any longer. Code words stand in for their claims. I think of the words of the Dead Fathers and Mothers woven into an array, a matrix, no longer binary but relational, like constellations of stars. The sound is like their visual shimmering, singular and multiple at once. Just like the people and animals that surround us, their words, ideas, and claims don't easily fall into two camps. They show many attitudes toward existence, agency, and obedience. This situation is much more complex than the DFs recognize.

I glance at Alina, who moves along the peak of the shed as if it's a gymnastics beam. She dances to a complex music I can't hear, her arms and legs reaching, fingers writhing, face focused. Even her eyebrows and mouth shift like flickering shadows from surprise to anger to pleasure. I have never seen her more focused and alive.

I walk toward the circle, but Emily pulls back on my hand. "You could die today. We could die. Use your head."

I point toward Alina, and Emily watches her. Her mouth drops open a little. "My sweet lord."

"I'm not running away from this," I say.

Thomas and Marie step to the edge of the circle. A porcupine waddles forward. I start to join them, but Sula comes from one side and bars my way. "You have been warned and warned, yet you persevere."

She's holding her trademark axe. Behind her I see Agnes. I turn to get away, but Emily's in the way. Sula focuses on her, frowning, a tactical mistake she'll certainly regret.

Emily's eyes open wide. She takes a step toward the woman. "Get the fuck out of my head. And get the fuck out of our way."

Sula doesn't move, but with her focus on Emily, I feel free to speak. "I have a place in this circle. I don't understand it, but I do know it has something to do with my nature, which is to pry into things."

From around Emily, Sula says, "Your curiosity will damn you."

"I don't think so," I say.

Emily and Sula glare at each other. Sula looks away. Emily takes my hand, and we walk around her. She raises her ax toward the three perched on the roof of the tin building—a clear threat. Delta and Marion simply smile. Emily lets go of my hand and steps back. Sula also takes her place on the edge of the circular space in the meadow. Thomas shakes his head, and the air blisters between them like heatwaves above asphalt. Sula glances up at the three on the roof and finally nods, reluctantly handing her axe to Agnes. I'm frightened of her even when she doesn't have a weapon. The air between Sula and Thomas, between all of us, radiates energy. Soon we will all burn as blue as the hottest star. The porcupine stands at Sula's side like a small, bristly dog. In a moment the fight will begin, and I have no weapon or desire to use one.

Suddenly I know what to do. I put my hand on my hat and push it tight, as I've seen rodeo cowboys do before the chute opens and the bull or bronco leaps out. I step forward to the center of the circle where there's a patch of dirt. With my walking stick, I draw in the dirt a human figure, a circle, a wavering line—none as simple and elegant as the archaic glyphs but similar to them. Thomas steps forward. I hand him the stick, and he draws more figures, all representing elemental life—water, people, animals, plants, rocks, fire. Sula's eyes widen with both fury and surprise. Thomas hands the stick to the porcupine, who grasps it in his hand-like paws but then lays it aside and draws with one claw, a series of concentric circles with some cross-bridges like a maze. I hear the sound of conversation, laughter even, rippling across the hillside. Thomas hands the stick to Marie, who draws a line of mountains with the sun or maybe the moon rising over them. Then she nods at me. I take the staff and draw again—a sun with rays extended and the head and curved horns of the pronghorn. I extend the staff toward Sula, and she looks at it as if it's a snake, and it is. She takes the head in one hand and the tail in the other and uses the rattles to draw jagged lines like steps, parallel lines with cross bars, like rungs in a ladder but even more like strands of DNA. She hands Thomas the snake, and he whispers in its ear and places it in the dirt, where it makes looping lines across the other drawings. I reach toward the snake and it's my stick again. I draw, then the porcupine, then Marie, then Sula. Soon there is just a tangle of lines, but they're also distinct, layered, and relating to each other, just as the four of us are connected in the act of drawing. Thomas smiles, adds a line. I add another that makes his into a branch. Sula frowns at the branch and at both of us, then draws a bud on the end of the branch. Emily steps forward and draws a leaf. Marie draws a flower coming from the branch. Sula adds more branches and buds. She's still not smiling, but she steps back and nods. Somehow, miraculously, her anger seems to have melted away.

The tension in the valley has shifted since I heard them arguing in choruses of single words. Now they are singing, but not only in human words. Some people hum, some sing in what sounds like Goshute. Birds chirp and caw and screech. Chipmunks chatter, elks bugle, bears grunt. It is both cacophony and symphony. It's sway and dance.

A strange memory comes into my head. In my kindergarten class we made a paper mural that showed aspects of our lives. I drew a butte in the desert and a wild horse running across the top of it. Everyone drew what they wanted—their houses, their families, pets, food they liked. It's the same feeling now as the day all our parents came to see our creation. Another story comes to mind. The valley reminds me of the vessel that appeared in the apostle Peter's dream in the Bible, full of creatures, no unclean thing. I whisper to myself, "Truly I understand that God shows no partiality."

The five of us still in the middle of the circle—Emily, me, Thomas, Marie, and Sula, who is no longer frowning and glaring—are just children, drawing pictures in the dirt. I draw a circle, and Sula draws a line. Thomas draws a doe deer, Marie a packrat. I draw a rattlesnake. Sula looks at my drawing for a moment and then smiles and draws a wolf. I look at what we've drawn, like a rock art panel, but in the dirt. A wind or spring floods will erase it. I'm no artist, but it feels finished, or finished for now. What does it all mean?

"Well argued," Sula says. "Never forget that predation is also natural." She touches my wrist and I know she could have scattered my atoms before my grandmother or Delta or Marion or anyone could react. For now, she chooses to let me exist. She turns toward Agnes, and they fade from my sight.

I wonder what she means—that hierarchies exist and that it's natural for the strong to prey on the weak? Or that I should still worry about her? If any creature is an apex predator, she is. I realize that her word "argued" might be a translation that communicates only part of its meaning. Our panel doesn't mean anything outside itself. It's not like words in a language where they mean something else. Nor are they a referent to an abstract truth. I think about my impulse to draw like the ancients did. It was not a burst of knowledge—a revelation or epiphany—but the settling of my mind. It's like the coming and going of the Dead Fathers, a gradual discovery. I can't point to a moment when my eyes saw or my ears heard. Knowledge blossomed all along the space-time continuum. And the others saw and heard as well, which is the real miracle. We engaged with each other in an act of drawing. We collaborated. That's the beginning and end of it. It was a strange nonbattle, such a relief to me. The drawing stick is mightier than the word or the axe.

Frowning, Hugh and Louis turn away from the clearing. I see others, mostly men, shaking their heads and drifting away. Not convinced by my *argument*, I suppose.

"Obedience," says Hugh in one last parting shot.

"Yes," I say. "Obedience to my best self."

"Authority," Louis says. "To maintaining order, you damned whelp."

"To love, agency, and intuition."

They both disappear. I look around and most of the people and animals are gone. A few stand in clusters, conversing. I see an elk listening to a small girl, probably someone who didn't get the chance to grow old. A coyote watches three cottontails as if she will gobble them up. Maybe in life she did. A pack rat and a meadowlark and a blowsnake disappear at the same time. More and more of the people and animals fade, exposing the brush and rock of the hillsides.

My mother stays. "Someone has to oppose or there's no balance." My father joins her, and they put their arms around each other—unexpected but nice.

"I don't understand what happened," says Emily, as more and more people and animals disappear, heading back to whatever they were doing before they gathered.

I hear slow clapping from the roof of the tin building.

"So sweet," calls Delta.

"We should all sing Hallelujah," says Marion.

"That would be insipid," says Delta.

"Logic and proportion haven't fallen sloppy dead."

"Christopher triumphed through redirection of energy."

Alina is still dancing, her face intent with effort. Suddenly I remember Bennie. I turn back to look at the truck, and he's walking toward us.

"Everyone assumed," says Marion, looking down at us on the ground, "that a war was coming. But you turned it."

They move their arm in a circle that includes all the creatures remaining. "Changed the narrative."

"The deeper balance and tension are between entropy and negentropy and anentropy," says Delta.

"And there's a deeper balance and tension than between those three."

"An eternity of dimensions, a symphony of tensions."

"Turtles all the way down."

"Still," they both say, "this was anticlimactic."

"Everyone got all wound up, but the result is like air slow-leaking from a tire."

"Kind of boring."

"Just as it should be. Never a pop."

"Well, occasionally there's a big bang," says Delta.

Marion grins. "Or a little whimper. But nothing is ever settled."

Bennie stands next to us. His eyes are wide, focused on Alina still moving slowly on the ridgeline of the building. His hand reaches toward her but then drops to his side. "Who the hell is she, really?"

Delta and Marion both turn to look at Alina, who hasn't noticed Bennie yet. She nods and stretches her arms forward, bending her wrists back and forth to loosen them. She rotates her head one way, then the other, stretching her neck.

I imagine that somewhere a black hole opens, somewhere else a universe expands to its limit and begins contracting again, Lucifer pulls humanity one way, the Mother and Father pull the other, Sula and Agnes, Cain and Abel, all exert their wills. There is balance and agency: a father beats his child and plants chaos in the child's mind, a child touches her parent's face; a man and woman kiss, another couple separate in anger, others maintain a comfortable distance from each other.

Delta, Marion, and Alina walk down the far side of the building and disappear from sight. After a moment Alina reappears around the corner. The walls are eight, ten, or twelve feet tall, and I wonder whether they jumped or floated to the ground, whether Delta and Marion became invisible and walked past us or stepped through a hidden doorway. After everything else, these details don't seem important.

I feel exhausted but there's nowhere to sit. I lean forward on the willow staff, and my leg throbs. I don't think I can take another step. Emily grabs my arm and Bennie the other, and they help me toward the double-cab truck. They help me lift myself into the passenger seat.

Bennie's still staring at Alina. He doesn't seem able to speak.

"You did it," says Alina. "You turned everyone's attention sideways, distracted them."

"What the hell just happened?" I say.

"My question exactly," says Bennie. "And you're going to take the time to tell me." I'm not sure whether he's talking to me or Alina.

"Seeing the petroglyphs gave you a clear hint," says Alina. She seems to be avoiding both Bennie's eyes and his question.

"You drawing in the dirt in the cave gave me a clearer one." I look around and see that everyone is gone, all the people and animals.

Emily drives down to her little pickup, and Alina and Bennie take off the two flat tires. Emily supervises. I want to help but can't squat or kneel, so I just sit on the same boulder I sat on before, right after I was shot.

"I want to sleep in our own house tonight," I say to Emily.

"Sounds good," she says.

"But I want to buy a truck like yours, so I can come back whenever I want."

"You can have this one," she says. "I think I may stick to paved roads from now on. Or I'll borrow it if I change my mind."

"Where are you going to live?" I say to Alina.

She puts one tire in the back of the bigger truck. "In the mine. You should see how nice their apartment is. They have a kitchen that would make Andrew jealous."

I wonder how it's powered and ventilated. And stocked with food.

She glances toward Bennie. "You should come visit sometime. I'll ask Delta and Marion."

"Who?"

"My—ah—employers." She turns back to me. "At least that's where I'll be for now. But someday I'll buy a van and fit it out."

"Where will you go?"

Alina smiles. "Wherever I please. I plan to roam to and fro upon the earth. And when I get tired of driving, I'll buy a backpack, park the van, and walk up and down the mountains."

"But—" says Bennie.

"But don't presume," Alina says to him. "I'm not someone you can expect to settle into something permanent with you."

He opens his mouth, but as I've said before, he's smart, so he shuts it again. I hope again that he won't be hurt too much by her.

She touches my arm and Emily's. "I'll visit you when I pass through Salt Lake, if that's all right."

"Yes," Emily and I say at the same time.

"Prime," I say, and Alina smiles, her eyebrows arch like a rainbow.

Bennie puts the other tire in the truck, and Emily helps me to my feet.

"I'm not driving down with you," says Alina. She turns to Bennie. "I'll see you soon."

"Where? When?"

"Soon," she says again. She gives him a quick hug.

Emily hugs her, and then I put my arms around them both.

"You are a marvel and a wonder," I say to Alina. "I'm so proud of you."

"Thanks, Father Twist," she says, her eyebrows ironic. Then she turns and walks back up toward the Valley of the Mines.

Bennie stands and watches her go while Emily helps me into the truck. "I'll never see her again."

"Oh, you probably will," I say.

"I'm ruined for any other woman," he says.

"I'm sorry," I say.

Tonight, while I'm lying on my bed waiting for Emily to get out of the shower, my mother and father visit.

"Nice," says my father, looking around. "You might be able to keep the pack rats out of this place."

"Pack rats and other vermin," says my mother.

"Now, Lucy, I'm not sure I like you calling my father and great-grandfather vermin."

"I was talking about you," she says. "We need to leave this boy alone and let him live his life."

My father scratches his head. "We'll see. I'm not going to make any promises I can't keep."

"Such a meddler," says my mother. "Constantly steadying the ark." She smiles at me. "You shaved your beard. It's nice to be able to see your face."

"It seemed time to get rid of that straggly thing and become a civilized person."

"Or as civilized as your nature allows you to be," says my father.

"Let yourself be happy," says my mother. "Whatever that takes."

They turn as if to go.

"Oh," says my mother, "I nearly forgot. We came to tell you that it was a false alarm."

"False alarm?" I ask.

"Yes," my father says. "All that about Mother and Father having a trial separation."

"The Great Divorce." My mother speaks in a dramatic voice and waggles her hands back and forth.

"They were just on a damn second honeymoon," says my father. "They found a place where nobody could bother them."

"Or maybe they've had more than one honeymoon," says my mother. "A hundred million getaways. You Twists didn't need to cause such an uproar."

I look up and they're gone.

Emily opens the door, wrapped in a towel, and it seems like Christmas morning. I feel my body getting ready for her.

"Who were you talking to?" she asks.

"Mom and Dad," I say. "They were basically saying so long."

"Good," she says. "I don't like interruptions."

I open my arms as she drops her towel.

ACKNOWLEDGMENTS

I thank Gabrielle Bond and Sue Bergin for their careful editing, and Tim Graves for his reliable copy editing. I also thank those who read drafts: Karla Bennion, Madeleine Dresden, Mel Henderson, Ann Dee Ellis, Cheri Earl, Dennis Clark, Valerie Clark, Charlotte England, Donna Jorgensen, Bruce Jorgensen, Diane Monson, and Roland Monson. I also thank Hannah Landeen for drawing the map and the Twist family tree.

Photo by Christopher Bennion

A native of the Utah desert, **JOHN BENNION** has published a collection of short fiction, *Breeding Leah and other Stories* (Signature Books, 1991), and five novels: *Falling Toward Heaven* (Signature Books, 2000), *An Unarmed Woman* (Signature Books, 2019), *Ezekiel's Third Wife* (Roundfire Books, 2019), *Spin* (BCC Press, 2022), and *Ruth at the End of the Earth* (BCC Press, 2023). Bennion has published short stories and essays in *Interdisciplinary Studies in Literature and Environment, Hotel Amerika, Southwest Review, AWP Chronicle, Hobart, Palaver, High Country News, Utah Historical Quarterly, Journal of Mormon History, Dialogue: A Journal of Mormon Thought, Sunstone Magazine* and others. He has retired from teaching creative writing in the English Department at Brigham Young University, and he lives in Provo with his wife Karla, a writer and retired psychotherapist.